A Man W

& Other Victorian Stories

Anonymous

Man With A Maid
And Other Victorian Stories

The Way Of A Man With A Maid

Volume 1:

"*The Tragedy*"

1.

*T*he Man, will not take up the time of my readers by detailing the circumstances under which Alice, the Maid, roused in me the desire for vengeance which resulted in the tale I am about to relate. Suffice it to say that Alice cruelly and unjustifiably jilted me! In my bitterness of spirit, I swore that if I ever had an opportunity to get hold of her, I would make her voluptuous person recompense me for my disappointment and that I would snatch from her by force the bridegroom's privileges that I so ardently coveted. But I dissemble! Alice and I had many mutual friends to whom this rupture was unknown; we were therefore constantly meeting each other, and if I gave her the slightest hint of my intentions towards her it would have been fatal to the very doubtful chances of success that I had! Indeed, so successfully did I conceal my real feelings under a cloak of genuine acceptance of her action that she had not the faintest idea (as she afterwards admitted to me) that I was playing a part.

But, as the proverb says, everything comes to the man who waits. For some considerable time, it seemed as if it would be wise on my part to abandon my desire for vengeance, as the circumstances of our daily lives were such as did not promise the remotest chance of my getting possession of Alice under conditions of either place or time suitable for the accomplishment of my purpose. Nevertheless, I controlled my patience and hoped for the best, enduring as well as I could the torture of unsatisfied desire and increasing lust.

It then happened that I had occasion to change my residence, and in my search for fresh quarters, I came across a modest suite consisting of a sitting room and two bedrooms, which would by themselves have suited me excellently; but with them the landlord desired to let what he termed a box or lumber room. I demurred to this addition, but as he remained firm, I asked to see the room. It was most peculiar both as regards access and appearance. The former was by a short passage from the landing and furnished with remarkably well-fitting doors at each end. The room was nearly square, of a good size and lofty, but the walls were unbroken, save by the one entrance, light and air being derived from a skylight, or rather lantern, which occupied the greater part of the roof and was supported by four strong and stout wooden pillars. Further, the walls were thickly padded, while iron rings were let into them at regular distances all 'round in two rows, one close to the door and the other at a height of about eight feet. From the roof beams, rope pulleys dangled in pairs between the pillars, while the two recesses on the entrance side, caused by the projection of the passage into the room, looked as if they had at one time been separated from the rest of the room by bars, almost as if they were cells. So strange indeed was the appearance of the whole room that I asked its history and was informed that the house had been built as a private lunatic asylum at the time that the now unfashionable square in which it stood was one of the centres of fashion, and that this was the old "mad room" in which violent patients were confined, the bolts, rings, and pulleys being used to restrain them when they were very violent, while the padding and the double doors made the room absolutely soundproof and prevented the ravings of the inmates from annoying the neighbors. The landlord added that the sound-proof quality was no fiction, as the room had frequently been tested by incredulous visitors.

Like lightning the thought flashed through my brain. Was not this room the very place for the consummation of my scheme of revenge? If I succeeded in luring Alice into it, she would be completely at my mercy—her screams for help would not be heard and would only increase my pleasure, while the bolts, rings, pulleys, etc., supplemented with a little suitable furniture, would enable me to secure her in any way I wished and to hold her fixed while I amused myself with her. Delighted with the idea, I agreed to include the room in my suite. Quietly, but with deep forethought and planning, I commissioned certain furniture made which, while in outward appearance most innocent, as well as most comfortable, was in truth full of hidden mechanisms planned for the special discomfiture of any woman or girl that I might wish to hold in physical control. I had the floor covered with thick Persian carpets and rugs, and the two alcoves converted into nominal photographic laboratories, but in a way that made them suitable for lavatories and dressing rooms.

When completed, the "Snuggery" (as I christened it) was really in appearance a distinctly pretty and comfortable room, while in reality it was nothing more or less than a disguised Torture Chamber!

And now came the difficult part of my scheme.

How to entrap Alice? Unfortunately she was not residing in London but a little way out. She lived with a married sister, and never seemed to come to town except in her sister's company. My difficulty, therefore, was how to get Alice by herself for a sufficiently long time to accomplish my designs. Sorely I cudgelled my brains over this problem!

The sister frequently visited town at irregular intervals as dictated by the contingencies of social duties or shopping. True to my policy of l'entente cordiale I had welcomed them to my rooms for rest and refreshment and had encouraged them to use my quarters; and partly because of the propinquity of the rooms to Regent Street, partly because of the very dainty meals I invariably placed before them, but mainly because of the soothing restfulness induced by the absolute quiet of the Snuggery after the roar and turmoil of the streets, it soon became their regular practice to honor me with their company for luncheon or tea whenever they came to town and had no special engagement. I need hardly add that secretly I hoped these visits might bring me an opportunity of executing my revenge, but for some months I seemed doomed to disappointment: I used to suffer the tortures of Tantalus when I saw Alice unsuspectingly braving me in the very room I had prepared for her violation, in very touch of me and of the hidden machinery that would place her at my disposal once I set it working. Alas, I was unable to do so because of her sister's presence! In fact, so keenly did I feel the position that I began to plan the capture of both sisters together, to include Marion in the punishment designed for Alice, and the idea in itself was not unpleasing, as Marion was a fine specimen of female flesh and blood of a larger and more stately type than Alice (who was "petite"). One could do much worse than to have her at one's disposal for an hour or two to feel and fuck! So seriously did I entertain this project, that I got an armchair made in such a way that the releasing of a secret catch would set free a mechanism that would be actuated by the weight of the occupant and would cause the arms to fold inwards and firmly imprison the sitter. Furnished with luxurious upholstery and the catch fixed, it made the most inviting of chairs, and, from its first appearance, Alice took possession of it, in happy ignorance that it was intended to hold her firmly imprisoned while I tackled and secured Marion!

Before, however, I resorted to this desperate measure, my patience was rewarded! And this is how it happened.

One evening, the familiar note came to say the sisters were travelling to town on the next day and would come for lunch. A little before the appointed hour Alice, to my surprise, appeared alone! She said that, after the note had been posted, Marion became ill and had been resting poorly all night and so could not come to town. The shopping engagement was one of considerable importance to Alice, and therefore she had come up alone. She had not come for lunch, she said, but had merely called to explain matters to me. She would get a cup of tea and a bun somewhere else.

Against this desertion of me, I vigorously protested, but I doubt if I would have induced her to stay had not a smart shower of rain come on. This made her hesitate about going out into it since the dress she was wearing would be ruined. Finally she consented to have lunch and leave immediately afterwards.

While she was away in the spare bedroom used by the sisters on their visits, I was in a veritable turmoil of excitement! Alice in my rooms by herself! It seemed too good to be true! But I remembered I yet had to get her into the Snuggery; she was absolutely safe from my designs everywhere but there! It was imperative that she should be in no way alarmed, and so, with a strong effort, I controlled my panting excitement and by the time Alice rejoined me in the dining room I was my usual self.

Lunch was quickly served. At first, Alice seemed a little nervous and constrained, but by tactful conversation, I soon set her at ease and she then chatted away naturally and merrily. I had craftily placed her with her back to the window so that she should not note that a bad storm was evidently brewing: and soon, with satisfaction, I saw that the weather was getting worse and worse! But it might at any moment begin to clear away, and so the sooner I could get her into my Snuggery, the better for me—and the worse for her! So by every means in my power, I hurried on the procedure of lunch.

Alice was leisurely finishing her coffee when a rattle of rain against the window panes, followed by an ominous growl of thunder, made her start from her chair and go to the casement. "Oh! just look at the rain!" she exclaimed in dismay. "How very unfortunate!"

I joined her at the window: "By Jove, it is bad!" I replied, then added, "and it looks like it's lasting. I hope that you have no important engagement for the afternoon that will keep you much in the open." As I spoke, there came a vivid flash of lightning closely followed by a peal of thunder, which sent Alice staggering backwards with a scared face.

"Oh!" she exclaimed, evidently frightened; then, after a pause, she said: "I am a horrid little coward in a thunderstorm: It just terrifies me!"

"Won't you then take refuge in the Snuggery?" I asked with a host's look of concern. "I don't think you will see the lightning there and you certainly won't hear the thunder, as the room is sound-proof. Shall we go there?" and I opened the door invitingly.

Alice hesitated. Was her guardian angel trying to give her a premonitory hint of what her fate would be if she accepted my seemingly innocent suggestion? But at that moment came another flash of lightning blinding in its intensity, and almost simultaneously a roar of thunder. This settled the question in my favour. "Yes, yes!" she exclaimed, then ran out, I closely followed her, my heart beating exultingly! Quickly she passed through the double doors into the Snuggery, the trap I had so carefully set for her was about to snap shut! Noiselessly I bolted the outer door, then closed the inner one. Alice was now mine! Mine!! At last I had trapped her! Now my vengeance was about to be consummated! Now her chaste virgin self was to be submitted to my lust and compelled to satisfy my erotic desires! She was utterly at my mercy, and promptly I proceeded to work my will on her!

2.

*T*he soothing stillness of the room after the roar of the storm seemed most gratifying to Alice. She drew a deep breath of relief and turning to me she exclaimed: "What a wonderful room it really is, Jack! Just look how the rain is pelting down on the skylight, and yet we do not hear a sound!"

"Yes! There is no doubt about it," I replied, "it is absolutely soundproof. I do not suppose that there is a better room in London for my special purpose!"

"What might that be, Jack?" she asked interestedly.

"Your violation, my dear!" I replied quietly, looking her straight in the face, "the surrender to me of your maidenhead!"

She started as if she had been struck. She colored hotly. She stared at me as if she doubted her hearing. I stood still and calmly watched her. Then indignation and the sense of outrage seized her.

"You must be mad to speak like that!" she said in a voice that trembled with concentrated anger. "You forget yourself. Be good enough to consider our friendship as suspended till you have recovered your senses and have suitably apologized for this intolerable insult.

Meanwhile I will trouble you only to call a cab so that I may remove myself from your hateful presence!" And her eyes flashed in wrathful indignation.

I quietly laughed aloud: "Do you really think I would have taken this step without calculating the consequences, Alice?" I rejoined coolly. "Do you really think I have lost my senses? Is there not a little account to be settled between us for what you did to me not very long ago? The day of reckoning has come, my dear; you have had your inning at my cost, now I am going to have mine at yours! You amused yourself with my heart, I am going to amuse myself with your body."

Alice stared at me, silent with surprise and horror! My quiet determined manner staggered her. She paled when I referred to the past, and she flushed painfully as I indicated what her immediate future would be. After a slight pause I spoke again:

"I have deliberately planned this revenge! I took these rooms solely because they would lend themselves so admirably to this end. I have prepared them for every contingency, even to having to subjugate you by force! Look!" And I proceeded to reveal to her astonished eyes the mechanism concealed in the furniture, etc. "You know you cannot get out of this room till I choose to let you go; you know that your screams and cries for help will not be heard. You now must decide what you will do. I give you two alternatives, and two only: You must choose one of them. Will you submit yourself quietly to me, or do you prefer to be forced?"

Alice stamped her little foot in her rage: "How dare you speak to me in this way?" she demanded furiously. "Do you think I am a child? Let me go at once!" and she moved in her most stately manner to the door.

"You are no child," I replied with a cruel smile, "you are a lusciously lovely girl possessing everything that I desire and able to satisfy my desires. But I am not going to let you waste time. The whole afternoon will hardly be long enough for the satisfaction of my whims, caprices, and lust. Once more, will you submit or will you be forced? Understand that if by the time the clock strikes the half-hour, you do not consent to submit, I shall, without further delay, proceed to take by force what I want from you! Now make the most of the three minutes you have left." And turning from her, I proceeded to get the room ready, as if I anticipated that I would have to use force.

Overcome by her feelings and emotions, Alice sank into an armchair, burying her face in her trembling hand. She evidently recognized her dreadful position! How could she yield herself up to me? And yet if she did not, she knew she would have to undergo violation! And possibly horrible indignities as well!! I left her absolutely alone, and when I had finished my preparation, I quietly seated myself and watched her.

Presently the clock chimed the half-hour. Immediately I rose. Alice quickly sprang to her feet and rushed to the far side of the large divan-couch on which I hoped before long to see her extended naked! It was evident that she was going to resist and fight me. You should know that I welcomed her decision, as now she would give me ample justification for the fullest exercising of my lascivious desires!

"Well, Alice, what is it to be? Will you submit quietly?"

A sudden passion seemed to possess her. She looked me squarely in the eyes for the first time, hers blazing with rage and indignation: "No! No!" she exclaimed vehemently, "I defy you! Do your worst. Do you think you will frighten me into satisfying your lust? Once and for all I give you my answer: No! No! No! Oh, you cowardly brute and beast!" And she laughed shrilly as she turned herself away contemptuously.

"As you please," I replied quietly and calmly, "let those laugh who win! I venture to say that within half an hour, you will not only be offering yourself to me absolutely and unconditionally, but will be begging me to accept your surrender! Let us see!"

Alice laughed incredulously and defiantly: "Yes, let us see! Let us see!" she retorted contemptuously.

Forthwith I sprang towards her to seize her, but she darted away, I in hot pursuit. For a short time she succeeded in eluding me, dodging in and out of the furniture like a butterfly, but soon I maneuvered her into a corner, and, pouncing on her, gripped her firmly, then half-dragged and half-carried her to where a pair of electrically worked rope-pulleys hung between two of the pillars. She struggled desperately and screamed for help. In spite of her determined resistance, I soon made the ropes fast to her wrists, then touched the button; the ropes tightened, and slowly but irresistibly, Alice's arms were drawn upwards till her hands were well above her head and she was forced to stand erect by the tension on her arms. She was now utterly helpless and unable to defend her person from the hands that were itching to invade and explore the sweet mysteries of her garments; but what with her exertions and the violence of her emotions, she was in such a state of agitation that I deemed it wise to leave her to herself for a few minutes, till she became more mistress of herself, when she would be better able to appreciate the indignities which she would now be compelled to suffer!

Here I think I had better explain the mechanical means I had at my disposal for the discomfiture and subjugation of Alice.

Between each two of the pillars that supported the lantern-skylight hung a pair of strong rope-pulleys working on a roller mechanism concealed in the beams and actuated by electricity. Should I want Alice upright, I had simply to attach the ropes to her wrists, and her arms would be pulled straight up and well over her head, thus forcing her to stand erect, and at the same time rendering her body defenseless and at my mercy. The pillars themselves I could utilize as whipping posts, being provided with rings to which Alice could be fastened in such a way that she could not move!

Close by the pillars was a huge divan-couch upholstered in dark leather that admirably enhanced the pearly loveliness of a naked girl. It stood on eight massive legs (four on each long side), behind each of which lay, coiled for use, a stout leather strap worked by rollers hidden in the upholstery and actuated by electricity. On it were piled a lot of cushions of various sorts and consistencies, with which Alice and Marion used to make nests for themselves, little dreaming that the real object of the "Turkish Divan" (as they had christened it) was to be the altar on which Alice's virginity was sacrificed to the Goddess of Love, the mission of the straps being to hold her in position while she was violated, should she not surrender herself quietly to her fate!

By the keyboard of the grand piano stood a duet-stool also upholstered in leather and with the usual mechanical power of adjustment for height, only to a much greater extent than usual. But the feature of the stool was its unusual length, a full six feet, and I one day had to satisfy Alice's curiosity by telling her that this was for the purpose of providing a comfortable seat to anyone who might be turning pages for the pianist! The real reason was that the stool was, for all practical purposes, a rack actuated by hidden machinery and fitted with a most ingenious arrangement of steps, the efficacy of which I looked forward to testing on Alice's tender self!

The treacherous armchair I have already explained. My readers can now perhaps understand that I could fix Alice in practically any position or attitude and keep her so fixed while I worked my sweet will on her helpless self!

All the ropes and straps were fitted with swivel snap-hooks. To attach them to Alice's limbs, I used an endless band of the longest and softest silk rope that I could find. It was an easy matter to slip a double length of the band 'round her wrist or ankle, pass one end through the other and draw tight, then snap the free end into the swivel hook. No amount of plunging or struggling would loosen this attachment, and the softness of the silk prevented Alice's delicate flesh from being rubbed or even marked.

3.

During the ten minute grace period I mentally allowed Alice in which to recover from the violence of her struggles, I quietly studied her as she stood helpless, almost supporting herself by resting her weight on her wrist. She was to me an exhilarating spectacle, her bosom fluttering, rising and falling as she caught her breath, her cheeks still flushing, her large hat somewhat disarranged, while her dainty well-fitting dress displayed her figure to its fullest advantage.

She regained command of herself wonderfully quickly, and then it was evident that she was stealthily watching me in horrible apprehension. I did not leave her long in suspense, but after going slowly 'round her and inspecting her, I placed a chair right in front of her, so close to her its edge almost touched her knees, then slipped myself into it, keeping my legs apart, so that she stood between them, the front of her dress pressing against the fly of my trousers. Her head was now above mine, so that I could peer directly into her downcast face.

As I took up this position, Alice trembled nervously and tried to draw herself away from me, but found herself compelled to stand as I had placed her. Noticing the action, I drew my legs closer to each other so as to loosely hold her between them, smiling cruelly at the uncontrollable shudder that passed through her, when she felt the pressure of my knees against hers! Then I extended my arms, clasped her gently 'round the waist, and drew her against me, at the same time tightening the clutch of my legs, till soon she was fairly in my embrace, my face pressing against her throbbing bosom. For a moment she struggled wildly, then resigned herself to the unavoidable as she recognized her helplessness.

Except when dancing with her, I had never held Alice in my arms, and the embrace permitted by the waltz was nothing to the comprehensive clasping between arms and legs in which she now found herself. She trembled fearfully, her tremors giving me exquisite pleasure as I felt them shoot through her, then she murmured: "Please don't, Jack!"

I looked up into her flushed face, as I amorously pressed my cheek against the swell of her bosom: "Don't you like it, Alice?" I said maliciously, as I squeezed her still more closely against me. "I think you're just delicious, dear, and I am trying to imagine what it will feel like, when your clothes have been taken off!"

"No! No! Jack!" she moaned, agonizingly, twisting herself in her distress, "let me go, Jack; don't...don't..." and her voice failed her.

For an answer, I held her against me with my left arm around her waist, then with my right hand I began to stroke and press her hips and bottom.

"Oh...! Don't, Jack! Don't!" Alice shrieked, squirming in distress and futilely endeavoring to avoid my marauding hand. I paid no attention to her pleading and cries, but continued my stroking and caressing over her full posteriors and thighs down to her knees, then back to her buttocks and haunches, she, all the while, quivering in a delicious way. Then I freed my left hand, and holding her tightly imprisoned between my legs, I proceeded with both hands to study, through her clothes, the configuration of her backside and hips and thighs, handling her buttocks with a freedom that seemed to stagger her, as she pressed herself against me, in an effort to escape from the liberties that my hands were taking with her charms.

After toying delightfully with her in this way for some time, I ceased and withdrew my hands from her hips, but only to pass them up and down over her bosom, which I began lovingly to stroke and caress to her dismay. Her color rose as she swayed uneasily on her legs. But her stays prevented any direct attack on her bosom, so I decided to open her clothes sufficiently to obtain a peep at her virgin breasts. I set to work unbuttoning her blouse.

"Jack, no! No!!" shrieked Alice, struggling vainly to get loose. But I only smiled and continued to undo her blouse till I got it completely open and threw it back onto her shoulders, only to be baulked as a fairly high bodice covered her bosom. I set to work opening this, my fingers revelling in the touch of Alice's dainty linen. Soon it also was open and thrown back—and then, right before my eager eyes, lay the snowy expanse of Alice's bosom, her breasts being visible nearly as far as their nipples!

"Oh!...oh!..." she moaned in her distress, flushing painfully at this cruel exposure. But I was too excited to take any notice; my eyes were riveted on the lovely swell of her breasts, exhibiting the valley between the twin-globes, now heaving and fluttering under her agitated emotions. Unable to restrain myself, I threw my arms 'round Alice's waist, drew her closely to me, and pressed my lips on her palpitating flesh which I kissed furiously.

"Don't, Jack" cried Alice, as she tugged frantically at her fastenings in her wild endeavors to escape from my passionate lips; but instead of stopping me, my mouth wandered all over her heaving delicious breasts, punctuating its progress with hot kisses that seemed to drive her mad, to such a pitch, in fact, that I thought it best to desist.

"Oh! my God!" she moaned as I relaxed my clasp and leaned back in my chair to enjoy the sight of her shame and distress. There was not the least doubt that she felt most keenly my indecent assault, and so I determined to worry her with lascivious liberties a little longer.

When she had become calmer, I passed my arms around her waist and again began to play with her posteriors, then, stooping down, I got my hands under her clothes and commenced to pull them up. Flushing violently, Alice shrieked to me to desist, but in vain! In a trice, I turned her petticoats up, held them thus with my left hand while with my right I proceeded to attack her bottom now protected only by her dainty thin drawers!

The sensation was delirious! My hand delightedly roved over the fat plump cheeks of her arse, stroking, caressing, and pinching them, revelling in the firmness and elasticity of her flesh under its thin covering, Alice all the time wriggling and squirming in horrible shame, imploring me almost incoherently to desist and finally getting so hysterical, that I was compelled to suspend my exquisite game. So, to her great relief, I dropped her skirts, pushed my chair back, and rose.

I had in the room a large plate glass mirror nearly eight feet high which reflected one at full length. While Alice was recovering from her last ordeal, I pushed this mirror close in front of her, placing it so that she could see herself in its centre. She started uneasily as she caught sight of herself, for I had left her bosom uncovered, and the reflection of herself in such shameful dishabille in conjunction with her large hat (which she still retained) seemed vividly to impress on her the horror of her position!

Having arranged the mirror to my satisfaction, I picked up the chair and placed it just behind Alice, sat down in it, and worked myself forward on it till Alice again stood between my legs, but this time with her back to me. The mirror faithfully reflected my movements, and her feminine intuition warned her that the front of her person was now about to become the object of my indecent assault.

But I did not give her time to think. Quickly I encircled her waist again with my arms, drew her to me till her bottom pressed against my chest, then, while my left arm held her firmly, my right hand began to wander over the junction of her stomach and legs, pressing inquisitively her groin and thighs, and intently watching her in the mirror.

Her color rose, her breath came unevenly, she quivered and trembled as she pressed her thighs closely together. She was horribly perturbed, but I do not think she anticipated what then happened.

Quietly dropping my hands, I slipped them under her clothes, caught hold of her ankles, then proceeded to climb up her legs over her stockings.

"No! no! for God's sake, don't, Jack!" Alice yelled, now scarlet with shame and wild with alarm at this invasion of her most secret parts. Frantically she dragged at her fastenings, her hands clenched, her head thrown back, her eyes dilated with horror. Throwing the whole of her weight on her wrists, she strove to free her legs from my attacking hands by kicking out desperately, but to no avail. The sight in the mirror of her struggles only stimulated me into a refinement of cruelty, for with one hand I raised her clothes waist high, exposing her in her dainty drawers and black silk stockings, while with the other I vigorously attacked her thighs over her drawers, forcing a way between them and finally working up so close to her cunt that Alice practically collapsed in an agony of apprehension and would have fallen had it not been for the sustaining ropes that were all that supported her, as she hung in a semi-hysterical faint.

Quickly rising and dropping her clothes, I placed an armchair behind her and loosened the pulleys till she rested comfortably in it, then left her to recover herself, feeling pretty confident that she was now not far from surrendering herself to me, rather than continue a resistance which she could not help but see was utterly useless. This was what I wanted to effect. I did not propose to let her off any single one of the indignities I had in store for her, but I wanted to make her suffering the more keen, through the feeling that she was, to some extent, a consenting party to actions that inexpressibly shocked and revolted her. The first of these I intended to be the removal of her clothes, and, as soon as Alice became more mistress of herself, I set the pulleys working and soon had her standing erect with her arms stretched above her head.

She glanced fearfully at me as if trying to learn what was now going to happen to her. I deemed it as well to tell her, and to afford her an opportunity of yielding herself to me, if she should be willing to do so. I also wanted to save her clothes from being damaged, as she was really beautifully dressed, and I was not at all confident that I could get her garments off her without using a scissors on some of them.

"I see you want to know what is going to happen to you, Alice," I said. "I'll tell you. You are to be stripped naked, utterly and absolutely naked; not a stitch of any sort is to be left on you!"

A flood of crimson swept over her face, invading both neck and bosom, which remained bare; her head fell forward as she moaned: "No!...No!...Oh! Jack...Jack...how can you..." and she swayed uneasily on her feet.

"That is to be the next item in the programme, my dear!" I said, enjoying her distress. "There is only one detail that remains to be settled first and that is, will you undress yourself quietly if I set you loose, or must I drag your clothes off you? I don't wish to influence your decision, and I know what queer ideals girls have about taking off their clothes in the presence of a man; I will leave the decision to you, only saying that I do not see what you have to gain by further resistance, and some of your garments may be ruined—which would be a pity. Now, which is it to be?"

She looked at me imploringly for a moment, trembling in every limb, then averting her eyes, but remaining silent, evidently torn by conflicting emotions.

"Come, Alice," I said presently, "I must have your decision or I shall proceed to take your clothes off you as best as I can."

Alice was now in a terrible state of distress! Her eyes wandered all over the room without seeming to see anything, incoherent murmurs escaped from her lips, as if she was trying to speak but could not, her breath came and went, her bosom rose and fell agitatedly. She was evidently endeavoring to form some decision, but found herself unable to do so.

I remained still for a brief space as if awaiting her answer; then, as she did not speak, I quietly went to a drawer, took out a pair of scissors and went back to her. At the sight of the scissors, she shivered, then with an effort, said, in a voice broken with emotion: "Don't...undress me, Jack! If you must...have me, let it be as I am...I will...submit quietly...oh! my God!!" she wailed.

"That won't do, dear," I replied, not unkindly, but still firmly, "you must be naked, Alice; now, will you or will you not undress yourself?"

Alice shuddered, cast another imploring glance at me, but seeing no answering gleam of pity in my eyes, but stern determination instead, she stammered out: "Oh! Jack! I can't! Have some pity on me, Jack, and...have me as I am! I promise I'll be...quiet!"

I shook my head, I saw there was only one thing for me to do, namely, to undress her without any further delay; and I set to work to do so, Alice crying piteously: "Don't, Jack; don't!...don't!"

I had left behind her the armchair in which I had allowed her to rest, and her blouse and bodice were still hanging open and thrown back on her shoulders. So I got on the chair and worked them along her arms and over her clenched hands onto the ropes; then gripping her wrists in turn one at a time, I released the noose, slipped the garments down and off it and refastened the noose. And as I had been quick to notice that Alice's chemise and vest had shoulder-strap fastenings and had merely to be unhooked, the anticipated difficulty of undressing her forcibly was now at an end! The rest of her garments would drop off her as each became released, and therefore it was in my power to reduce her to absolute nudity! My heart thrilled with fierce exultation, and without further pause, I went on with the delicious work of undressing her.

Alice quickly divined her helplessness and in an agony of apprehension and shame cried to me for mercy! But I was deaf to her pitiful pleadings! I was wild to see her naked!

Quickly I unhooked her dress and petticoats and pulled them down to her feet thus exhibiting her in stays, drawers, and stockings—a bewitching sight! Her cheeks were suffused with shamefaced blushes, she huddled herself together as much as she could, seemingly supported entirely by her arms; her eyes were downcast and she seemed dazed both by the rapidity of my motions and their horrible success!

Alice now had on only a dainty Parisian corset which allowed the laces of her chemise to be visible, just hiding the nipples of her maiden breasts, and a pair of exquisitely provoking drawers, cut wide especially at her knees and trimmed with a sea of frilly lace, from below which emerged her shapely legs encased in black silk stockings and terminated in neat little shoes. She was the daintiest sight a man could well imagine, and, to me, the daintiness was enhanced by her shame-faced consciousness, for she could see herself reflected in the mirror in all her dreadful dishabille!

After a minute of gloating admiration, I proceeded to untie the tapes of her drawers so as to take them off her. At this she seemed to wake to the full sense of the humiliation in store for her; wild at the idea of being deprived of this most intimate of garments to a girl, she screamed in her distress, tugging frantically at her fastenings in her desperation! But the knot gave way, and her drawers, being now unsupported, slipped down to below her knees where they hung for a brief moment, maintained only by the despairing pressure of her legs against each other. A tug or two from me, and they lay in snowy loads 'round her ankles and rested on her shoes!

Oh that I had the pen of a ready writer with which to describe Alice at this stage of the terrible ordeal of being forcibly undressed, her mental and physical anguish, her frantic cries and impassioned pleadings, her frenzied struggles, the agony in her face, as garment after garment was removed from her and she was being hurried nearer and nearer to the appalling goal of absolute nudity! The accidental but unavoidable contact of my hands with her person, as I undressed her, seemed to upset her so terribly that I wondered how she would endure my handling and playing with the most secret and sensitive parts of herself when she was naked! But acute as was her distress while being deprived of her upper garment, it was nothing to her shame and anguish when she felt her drawers forced down her legs and the last defense to her cunt thus removed. Straining wildly at the ropes with cheeks aflame, eyes dilated with terror, and convulsively heaving bosom, she uttered inarticulate cries, half-choked by her emotions and panting under her exertions.

I gloated over her sufferings and I would have liked to have watched them—but I was now mad with desire for her naked charms and also feared that a prolongation of her agony might result in a faint, when I would lose the anticipated pleasure of witnessing Alice's misery when her last garment was removed and she was forced to stand naked in front of me. So, unheeding her imploring cries, I undid her corset and took it off her, dragged off her shoes and stockings and with them her fallen drawers. During this process I intently watched her struggles in the hope of getting a glimpse of her Holy of Holies, but vainly, then slipped behind her; unbuttoning the shoulder-fastenings of her chemise and vest, I held these up for a moment, then watching Alice closely in the mirror, I let go! Down they slid with a rush, right to her feet! I saw Alice flash one rapid stolen half-reluctant glance at the mirror, as she felt the cold air on her now naked skin. I saw her reflection stark naked, a lovely gleaming pearly vision; then instinctively she squeezed her legs together, as closely as she could, huddled herself cowering as much as the ropes permitted—her head fell back in the first intensity of her shame, then fell forward suffused with blushes that extended right down to her breasts, her eyes closed as she moaned in heartbroken accents: "Oh! oh! oh!" She was naked!!

Half delirious with excitement and the joy of conquest, I watched Alice's naked reflection in the mirror. Rapidly and tumultuously, my eager eyes roved over her shrinking, trembling form, gleaming white, save for her blushing face and the dark triangular mossy-looking patch at the junction of her belly and thighs. But I felt that, in this moment of triumph, I was not sufficiently master of myself to fully enjoy the spectacle of her naked maiden charms now so fully exposed; besides which, her chemise and vest still lay on her feet. So I knelt down behind these garments, noting, as I did so, the glorious curves of her bottom and hips. Throwing these garments onto the rest of her clothes, I pushed the armchair in front of her, and then settled myself down to a systematic and critical inspection of Alice's naked self!

As I did so, Alice colored deeply over face and bosom and moved herself uneasily. The bitterness of death (so to speak) was past, her clothes had been forced off her and she was naked; but she was evidently conscious that much indignity and humiliation was yet in store for her, and she was horribly aware that my eyes were now taking in every detail of her naked self! Forced to stand erect by the tension of the ropes on her arms, she could do nothing to conceal any part of herself, and, in an agony of shame, she endured the awful ordeal of having her naked person closely inspected and examined!

I had always greatly admired her trim little figure, and in the happy days before our rupture, I used to note with proud satisfaction how Alice held her own, whether at garden parties, at afternoon teas, or in the theatre or ballroom. And after she had jilted me and I was sore in spirit, the sight of her invariably added fuel to the flames of my desire, and I often caught myself wondering how she looked in her bath! One evening, she wore at dinner a low-cut evening dress and she nearly upset my self-control by leaning forward over the card table by which I was standing, and unconsciously revealing to me the greater portion of her breasts! But my imagination never pictured anything as glorious as the reality now being so reluctantly exhibited to me!

Alice was simply a beautiful girl and her lines were deliciously voluptuous. No statue, no model, but glorious flesh and blood allied to superb femininity! Her well-shaped head was set on a beautifully modelled neck and bosom from which sprang a pair of exquisitely lovely breasts (if anything too full), firm, upstanding, saucy and invit-ing. She had fine rounded arms with small well-shaped hands, a dainty but not too small waist, swelling grandly downwards and outwards and melting into magnificent curves over her hips and haunches. Her thighs were plump and 'round, and tapered to the neatest of calves and ankles and tiny feet, her legs being the least trifle too short for her, but adding by this very defect to the indescribable fascination of her figure. She had a graciously swelling belly with a deep navel, and, framed by the lines of her groin, was her Mount Venus, full, fat, fleshy, prominent, covered by a wealth of fine silky dark curly hairs through which I could just make out the lips of her cunt. Such was Alice as she stood naked before me, horribly conscious of my devouring eyes, quiv-ering and trembling with suppressed emotion, tingling with shame, flushing red and white, knowing full well her own loveliness and what its effect on me must be; and in dumb silence I gazed and gazed again at her glorious naked self till my lust began to run riot and insist on the gratification of senses other than that of sight!

I did not however consider that Alice was ready to properly appre-ciate the mortification of being felt. She seemed to be still absorbed in the horrible consciousness of one all-pervading fact, namely, that she was utterly naked, that her chaste body was the prey of my lascivious eyes, that she could do nothing to hide or even screen any part of herself, even her cunt, from me! Every now and then, her downcast eyes would glance at the reflection of herself in the faithful mirror only to be hastily withdrawn with an excess of color to her already shame-suffused cheeks at these fresh reminders of the spectacle she was offering to me!

Therefore with a strong effort, I succeeded in overcoming the temptation to feel and handle Alice's luscious body there and then, and being desirous of first studying her naked self from all points of view, I rose and took her in strict profile, noting with delight the arch of her bosom, the proudly projecting breasts, the glorious curve of her belly, the conspicuous way in which the hairs on the Mount of Venus stood out, indicating that her cunt would be found both fat and fleshy, the magnificent swell of her bottom! Then I went behind her, and for a minute or two, revelled in silent admiration of the swelling lines of her hips and haunches, her quivering buttocks, her well-shaped legs! Without moving, I could command the most perfect exhibition of her naked loveliness, for I had her back view in full sight while her front was reflected in the mirror!

Presently I completed my circuit, then standing close to her, I had a good look at her palpitating breasts, noting their delicious fullness and ripeness, their ivory skin, and the tiny virgin nipples pointing outward so prettily, Alice coloring and flushing and swaying uneasily under my close inspection. Then I peered into the round cleft of her navel while she became more uneasy than ever, seeing the downward trend of my inspection. Then I dropped on my knees in front of her and from this vantage point I commenced to investigate with eager eyes the mysterious region of her cunt so deliciously covered with a wealth of close curling hairs, clustering so thickly 'round and over the coral lips as almost to render them invisible! As I did so, Alice desperately squeezed her thighs together as closely as she could, at the same time drawing in her stomach in the vain hope of defeating my purpose and of preventing me from inspecting the citadel wherein reposed her virginity!

As a matter of fact, she did to a certain extent thwart me, but as I intended before long to put her on her back and tie her down, with her legs wide apart, I did not grudge her partial success, but brought my face close to her belly. "Don't! Oh, don't!" she cried, as if she could feel my eyes as they searched this most secret part of herself; but disregarding her pleadings, I closely scanned the seat of my approaching pleasure, noting delightedly that her Mount Venus was exquisitely plump and fleshy and would afford my itching fingers the most delicious pleasure when I allowed them to wander over its delicate contours and hide themselves in the forest of hairs that so sweetly covered it!

At last I rose. Without a word, I slipped behind the mirror and quickly divested myself of my clothes, retaining only my shoes and socks. Then, suddenly, I emerged and stood right in front of Alice. "Oh," she ejaculated, horribly shocked by the unexpected apparition of my naked self, turning rosy red and hastily averting her eyes—but not before they had caught sight of my prick in glorious erection! I watched her closely. The sight seemed to fascinate her in spite of her alarmed modesty, she flashed rapid glances at me through half-closed eyes, her color coming and going. She seemed forced, in spite of herself, to regard the instrument of her approaching violation, as if to assess its size and her capacity!

"Won't you have a good look at me, Alice?" I presently remarked maliciously. "I believe I can claim to possess a good specimen of what is so dear to the heart of a girl!" (She quivered painfully.) After a moment I continued: "Must I then assume by your apparent indifference that you have, in your time, seen so many naked men that the sight no longer appeals to you?" She colored deeply, but kept her eyes averted.

"Are you not even curious to estimate whether my prick will fit in your cunt?" I added, determined, if I possibly could, to break down the barrier of silence she was endeavoring to protect herself with.

I succeeded! Alice tugged frantically at the ropes which kept her upright, then broke into a piteous cry: "No, no...my God, no!" she supplicated, throwing her head back but still keeping her eyes shut as if to exclude the sight she dreaded, "Oh!...you don't really mean to...to..." she broke down, utterly unable to clothe in words the overwhelming fear that she was now to be violated!

I stepped up to her, passed my left arm 'round her waist and drew her trembling figure to me, thrilling at the exquisite sensation caused by the touch of our naked bodies against each other. We were now both facing the mirror, both reflected in it.

"D-don't touch me!" she shrieked as she felt my arm encircle her, but holding her closely against me with my left arm, I gently placed my right forefinger on her navel, to force her to open her eyes and watch my movements in the mirror, which meant that she would also have to look at my naked self, and gently I tickled her.

She screamed in terror, opening her eyes, squirming deliciously: "Don't! oh, don't!" she cried agitatedly.

"Then use your chaste eyes properly and have a good look at the reflection of the pair of us in the mirror," I said somewhat sternly: "Look me over slowly and thoroughly from head to foot, then answer the questions I shall presently put to you. May I call your attention to that whip hanging on that wall and to the inviting defenselessness of your bottom? Understand that I shall not hesitate to apply one to the other if you don't do as you are told! Now have a good look at me!"

Alice shuddered, then reluctantly raised her eyes and shamefacedly regarded my reflection in the mirror, her color coming and going. I watched her intently (she being also reflected, my arm was still 'round her waist holding her against me) and I noted with cruel satisfaction how she trembled with shame and fright when her eyes dwelt on my prick, now stiff and erect!

"We make a fine pair, Alice, eh?" I whispered maliciously. She colored furiously, but remained silent.

"Now answer my questions: I want to know something about you before going further. How old are you?"

"Twenty-five," she whispered.

"In your prime then! Good! Now, are you a virgin!"

Alice flushed hotly and painfully, then whispered again: "Yes!"

Oh, my exultation! I was not too late! The prize of her maidenhead was to be mine! My prick showed my joy! I continued my catechism.

"Absolutely virgin?" I asked. "A pure virgin? Has no hand wandered over those lovely charms, has no eye but mine seen them?"

Alice shook her head, blushing rosy red at the idea suggested by my words. I looked rather doubtingly at her.

"I include female eyes and hands as well as male in my query, Alice," I continued, "you know that you have a most attractive lot of girl and woman friends and that you are constantly with them. Am I to understand that you and they have never compared your charms, have never, when occupying the same bed..." but she broke in with a cry of distress. "No, no, not I, not I, oh! how can you talk to me like this, Jack?"

"My dear, I only wanted to find out how much you already knew so that I might know what to teach you now! Well, shall we begin your lessons?" And I drew her against me, more closely than ever, and again began to tickle her navel.

"Jack, don't!" she screamed, "oh, don't touch me! I can't stand it! really I can't!"

"Let me see if that is really so," I replied, as I removed my arm from her waist and slipped behind her, taking up a position from which I could command the reflection of our naked figures in the mirror, and thus watch her carefully and noted the effect on her of my tender mercy.

4.

commenced to feel Alice by placing my hands one on each side of her waist, noting with cruel satisfaction the shiver that ran through her at their contact with her naked skin. After a few caresses, I passed them gently but inquisitively over her full hips which I stroked, pressed, and patted lovingly, then bringing my hands downward behind her, I roved over her plump bottom, the fleshy cheeks of which I gripped and squeezed to my heart's content. Alice the while arching herself outwards in a vain attempt to escape my hands. Then I descended to the underneath portion of her soft round thighs and finally worked my way back to her waist running my hands up and down over her loins and finally arriving at her armpits.

Here I paused, and to try the effect on Alice, I gently tickled these sensitive spots of herself. "Don't!" she exclaimed, wriggling and twisting herself uneasily. "don't, I am dreadfully ticklish, I can't stand it at all!" At once I ceased but my blood went on fire, as through my brain flashed the idea of the licentiously lovely spectacle Alice would afford, if she was tied down with her legs fastened widely apart, and a pointed feather-tip cleverly applied to the most sensitive part of her—her cunt—

sufficient slack being allowed in her fastenings to permit of her wriggling and writhing freely while being thus tickled, and I promised to give myself presently this treat together with the pleasure of trying on her this interesting experiment!

After a short pause, I again placed my hands on her waist played for a moment over her swelling hips, then slipped onto her stomach, my right hand taking the region below her waist while my left devoted itself to her bosom, but carefully avoiding her breasts for the moment.

Oh! what pleasure I tasted in thus touching her pure sweet flesh, so smooth, so warm, so essentially female! My delighted hands wandered all over her body, while the poor girl stood quivering and trembling, unable to guess whether her breast or cunt was next to be attacked.

I did not keep her long in suspense. After circling a few times over her rounded belly, my right hand paused on her navel again, and while my forefinger gently tickled her, my left hand slid quietly onto her right breast which it then gently seized.

She gave a great cry of dismay! Meanwhile my right hand had in turn slipped up to her left breast, and another involuntary shriek from Alice announced that both of her virgin bubbies had become the prey of my cruel hands!

Oh, how she begged me to release them, the while tossing herself from side to side in almost uncontrollable agitation as my fingers played with her delicious breasts, now squeezing, now stroking, now pressing them against each other, now rolling them upwards and downwards, now gently irritating and exciting their tiny nipples! Such delicious morsels of flesh I had never handled so firm and yet so springing, so ripe and yet so maidenly, palpitating under the hitherto unknown sensations communicated by the touch of masculine hands on their virgin surfaces. Meanwhile Alice's telltale face reflected in the mirror clearly indicated to me the mental shame and anguish she was feeling at this terrible outrage; her flushed cheeks, dilated nostrils, half-closed eyes, her panting, heaving bosom all revealing her agony under this desecration of her maiden self. In rapture, I continued toying with her virgin globes, all the while gloating on Alice's image in the mirror, twisting and contorting in the most lasciviously ravishing way under her varying emotions!

At last I tore my hands away from Alice's breasts. I slipped my left arm 'round her waist, drew her tightly against me, then while I held her stomach and slowly approached her cunt, Alice instantly guessed my intention! She threw her weight on one leg, then quickly placed the other across her groin to foil my attack, crying: "No, no, Jack!...not there...not there!" At the same time endeavoring frantically to turn herself away from my hand. But the close grip of my left arm defeated her, and disregarding her cries, my hand crept on and on till it reached her hairs! These I gently pulled, twining them 'round my fingers as I revelled in their curling silkiness. Then amorously, I began to feel and press her gloriously swelling Mount Venus, a finger on each side of its slit! Alice now simply shrieked in her shame and distress, jerking herself convulsively backwards and twisting herself frenziedly! As she was forced to stand on both legs in order to maintain her balance, her cunt was absolutely defenseless, and my eager fingers roved all over it, touching, pressing, tickling, pulling her hairs at their sweet will. Then I began to attack her virgin orifice and tickle her slit, passing my fore-finger lightly up and down it, all the time watching her intently in the mirror! Alice quivered violently, her head fell backwards in her agony as she shrieked: "Jack don't!...for God's sake, don't!...stop! ...stop!" But I could feel her cunt opening under my lascivious titillation and so could she! Her distress became almost uncontrollable. "Oh, my God!" she screamed in her desperation as my finger found its way to her clitoris and lovingly titillated it, she spasmodically squeezing her thighs together in her vain attempts to defend herself. Unheeding her agonized pleading, I continued to tickle her clitoris for a few delicious moments, then I gently passed my finger along her cunt and between its now half-opened lips till I arrived at her maiden orifice up which it tenderly forced its way, burying itself in Alice's cunt till it could penetrate no further into her! Alice's agitation now became uncontrollable, she strug-gled so violently that I could hardly hold her still, especially when she felt the interior of her cunt invaded and my finger investigate the mysteries of its virgin recesses!

Oh! My voluptuous sensations at that moment! Alice's naked quiv-ering body clutched tightly against mine! My finger, half-buried in her maiden cunt, enveloped in her soft, warm, throbbing flesh and gently exploring its luscious interior!! In my excitement I must have pushed my inquisitiveness too far, for Alice suddenly screamed: "Oh!...Oh!... you're hurting me!...stop!...stop!" her head falling forward on her bosom as she did so! Delighted at this unexpected proof of her virginity and fearful of exciting her sexual passions beyond her powers of control, I gently withdrew my finger and soothed her by passing it lovingly and caressingly over her cunt; then releasing her from my encircling arm, I left her to recover herself. But, though visibly relieved at being at last left alone, Alice trembled so violently that I hastily pushed her favorite armchair (the treacherous one) behind her, hastily released the pulley-ropes and let her drop into the chair to rest and recover herself, for I knew that her distress was only temporary and would soon pass away and leave her in a fit condition to be again fastened and subjected to some other torture, for so it undoubtedly was to her.

5.

O n this occasion, I did not set free the catch which permitted the arms of the chair to imprison the occupant. Alice was so upset by her experiences that I felt sure she would not give me any trouble worth mentioning when it became time for her torturing to recommence, provided, of course, that I did not allow her too long a respite, and this, from my own point of view, I did not propose to do as I was wildly longing to play again with her naked charms!

I therefore let her coil herself up in the chair with her face buried in her hands, and greedily gloated over the voluptuous curves of her haunches and bottom which she was unconsciously exhibiting, the while trying to make up my mind as to what I should next do to her. This I soon decided. My hands were itching to again handle her virgin flesh, and so I determined to tie Alice upright to one of the pillars and while comfortably seated close in front of her, to amuse myself by playing with her breasts and cunt again!

She was now lying quietly and breathing normally and regularly, the trembling and quivering that had been running intermittently through her having, by now, ceased. I did not feel quite sure she had recovered herself yet, but as I watched her, I noticed an attempt on her part to try and slip her wrists out of the silken nooses that attached the ropes to them. This settled the point, and, before she could free her hands, I set the ropes working, remarking as I did so: "Well, Alice, shall we resume?"

She glanced at me fearfully, then averted her eyes as she exclaimed hurriedly: "Oh, no, Jack! Not again, not again!" and shuddered at the recollection of her recent ordeal!

"Yes, my dear!" I replied, "the same thing, though not quite in the same way; you'll be more comfy this time! Now, Alice, come along, stand up again!"

"No!" she cried, fighting vainly the now fast tightening ropes that were inexorably raising her to her feet! "Oh, Jack! no!...no!!" she pitifully pleaded, while opposing the upward pull with all her might but to no avail! I simply smiled cruelly at her as I picked up a leather strap and awaited the favorable moment to force her against the nearest pillar. Presently she was dragged off the chair and now was my time. I pounced on her and rushed her backwards to the pillar, quickly slipping the strap 'round it and her waist and buckling it, and thus securing her. Then I loosened the pulleys and, lowering her arms, I forced them behind her and 'round the pillar, till I got her wrists together and made them fast to a ring set in the pillar. Alice was now helpless: The whole of the front of her person was at my disposal. She was securely fastened, but, with a refinement of cruelty, I lashed her ankles together and bound them to the pillar! Then I unbuckled the strap 'round her waist and threw it away, it being no longer needed, placed the armchair in front of her, and sitting down in it, I drew it so close to her that she stood between my parted legs and within easy touch, just as she did when she was being indecently assaulted before she was undressed, only then we both were fully clothed, while now we both were stark naked! She could not throw her head back because of the pillar, and if she let it droop, as she naturally wanted to do, the first thing that her innocent eyes would rest upon would be my excited prick in glorious erection, its blushing head pointing directly towards her cunt as if striving to make the acquaintance of its destined bride!

Confused, shamefaced, and in horrible dread, Alice stood trembling in front of me, her eyes tightly closed as if to avoid the sight of my naked self, her bosom agitatedly palpitating till her breasts seemed almost to be dancing! I leant back in my chair luxuriously as I gloated over the voluptuously charming spectacle, allowing her a little time in which to recover herself somewhat, before I set to work to feel her again!

Before long, the agitations of her bosom died away; Alice's breathing became quieter. She was evidently now ready for another turn, and I did not keep her waiting, but gently placed my hands on her breasts.

"No, Jack, don't!" she pleaded piteously, moving herself uneasily. My only response was to stroke lovingly her delicious twin-globes. As her shoulders were of necessity drawn well back by the pull of her arms her bust was thrown well forward, thus causing her breasts to stand out saucily and provokingly; and I took the fullest advantage of this. Her flesh was delicious to the touch, so smooth and soft and warm, so springy and elastic! My fingers simply revelled in their contact with her skin! Taking her tempting bubbies between my fingers and thumbs, I amorously pressed and squeezed them, pulled them this way and that way, rubbed them against each other, finally taking each delicate nipple in turn in my mouth and sucking it while my hands made as if they were trying to milk her! Alice all the while involuntarily shifting herself nervously as if endeavoring to escape from my audaciously inquisitive fingers, her face scarlet with shame.

After a delicious five minutes of lascivious toying with her maiden breasts, I reluctantly quitted them, first imprinting on each of her little nipples a passionate kiss which seemed to send a thrill through her. As I sank back into my chair she took a long breath of relief, at which I smiled, for I had only deserted her breasts for her cunt!

Alice's legs were a trifle short, and her cunt therefore lay a little too low for effective attack from me in a sitting position. I therefore pushed the chair back and knelt in front of her. My intentions were now too obviously plain to her and she shrieked in her dismay, squirming deliciously!

For some little time, I did not touch her, but indulged in a good look, at close quarters, at the sweet citadel of her chastity!

My readers will remember that immediately after I had stripped Alice naked, I had closely inspected her cunt from a similar point of view. But then it was unsullied, untouched; now it had experienced the adoring touch of a male finger, and her sensitive body was still all aquiver from the lustful handling her dainty breasts had just endured! Did her cunt share in the sexual excitement that my fingers had undoubtedly aroused in her?

It seemed to me that it did! The hair seemed to stand out as if ruffled, the Mount of Venus certainly looked fuller, while the coral lips of the cunt itself were distinctly more apart! I could not see her clitoris, but I concluded that it participated in the undoubted excitement that was prevailing in this sweet portion of Alice's body, and of which she evidently was painfully aware, to judge by her shrinking, quivering movements!

I soon settled the point by gently placing my right forefinger on her slit and lovingly stroking it! An electric shock seemed to send a thrill through Alice, her limbs contracted, her head fell forward as she screamed: "Don't, Jack!…oh, my God! How can you treat me so!!" while she struggled frantically to break the ropes which lashed her legs to the pillar to which she was fastened!

"Don't you like it, dear?" I asked softly with a cruel smile, as I continued to gently play with her cunt!

"No, no," she shrieked, "oh, stop!…I can't stand it!" And she squirmed horribly! The crack of her cunt now began to open visibly!

I slipped my finger in between the parted lips: Another despairing shriek from Alice, whose face now was scarlet! Again I found my progress barred by the membrane that proved her virgin condition! Revelling in the warm moistness of her throbbing flesh, I slowly agitated my finger in its delicious envelope, as if frigging her: "Jack! don't!" Alice yelled, now mad with distress and shame, but I could not for the life of me stop, and with my left forefinger, I gently attacked her virgin clitoris!

Alice went off into a paroxysm of hysterical shrieks, straining at her fastenings, squirming, wriggling, writhing like one possessed. She was a lovely sight in herself and the knowledge that the struggling, shrieking girl I was torturing was Alice herself and none but Alice added zest to my occupation!

Disregarding her cries, I went on slowly frigging her, but carefully refrain from carrying her sexual excitement to the spending point, till I had pushed her powers of self-control to their utmost. I did not want her to spend yet, this crowning humiliation I intended to effect with my tongue. Presently, what I wished was to make Alice endure the most outrageously indecent indignities I could inflict on her virgin person, to play on her sexual sensitiveness, to provoke her nearly into spending, and then deny her the blessed relief. So, exercising every care, and utilizing to the utmost the peculiarly subtle power of touch I possessed, I continued to play with her cunt using both my hands, till I drove her nearly frantic with the sexual cravings and excitement I was provoking!

Just then I noticed certain spasmodic contortions of her hips and buttocks, certain involuntary thrusting out of her belly, as if begging for more close contact with my busy fingers; I knew this meant that her control over her sexual organs was giving out and that she would be driven into spending if I did not take care. Then, most reluctantly, I stopped torturing her for the moment, and, leaning back in my chair, I gloatingly watched Alice as little by little she regained her composure, my eyes dwelling delightedly on her trembling and quivering naked body so gloriously displayed!

She breathed a long sigh of heartfelt relief as she presently saw me rise and leave her. She did not, however, know that my object in doing so was to prepare for another, and perhaps more terrible, ordeal for her virgin cunt!

From a drawer, I took out a long glove box, then returned and resumed my seat in front of her with the box in my hand. She watched me with painful intensity, her feminine intuition telling her that something horrible was in store for her, and she was not wrong!

Holding the box in such a way that she could see the contents, I opened it. Inside were about a dozen long and finely pointed feathers. Alice at once guessed her fate—that her cunt was to be tickled. Her head fell back in her terror as she shrieked: "Oh, my God! not that, Jack!...not that!...you'll kill me! I can't stand it!" I laughed cruelly at her and proceeded to pick out a feather, whereupon she frantically tugged at her fastenings, screaming frenziedly for mercy!

"Steady, dear, steady now, Alice!" I said soothingly, as if addressing a restive mare, then touched her palpitating breasts with the feather's point.

"Jack, don't!" she yelled, pressing herself wildly back against the pillar in an impotent effort to escape the torture caused by the maddeningly gentle titillation, her face crimson. For response, I proceeded to pass the tip of the feather along the lower portion of her glorious bubbies, touching the skin ever so lightly here and there, then tickling her maiden nipples! With redoubled cries, Alice began to squirm convulsively as much as her fastenings would permit, while the effect of the fiendishly subtle torture on her became manifest by the sudden stiffening of her breasts, which now began to stand out tense and full! Noting this, I thought it as well to allow her a little respite; so I dropped my hand, but, at the same time, leaned forward till my face touched her breasts, which I then proceeded to kiss lovingly in turn, finally sucking them amorously till they again became soft and yielding. I then made as if I would repeat the torture, but after a touch or two (which produced piteous cries and contortions) I pretended to be moved by her distress, and again dropping my hand leaned back in the chair till she became less agitated!

But as soon as the regular rise and fall of her lovely bosom indicated the regaining of her composure, I proceeded to try the ardently longed for experiment: The effect of a feather applied to a girl's cunt! And no one could have desired a more lovely subject on which to test this much debated question than was being offered by the naked helpless girl now standing terrified between my legs!

Pushing my chair back as much as was desirable, I leant forward, then slowly extended my right arm in the direction of Alice's cunt. A great cry of despair broke from her as she noted the movement, and she flattened her bottom against the pillar in a vain attempt to draw herself back out of reach. But the only effect of her desperate movement was to force forward her Mount Venus, and thereby render her cunt more open to the attack of the feather than it previously was!

Carefully regulating my motions, I gently brought the tip of the feather against the lowest point of Alice's cunt hole, then very softly and gently began to play up and down, on and between its delicate coral lips! Alice's head had dropped onto her breast, the better, I fancy, to watch my movements; but as soon as the feather touched her cunt, she threw her head backwards, as if in agony, shrieking at the top of her voice, her whole body twisting and contorting wildly. Not heeding her agonized appeals, I proceeded to work along her slit towards her clitoris, putting into play the most subtle titillation I was capable of, sometimes passing the feather all along the slit from one end to the other, sometimes tickling the orifice itself, not only outside but inside, then ascending towards her clitoris, I would pass the tip of the feather all 'round it, irritating it without so much as touching it. The effect of my manipulation soon became evident. First the lips of Alice's cunt began to pout, then to gape a little, then a little more as if inviting the feather to pass into it—which it did! Then Alice's clitoris commenced to assert itself and to become stiff and turgid, throbbing excitedly; then her whole cunt seemed as if possessed by an irresistible flood of sexual lust and almost to demand mutely the immediate satisfaction of its cravings! Meanwhile Alice, firmly attached to the pillar, went into a paroxysm of contortions and convulsions, wriggling, squirming, writhing, tugging frantically at her fastenings, shrieking, praying, utterly incoherent exclamations and ejaculations, her eyes starting out of her head, her quivering lips, her heaving bosom with its wildly palpitating breasts all revealing the agony of body and mind that she was enduring! Fascinated by the spectacle, I continued to torture her by tickling her cunt more and more scientifically and cruelly, noting carefully the spots at which the tickling seemed most felt and returning to those ultra-sensitive parts of her cunt avoiding only her clitoris—as I felt sure that, were this touched, Alice would spend—till her strength became exhausted under the double strain! With a strangled shriek Alice collapsed just as I had forced the feather up her cunt and was beginning to tickle the sensitive interior! Her head fell forward on her bosom, her figure lost its self-supporting rigidity, she hung flaccidly, prevented from falling only by her wrists being shackled together 'round the pillar! There was nothing to be gained by prolonging the torture, so quickly I unfastened her, loosed her wrists and ankles from their shackles, and carried her to the large divan-couch, where I gently laid her, knowing that she would soon recover herself and guessing that she now would not need to be kept tied and that she had realized the futility of resistance.

6.

The couch on which I had placed Alice was one of the cunning pieces of furniture that I had designed for use, should I succeed in capturing her. It was unusually long, nearly eight feet, and more than three feet wide, upholstered in dark green satin and stuffed in such a way as to be delightfully soft and springy and yet not to allow one's body to sink into it. In appearance it resembled a divan, but in stern reality it was a rack, for at each end, there was concealed a mechanism that worked stout leather straps, its object being to extend Alice flat at full length either on her back or her front (as I might wish) and to maintain her fixed thus, while I amused myself with her or worked my cruel will on her! From about halfway down the sides, there issued a pair of supplementary straps also worked by a mechanism, by which means Alice's legs could be pulled widely apart and held so, should I want to devote myself to her cunt or to, dare I actually say it, fuck her against her will!

I did not wish to fatigue her with another useless struggle, so before she recovered the use of her faculties, I attached the corner straps to her wrists and ankles, leaving them quite loose and slack, so that she could move herself freely. Hardly had I effected this when Alice began to come to herself; immediately I quitted her and went to a part of the room where my back would be turned to her, but from which I could nevertheless watch her by means of a mirror.

I saw her take a deep breath, then slowly open her eyes and look about her as if puzzled. Then, almost mechanically, one of her hands stole to her breasts and the other to her cunt, and she gently soothed these tortured parts by stroking them softly, as if to relieve them of the terrible tickling to which they had been subjected! Presently she rose to a sitting position, then tried to free herself from the straps on her wrists and ankles.

I now considered that she must have fully recovered, so I returned to her and without a word I touched the spring that set the mechanism working noiselessly. Immediately the straps began to tighten. As soon as she observed this, Alice started up in a fright, at once detecting that she would be spread-eagled on her back if she did not break loose! "No, no, no!" she cried, terrified at the prospect; then she desperately endeavored to slip out of her fastenings, but the straps were tightening quickly and in the struggle she lost her balance and fell backwards on the couch, and before she could recover herself, she was drawn into a position in which resistance was impossible! With cruel satisfaction, I watched her, disregarding her frenzied appeals for mercy! Inch by inch, she was pulled flatter and flatter, till she rested on her back, then, inch by inch, her dainty legs were drawn asunder, till her heels rested on the edges of the couch! Then I stopped the machinery. Alice was now utterly helpless! In speechless delight, I stood gazing at her lovely body as she lay on her back, panting after her exertions, her bosom heaving and fluttering with her emotions, her face rosy red with shame, her lovely breasts and virgin cunt conspicuously exposed, stark naked, a living Maltese Cross!

When I had sufficiently gratified my sense of sight and she had become a little calmer, I quietly seated myself by her waist, facing her feet, then, bending over her, I began delightedly to inspect the delicious abode of Alice's maidenhead, her virgin cunt, now so fully exhibited! With sparkling eyes, I noted her full, fleshy Mount Venus, the delicately tinted coral lips quivering under sensations hitherto a stranger to them, the wealth of close-clustering curly hair; with intense delight, I saw that, for a girl of her height and build, Alice had a large cunt, and that her clitoris was well-developed and prominent, that the lips were full and her slit easy to open! Intently I scanned its every feature, the sweet junction of her belly and thighs, her smooth plump thighs themselves, the lines of her groin, while Alice lay trembling in an agony of shame and fright, horribly conscious of the close investigation her cunt was undergoing and in terrible dread of the sequel!

Shakespeare sings (in *Venus and Adonis*):

> *Who sees his true love in her naked bed,*
> *Teaching the sheets a whiter hue than white;*
> *But when his glutton eye full gorged hath fed,*
> *His other agents aim at like delight!*

So it was with me! My hands were tingling to explore the mysteries of Alice's cunt, to wander unchecked over her luscious belly and thighs. My prick was in a horrible state of erection! I could hardly restrain myself from falling on her and ravishing her as she lay there so temptingly helpless! But with a strong effort, I did suppress my rioting lustful desires and tore myself away from Alice's secret charms for a brief spell!

I turned 'round so as to face her, still seated by her waist, and placed my hands on her lovely breasts. As I lovingly squeezed them I lowered my face till I almost touched hers, then whispered: "You delicious beauty, kiss me!" at the same time placing my lips on hers. Alice flushed hotly, but did not comply! I had never yet either kissed her or received a kiss from her and was mad for one!

"Alice, kiss me!" I repeated somewhat sternly, looking threateningly at her and replacing my lips on her mouth. Reluctantly she complied, I felt her lips open as she softly kissed me! It was delicious! "Give me another!" I demanded, putting my right cheek in position to receive it. She complied. "Yet another!" I commanded, tendering my left cheek. Again she complied. "Now give me two more, nice ones, mouth to mouth!" Again came the sweet salute, so maddeningly exciting that, hastily quitting her breasts, I threw my arms 'round her neck, drew her face to mine, then showered burning kisses on her mouth, eyes and cheeks till she gasped for breath, blushing rosy red! Reluctantly I let her go; then to her dismay, I again turned 'round and bent over her cunt, and after a long look at it, expressive of the deepest admiration, I gently placed my hands on her belly and after softly stroking it, began to follow the converging lines of her groin. Alice shrieked in sudden alarm! "No, no—Oh! my God, no, no…don't touch me there!…Oh! no! not there!" and struggled desperately to break loose. But I disregarded her cries and continued my invasion; soon my itching fingers reached the forest of hairs that covered her Mons Veneris, she squirming deliciously, then rested on her cunt itself. An agonized shriek of "Oh!...Oh!!" from Alice, as she writhed helplessly with quivering hips, proclaimed my victory and her shame!

Shall I ever forget the sensations of that moment! At last, after all that longing and waiting, Alice's cunt was finally at my mercy, I not only had it in the fullest possible view, but was actually touching it! My fingers, ranged on each side of the delicate pinky slit, were busy amorously pressing and feeling it, now playing with its silky curly hairs and gently pulling them, now tenderly stroking its sweet lips, now gently opening them so as to expose its coral orifice and its throbbingly agitated clitoris! Resting as I was on Alice's belly, I could feel every quiver and tremor as it passed through her, every involuntary contortion induced by the play of my fingers on this most delicate and susceptible part of her anatomy, the fluttering of her palpitating and heaving bosom! I could hear the involuntary ejaculation, the "ohs!" and the "ahs!" that broke from her in her shame and mental anguish at thus having to endure such handling and fingering of her maiden cunt and the strange half-terrifying sensations thereby provoked.

Half-mad with delight, I continued to toy sweetly with Alice's cunt, till sudden unmistakable wriggles of her bottom and hips and her incoherent exclamations warned me that I was trying her too much, if not goading her into spending, and as I had determined that Alice's first sacrifice to Venus should be induced by the action of my tongue on her cunt, I reluctantly desisted from my delightful occupation, to her intense relief!

Turning 'round, I again clasped her in my arms, rained hot kisses on her unresisting lips and cheeks, murmuring brokenly: "Oh, Alice!...Oh, Alice!..." Then pressing my cheek against hers, I rested with her clasped in my arms, her breasts quivering against my chest, till we both grew calmer and her trembling ceased.

For about five minutes there was dead silence, broken only by Alice's agitated breathing. Soon this ceased, and she seemed to have recovered command of herself again. Then softly I whispered to her: "Will you not surrender yourself to me now, Alice dear!. surely it is plain to you that you cannot help yourself?"

She drew her face away from me, and murmured: "No, no, I can't, I can't...let you...have me! Oh, let me go!...Let me go!!!"

"No," I replied sternly, releasing my clasp of her and resuming my sitting position by her waist, "No, my dear, you shan't go till you've been well punished and well fucked! But as I said before, I think you will change your mind presently!"

She looked questioningly at me, fear in her eyes. I rose. Her eyes followed me, and when she saw me select another fine-pointed feather and turn back to her, she instantly divined my intentions and frantically endeavored to break the ropes that kept her thighs apart shrieking: "Oh no, no, my God no, I can't stand it!...you'll kill me!"

"Oh, no, I won't!" I replied quietly, seating myself by her knees, so as to command both her cunt and a view of her struggles which I knew would prove most excitingly delicious! Then without another word, I gently directed the point of the feather against the lowest part of her cunt's virgin orifice, and commenced to tickle her!

7.

A fearful scream broke from Alice, a violent quivering spasm shook her from head to foot! Her muscles contracted, as she vainly strove to break free! Arching her back she endeavored to turn herself first on one side and then on the other, tugging frantically at the straps, anything as long as she could dodge the feather! But she could do nothing! The more she shrieked and wriggled, the greater was the pleasure she was affording me; so, deaf to her cries and incoherent pleadings, I continued to tickle her cunt, sometimes up and down the slit, sometimes just inside, noting with cruel delight how its lips began to gape open under the sexual excitement now being aroused and how her throbbing clitoris began to erect itself!

Alice presented a most voluptuous spectacle; clenched hands, half-closed eyes, heaving breasts, palpitating bosom, plunging hips, tossing bottom, jerking thighs—wriggling and squirming frantically. uttering broken and incoherent ejaculations, shrieking, praying.

I thought it wise to give her a pause for rest and partial recovery, and withdrew the feather from between the lips of her cunt, then gently stroked them caressingly. "Ah!…Ah!…" she murmured half unconsciously, closing her eyes. I let her lie still, but watched her closely.

Presently her eyes opened half-dreamily, she heaved a deep breath. I made as if to resume the tickling. "No, no," she murmured faintly, "it's no use!…I can't stand it!…don't tickle me any more!"

"Well, will you yield yourself to me?" I asked.

Alice lay silent for a moment, then with an evident effort said, "Yes!"

Letting the feather fall between her parted legs, I leaned forward and took her in my arms: "There must not be any mistake, Alice," I said softly, "are you willing to let me do to you anything and everything that I may wish?"

Half-opening her eyes, she nodded her head in assent. "And do you promise to do everything and anything that I may wish you to do?"

She hesitated: "What will you want me to do?" she murmured.

"I don't know," I replied, "but whatever it may be, you must do it. Do you promise?"

"Yes," she murmured, reluctantly.

"Then kiss me, kiss me properly in token of peace!" I whispered in her ear, placing my lips on hers; and deliciously she kissed me, receiving at the same time my ardent reciprocations. Then I unclasped her and began to play with her breasts.

"May I get up now?" she murmured, moving herself uneasily as she felt her breasts being squeezed.

"Not just yet, dear," I replied. "I've excited you so terribly that it is only fair to you that I should give you relief, and as I know that in spite of your promise you will not behave as you should do, simply from inexperience, I will keep you as you are, till I have solaced you!"

"Oh, what are you going to do to me?" she asked in alarm, in evident fear that she was about to be violated!

"Restore you to ease, dear, by kissing you all over; now lie still and you will enjoy the greatest pleasure a girl can taste and yet remain virgin!"

With heightened color she resigned herself to her fate. I took her again in my arms, and sweetly kissed her on her eyes, her cheeks, her hair! Then releasing her, I applied my lips to her delicious breasts, and showered burning kisses all over them, revelling in their sweet softness and their exquisite elasticity. Taking each breast in turn, I held it between finger and thumb, then enveloping the dainty little nipple between my lips, I alternately played on it with my tongue and sucked it, all the while squeezing and toying with the breast, causing Alice to experience the most lascivious sensation she had yet known, except perhaps when her cunt was being felt.

"Stop! Oh, for God's sake stop!" she ejaculated in her confusion and half-fright as to what might happen, "for heaven's sake, stop!" she screamed as I abandoned one breast only to attack the other. But the game was too delightful: To feel her glorious throbbing ripe bubbies in my mouth and quivering under my tongue, while Alice squirmed in her distress, was a treat for a god; so disregarding her impassioned plead-ings, I continued to suck and tongue-tickle them till their sudden stiffening warned me that Alice's sexual instincts were being roused and the result might be a premature explosion when she felt the grand assault on her cunt.

So I desisted reluctantly. Again I encircled her neck with my arms, kissed her pleading mouth and imploring eyes as she lay helpless, then with my tongue, I touched her navel. She cried "No, no, oh! don't," struggling desperately to get free, for it began to dawn on her innocent mind what her real torture was to be.

I did not keep her in suspense. Thrusting my hands under her and gripping the cheeks of her bottom so as to steady her plunging, I ran my tongue down lightly over the lines of her abdomen, then began to tenderly kiss her cunt. She shrieked in her terror as she felt my lips on her cunt, and with frantic wriggling endeavored to escape my pursu-ing mouth. At this critical moment, I lightly ran my tongue along Alice's slit. The effect was astounding! For a moment she seemed to swoon under the subtle titillation, but on my tongue again caressing her cunt, only this time darting deeper between its lips, she went off into a paroxysm of shrieks and cries, wriggling and squirming in a most wonderful way, considering how strongly I had fastened her down; her eyes seemed to start out of her head under the awful tickling that she was experiencing; she plunged so frantically that although I was tightly gripping her buttocks, she almost dislodged my mouth, the rigid muscles of her lovely thighs testifying to the desperate effort she was making to get loose. But the subtle titillation had aroused her sexual desires, without her recognizing the fact in her distress. Her cunt began to open of its own accord, soon the clitoris was revealed turgid and stiff, quivering in sexual excitement, then her orifice began to yawn and show the way to Paradise; deeper and deeper plunged my tongue into its satiny recess, Alice mechanically and unconsciously thrusting herself upwards as if to meet my tongue's downward darting and strokes. Her head rolled from side to side, as, with half-closed eyes, she struggled with a fast-increasing feeling that she must surrender herself to the imperious call of her sexual nature, yet endeavoring desperately not to do so, hampered by long-established notions of chastity. Her breath came in snatches, her breasts heaved and panted, half-broken ejaculations escaped from her quivering lips. The time had arrived for the sacrifice and the victim was ready. Thrusting my tongue as deeply into her cunt as I could force it, I gave her one final and supreme tickling, then taking her clitoris between my lips, I sucked hard on it, all the while tickling it with my tongue.

It was too much for Alice. "Stop…stop…it's coming!…it's coming!" she gasped. An irresistible wave of lust swept away the last barriers of chastity, and, with a despairing wail: "Oh…Oh! I can't help…it! Oh…Oh…Oh!!!" she spent frantically!

Feeling her go, I sprang to my feet to watch Alice as she spent. It was a wonderful sight! There she lay on her back, completely naked, forced to expose her most secret charm, utterly absorbed in the sensations of the moment, her body pulsating and thrilling with each sexual spasm, her closed eyes, half-open lips, and stiff breasts indicating the intensity of the emotions that possessed her. And so she remained for a minute or two, as if in a semi-swoon.

Presently I noticed a relaxing of her muscles; then she drew a long breath and dreamily opened her eyes. For a moment she seemed dazed and almost puzzled about where she was: then her eyes fell on me, and in a flash she remembered everything. A wave of color surged furiously over her face and bosom at the thought that I had witnessed her unconscious transports and raptures as she yielded herself to her sexual passions in spite of herself. Stirring uneasily, she averted her eyes, flushing hotly again. I stooped down and kissed her passionately; then, without a word, I unfastened her, raised her from the settee and supported her to the large armchair, where she promptly curled herself up, burying her blushing face in her hands.

I thought it wisest to leave her undisturbed for a brief space, so I busied myself quietly in pouring out two glasses of wine, and knowing what severe calls were going to be made on Alice's reproductive powers, I took the opportunity to fortify these by dropping into her glass the least possible dose of cantharides.

8.

*M*y readers will naturally wonder what my condition of mind and body was after both had been subjected to such intense inflammation as was inevitable from my close association with Alice dressed and Alice naked.

Naturally I had been in a state of considerable erotic excitation from the moment that Alice's naked charms were revealed, especially when my hands were playing with her breasts and toying with her cunt. But I had managed to control myself. The events recorded in the last chapter however proved too much for me. The contact of my lips and tongue with Alice's maiden lips, breasts, and cunt and the sight of her as she spent were more than I could stand, and I was nearly mad with lust and an overpowering desire that she should somehow satisfy for the time this lust after her.

But how could it be arranged? I wanted to keep her virgin as long as I possibly could, for I had not nearly completed my carefully prepared programme of fondling and quasi-tortures that gain double spice and salaciousness when perpetrated on a virgin. To fuck her therefore was out of the question. Of course there was her mouth, and my blood boiled at the idea of being sucked by Alice; but it was patent that she was too innocent and inexperienced to give me this pleasure. There were her breasts: One could have a delicious time no doubt by using them to form a tunnel and to work my prick between them, but this was a game better played later on. There were her hands, and sweetly could Alice frig me, if she devoted one dainty hand to my prick, while the other played with my testicles, but nothing would be easier than for her to score off me heavily, by giving the latter an innocent wrench that would throw me out of action entirely. The only possible remaining method was her bottom, and while I was feverishly debating its advisability, an innocent movement of hers and the consequent change of attitude suddenly displayed the superb curves and general lusciousness of her posteriors. In spite of my impatience, I involuntarily paused to admire their glorious opulence! Yes, I would bottom-fuck Alice: I would deprive her of one of her maidenheads.

But would she let me do so? True, she had just sworn to submit herself to my caprices whatever they might be, but such a caprice no doubt never entered into her innocent mind, and unless she did submit herself quietly, I might be baffled and in the excitement of the struggle and the contact with her warm naked flesh, I might spend, "waste my sweetness on the desert air!" Suddenly a cruelly brilliant idea struck me, and at once I proceeded to act on it.

She was still lying curled up in the armchair. I touched her on the shoulder; she looked up hurriedly.

"I think you have rested long enough, Alice," I said, "now get up, I want you to put me right!" And I pointed to my prick now in a state of terrible erection! "See!" I continued, "you must do something to put it out of its torment, just as I have already so sweetly allayed your lustful cravings!" She flushed painfully! "You can do it either with your mouth or by means of your bottom. Now say quick—for I am just bursting with lust for you!"

She hid her face in her hands! "No, no," she ejaculated—"No. Oh, no! I couldn't, really I couldn't!"

"You must!" I replied somewhat sternly, for I was getting mad with unsatisfied lust, "remember the promises you have just made! Come now, no nonsense! Say which you'll do!"

She threw herself at my feet: "No, no," she cried. "I can't!"

Bending over her, I gripped her shoulders: "You have just sworn that you would let me do to you anything I pleased, and that you would do anything I might tell you to do, in other words, that you would both actively and passively minister to my pleasures. I have given you your choice! If you prefer to be active, I will lie on my back and you can suck and excite me into spending: If you would rather be passive, you can lie on your face and I will bottom-fuck you! Now which shall it be?"

"No, no, no!" she moaned in her distress. "I can't do either. Really I can't!"

Exasperated by her non-compliance, I determined to get by force what I wanted, and before she could guess my intentions, I had gripped her firmly 'round her body, then half-carried and half-dragged her to the piano duet-stool which also contained a hidden mechanism. I forced her onto it, face downwards, and in spite of her resistance, I soon fixed the straps to her wrists and ankles; then I set the mechanism working, sitting on her in order to keep her in the proper position, as she desperately fought to get loose. Cleverly managing the straps, I soon forced Alice into the desired position, flat on her face and astride the stool, her wrists and ankles being secured to the longitudinal wooden bars that maintained the rigidity of the couch.

Alice was now fixed in such a way that she could not raise her shoulders or bosom, but by straightening her legs, she could heave her bottom upwards a little. Her position was perfect for my purpose, and lustfully I gloated over the spectacle of her magnificent buttocks, her widely parted thighs affording me a view of both of her virgin orifices—both now at my disposal!

I passed my hands amorously over the glorious backside now at my mercy, pinching, patting, caressing, and stroking the glorious flesh; my hands wandered along her plump thighs, revelling in their smoothness and softness, Alice squirming and wriggling deliciously! Needless to say her cunt was not neglected, my fingers tenderly and lovingly playing with it and causing her the most exquisitely irritating titillation.

After enjoying myself in this way for a few minutes and having thoroughly felt her bottom, I left her to herself for a moment while I went to a cupboard, Alice watching my movements intently. After rummaging about, I found what I sought, a riding whip of some curious soft substance, very springy and elastic, calculated to sting but not to mark the flesh. I was getting tired of having to use force on Alice to get what I wanted and considered it would be useful policy to make her learn the result of not fulfilling her promises. There is no better way to bring a girl to her senses than by whipping her soundly, naked if possible! And here was Alice, naked; fixed in the best possible position for a whipping!

As I turned towards her, whip in hand, she instantly guessed her fate and shrieked for mercy, struggling frantically to get loose. Deaf to her pitiful pleading, I placed myself in position to command her backside, raised the whip, and gave her a cut right across the fleshiest part!

A fearful shriek broke from her! Without losing time, I administered another, and another, and another, Alice simply now yelling with the pain, and wriggling in a marvelous way, considering how tightly she was tied down. I had never before whipped a girl, although I had often read and been told of the delights of the operation to the operator, but the reality far surpassed my most vivid expectations! And the naked girl I was whipping was *Alice*, the object of my lust, the girl who had jilted me, the girl I was about to ravish! Mad with exultation, I disregarded her agonized shrieks and cries. With cruel deliberation, I selected the tenderest parts of her bottom for my cuts, aiming sometimes at one luscious cheek, then the other, then across both, visiting the tender inside of her widely parted thighs! Her cries were music to my ear in my lustful frenzy, while her wiggles and squirms and the agitated plunging of her hips and buttocks enthralled my eyes. But soon, too soon, her strength began to fail her, her shrieks degenerated into inarticulate ejaculations! There was now little pleasure in continuing her punishment, so, most reluctantly, I ceased!

Soothingly I passed my right hand over Alice's quivering bottom and stroked it caressingly, alleviating, in a wonderfully short time, the pain. In spite of the severity of the whipping she had received, she was not marked at all! Her flesh was like that of a baby, slightly pinker perhaps, but clean and fresh. As I tenderly restored her to ease, her trembling died away, her breath began to come more freely and normally, and soon she was herself again.

"Has the nonsense been whipped out of you, Alice?" I asked mockingly. She quivered, but did not answer.

"What, not yet?" I exclaimed, pretending to misunderstand her. "Must I give you another turn?" and I raised the whip as if to commence again.

"No, no!" she cried in genuine terror, "I'll be good!"

"Then lie still and behave yourself," I replied, throwing the whip away into a corner of the room.

From a drawer I took a pot of cold cream. Alice, who was fearsomely watching every movement of mine, cried in alarm: "Jack, what are you going to do to me?...oh, tell me!" My only response was to commence lubricating her arse-hole, during which operation she squirmed delightfully, then placing myself full in her sight, I set to work anointing my rampant prick. "Guess, dear!" I said.

She guessed accurately! For a moment she was struck absolutely dumb with horror, then struggling desperately to get free, she cried, "Oh! my God...no, Jack...no!...you'll kill me!"

"Don't be alarmed," I said quietly, as I caressed her quivering buttocks, "think a moment; larger things have come out than what is going in! Lie still, Alice, or I shall have to whip you!" Then placing myself in position behind her, I leant forward till the head of my prick rested against her arse-hole.

"My God!—no, no!" she shrieked, frantically wriggling her buttocks in an attempt to thwart me. But the contact of my prick with Alice's flesh maddened me; thrusting fiercely forward, I, with very little difficulty, shoved my prick halfway up Alice's bottom with apparently little or no pain to her; then falling on her, I clasped her in my arms and rammed myself well into her, till I felt my balls against her and the cheeks of her bottom against my stomach!

My God! it was like heaven to me! Alice's naked quivering body was closely pressed to mine! My prick was buried to its hairs in her bottom, revelling in the warmth of her interior! I shall never forget it! Prolonging my rapturous ecstasy, I rested motionless on her, my hands gripping and squeezing her palpitating breasts so conveniently placed for their delectation, my cheek against her averted face, listening to the inarticulate murmurs wrung unconsciously from her by the violence of her emotions and the unaccountably strange pleasure she was experiencing, and which she confessed to by meeting my suppressed shoves with spasmodic upward heavings of her bottom—oh! it was Paradise!

Inspired by a sudden thought, I slipped my right hand down to Alice's cunt and gently tickled it with my forefinger, but without penetrating. The effect was marvelous! Alice plunged wildly under me with tumultuous quivering, her bosom palpitating and fluttering: "Ah!...Ah!..." she ejaculated, evidently falling prey to uncontrollable sexual cravings! Provoked beyond endurance, I let myself go! For a few moments there was a perfect cyclone of frenzied upheavings from her, mixed with fierce down-thrustings from me, then blissful ecstasy, as I spent madly into Alice, flooding her interior with my boiling tribute! "Ah!...Ah!..." she gasped, as she felt herself inundated by my hot discharge! Her cunt distractedly sought my finger, a violent spasm shook her, and, with a scarcely articulate cry but indicative of the intense rapture, Alice spent on my finger with quivering vibrations, her head falling forward as she half-swooned in her ecstasy! She had lost the maidenhood of her bottom!!!

For some seconds we both lay silent and motionless save for an occasional tremor; I utterly absorbed in the indescribable pleasure of spending into Alice as she lay tightly clasped in my arms! She was the first to stir (possibly incommoded by my weight), gently turning her face towards me, coloring furiously as our eyes met! I pressed my cheek against hers, she did not flinch but seemed to respond. Tenderly I kissed her, she turned her face fully towards me and of her own accord she returned my kiss! Was it that I had tamed her? Or had she secretly tasted certain pleasure during the violation of her bottom? Clasping her closely to me I whispered: "You have been a good girl this time, Alice, very good!!" She softly rubbed her cheek against mine! "Did I hurt you?" I asked.

She whispered back: "Very little at first, but not afterwards!"

"Did you like it?" I inquired maliciously. For answer she hid her face in the settee, blushing hotly! But I could feel a small thrill run through her!

After a moment's silence, she raised her head again, moved uneasily, then murmured: "Oh! let me get up now!"

"Very well," I replied, and unclasping my arms from 'round her, I slowly drew my prick out of her bottom, untied her—then taking her into one of the alcoves I showed her a bidet all ready for her use and left her. Passing into the other, I performed the needful ablutions to myself, then radiant with my victory and with having relieved my overcharged desires, I awaited Alice's re-appearance.

9.

*P*resently Alice emerged from her screen, looking much freshened up by her ablutions. She had taken the opportunity to put her hair in order, it having become considerably disarranged and rumpled from her recent struggling.

Her face had lost the woebegone look, and there was a certain air of almost satisfaction about her that I could not understand, for she smiled as our eyes met, at the same time faintly coloring and concealing her cunt with her left hand as she approached me.

I offered her a glass of wine, which she drank, then I passed my left arm 'round her waist and drew her to the armchair, into which I placed myself, making her seat herself on my thighs and pass her right arm 'round my neck. Then, drawing her closely to me, I proceeded to kiss her ripe lips. She made no resistance; nor did she respond.

We sat in silence for a minute or two, I gently stroking her luscious breasts while unsuccessfully trying to read in her eyes what was her present frame of mind. Undoubtedly, during the ravishment of her bottom, she had tasted some pleasure sufficiently delicious to make her condone for its sake her *violation à la derrière* and practically to pardon her violator!—what could it be?

I thought I would try a long shot, so presently I whispered in her ear, "Wouldn't you like that last all over again?"

I felt her quiver. She was silent for a moment, then asked softly, "Do you mean as a further punishment?" steadily keeping her eyes averted from me and flushing slightly.

"Oh! no," I replied, "it was so very evident that it was not 'punishment' to you" and I tried to catch her eyes as I pressed her amorously to me! "I meant as a little entr'acte."

Alice blushed furiously! I felt her arm 'round my neck tighten its embrace, and she nestled herself closer to me! "Not all!" she murmured gently.

"How much then?...or which part?" I whispered again.

"Oh! how can I possibly tell you!" she whispered back, dropping her face onto my shoulder and snuggling up to me, then throwing her left arm also 'round me, thereby uncovering her cunt!

I took the hint! "May I guess?" I whispered.

Without waiting for a reply, I slipped my right hand down from her breast and over her rounded belly, then began gently to toy with her hairs and caress her slit! Alice instantly kissed me twice passionately! She was evidently hot with lust, inflamed possibly by the dose of cantharides she had unknowingly swallowed!

"Then let me arrange you properly," I said. "Come we'll sit in front of the mirror and look at ourselves!" Alice blushed, not quite approving of the idea, but willing to please me!

So I moved the armchair in front of the mirror and seated myself in it. I then made Alice place herself on my thighs, her bottom being right over my prick, which promptly began to return to life, raising its drooping head until it rested against her posteriors. Passing my left arm around her waist, I held her firmly to me. Then I made her part her legs, placing her left leg between mine while her right leg rested against the arm of the chair, my right thigh, in fact, separating her thighs.

Alice was now reflected in the mirror in three-quarter profile, but her parted legs allowed the whole of her cunt, with its glorious wealth of hair, to be fully seen! Her arms hung idly at her sides—I had made her promise not to use them!

We gazed at our reflection for a moment, our eyes meeting in the glass! Alice looked just lovely in her nakedness!

"Are you ready" I asked, with a significant smile! Alice wriggled a little as if to settle herself down more comfortably, then turning her face (now all aflame and rosy red) to me she shamefacedly nodded, then kissed me!

"Keep your cheek against mine, and watch yourself in the glass, Alice," I whispered, then I gently placed my right hand on her sweet belly and slowly approached her cunt!

A thrill, evidently of pleasure, quivered through her as she felt my fingers pass through her hairs and settle on her cunt! "Ah!" she murmured, moving deliciously over my prick as I commenced to tenderly frig her, now fingering her slit, now penetrating her still virgin orifice, now tickling her clitoris—causing her all the time the most deliciously lascivious transports, to which she surrendered herself by licentiously oscillating and jogging herself backwards and forwards as if to meet and stimulate my finger!

Presently Alice became still more excited; her breasts stiffened, her nostrils dilated! Noting this, I accelerated the movements of my finger, at the same time clasping her more firmly to me, my eyes riveted on her image in the glass and gloating over the spectacle she presented in her voluptuous raptures! Suddenly she caught her breath! Quickly I tickled her on her clitoris! "Oh!...Oh!...Oh!...Oh!" she ejaculated—then spent in ecstasy, maddening me by the quivering of her warm buttocks, between which my now rampant prick raged, held down!

I did not remove my finger from Alice's cunt, but kept it in her while she spent, slightly agitating it from time to time, to accentuate her ecstasy. But, as soon as I considered her sexual orgasm had exhausted itself, I began again to frig her. Then an idea flashed through my brain: why should I not share her raptures? Carefully I watched for an opportunity! Soon I worked her again into an awful state of desire, panting with unsatisfied lust and furiously excited, obviously the result of the cantharides! Alice jerked herself about madly and spasmodically on my thighs! Presently an unusually violent movement of hers released my prick from its sweet confinement under her bottom; promptly it sprang up stark and stiff!

Quick as thought, I gripped Alice tightly and rammed myself fiercely into her bottom!!

"No!...no!...no!..." she cried and strove to rise and so dislodge me, but I pressed her firmly down on my thighs and compelled her to remain impaled on my prick, creating a diversion by frigging her harder than ever!!

"Kiss me," I gasped, frantic with lust under my sensations in Alice's bottom and the sight of her naked self in the glass, quivering, palpitating, wriggling!! Quickly Alice pressed her lips on mine, our breaths mingled, our tongues met, my left hand caught hold of one of her breasts and squeezed it as her eyes closed. An electric shock ran through her!...then Alice spent frantically, plentifully bedewing my finger with her virgin distillation—at the same moment receiving inside her my boiling essence, as I shot it madly into her, my prick throbbing convulsively under the contractions of her rear sphincter muscles agitated and actuated by her ecstatic transports!!

Oh! the sensations of the moment! How Alice spent! How I discharged into her!!

It must have been a full minute before either of us moved, save for the involuntary tremors, which, from time to time, ran through us as our sexual excitement died away! Alice, now limp and nerveless, but still impaled on my prick, reposed on me, my finger dwelt motionless in her cunt, luxuriating in its envelope of warm, throbbing flesh! And so we rested, exhausted after our lascivious orgy, both half-conscious!

I was the first to come to myself, and, as I caught sight of our reflection in· the mirror, the licentious tableau we presented sent an involuntary quiver through me that my prick communicated to Alice, thus rousing her! As she dreamily opened her eyes, her glance also fell on the mirror! She started, became suddenly wide-awake, flushed rosy red, then hid her face in her hands, murmuring brokenly: "Oh!...how horrible!...how horrible!...what...have you... made me do?..." half-sobbing in her shame; now that her sexual delirium had subsided and horribly conscious that my prick was still lodged in her bottom and impaling her! Foreseeing her action, I brought my right arm to the assistance of my left and held her forcibly down and so prevented her from rising and slipping off me! "What's the matter, Alice?" I asked soothingly, as she struggled to rid herself of my prick!

"Oh, let me go!—let me go!" she begged still with her face in her hands, in such evident distress that I deemed it best to comply and let her hurry off to her bidet, as she clearly desired.

So I released Alice: she slowly drew her bottom off my prick and rushed behind her screen. Following her example, I repaired to my corner and, after the necessary ablutions, I awaited Alice's return.

10.

*P*ending Alice's re-appearance, I asked with myself the important question: 'what next should I do to her?' There was no doubt that I had succeeded in taming her, that I had now only to state my wishes and she would comply with them! But this very knowledge seemed to destroy the pleasure I had anticipated in having her in such utter subjection, the spice of the proceedings up to now undoubtedly lay in my forcing her to endure my salacious and licentious caprices, in spite of the most determined and desperate resistance she could make! Now that she had become a dull passive representative of the proud and voluptuous girl I had wanted, I should practically be flogging a dead horse were I to continue my programme!

But there was one experience which on no account was to be omitted, forming as it did the culmination of my revenge as well as of my lust, one indignity which she could not and would not passively submit to, one crowning triumph over her which she could never question or deny—and this was...her violation!—the ravishing of her maidenhead!!

Alice was now fully educated to appreciate the significance of every detail of the process of transforming a girl into a woman; my fingers and lips had thoroughly taught her maiden cunt its duty, while my prick, when lodged in the throbbing recesses of her bottom, had acquainted her with the phenomenon of the masculine discharge at the crisis of pleasure, of the feminine ecstasy in receiving it, while her transports in my arms, although somewhat restricted by the circumstances, had revealed to her the exquisitely blissful sensations mutually communicated by such close clinging contact of male and female flesh! Yes! I would now devote the rest of the afternoon to fucking her.

Hardly had I arrived at this momentous decision when Alice came out of her alcove after an unusually prolonged absence. She had evidently thoroughly refreshed and freshened herself, and she looked simply fetching as she halted hesitatingly on pressing through the curtains, shielding her breasts with one hand and her cunt with the other, in charming shamefaced confusion. Obedient to my gesture, she came timidly towards me; she allowed me to pass my arm 'round her waist and kiss her, and then to lead her to the table where I made her drink a small tumbler of champagne that I had previously poured out for her, and for which she seemed most grateful. Then I gently whispered to her that we should lie down together on the couch for a little rest, and soon we were closely lying at our ease, she pressed and held amorously against me by my encircling arms.

For a minute or two we rested in silence, then the close conjunction of our naked bodies began to have the inevitable result on me—and I think also on her! Clasping her closely against me, I murmured: "Now, Alice, darling, I think the time has come for you to surrender to me your maidenhead...for you to be my bride!" And I kissed her passionately.

She quivered, moved herself uneasily as if trying to slip out of my encircling arms, trembling exceedingly, but remained silent.

I made as if to place her on her back, whispering: "Open your legs, dear!"

"No! No! Jack" Alice ejaculated, struggling to defend herself, and successfully resisting my attempt to roll her over onto her back, "let me go, dear Jack!...surely you have revenged yourself on me sufficiently!"...And she endeavored to rise.

I held her down firmly, and, in spite of her determined resistance, I got Alice on her back and myself on top of her. But she kept her legs so obstinately closed, and, in that position, I could not get mine between them! I began to get angry! Gripping her to me till her breasts flattened themselves against my chest, I raised my head and looked her sternly in the eyes.

"Now, Alice, no more nonsense," I said brusquely. "I'm going to fuck you! Yield yourself at once to me and do as I tell you—or I shall tie you down on this couch and violate you by force in a way you won't like! Now, once and for all, are you going to submit or are you not?"

She closed her eyes in an agony of distress!

"Jack!...Jack!..." she murmured brokenly, then stopped as if unable to speak because of her overwhelming emotion!

"I can only take it that you prefer to be ravished by force rather than to be treated as a bride! Very well!" I rejoined. And I slipped off her as if to rise and tie her down. But she caught my hand; looked at me so pleadingly and with so piteous an expression in her lovely eyes that I sat down by her side on the couch.

"Upon my word I don't understand you, Alice!" I said, not unkindly. "You have known all along that you were to lose your maidenhead and you have solemnly promised to yield it to me and to conform to all my desires, whatever they might be. Now, when the time has arrived for you to be fucked, you seem to forget all your promises!"

"But...but..." she stammered, "I didn't know...then! I thought... there was only one way!...so...I promised!...But you...have...had me...twice...another way!...oh! let me off!...do let me off!...I can't submit!...truly I can't...have me again...the...other way...if...you must!...but not...this way!...oh!...not this way!!!"

With my right hand I stroked her cunt gently, noting how she flinched when it was touched! "I want *this* virginity Alice! This virginity of your cunt! Your real maidenhead! And you must let me have it! Now am I to whip you again into submission? Don't be foolish! You can guess how this whip will hurt when properly applied, as it will be. You know you'll then have to give in! Why not do so at once, and spare yourself the pain and indignity of a severe whipping?"

Alice moaned pitifully: "Oh, my God!"—then was silent for a few seconds, her face working painfully in her distress! Then she turned to me: "I must give in!" she murmured brokenly, "I couldn't endure...to be whipped...naked as I am!...so take me...and do what you desire!...only treat me as kindly as you can! Now...I don't know why I ask it...but...kiss me...let me think I'm your wife...and on my wedding night!...not...." She stopped, struggling with her emotions, then bravely put up her mouth with a pitiful smile to be kissed!

Promptly I took her lovely naked form lovingly in my arms, and pressing her to me till her breasts flattened against me, I passionately kissed her trembling lips again and again, until she gasped for breath.

Then stooping, I repeated the caress on each breast and then on her quivering cunt, kissing the latter over and over again and interspersing my kisses with delicate lingual caresses! Then I succeeded in soothing her natural agitation at thus reaching the critical point of her maiden existence.

11.

Thus, at last, Alice and I found ourselves together naked on the Couch
of Love!—she, ill at ease and down-
cast at having to thus yield up her virginity and dreading horribly the
process of being initiated by me into the mysteries of sexual love!—I,
overjoyed at the prospect of ravishing Alice and conquering her maidenhead! Side by side on our backs, we lay in silence, my left hand
clasping her right till she had regained her composure a little.

As soon as I saw she had become calmer, I slipped my arms 'round
her, and, turning on my side towards her, I drew her tenderly to me, but
still keeping her flat on her back; then I kissed her lips again and
again ardently, murmuring lovingly between my kisses: "My little
wife...my wee wife!"—noting delightedly how her downcast face bright-
ened at my adoption of her fantasy, and feeling her respond almost
fondly to my kisses.

"May I learn something about my wife?" I whispered as I placed
my right hand on Alice's maiden breasts and began feeling them as if
she were, indeed, my bride! Alice smiling tenderly, yielding herself to
my caprice, and quivering anew under the voluptuous sensations

communicated to her by my inquisitive fingers! "Oh! what little beauties! oh! what darling bubbies!" I murmured amidst fresh kisses. Alice was now beginning to look quite pleased at my using her own pet name for her treasures: She joined almost heartily into my game. I continued to fondle and squeeze her luscious breasts for a little longer, then carried my hand lower down, but suddenly arrested it, whispering: "May I?"

At this absurd travesty of a bridegroom's chivalrous respect to his bride, Alice fairly laughed (poor girl, her first laugh in that room all day!) then gaily nodded, putting up her lips for more kisses! Overjoyed to see her thus forgetting her woes, I pressed my lips on hers and kept them there, punctuating the kisses with feignedly timid advance of my hand over her belly, till it invaded the precincts of her cunt! "Oh! my darling! oh! my sweetheart, oh, my wife!" I murmured passionately as my fingers roved wantonly all over Alice's virgin cunt, playing with her hairs, feeling and pressing its fleshiness insidiously, and toying with her slit—but not yet penetrating it! Alice all the while abandoned herself freely to the lascivious sensations induced by my fingerings, jogging her buttocks upwards and waggling her hips, ejaculating, "Ah!" and "Oh!" in spite of my lips being glued to hers, nearly suffocating her with kisses!

After a few minutes of this delicious exploitation of the most private part of Alice's body, I stopped my finger on her virgin orifice! "Pardon me, sweet," I whispered; then gently inserted it into Alice's cunt as far as I could, as if to assure myself as to her virgin condition, all the time smothering her with kisses. Keenly appreciating the humor of the proceedings, in spite of the serious lover-like air I was assuming, Alice laughed out heartily, unconsciously heaving herself up so as to meet my finger and slightly opening her thighs to allow it freer access to her cunt. My tongue took advantage of her laughter to dart through her parted lips in search of her tongue, which she then sweetly resigned to my ardent homage! "Oh! wife…my wife! my sweet wife, my virgin wife!" I murmured, as if enchanted to find her a maiden! "Oh what a delicious cunny you have—so fat! so soft, so juicy!—my wife, oh, wife." I breathed passionately into her ear, as I agitated my finger inside her cunt half frigging her and stopping her protests with my kisses, till I saw how I was exciting her! "Little wife" I whispered with a grin I could not for the life of me control. "Little wife, shall I make you come?"

In spite of her almost uncontrollable and self-absorbing sexual irritation, Alice laughed out, then nodded, closing her eyes as if in anticipation of her now fast-approaching ecstasy! A little more subtle titillation and Alice spent blissfully on my finger, jerking herself about lasciviously and evidently experiencing the most voluptuous raptures and transports.

I waited till her sexual spasm had ceased: "Wife," I whispered, rousing her with my kisses, "Little wife! oh you naughty girl. How you seemed to enjoy it. Tell me wife, was it then so good?"

As she opened her eyes, Alice met mine brimming with merriment: she blushed, then clasped me in her soft arms and kissed me passionately, murmuring: "Darling, oh, darling!" Then she burst out laughing at our ridiculousness! And so we lay for a few delicious moments, clasped in each other's arms.

Presently I murmured: "Now, wife, you'll like to learn something about me, eh?"

Alice laughed merrily at the quaint conceit, then colored furiously as she remembered that it would mean the introduction of her virgin hands to my virile organs. "Sit up, wife, dear, and give me your pretty hands." I said.

Alice, now glowing red with suppressed excitement and lust, quickly raised herself to a sitting position at my side. I took her dainty hands, which she yielded rather coyly into mine, turned on my back, opened my legs, and then guided her right hand onto my prick and her left to my testicles, then left her to indulge and satisfy in any manner she saw fit her senses of sight and touch, wondering whether it would occur to her that the fires she was about to excite in me would have to be extinguished in her virgin self when she was being ravished, as before long she would be!

For certainly half a minute, Alice intently inspected my organs of generation, leaning over me and supporting herself by placing her right hand on my stomach and her left on my thigh. I wondered what thoughts passed through her mind as she gazed curiously on what very soon would be the instruments of her violation and the conquerors of her virginity! But she made no sign.

Presently she steadied herself on her left hand, then timidly, with her right hand, she took hold of my prick gently, glancing curiously at me as if to note the effect of the touch of her soft hand on so excitable a part of my person, then smiling wickedly and almost triumphantly as she saw me quiver with pleasure. Oh! the exquisite sensations that accompanied her touch. Growing bolder, she held my prick erect and gently touched my balls with her slender forefinger, as if to test their substance, then took them in her hand, watching me eagerly out of the corners of her eyes to note the effect on me! I was simply thrilling with the pleasure. For a few minutes she lovingly played with my organs, generally devoting a hand to each, but sometimes she would hold my prick between one finger and thumb, while with her other hand, she would amuse herself by working the loose folds of skin off and on the knob! At another time, she would place my prick between her soft warm palms and pretend to roll it. Another time she seized a testicle in each hand, oh so sweetly and gently, and caressed them. Had I not taken the edge off my sexual ardor by the two spendings in Alice's bottom, I would surely have discharged under the tenderly provocative ministration of her fingers. As it was, I had to exercise every ounce of my self-control to prevent an outbreak.

Presently I said quietly but significantly: "Little wife, may I tell you that between husband and wife, kissing is not only sanctioned but is considered even laudable!"

Alice laughed nervously, glanced quickly at me, then with heightening color, looked intently at my prick, which she happened at that moment to be grasping tightly in her right hand, its head protruding above her thumb and fingers, while with her left forefinger she was delicately stroking and tickling my balls! After a moment's hesitation, she bent down and squeezed my prick tightly (as if to prevent anything from issuing out of it) then softly kissed its head! Oh, my delicious sensations as her lips touched my prick! Emboldened by the success of her experiment, Alice set to work to kiss my balls sweetly, then passed her lips over the whole of my organ, showering kisses on them, but favouring especially my balls, which had for her a wonderful attraction, burying her lips in my scrotum, and (I really believe) tonguing them! Such attentions could only end in one way. Inflamed almost beyond endurance by the play of her sweetly irritating lips, my prick became so stiff and stark that Alice, in alarm, thought she had better cease her ministrations, and with blushing cheeks and a certain amount of trepidation, she lay herself down alongside of me.

By this time I was so mad with lust that I could hardly control myself, and as soon as Alice lay down I seized her by the arms, drew her to me, showered kisses on her lips, then with an abrupt movement, I rolled her over onto her back, slipping on top of her. In an effort to counteract my attack she separated her legs the better to push me back! Quick as thought, I forced myself between them!

> *Now I was in the very lists of Love,*
> *Her champion, mounted for the hot encounter!*
>> (Shakespeare, in *Venus and Adonis*.)

Alice was at my mercy! I could not have her at better advantage. She struggled desperately to dislodge me, but to no avail.

Gripping her tightly, I got my stiff and excited prick against the lips of her cunt, then pushing steadily, I drove it into Alice, burying its head in her! Despite her fearful struggles and rapid movements of her buttocks and hips, I made another thrust, entering still further into her cunt, then felt myself blocked! Alice screamed agonizingly: "Oh...oh, stop, you're hurting me!" throwing herself wildly about in her pain and despair, for she recognized that she was being violated. Knowing that it was her maiden membrane that was stopping my advance into her, and that this now was the last defense of her virginity, I rammed into her vigorously! Suddenly I felt something give way inside her. Finally my prick glided well up her cunt and it did not require the despairing shriek that came from Alice to tell me that I had broken through the last barriers and had conquered her virginity!

Oh, my exultation! At last I had ravished Alice, I had captured her maidenhead and was now actually fucking her in spite of herself! She, poor girl, lay beneath me tightly clasped in my arms, a prey to the keenest shame, deprived of her maidenhead, transfixed with my prick, her cunt suffering martyrdom from its sudden distension and smarting with the pain of her violation! Pitying her, I lay still for some seconds so as to allow the interior of her cunt to stretch a bit, but I was too wrought up and mad with lust to long remain inactive in such surroundings.

With a final thrust, I sent my prick well home, Alice's hair and mine interweaving. She shrieked again! Then agitating myself gently on her, I began to fuck her, first with steady strokes of my buttocks, then with more rapid and uneven strokes and thrusts, she quivering under me, overwhelmed by her emotions at thus finding her pure body compelled to become the recipient of my lust and by the strangely delicious pleasures that the movements of my prick inside her cunt were arousing within her. Alice no longer struggled, but lay passive in my arms, unconsciously accommodating herself to my movements on her, and involuntarily working her hips and bottom, instinctively yielding to the prompting of her now fast-increasing sexual cravings by jogging herself up as if to meet my downward thrusts!

Shall I ever forget my sensations at that moment? Alice, the long
desired Alice, the girl of all girls, the unconscious object of all my
desires—Alice lay beneath me, tightly clasped in my arms, naked,
quivering, her warm flesh throbbing against mine, my prick lodged in
her cunt, her tearful face in full sight, her breasts palpitating and her
bosom heaving in her agitation!—gasping, panting in the acutest shame
and distress at being violated, yet unconsciously longing to have her
sexual desires satisfied while dreading the consummation of her
deflowering! I could no longer control myself! Clasping her yielding
figure still more closely against me, I let myself go!—thrusting, ramming,
shoving and agitating my prick spasmodically in her, I frenziedly set
to work to fuck her! A storm of rapid tumultuous jogs, a half-strangled
"oh—oh! Oh!!" from Alice as I spent deliriously into her with my hot
discharge, at the same moment feeling the head of my prick christened
by the warm gush that burst from Alice as she also frantically spent,
punctuating the pulsations of her discharge by voluptuous upheavings
of her wildly agitated bottom.

I remained master of myself, notwithstanding my ecstatic delirium, but Alice fainted under the violence of the sexual eruption for the
first time legitimately induced within her! My warm kisses on her
upturned face, however soon revived her. When she came to and
found herself still lying naked in my arms and harboring my prick in
the freshly opened asylum of her cunt, she begged me to set her free.
But she had not yet extinguished the flames of lust and desire her
provocative personality and appetizing nakedness had kindled and
which she had stimulated to white heat by the tender manipulations
and kisses she had bestowed on my testicles and prick! The latter still
remained rampant and stiff and burned to riot again within the deliciously warm and moist recesses of Alice's cunt—while I longed to
make her expire again in the sweet agonies of satisfied sexual desire
and to witness and share her involuntary transports and wondrous
ecstasies as she passed from sexual spasm while being sweetly fucked.

So I whispered amidst my kisses: "Not yet, Alice! Not yet! Once
more, Alice! you'll enjoy it this time," I then began gently to fuck her
again.

"No, no," she cried, plunging wildly beneath me in her vain endeavors to dislodge me. "Not again, oh, not again. Let me go! stop! oh,
please, do stop," she implored, almost in tears, and in terrible distress
at the horrible prospect of being ravished a second time.

I only shook my head and endeavored to stifle her cries with my kisses! Seeing that I was determined to enjoy her again, Alice, now in tears, ceased her pleading and resigned herself to her fate!

In order to more easily control her struggles, I had thrown my arms over hers, thus pinioning them. Seeing now that she did not intend to resist me, except perhaps passionately, I relaxed my embrace, set her arms free, passed mine 'round her body, then whispered: "Hug me tightly, you'll be more comfy now, Alice!" She did so. "That's much better, isn't it?" I murmured. She tearfully smiled, then nodded affirmatively, putting up her lips to be kissed.

"Now just lie quietly and enjoy yourself," I whispered, then began to fuck her with slow and steady piston-like thrusts of my prick up and down her cunt! At once Alice's bosom and breasts began to flutter deliciously against my chest. Exercising the fullest control I possibly could bring to bear on my seminal reserves, so that Alice should have every opportunity of indulging and satisfying her sexual appetites and cravings and of fully tasting the delights of copulation, I continued to fuck her steadily, watching her blushing up-turned face and learning from her telltale eyes how she was getting on. Presently she began to agitate her hips and jog herself upwards, then her breath came and went quickly, her eyes turned upwards and half-closed, a spasm convulsed her. She spent! I stopped for a moment. After a few seconds, Alice opened her eyes, blushing rosy red as she met mine. I kissed her lips tenderly, whispering: "Good?" She nodded and smiled. I resumed. Soon she was again quivering and wriggling under me, as a fresh wave of lust seized her; again her eyes closed and again Alice spent blissfully! I saw that I had now thoroughly roused her sexual desires and that she had surrendered herself to their domination and that they were imperiously demanding satisfaction!

I clasped her closely to me, and whispered quickly: "Now, Alice, let yourself go!" I set to work in real earnest, thrusting rapidly and ramming myself well into her! Alice simply abandoned herself to her sensations of the moment! Hugging me to her, she agitated herself wildly under me, plunging madly, heaving herself furiously upwards, tossing her head from side to side, she seemed as if overcome and carried away by a torrent of lust and madly endeavoring to satisfy it! I could hardly hold her still. How many times she spent I do not know, but her eyes were constantly half-closing and opening again as spasm after spasm convulsed her! Suddenly she ejaculated frenziedly: "Now! Now, let me have it! Oh, God! Let me have it all!" Immediately I responded—a few furious shoves, and I poured my boiling essence into Alice, spending frantically in blissful ecstasy. "Ah! Ah!..." she cried, quivering in rapturous transports as she felt herself inundated by my warm discharge!—then a paroxysm swept through her, her head fell back, her eyes closed, her lips opened as she spent convulsively in her turn!

She fainted right away; it had been too much for her! I tried to bring her to by kisses and endearments, but did not succeed. So I drew my prick cautiously out of Alice's cunt, all bloodstained, staunched with a handkerchief the blood—unimpeachable evidence of the rape that had been committed on her virginity. When she soon came to, I assisted her to rise, and, as she seemed half-dazed, supported her as she tottered to her alcove, where she half-fell into a low chair. I brought her a glass of wine, which she drank gratefully, and which greatly revived her. Then I saw that she had everything she could want, water, soap, syringe, and towels. She asked me to leave her, adding she was now all right. Before doing so, I stooped down to receive the first kiss she would give as a woman, having had her last as a girl. Alice threw her arms 'round my neck, drew my face to hers, then kissed me passionately over and over again, quite unable to speak because of her emotion! I returned her kisses with interest, wondering whether she wished to pardon me for violating her!

Presently Alice whispered: "May I dress now?"

I had intended to fuck her again, but I saw how overwrought she was; besides that, the afternoon was late and there was just comfortable time left for her to catch her first train home. So I replied: "Yes, dear, if you like, shall I bring your clothes here?" She nodded gratefully. I carefully collected her garments and took them to her, then left her to herself to dress; pouring out a bumper of champagne, I celebrated silently but exultingly the successful completion of my vengeance and my victory over Alice's virginity, then retired to my alcove and donned my own garments.

In about a quarter of an hour Alice appeared, fully dressed, hatted, and gloved. I threw open the doors and she passed without a word but cast a long glance 'round the room in which she had passed so memorable an afternoon. I called a hansom, placed her in it, and took her to her station in comfortable time for her train. She was very silent during the drive, but made no opposition when I took her hand in mine and stroked it gently. As the train started, I raised my hat with the customary salute, to which she responded in quite her usual pleasant way. No one who witnessed our parting would have dreamt that the pretty ladylike girl had just been forcibly ravished by the quiet gentle-manly man, after having first been stripped naked and subjected to shocking indignities! And as I drove home, I wondered what the outcome of that afternoon's work would be!

Volume 2:

"*The Comedy*"

1.

I will now tell my readers that four months have elapsed since the events recorded in the previous volume. During this period, Alice and I had frequently met at the houses of mutual friends who were under the impression that by thus bringing us together, they were assisting in making a match between us. Our rapture was known only to our two selves, and Alice had quickly recognized that complete silence as to what had happened to her in my Snuggery was her safest policy. And really, there was some excuse for the incorrect impression under which our friends were labouring, for our mutual embarrassment, when we first met after her violation, and her inability to altogether subdue on subsequent occasions a certain agitation and heightened color when I appeared on the scene, were to be symptoms of the "tender passion" that was supposed to be consuming us both.

But Alice's manner to me insensibly became kinder and kinder as time went on. Unknown to herself, there was in her composition a strain of strong sensuality which had lain dormant under the quiet peacefully virtuous life of an English Miss that she had hitherto led;

and it only wanted some fierce sexual stimulant to fan into flame the smouldering fires of her lust. This now had been supplied.

She afterwards confessed to me that, when the sense of humiliation and the bitter regrets for her ravished virginity had died down, she found herself recalling certain moments in which she had tasted the most exquisite pleasure, in spite of the dreadful indignities to which her stark naked self was being submitted, and then unconsciously beginning to long to experience them again till a positive, though unacknowledged, craving sprang up, which she was quite unable to stifle but did not know how to satisfy! When such promising conditions prevail, kind Mother Nature and sweet lady Venus generally come into operation. Soon Alice began to feel towards me the tender regard that every woman seems to cherish towards the fortunate individual who has taken her maidenhead! As I have just stated, she became kinder and kinder, till it was evident to me that she had pardoned my brutality; instead of almost shrinking from me, she undoubtedly seemed to welcome me and was never averse to finding herself alone with me in quiet corners and nooks for two.

On my side, I was beginning to experience a fierce desire once more to hold her naked in my arms and revel in the delights of her delicious person, to taste her lips as we mutually spent in each other's clasped embrace, in other words, to fuck her! Kind Mother Nature had taken us both into her charge: now sweet lady Venus came on the scene.

One evening, Alice and I met at the house of a lady hostess, who placed us together at the dinner table: I naturally devoted myself to Alice afterwards in the drawing room. When the guests began to depart, our hostess asked me if I would mind seeing Alice home in my taxicab, which, of course, I was delighted to do. Strangely enough, the possibilities of a tête-à-tête did not occur to me; and it was only when Alice returned to the hall cloaked and veiled and our hostess had told her that I had very kindly offered to take her home in my taxi that the opportunity of testing her real feelings was suggested to me by the vivid blush that, for a moment, suffused her face and elicited a sympathetic but significant smile from our hostess, who evidently thought she had done us both a good turn. And so she had, but not in the direction she fondly thought!

The taxi had hardly begun to move when we both seemed to remember that we were alone together for the first time since the afternoon on which Alice had been first tortured scientifically, and then ravished! Overcome by some sudden inspiration, our eyes sought each other. In the dim light, I saw Alice's face working under the rush of her emotion, but she was looking at me with eyes full of love and not of anger; she began to cuddle up against me perhaps unconsciously, at the same time turning her face up as if seeking a kiss. I could not resist the mute invitation. Quickly I slipped my left arm 'round her, drew her to me (she yielding to me without a struggle), pressed my lips on hers and fondly rained kisses on her mouth. "Jack!" she murmured lovingly. I felt her thrill under my kisses, then catch her breath and quiver again! I recognized the symptoms. Promptly I slipped my right hand under her clothes, and before she could offer any resistance (even had she desired to do so, which she evidently did not) my hand had reached the sweet junction of her belly and thighs and my fingers began to attack the folds of her chemise through the opening of her drawers in their feverish impatience to get at her cunt! "Jack! Oh, Jack!" Alice again murmured as she pressed herself against me as closely as she could, while at the same time she began to open her thighs slightly, as if to facilitate the operations of my ardent fingers, which, just at that moment, succeeded in displacing the last obstacle and were now resting on her cunt itself.

Alice quivered deliciously at the touch of my hand on her bare flesh as I gently and tenderly stroked her cunt, playing lovingly on its moist palpitating lips and twining her hairs 'round my fingers, but as soon as she felt me tickle her clitoris (time was short and we were fast nearing her rooms, besides which it would have been cruel to have aroused her sexual passions without satisfying them) she threw all restraint to the winds and madly agitated her cunt against my hand, wiggling divinely as I set to work frigging her. Soon came the first blissful ecstasy; a delicious spasm thrilled through her as she spent deliriously on my fingers—then another—and another—and yet another —till, unable to spend any more, she gasped brokenly: "Stop, Jack!...I can't go on!" only half-conscious and utterly absorbed in the overpoweringly exquisite sensations of the moment and the delicious satisfying of the longings and cravings which had been tormenting her. It was full time that we stopped, for the taxi was now turning into her street. Quickly (but reluctantly) I withdrew my hand from Alice's cunt, now moist with her repeated spendings, and I just managed to get her clothes into some sort of order when the cab stopped at her door. I sprang out first and assisted Alice to alight, which she did almost totteringly as she had not yet recovered from her trance of sexual pleasure.

"I'll see you right into your rooms, so that I may be able truly to report that I have faithfully executed the orders," I said laughingly, more for the benefit of the chauffeur than of Alice.

"Thanks very much!" she replied quietly, and, having collected her wraps, I followed her into the house and up the staircase to her apartments on the first floor, carefully closing the door after me.

Alice threw herself into my arms in an ecstasy of delight. I rather think that she expected me to take the opportunity to fuck her—and gladly would I have done so, as I was in a terrible state of lust: but I always hated "snatch-fucking" and if I started with her long enough for her to undress and be properly fucked, it might arouse suspicions that would damage her reputation.

So after a passionate embrace, I whispered: "I must not stop here, darling: when will you come to lunch?"

Alice blushed deliciously, instantly comprehending the significance of my invitation. "Tomorrow!" she murmured, hiding her face on my shoulder.

"Thanks, sweetheart—tomorrow then!" Now get to bed and have a good night's rest: good night my darling!" and after a few more passionate kisses, I left her and rejoined my taxi.

Next morning, after ordering a lunch cunningly calculated to excite and stimulate Alice's lascivious instincts, I made the usual tour of inspection 'round my flat; and from sheer force of habit, I began to test the mechanism concealed in the Snuggery furniture, then suddenly remembered that its assistance was now no longer needed; it had done its duty faithfully; with its help I had stripped, tortured, and violated Alice—and today she was coming of her own free will to be fucked.

The reflection that I would now have to dismantle all this exquisite machinery caused me quite a pang—then I found myself wondering whether it would not be as well to let it remain—on the off chance of its being useful on some later occasion.

In my circle of acquaintances, there were many pretty and attractive girls, married and unmarried, and, if I could only lure some of them into the Snuggery, the torturing and ravishing of them would afford me the most delicious of entertainment, although the spice of revenge that pervaded my outraging of Alice would be absent!

But how was I to effect the luring? They were not likely to come to lunch alone with me, and if accompanied by anyone, it would simply mean that I should again experience the irritating disappointments that I suffered when Marion used to accompany Alice, and, by her presence, prevent the accomplishment of my desires. Besides this, many of the girls I lusted after were hardly more than casual acquaintances whom I could not venture to invite to my flat, except in the company of some mutual friend.

Therein came my inspiration—why not try and induce Alice herself to act as decoy and assistant? If I could only instill in her a taste for Sadism and Sadique pleasures and a penchant for her own sex, and let her see how easily she could satisfy such lascivious fancies by cooperating with me, the possibilities were boundless!

A luncheon invitation to her and our selected victim would, in nine cases out of ten, be accepted by the latter; after lunch the adjournment to the Snuggery would follow as a matter of course at her suggestion— and then her assistance in stripping the girls would be invaluable, after which we could, together, put the girl through a course of sexual torture, painless but distressingly effective, and quench in each other the fires of lust which would spring up as we gloated over our victim's shame and mental agony! Yes! here was the solution of the difficulty; somehow or other, I must induce Alice to give me her cooperation.

2.

I will not take up my readers' time by detailing the incidents of Alice's visit. She was exceedingly nervous and so timid that I saw it was absolutely necessary for me to treat her with the greatest tenderness and delicacy and in no way to offend her susceptibility. She yielded herself to me with pretty bashfulness, blushing divinely when I drew off her last garment and exposed her naked body to my eager eyes; and her transports of delirious pleasure during her first fucking were such that I shall never forget! I had her four delicious times—and when she left, I felt certain that it only wanted a little diplomacy to secure her cooperation!

She, naturally, was more at her ease on her next visit, and I ventured to teach her the art of sucking! When her sweet lips for the first time received my eager prick between them and her warm tongue made its first essays in the subtle art of titillation, I experienced the most heavenly bliss—such as I had never tasted before at the mouth of any woman; and when, after prolonging my exquisite rapture till I could no longer restrain myself, I spent in her mouth in a delirium of pleasure, her pretty confusion was something to be remembered!

I thought I might safely venture to convert her when she paid her third visit, and to this end, I selected from my collection of indecent photographs several that told their tale better than could be expressed by words. Among these was a series known as the "Crucifixion," in which a lovely girl (evidently a nun from her despoiled garments scattered on the floor) was depicted bound naked to a cross, while sometimes the Lady Abbess (in her robes), alone, and sometimes in conjunction with one of the Sisters, indulged their wanton fancies and caprices on the poor girl's breasts and cunt as she hung helpless! One photograph showed the girl fastened naked to a Maltese Cross, the Lady Abbess had inserted her finger into the Nun's cunt while the Sister tickled the Nun's clitoris! In another photograph, a monk was introduced who, kneeling before the Nun (still fastened on a Maltese Cross) sucked her cunt while his uplifted hands, in the attitude of prayer, attacked her helpless breasts! Another series, entitled "La Barrière" depicted various phases in the ravishment of a girl by two ruffians in a solitary part of the Bois de Boulogne. The rest were mostly scenes of Tribadism and of Lesbian love, and interspersed with them were a few representing flagellation by a girl on a girl, both being stark naked!

I was puzzled how best to lead up to the subject, when Alice herself gave me the desired opening. We had just finished our first fuck and were resting on the broad couch, lying in each other's arms, her gentle hand caressing my prick with a view to its restoration to life. She had been rather more silent than usual, for she generally was full of questions which she used to ask with pretty hesitation and delicious naivety—and I was cudgelling my brains to invent a suitable opening.

Suddenly Alice turned to me and said softly: "Jack, I'd awfully like to know one thing!—when you had me tied up tight on that dreadful afternoon and...did all sorts of awful things to me, did it give you any pleasure besides the satisfaction of revenging yourself on me?"

"Will you hate me if I confess, dear, that the sight of your agony, shame, and distress, as you struggled naked, gave me intense pleasure!" I replied as I drew her once more closely against me. "I knew I wasn't hurting you or causing you bodily pain; and the knowledge that your delicious wriggling and writhing, as you struggled naked to get loose, was instigated by your shame at being naked and your distress at finding your sexual passions and instincts aroused in spite of yourself, and irritated till you could no longer control them, and so felt yourself being forced to do what was so horribly repugnant to you, in other words...to...spend!—and not only to spend, but to spend with me watching you! All this gave me the most extraordinary pleasure! When I stopped to let you have a little rest or else put you into another position, I felt the pleasure arising from vengeance gratified, but when I began again to torture you, especially when I was tickling your cunt with a feather, while you were fastened down on your back with legs tied widely apart, I must confess that the pleasure was the pleasure of cruelty! My God! darling, how you did wriggle then!"

"I thought I would have died!" Alice whispered, as she snuggled up against me (apparently not displeased by my confession), yielding herself sweetly to the pressure of my encircling arm. "I wasn't in pain at all, but oh! my sensations! My whole self seemed to be concentrated just...where you were tickling me! and I was nearly mad at being forced to endure such indignity; and on top of it all came that awful tickling, tickling, tickling!"

She shuddered at the recollection; I pressed her still more tightly against me and kissed her tenderly, but held my tongue—for I knew not what to say!

Presently Alice spoke again. "And so it really gave you pleasure to torture me, Jack?" she asked almost cheerfully, adding before I could reply: "I was very angry with my maid this morning and it would have delighted me to have spanked her severely. Now, would such delight arise from revenge or from being cruel?"

"Undoubtedly from being cruel," I replied, "the infliction of the punishment is what would have given you the pleasure, and behind it would come the feeling that you were revenging yourself. Here's another instance—you women delight in saying nasty, cutting things to each other in the politest of ways; why? Not from revenge, but from the satisfaction afforded by the shot going home. If you had given your maid a box on the ears this morning you would have satisfied your revenge without any pleasure whatever; but if I had been there and held your maid down while you spanked her bottom, your pleasure would have arisen from the infliction of the punishment. Do you follow me, dear?"

"Yes, I see it now," Alice replied, then added archly: "I wish you had been there, Jack! it would have done her a lot of good!"

"I sometimes wonder why you keep her on," I said musingly. "She's a pert minx and at times must be very aggravating. Let me see—what's her name?"

"Fanny."

"Yes, of course—a case of 'pretty Fanny's way,' for she certainly is a pretty girl and a well-made one. My dear, if you want to do bottom slapping, you won't easily find a better subject, only I think she will be more than you can manage single-handed, and it may come to *her* slapping *your* bottom, my love!"

Alice laughed. "Fanny is a most perfect maid, a real treasure, or I would not keep her on—for as you say, she is too much for me. She's very strong and very high-spirited, but wants taming badly."

"Bring her some afternoon, and we'll tame her between us!" I suggested, seemingly carelessly, but with well-concealed anxiety, for was I not now making a direct attempt to seduce Alice into Sadism?

Alice started, raised herself on her elbows, and regarded me questioningly. I noticed a hard glitter in her eyes, then she caught her breath, colored, then exclaimed softly: "Oh, Jack, how lovely it would be!"

I had succeeded! Alice had succumbed to the sudden temptation! For the second time her strain of lascivious sexuality had conquered.

"Shall we try?" I asked with a smile, secretly delighted at her unconcealed eagerness and noting how her eyes now brimmed over with lust and how her lovely breasts were heaving with excitement.

"Yes! Yes! Jack!" she exclaimed feverishly, "but how can it be managed?"

"That shouldn't be much trouble," I replied. "Take her out with you shopping some afternoon close by here, then say you want to just pop in to see me about something. En route tell her about this room, how it's sound-proof, it will interest her and she will at the same time learn information that will come in useful later on. Once in here follow my lead. I suppose you would like to have a hand in torturing her?"

"Oh! Jack! will you really torture Fanny?" exclaimed Alice, her eyes sparkling with eagerness, "will you fasten her down as you did me?"

I nodded.

"Yes! yes! let me have a turn at her!" she replied vivaciously. Then after a pause she looked queerly at me and added, "and will you...?" at the same moment she significantly squeezed my prick.

"I think so, unless of course you would rather I didn't, dear," I replied with a laugh; "I suppose you have no idea whether she is a virgin or not?"

"I can't say!" Alice replied, blushing a little. "I've always fancied she was and have treated her as such."

"And what sort of treatment is that?" I queried mischievously, and was proceeding to cross-question Alice when she stopped me by putting her hand over my mouth.

"Well, we'll soon find out when we get her here," I remarked philosophically, much to her amusement. "But, darling, your lessons in the Art of Love are being neglected; let us resume them. There is just time for one—I think you must show me that you haven't forgotten Soixante-neuf!"

Alice blushed prettily and slipped out of my embrace, and soon her cunt was resting on my lips while her gentle hands and mouth busied themselves with my delighted prick and balls! She worked me so deliciously that she made me spend twice in her mouth, by which time I had sucked her completely dry! Then we reluctantly rose to perform the necessary ablutions and resume our clothes.

"When shall I bring Fanny here, Jack?" asked Alice as she was saying good-bye to me.

"Oh! You naughty, lustful, cruel girl!" I exclaimed with a laugh in which she somewhat shamefacedly joined. "When do you think?"

"Will...tomorrow afternoon do?" she asked, avoiding my eyes.

"Yes, certainly," I replied, kissing her tenderly. "Let it be tomorrow afternoon!" And so we parted.

This is how it came to pass that Alice's first experiments in Sadique pleasures were to be made on the person of her own maid.

3.

Next afternoon, after seeing that everything was in working order in the Snuggery, I threw open both doors as if carelessly, and taking off my coat as if not expecting any visitors, I proceeded to potter about the room, keeping a vigilant eye on the stairs. Before long, I heard footsteps on the landing but pretended not to know that any one was there till Alice tapped merrily on the door saying: "May we come in, Jack?"

"Good Heavens! Alice?" I exclaimed in pretended surprise as I struggled hurriedly to get into my coat. "Come in! How do you do? Where have you dropped from?"

"We've been shopping—this is my maid, Jack"—(I bowed and smiled, receiving in return a distinctly pert and not too respectful nod from Fanny)—"and as we were close by, I thought I would take the chance of finding you in and take that enlargement if it is ready."

By this time I had struggled into my coat: "It's quite ready," I replied, "I'll go and get it, and I don't know why those doors should stand so unblushingly open," I added with a laugh.

Having closed them, noiselessly locking them, I disappeared into the alcove I used for myself, and pretended to search for the enlargement—my real object being to give Alice a chance of letting Fanny know the nature of the room. Instinctively she divined my idea, and I heard her say: "This is the room I was telling you about, Fanny—look at the double doors, the padded walls, the rings, the pillars, the hanging pulley straps! Isn't it queer?"

Fanny looked about her with evident interest: "It is a funny room, Miss! And what are those little places for?" She asked, pointing to the two alcoves.

"We do not know, Fanny," Alice replied, "Mr. Jack uses them for his photographic work now."

As she spoke, I emerged with a large print which was to represent the supposed enlargement, and gave it to Alice who at once proceeded to closely examine it.

I saw that Fanny's eyes were wandering all over the room, and I moved over to her: "A strange room Fanny, eh?" I remarked. "Is it not still; no sound from outside can get in, and no noise from inside can get out! That's a fact, we've tested it thoroughly!"

"Lor', Mr. Jack!" she replied in her forward familiar way, turning her eyes on me in a most audacious and bold way, then resuming her survey of the room.

While she was doing so, I hastily inspected her. She was a distinctly pretty girl, tall, slenderly but strongly built, with an exquisitely well-developed figure. A slightly turned-up nose and dark flashing eyes gave her face a saucy look, which her free style of moving accentuated, while her dark hair and rich coloring indicated a warm-blooded and passionate temperament. I easily could understand that Alice, with her gentle ways, was no match for Fanny: and I fancied that I should have my work cut out for me before I got her arms fastened to the pulley ropes.

Alice now moved towards us, print in hand: "Thanks awfully, Jack, it's lovely!" and she began to roll it up. "Now, Fanny, we must be off!"

"Don't bother about the print, I'll send it after you," I said. "And where are you off to now?"

"Nowhere in particular," she replied, "we'll look at the shops and the people. Good-bye, Jack!"

"One moment," I interposed. "You were talking the other day about some perfection of a lady's maid that you didn't want to lose"—(Fanny smiled complacently)—"but whose tantrums and ill tempers were getting to be more than you could stand." (Fanny here began to look angry.) "Somebody suggested that you should give her a good spanking"—(Fanny assumed a contemptuous air)—"or, if you couldn't manage it yourself, you should get someone to do it for you!" (Fanny here glared at me.) "Is this the young lady?"

Alice nodded, with a curious glance at Fanny, who was now evidently getting into one of her passions.

"Well, as you've nothing to do this afternoon, and she happens to be here, and this room is so eminently suitable for the purpose, shall I take the young woman in hand for you and teach her a lesson?"

Before Alice could reply, Fanny with a startled exclamation darted to the door, evidently bent on escape, but in spite of her vigorous twists of the handle, the door refused to open, for the simple reason that, unnoticed by her, I had locked it! Instantly divining that she was a prisoner, she turned hurriedly 'round to watch our movements, but she was too late! With a quickness learnt on the football field, I was onto her and pinned her arms to her sides in a grip that she could not break out of, despite her frantic struggles: "Let me go!…Let me go, Mr. Jack!" she screamed; I simply chuckled as I knew I had her safe now! I had to exert all my strength and skill for she was extraordinarily strong and her furious rage added to her power; but in spite of her desperate resistance, I forced her to the hanging pulleys where Alice was eagerly waiting for us. With astonishing quickness she made fast the ropes to Fanny's wrists and set the machinery going—and in a few seconds the surprised girl found herself standing erect with her arms dragged up taut over her head!

"Well done, Jack!" exclaimed Alice, as she delightedly surveyed the still-struggling Fanny! The latter was indeed a lovely subject of contemplation, as with heaving bosom, flushed cheeks, and eyes that sparkled with rage, she stood panting, endeavoring to get back her breath, while her agitated fingers vainly strove to get her wrists free from the pulley ropes. We watched her in victorious silence, waiting for the outbursts of wrathful fury that we felt would come as soon she was able to speak!

It soon came! "How dare you, Mr. Jack!" Fanny burst out as she flashed her great piercing eyes at us, her whole body trembling with anger; "How dare you treat me like this! Let me loose at once, or, as sure as I am alive, I'll have the law on you and also on that mealy-mouthed smooth-faced demure hypocrite who calls herself my mistress. Indeed!—She who looks on while a poor girl is vilely treated and won't raise a finger to help her! Let me go at once, Mr. Jack! and I'll promise to say and do nothing; but my God!"—(here her voice became shrill with overpowering rage)—"my God! if you don't, I'll make it hot for the pair of you when I get out!" And she glared at us in her impotent fury.

"Your Mistress has asked me to give you a lesson, Fanny," I replied calmly, "and I'm going to do so! The sooner you recognize how helpless you really are, and submit yourself to us, the sooner it will be over; but if you are foolish enough to resist, you'll have a long doing and a bad time! Now, if I let you loose, will you take your clothes off quietly?"

"My God! No!" she cried indignantly, but, in spite of herself she blushed vividly!

"Then we'll take them off for you!" was my cool reply. "Come along, Alice, you understand girl's clothes, you undo them and I'll get them off somehow!"

Quickly Alice sprang up, trembling with excitement, and together we approached Fanny, who shrieked defiance and threats at us in her impotent fury as she struggled desperately to get free. But, as soon as she felt Alice's fingers unfastening her garments, her rage changed to horrible apprehension: and as one by one they slipped off her, she began to realize how helpless she was! "Don't, Miss!" she ejaculated pitifully; "My God! Stop her, Sir!" she pleaded, the use of these more respectful terms of address sufficiently proclaiming her changed attitude. But we were obdurate, and soon Fanny stood with nothing but her chemise left on, her shoes and stockings having been dragged off her at the special request of Alice, whose uncontrolled enjoyment of the work of stripping her maid was delicious to witness.

She now took command of operations. Pointing to a chair just in front of Fanny she exclaimed: "Sit there, Jack, and watch Fanny as I take off her last garments."

"For God's sake, Miss, don't strip me naked!" shrieked Fanny, who seemed to expect that she would be left in her chemise and to whom the sudden intimation that she was to be exposed naked came with an appalling shock! "Oh, Sir! For God's sake, stop her!" she cried, appealing to me as she saw me take my seat right in front of her and felt Alice's fingers begin to undo the shoulder-strap fastenings which alone kept her scanty garments on her. "Miss Alice!…Miss Alice! don't!…for God's sake, don't," she screamed, in a fresh outburst of dismay as she felt her vest slip down her body to her feet and knew now her only covering was about to follow. In despair she tugged frantically at the ropes which made her arms so absolutely helpless, her agitated, quivering fingers betraying her mental agony!

"Steady, Fanny, steady!" exclaimed Alice to her struggling maid as she proceeded to unfasten the chemise, her eyes gleaming with lustful cruelty: "Now, Jack!" she said warningly, then let go, stepping back a pace herself the better to observe the effect! Down swept the chemise, and Fanny stood stark naked!!

"Oh! oh!!" she wailed, crimson with shame, her face hidden on her bosom which now was wildly heaving in agitation. It was a wonderful spectacle!—in the foreground Fanny, naked, helpless, in an agony of shame—in the background but close to her was Alice, exquisitely costumed and hatted, gloating over the sight of her maid's absolute nudity, her eyes intently fixed on the gloriously luscious curves of Fanny's hips, haunches, and bottom!

I managed to catch her eye and motioned to her to come sit on my knees that we might, in each other's close company, study her maid's naked charms, which were so reluctantly being exhibited to us. With one long, last look she obeyed my summons. As she seated herself on my knees she threw her arms around my neck and kissed me rapturously, whispering: "Jack! Isn't she delicious!" I nodded smiling, then in turn muttered in her ear: "And how do you like the game, dear?"

Alice blushed divinely: a strange languishing voluptuous half-wanton, half-cruel look came into her eyes. Placing her lips carefully on mine, she gave me three long-drawn-out kisses, the significance of which I could not possibly misunderstand, then whispered almost hoarsely: "Jack, let me do all the...torturing and be content this time, with...fucking Fanny...and me, too, darling!"

"She's your maid, and so-to-speak your property, dear," I replied softly, "so arrange matters just as you like: I'll leave it all to you and won't interfere unless you want me to do anything."

She kissed me gratefully, then turned her eyes on Fanny, who during this whispered conference had been standing trembling, her face still hidden from us, her legs pressed closely against each other as if to shield her cunt as much as possible from our sight.

I saw Alice's eyes wander over Fanny's naked body with evident pleasure, dwelling first on her magnificent lines and curves, then on her lovely breasts, and finally on the mass of dark curling moss-like hair that covered her cunt. She was a most deliciously voluptuous girl, one calculated to excite Alice to the utmost pitch of lust of which she was capable, and while secretly regretting that my share in the process of taming Fanny was to be somewhat restricted, I felt that I would enjoy the rare opportunity of seeing how a girl, hitherto chaste and well-mannered, would yield to her sexual instincts and passions when she had, placed at her absolute disposal, one of her own sex in a state of absolute nakedness!

Presently Alice whispered to me: "Jack, I'm going to feel her!" I smiled and nodded. Fanny must have heard her, for as Alice rose, she for the first time raised her head and cried in fear: "No, Miss, please, Miss, don't touch me!" and again she vainly strained at her fastenings, her face quivering and flushed with shame. But disregarding her maid's piteous entreaties, Alice passed behind her, then kneeling down began to stroke Fanny's bottom, a hand to each cheek!

"Don't, Miss!" yelled Fanny, arching herself outwards and away from Alice, and thereby, unconsciously, throwing the region of her cunt into greater prominence! But with a smile of cruel satisfaction, Alice continued her sweet occupation, sometimes squeezing, sometimes pinching Fanny's glorious half-moons, now and then extending her excursions over Fanny's round, plump thighs, once, indeed, letting her hands creep up them till I really thought (and so did Fanny from the way she screamed and wriggled) that she was about to feel Fanny's cunt!

Suddenly Alice rose, rushed to me, and, kissing me ardently, whispered excitedly: "Oh, Jack! she's just lovely! Such flesh, such a skin! I've never felt a girl before, I've never touched any girl's breasts or...cunt...except, of course, my own," she added archly, "and I'm wild at the idea of handling Fanny. Watch me carefully, darling, and if I don't do it properly, tell me!" And back to Fanny she rushed, evidently in a state of intense eroticism!

This time Alice didn't kneel, but placed herself close behind Fanny (her dress in fact touching her) then suddenly she threw her arms around Fanny's body and seized her breasts: "Miss Alice...don't!" shrieked Fanny, struggling desperately, her flushed face betraying her agitation. "Oh! how lovely!...how delicious!...how sweet!..." cried Alice, wild with delight and sexual excitement as she squeezed and played with Fanny's voluptuous breasts! Her head with its exquisite hat was just visible over Fanny's right shoulder, while her dainty dress showed on each side of the struggling, agitated girl, throwing into bold relief her glorious shape and accentuating in the most piquant way Fanny's stark nakedness! Entranced, I gazed at the voluptuous spectacle, my prick struggling to break through the fly of my trousers! Fanny had now ceased her cries and was enduring in silence, broken only by her involuntary "Ohs," the violation of her breasts by Alice, whose little hands could scarcely grasp the luscious morsels of Fanny's flesh that they were so subtly torturing, but which, nevertheless, succeeded in squeezing and compressing them and generally playing with them till the poor girl gasped in her shame and agony: "Oh! Miss Alice!...Miss Alice!...stop!... stop!" her head falling forward in her extreme agitation.

With a smile of intense satisfaction, Alice suspended her torturing operations and gently stroked and soothed Fanny's breasts till the latter indicated that she had, in a great degree, regained her self-control. Then Alice's expression changed. A cruel hungry light came into her eyes as she smiled wickedly at me, then I saw her hands quit Fanny's breasts and glide over Fanny's stomach till they arrived at her maid's cunt!

Fanny shrieked as if she had been stung: "Miss Alice...Miss Alice!...Don't! Don't touch me there! Oh!...oh! My God, Miss Alice...oh! Miss Alice! Take your hands away!..." at the same time twisting and writhing in a perfectly wonderful way in her frantic endeavors to escape from her mistress's hands, the fingers of which were now hidden in her cunt's mossy covering as they inquisitively traveled all over her Mount Venus and along the lips of the orifice itself. For some little time they contented themselves with feeling and pressing and toying caressingly with Fanny's cunt, then I saw one hand pause while the first finger of the other gently began to work its way between the pink lips, which I could just distinguish, and disappear into the sweet cleft. "Don't, Miss!" yelled Fanny, her agonized face now scarlet while in her distress she desperately endeavored to defend her cunt by throwing her legs in turn across her groin, to Alice's delight—her telltale face proclaiming the intense pleasure she was tasting in thus making her maid undergo such horrible torture!

Presently I noted an unmistakable look of surprise in her eyes; her lips parted as if in astonishment, while her hand seemed to redouble its attack on Fanny's cunt, then she exclaimed: "Why Fanny? What's this?"

"Oh! Don't tell Mr. Jack, Miss!" shrieked Fanny, letting her legs drop as she could no longer endure the whole weight of her struggling body on her slender wrists, "don't let him know!"

My curiosity was naturally aroused and intently I watched the movements of Alice's hand, which the fall of Fanny's legs brought again into full view. Her forefinger was buried up to the knuckle in her maid's cunt! The mystery was explained: Fanny was not a virgin!

Alice seemed staggered by her discovery. Abruptly she quit Fanny, rushed to me, threw herself on my knees, then, flinging her arms 'round my neck, she whispered excitedly in my ear: "Jack! she's been...had by someone...my finger went right in!"

"So I noticed, darling!" I replied quietly as I kissed her flushed cheek, "it's rather a pity! but she'll stand more fucking than if she had been a virgin, and you must arrange your programme accordingly! I think you'd better let her rest a bit now, her arms will be getting numb from being kept over her head; let's fasten her to that pillar by passing her arms 'round it and shackling her wrists together. She can then rest a bit; and, while she's recovering from her struggles, hadn't you better...slip your clothes off also—for your eyes hint that you'll want...something before long!"

Alice blushed prettily, then whispered as she kissed me ardently, "I'd like...something now, darling!" Then she ran away to her dressing room.

Left alone with Fanny, I proceeded to transfer her from the pulley to the pillar; it was not a difficult task as her arms were too numb (as I expected) to be of much use to her and she seemed stupefied at our discovery that her maidenhead no longer existed. Soon I had her firmly fastened with her back pressing against the pillar. This new position had two great advantages: She could no longer hide her face from us, and the backwards pull of her arms threw her breasts out. She glanced timidly at me as I stood admiring her luscious nakedness while I waited for Alice's return.

"When did this little slip happen, Fanny?" I asked quietly.

She colored vividly: "When I was seventeen, Sir," she replied softly but brokenly: "I was drugged...and didn't know till after it was done! It's never been done again, Mr. Jack," she continued with pathetic earnestness in her voice, "never! I swear it, Sir!" Then after a short pause she whispered: "Oh! Mr. Jack! let me go!...I'll come to you whenever you wish...and let you do what you like but...I'm afraid of Miss Alice today...she seems so strange!...Oh! my God! She's naked!" she screamed in genuine alarm as Alice came out of her toilet room with only her shoes and stockings on, and her large matinee hat, a most coquettishly piquantly indecent object! Poor Fanny went red at the sight of her mistress and didn't know where to look as Alice came dancing along, her eyes noting with evident approval the position into which I had placed her maid.

"Mes compliments, mademoiselle!" I said with a low bow as she came up.

She smiled and blushed, but was too intent on Fanny to joke with me. That's lovely, Jack!" she exclaimed after a careful inspection of her now-trembling maid, "but surely she can get loose!"

"Oh, no!" I replied with a smile, "but if you like I'll fasten her ankles together!"

"No, no, Sir!" Fanny cried in terror.

"Yes, Jack, do!" exclaimed Alice, her eyes gleaming with lust and delight. She evidently had thought out some fresh torture for Fanny, and with the closest attention, she watched me as I linked her maid's slender ankles together in spite of the poor girl's entreaties!

"I like that much better, Jack," said Alice, smiling her thanks; then catching me by the elbow, she pushed me towards my alcove saying: "We both will want you presently, Jack!" Looking roguishly at me: "So get ready! But tell me first where are the feathers?"

"Oh, that's your game!" I replied with a laugh. She nodded, coloring slightly, and I told her where she would find them.

I had a peep-hole in my alcove through which I could see all that passed in the room, and being curious to watch the two girls, I placed myself by it as I slowly undressed myself.

Having found the feathers, Alice placed the box near her, then going right up to Fanny, she took hold of her own breasts, raised them till they were level with the trembling girl's, then leaning on Fanny so that their stomachs were in close contact, she directed her breasts against Fanny's, gently rubbing her nipples against her own while she looked intently into Fanny's eyes! It was a most curious sight! The girl's naked bodies were touching from their ankles to their breasts, their cunts were so close to each other that their hairs formed one mass, while their faces were so near to each other that the brim of Alice's matinee hat projected over Fanny's forehead!

Not a word was said! For about half a minute Alice continued to rub her breasts gently against Fanny's with her eyes fixed on Fanny's downcast face, then suddenly I saw both naked bodies quiver, and then Fanny raised her head and for the first time responded to Alice's glance, her color coming and going! At the same moment, a languorous voluptuous smile swept over Alice's face, and gently she kissed Fanny, who flushed rosy red, but, as far as I could see, did not respond.

"Won't you...love me, Fanny?" I heard Alice say softly but with a curiously strained voice! Immediately I understood the position. Alice was lusting after Fanny! I was delighted! It was clear that Fanny had not yet reciprocated Alice's passion, and I determined that Alice should have every opportunity of satisfying her lust on Fanny's naked helpless body, till the latter was converted to Tribadism with Alice as the object.

"Won't you...love me, Fanny!" again asked Alice softly, now supplementing the play of her breasts against Fanny's by insinuating and significant pressings of her stomach against Fanny's, again kissing the latter sweetly. But Fanny made no response, and Alice's eyes grew hard with a steely cruel glitter that boded badly for Fanny!

Quitting Fanny, Alice went straight to the box of feathers, picked out one, and returned to Fanny, feather in hand. The sight of her moving about thus, her breasts dancing, her hips swaying, her cunt and bottom in full view, her nakedness intensified by her piquant costume of hat, shoes and stockings, was enough to galvanize a corpse: it set my blood boiling with lust and I could hardly refrain from rushing out and compelling her to let me quench my fires in her! I, however, did resist the temptation, and rapidly undressed to my shoes and socks so as to be ready to take advantage of any chance that either of the girls might offer; but I remained in my alcove with my eye to the peep-hole as I was curious to witness the denouement of this strangely voluptuous scene, which Alice evidently wished to play single-handed.

No sooner did Fanny catch sight of the feather than she screamed: "No!…no! Miss Alice!…don't tickle me!" at the same time striving frantically to break the straps that linked together her wrists and her ankles. But my tackle was too strong! Alice meanwhile had caught up a cushion which she placed at Fanny's feet and right in front of her, she knelt on it, resting her luscious bottom on her heels, and, having settled herself down comfortably, she, with a smile in which cruelty and malice were strangely blended, gloatingly contemplated her maid's naked and agitated body, then slowly and deliberately applied the tip of the feather to Fanny's cunt!

"Oh, my God! Miss Alice, don't!" yelled Fanny, writhing in delicious contortions in her desperate endeavors to dodge the feather. "Don't, Miss!" she shrieked, as Alice, keenly enjoying her maid's distress and her vain efforts to avoid the torture, proceeded delightedly to pass the feather lightly along the sensitive lips of Fanny's cunt and finally set to work to tickle Fanny's clitoris, thereby sending her so nearly into hysterical convulsions that I felt it time I interposed.

As I emerged from my alcove Alice caught sight of me and dropped her hand as she turned towards me, her eyes sparkling with lascivious delight! "Oh, Jack! did you see her?" she cried excitedly.

"I heard her, dear!" I replied ambiguously, "and began to wonder whether you were killing her, so came out to see."

"Not to worry!" she cried, hugely pleased, "I'm going to give her another turn!" that declaration produced from Fanny the most pitiful pleadings, which seemed, however, only to increase Alice's cruel satisfaction, and she was proceeding to be as good as her word when I stopped her.

"You'd better let me first soothe her irritated senses, dear," I said, and, with one hand, I caressed and played with Fanny's full and voluptuous breasts, which I found tense and firm under her sexual excitement, while with the other, I stroked and felt her cunt, a procedure that evidently afforded her considerable relief although, at another time, it doubtless would have provoked shrieks and cries! She had not spent, though she must have been very close to doing it; and I saw that I must watch Alice very closely indeed during the "turn" she was going to give Fanny for my special delectation, lest the catastrophe I was so desirous of avoiding should occur, for in my mind, I had decided that when Alice had finished tickling Fanny, she should have an opportunity of satisfying her lustful cravings on her, when it would be most desirable that Fanny should be in a condition to show the effect on her of Alice's lascivious exertions.

While feeling Fanny's cunt, I naturally took the opportunity to see if Alice's penetrating finger had met with any difficulty entering and had thus caused Fanny the pain that her shrieks and wriggles had indicated. I found the way in intensely tight, a confirmation of her story and statement that nothing had gone in since the rape was committed on her. Although therefore I could not have the gratification of taking her virginity, I felt positive that I should have a delicious time and that practically, I should be violating her, and I wondered into which of the two delicious cunts now present I would shoot my surging and boiling discharge as it dissolved in Love's sweetest ecstasies!

"Now, Alice, I think she is ready for you!" I said when I had stroked and felt Fanny to my complete satisfaction.

"No, no, Miss Alice!" shrieked Fanny in frantic terror, "for God's sake, don't tickle me again!"

Disregarding her cries, Alice, who had with difficulty restrained her impatience, quickly again applied the feather to Fanny's cunt, and a wonderful spectacle followed; Fanny's shrieks, cries, and entreaties, filled the room while she wiggled and squirmed and twisted herself about in the most bewitchingly provocative manner, while Alice, with parted lips and eyes that simply glistened with lust, remorselessly tickled her maid's cunt with every refinement of cruelty, every fresh shriek and convulsion bringing a delightful look on her telltale face. Motionless, I watched the pair, till I noticed Fanny's breasts stiffen and become tense.

Immediately I covered her cunt with my hand, saying to Alice: "Stop, dear, she's had as much as she can stand!" Then, reluctantly, she desisted from her absorbing occupation and rose, her naked body quivering with aroused but unsatisfied lust.

Now was the time for me to try and effect what I had in mind: The introduction of both girls to Tribadism! "Let us move Fanny to the large couch and fasten her down before she recovers herself," I hastily whispered to Alice. Quickly we set her loose, between us we carried her, half-fainting, to the large settee couch where we lay her on her back and made fast her wrists to the two top corners and her ankles to the two lower ones. We now had only to set the machinery going and she would lie in the position I desired, namely spread-eagled!

Alice, now clutched me excitedly and whispered hurriedly: "Jack, do me before she comes to herself and before she can see us! I'm just mad for it!" And, indeed, with her flushed cheeks, humid eyes, and heaving breasts this was very evident!

But although I was also bursting with lust and eager to fuck either Alice or her maid, it would not have suited my programme to do so! I wanted Alice to fuck Fanny! I wanted the first spending of both girls to be mutually provoked by the friction of their excited cunts one against the other! This was why I stopped Alice from tickling her maid into spending, and it was for this reason that I had extended Fanny on her back in such a position that her cunt should be at Alice's disposal!

"Hold on, darling, for a bit!" I whispered back, "you'll soon see why! I want it as badly as you do, my sweet, but am fighting it till the proper time comes! Run away now, and take off your hat, for it will now only be in the way," and I smiled significantly as I kissed her.

Alice promptly obeyed. I then seated myself on the couch by the side of Fanny, who was still lying with eyes closed, but breathing almost normally. Bending over her, I closely inspected her cunt to ascertain whether she had or had not spent under the terrific tickling she had just received! I could find no traces whatever, but to make sure I gently drew the lips apart and peered into the sweet coral cleft, but again saw no traces. The touch of my fingers on her cunt however had roused Fanny from her semi-stupor and she dreamily opened her eyes, murmuring: "Oh, Sir, don't!" as she recognized that I was her assailant, then she looked hurriedly 'round as in search of Alice.

"Your mistress will be here immediately," I said with a smile, "she has only gone away to take off her hat!" The look of terror returned to her eyes, and she exclaimed: "Oh, Mr. Jack, do let me go, she'll kill me!"

"Oh, no!" I replied as I laughed at her agitation, "oh, no, Fanny, on the contrary she's now going to do to you the sweetest, nicest, and kindest thing one girl can do to another! Here she comes!"

I rose as Alice came up full of pleasurable excitement as to what was now going to happen, and slipped my arm lovingly 'round her waist. She looked eagerly at her now trembling maid, then whispered: "Is she ready for us again, Jack?"

"Yes, dear!" I answered softly. "While you were away taking off your hat, I thought it as well to see in what condition her cunt was after its tickling! I found it very much irritated and badly in want of Nature's soothing essence! You, darling, are also much in the same state, your cunt also wants soothing! So I want you girls to soothe each other! Get onto Fanny, dear, take her in your arms; arrange yourself on her so that your cunt lies on hers! and then gently rub yours against hers! and soon both of you will be tasting the sweetest ecstasy!! In other words, fuck Fanny, dear."

Alice looked at me in wondrous admiration! As she began to comprehend my suggestion, her face broke into delightful smiles; and when I stooped to kiss her she exclaimed rapturously: "Oh, Jack! how sweet!...how delicious!" as she gazed eagerly at Fanny. But the latter seemed horrified at the idea of being submitted thus to her mistress's lustful passion and embraces, and attempted to escape, crying in her dismay: "No, no, Sir!—oh, no, Miss!—I don't want it, please!"

"But I do, Fanny," cried Alice with sparkling eyes as she gently, but firmly, pushed her struggling maid onto her back and held her down forcibly, till I had pulled all four straps tight, so that Fanny lay flat with her arms and legs wide apart in Maltese-Cross fashion, a simply entrancing spectacle! Then slipping my hands under her buttocks, I raised her middle till Alice was able to push a hard cushion under her bottom, the effect of which was to make her cunt stand out prominently; then turning to Alice, who had assisted in these preparations with the keenest interest but evident impatience, I said: "Now dear, there she is! Set to work and violate your maid!"

In a flash Alice was on the couch and on her knees between Fanny's widely parted legs—excitedly she threw herself on her maid, passed her arms 'round her and hugged her closely as she showered kisses on Fanny's still-protesting mouth till the girl had to stop for breath. With a few rapid movements she arranged herself on her maid so that the two luscious pairs of breasts were pressing against each other, their stomachs in close contact, and their cunts touching!

"One moment, Alice!" I exclaimed, just as she was beginning to agitate herself on Fanny, "Let me see that you are properly placed before you start!"

Leaning over her bottom, I gently parted her thighs, till between them I saw the cunts of the mistress and the maid resting on each other, slit to slit, clitoris to clitoris, half hidden by the mass of their closely interwoven hairs, the sweetest of sights! Then, after restoring her thighs to their original position, closely pressed against each other, I gently thrust my right hand between the girl's navels, and worked it along amidst their bellies till it lay between their cunts! "Press down a bit, Alice!" I said, patting her bottom with my disengaged hand; promptly she complied with two or three vigorous downward thrusts which forced my palm hard against Fanny's cunt while her own pressed deliciously against the back of my hand. The sensation of thus feeling at the same time these two full, fat, fleshy, warm and throbbing cunts between which my hand lay in sandwich fashion was something exquisite; and it was with the greatest reluctance that I removed it from the sweetest position it is ever likely to find herself in, but Alice's restless and involuntary movements proclaimed that she was fast yielding to her feverish impatience to fuck Fanny and to taste the rapture of spending on the cunt of her maid, the emission provoked by its sweet contact and friction against her own excited organ!

She still held Fanny closely clasped against her and with head slightly thrown back, she kept her eyes fixed on her maid's terrified averted face with a gloating hungry look, murmuring softly: "Fanny, you shall now...love me!" Both the girls were quivering, Alice from overwhelming and unsatisfied lust, Fanny from shame and horrible apprehension!

Caressing Alice's bottom encouragingly, I whispered: "Go ahead, dear!" In a trice her lips were pressed to Fanny's flushed cheeks on which she rained hot kisses as she slowly began to agitate her cunt against her maid's with voluptuous movements of her beautiful bottom.

"Oh! Miss..." gasped Fanny, her eyes betraying the sexual emotion that she felt beginning to overpower her, her color coming and going!

Alice's movements became quicker and more agitated; soon she was furiously rubbing her cunt against Fanny's with strenuous downward thrusting strokes of her bottom, continuing her fierce kisses on her maid's cheeks as the latter lay helpless with half-closed eyes, tightly clasped in her mistress's arms!

Then a hurricane of sexual rage seemed to seize Alice! Her bottom wildly oscillated and gyrated with confused jerks, thrusts, and shoves as she frenziedly pressed her cunt against Fanny's with a rapid jogging motion: suddenly Alice seemed to stiffen and become almost rigid, her arms gripped Fanny more tightly than ever; then her head fell forward on Fanny's shoulder as an indescribable spasm thrilled through her, followed by convulsive vibrations and tremors! Almost simultaneously Fanny's half-closed eyes turned upwards till the whites were showing, her lips parted, she gasped brokenly: "Oh!...Miss...Alice!... Ah...ah!" then thrilled convulsively while quiver after quiver shot through her! The blissful crisis had arrived! Mistress and maid were deliriously spending, cunt against cunt, Alice in rapturous ecstasy at having so deliciously satisfied her sexual desires by means of her maid's cunt, while forcing the latter to spend in spite of herself, while Fanny was quivering ecstatically under heavenly sensations hitherto unknown to her (owing to her having been unconscious when she was ravished) and now communicated to her wondering senses by her mistress whom she still felt lying on her and in whose arms she was still clasped!

Intently I watched both girls, curious to learn how they would regard each other when they had recovered from their ecstatic trance. Would the mutual satisfaction of their overwrought sexual cravings wipe out the animosity between them, which had caused the strange events of this afternoon, or would Alice's undoubted lust for her maid be simply raised to a higher pitch by this satisfying of her sexuality on her maid's body, and would Fanny consider that she had been violated by her mistress and therefore bear a deeper grudge than ever against her! It was a pretty problem and I eagerly awaited the situation.

Alice was the first to move. With a long-drawn breath, indicative of intense satisfaction, she raised her head off Fanny's shoulder. The slight movement roused Fanny, who mechanically turned her averted head towards Alice, and as the girls languidly opened their humid eyes, they found themselves looking straight at each other! Fanny colored like a peony and quickly turned her eyes away; Alice on the contrary continued to regard the blushing face of her maid; a look of gratification and triumph came into her eyes, then she deliberately placed her lips on Fanny's and kissed her, saying softly but significantly: "Now it's Mr. Jack's turn, my dear!" Then raising her head, she, with a malicious smile, watched Fanny to see how she would receive the intimation.

Fanny darted a startled, horrified glance at me, another at her mistress, then seeing that both our faces only confirmed Alice's announcement, she cried pitifully: "No, no, Mr. Jack! no, no! Miss Alice! oh, Miss, how can you be so cruel?"

With a malicious smile, Alice again kissed her horrified maid, saying teasingly: "You must tell us afterwards which of us you like best, Fanny, and, if you're very good and let Mr. Jack have as good a fuck as you have just given me, we'll have each other in front of you for your special edification!"

She kissed Fanny once more, then rose slowly off her, exposing as she did so her own cunt and that of her maid. I shot a quick glance at both in turn. The girls had evidently spent profusely, their hairs glistened with tiny drops of love-dew, while, here and there, bits were plastered down.

Alice caught my glance and smiled merrily. "I let myself go, Jack!" she laughed. "But there will be plenty when you are ready!" she added wickedly. "I'll just put myself right, then I'll do lady's maid to Fanny and get her ready for you!" Then with a saucy look she whispered: "Haven't I sketched out a fine programme!"

"You have indeed!" I replied as I seized and kissed her. I wish only that I was to have you first, dear, while I'm so rampant!"

"No, no," she whispered, kissing me again: "I'm not ready yet! Fuck Fanny well, Jack! It will do her good, and you'll find her a delicious mover!" And she ran off to her alcove.

I sat down on the couch by Fanny's side and began to play with her breasts, watching her closely. She was in a terrible state of agitation, her head rolling from side to side, her eyes closed, her lips slightly apart, while her bosom heaved wildly. As my hands seized her breasts gently she started, opened her eyes, and seeing that it was me she piteously pleaded: "Oh, Mr. Jack! don't...don't..." she could not bring herself to say the dreadful word that expressed her fate.

"Don't...what, Fanny?" I asked maliciously. With effort she brought out the word. "Oh! Sir! Don't...fuck me!"

"But your mistress has ordered it, Fanny, and she tells me you are very sweet, and so I want it! And it will be like taking your maidenhead, only much nicer for you, as you won't have the pain that girls feel when they are first ravished and you'll be able to taste all the pleasure!"

"No, no, Mr. Jack," she cried, "don't...fuck me."

Just then Alice came up with water, a sponge, and a towel. "What's the matter, Jack?" she asked.

"Your maid says she doesn't want to be fucked, dear; perhaps you can convince her of her foolishness!"

Alice was now sponging Fanny's cunt with sedulous care, and her attentions were making Fanny squirm and wriggle involuntarily in the most lovely fashion, much to her mistress's gratification. When Alice had finished she turned to me and said: "She's quite ready, Jack! Go ahead!"

"No, no, Sir!" yelled Fanny in genuine terror, but I quickly got between her legs and placed myself on her palpitating stomach, clasped her in my arms; then directed my prick against her delicious cleft. I got its head inside without much difficulty. Fanny was now wild with fright and shrieked despairingly as she felt me effect an entrance into her; and as my prick penetrated deeper and deeper, she went off into a paroxysm of frantic plunging in the hope of dislodging me.

I did not experience half the difficulty I had anticipated in getting into Fanny, for her spendings under Alice had lubricated the passage; but she was exceedingly tight and I must have hurt her for her screams were terrible! Soon, however, I was into her till our hairs mingled, then I lay still for a little while to allow her to recover a bit; and before long her cries ceased and she lay panting in my arms.

Alice, who was in my full sight and had been watching—with the closest attention and the keenest enjoyment—this violation of her maid, now bent forward and said softly: "She's all right, Jack! Go on dear!" Promptly I set to work to fuck Fanny, at first with long, slow, pistonlike strokes of my prick, then more and more rapid thrusts and shoves, driving myself well up into her. Suddenly I felt Fanny quiver deliciously under me...she had spent! Delightedly I continued to fuck her...soon she spent again, then again, and again, quivering with the most exquisite tremors and convulsions as she lay clasped tightly in my arms, uttering almost inarticulate "Ahs" and "Ohs" as the spasm of pleasure thrilled her. Now I began to feel my own ecstasy quickly approaching! Hugging Fanny against me more closely than ever, I let myself go and rammed furiously into her as she lay quivering under me till the rapturous crisis overtook me, then madly I shot her my pent-up torrent of boiling virile balm, inundating her sweetly excited interior and evidently causing her the most exquisite bliss, for her head fell backwards, her eyes closed, her nostrils dilated, her lips parted, as she ejaculated: "Ah!...Ah!... Ah!..." when feeling each jet of my hot discharge shoot into her. Heavens! How I spent! The thrilling, exciting and provocative events of the afternoon had worked me up into a state of sexual excitement that even the ample discharge I had spent into Fanny did not quench my ardor; and as soon as the delicious thrills and spasms of pleasure had died away, I started fucking her a second time. But Alice intervened: "No, Jack!" she exclaimed softly, adding archly, "you must keep the rest for me! Get off quickly, dear, and let me attend to Fanny!"

Unable to challenge her veto, I reluctantly withdrew my prick from Fanny's cunt after kissing her ardently. I then rose and retired to my alcove, while Alice quickly took Fanny into her charge and attended to her with loving care!

When I returned, Fanny was still lying on her back, fastened down to the couch, and Alice was sitting by her and talking to her with an amused smile as she gently played with her maid's breasts. As soon as Fanny caught sight of me she blushed rosy red, while Alice turned and greeted me with a welcoming smile.

"I've been trying to find out from Fanny which fuck she liked best," she said with a merry smile, "but she won't say! Did she give you a good time, Jack?"

"She was simply divine!" I replied as I stopped and kissed the still-blushing girl!

"Then we'll give her the reward we promised," replied Alice, looking sweetly at Fanny. "She shan't be tied up any more and she'll see you fuck me presently! Set her free, Jack," she added, and soon Fanny rose confusedly from the couch on which she had tasted the probably unique experience of being fucked in rapid succession first by a girl and then by a man!" She was very shamefaced and her limbs were very stiff from having been retained so long in one position; but we supported her to the sofa where we placed her between us: then we gently chafed and massaged her limbs till they regained their powers and soothed her with our kisses and caresses, while our hands wandered all over her naked and still trembling body, and soon she was herself again.

"Now!" exclaimed Alice, who was evidently in heat again, "are you ready?"

"Look, dear!" I replied, holding up my limp prick for her inspection, adding with a smile: "Time, my Christian friend!"

She laughed, took my prick gently in her hands and began to fondle it, but as it did not show the signs of returning life she so desired to see, she caught hold of Fanny's hand and made it assist hers, much to Fanny's bashful confusion. But her touch had the desired effect, and soon I was stiff and rampant again!

"Thanks, Fanny!" I said as I lovingly kissed her blushing face, "Now, Alice, if you will!"

Quickly Alice was on her back with parted legs. Promptly I got onto her and drove my prick home up her cunt; then, clasping each other closely, we set to work and fucked each other deliciously, till we both spent in delirious transports of pleasure which heightened Fanny's blushes, as with humid eyes she watched us in wondering astonishment and secret delight!

After exchanging ardent kisses, we rose. "Come, Fanny, we must dress and be off, I didn't know it was so late!" exclaimed Alice. Off the girls went together to Alice's alcove while I retired to mine. I was delighted that their departure should be thus hurried as it would bypass the possible awkwardness of a more formal leave-taking. Soon we all were dressed. I called a taxi and put the girls into it, their faces discreetly veiled; and as they drove off, I felt that the afternoon had not been wasted!

4.

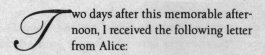wo days after this memorable after-
noon, I received the following letter
from Alice:

My darling Jack,

I must write and tell you the sequel to yesterday's lovely
afternoon at the Snuggery.

Fanny didn't say a word on the way home, but was evidently
deeply thinking and getting more and more angry. She went
straight to her room and I to mine. I did not expect she would
resume her duties, in fact I rather anticipated she would come in
to say she was going away at once! But in about ten minutes
she came in as if nothing had happened, only she wouldn't speak
unless it was absolutely necessary.

At eight o'clock she brought me the dinner menu as usual for
my orders. I told her I felt too tired to dress and go down, so would
dine in my own room and that she must dine with me, as she was
looking so tired and upset generally. She looked surprised, and
I think she hesitated about accepting my invitation, but did so.

At dinner, of course, she had to talk. I saw she had refreshing and appetizing food and she made a good dinner. I also induced her to drink a little Burgundy, which seemed to do her a lot of good, and she gradually became less sulky.

When the table was cleared, she was going away, but I asked her to stay and rest comfortably if she had done her work for the day. To my surprise she seemed glad to do so. I installed her in a comfortable chair and made her chat with me about things in general, carefully avoiding anything that might recall the events of the afternoon!

After some little time so passed, she rose and stood before me in a most respectful attitude and said: "Miss Alice, you've always been a very kind mistress to me: You've treated me with every consideration, you've paid me well, you've given me light work. Would you mind telling me why you were so awfully cruel to me this afternoon?"

I was very surprised, but fortunately ideas came!

"Certainly I will, Fanny," I replied, "I think you are entitled to know. Come and sit by me and we can talk it over nicely."

I was then on the little sofa with padded back and ends, and which you know just holds two nicely. Fanny hesitated for a moment and then sat down.

"I've tried to be a good mistress to you, Fanny," I said gravely, "because you have been a very good maid to me. But, of late, there has been something wrong with you; your temper has been so queer that, though you have never disobeyed me, you have made your obedience very unpleasant; and I found myself wondering whether I had not better send you away. But I very much didn't want to lose you—(here she half moved toward me)—and so I thought I'd talk the case over with Mr. Jack, who is one of my best friends and always helps me in all troublesome matters. He said something must be wrong with you, and there undoubtedly is—and you must presently tell me what it is—and advised that he should give you a good shock, which he has done!"

"My God, yes, Miss Alice!" Fanny replied almost tearfully.

"But there is a second reason, Fanny," I continued, "which will explain to you why you were forced to submit yourself to me and to Mr. Jack. Am I wrong in guessing that your queer temper has been caused by your not being able to satisfy certain sexual cravings and desires? Tell me frankly!"

"Yes!" she whispered bashfully.

"We felt sure of it!" I continued. "Mr. Jack said to me: 'Look here, Alice, isn't it absurd that you two girls should be living in such close relations as mistress and maid, and yet should go on suffering from stifled natural sexual functions when you could and should so easily soothe each other?' Then he explained to me how!"

I gently took her hand, she yielded it to me without hesitation "Now, Fanny, do you understand? Shall we not agree to help each other, to make life pleasanter and more healthy for us both? We tried each other this afternoon, Fanny! Do you like me sufficiently?"

She blushed deeply, then glanced shyly but lovingly at me. I took the hint. I slipped my arm 'round her, she yielded to my pleasure. I drew her to me and kissed her fondly, whispering: "Shall we be sweethearts, Fanny?"

She sank into my arms murmuring: "Oh, Miss Alice!" her eyes shining with love! Our lips met, we sealed our pact with kisses!

Just then ten o'clock struck: "Now we'll have a nightcap and go to bed," I said to her, "will you get the whiskey and siphon, dear, and mix my allowance and also one for yourself, as it will do you good?"

Fanny rose and served me with the "grog" as I call it, and when we had finished, we turned out the lights and went to my bedroom.

After she had done my hair and prepared me for bed as usual I said to her softly: "Now go and undress dear, and come back," and significantly kissed her. She blushed sweetly and withdrew. I undressed.

Presently there was a timid tap on the door, and Fanny came in shyly in her "nightie." "Take it off, dear, please," I said softly, "I want to see you, I was too excited to do so this afternoon!" Bashfully and with pretty blushes she complied. I made her lie on my bed naked and had a good look at her all over, back, front, everywhere! Jack, she is a little beauty! When I kissed her after I had thoroughly examined her, she put her arms around my neck and whispered: "May I look at you, Miss?" So in turn I lay down naked and she looked me all over and played with me, kissed me here and there, till the touch of her lips and hands set my blood on fire. "Come, darling!" I whispered. In a moment she was on the bed by me with parted legs; I got between them and on her, and in each other's arms we lay spending, she sometimes on me, I oftener on her, till we fell asleep still clasped against each other! Oh, Jack, you don't know what a good turn you did us yesterday afternoon!

Today Fanny is another person, so sweet and gentle and loving! An indescribable thrill comes over me when I think that I have this delicious girl at my command whenever I feel like I'd like to be—naughty! You must come and see us soon, and have some tea, and my maid and me!

> Your loving sweetheart,
> Alice

P.S.—I cross-questioned Fanny last night as to her experiences of that afternoon. I must tell you some day how she described what she went through, it will thrill you! But one thing I must tell you now! She says that she never felt anything so delicious as her sensations when in your arms, after you had got into her! I then asked her if she would go to you, some afternoon, if you wanted a change from me? She blushed sweetly and whispered: "Yes, Miss, if you didn't mind!"

5.

*A*mong our friends was a very pretty lady, Connie Blunt, a young widow whose husband died within a few weeks of the marriage. She had been left comfortably off and had no children.

She was a lovely golden-haired girl of about twenty-two years, slight, tall, and beautifully formed, a blue-eyed beauty, with a dazzling skin and pure complexion.

She and Alice were great friends and she was Alice's pet chaperone. The two were constantly together, Alice generally passing the night at Mrs. Blunt's flat, when they were going to a ball or any late entertainment; and I suppose that the sweet familiarity that exists between girl friends enabled Alice to see a good deal of her friend's physical charms, with the result that she fell in love with her. But hint as delicately and as diplomatically as she dared of the pleasures tasted by girl sweethearts, Mrs. Blunt, never by word or deed or look, gave Alice any encouragement. In fact, she seemed ignorant that such a state of affection could or did exist.

I used to tease Alice about her ill-success and she took my chaff very good-naturedly; but I could see that she was secretly suffering from the "pangs of ill-requited love," and had it not been for the genuine affection that existed between her and her maid Fanny, which enabled Alice to satisfy with the help of Fanny's cunt the desires provoked by Mrs. Blunt, things might have fared badly with Alice.

Among ardent girls, an unrequited passion of this sort is apt to become tinged with cruel desire against the beloved one; and one day, when Alice was consoling herself with me, I saw that this was getting to be the case with her passion for Mrs. Blunt, and my fertile imagination suggested to me means by which she might attain to the desired end.

We were discussing Mrs. Blunt. "I am getting hungry for Connie, Jack!" Alice had said mournfully. "Very hungry!"

"Dear, I'd like to help you, and I believe I can," I remarked sympathetically, "but I shall want a lot of help from you. Could you bring yourself to torture her?"

"Oh, yes!" replied Alice briskly, "and I'd dearly like to do it!" And into her eyes came the Sadique glint I knew so well! "But it would never do, Jack! She'd never have anything to do with me again. I thought of this, but it won't do!"

"I'm not so sure!" I said reflectively. "Let me give you my ideas as clearly as I can, and you can tell me if you think them workable."

"Wait a moment, Jack!" she exclaimed, now keenly interested. "Let me get on you, it's better for both of us," she added archly: and soon she was lying flat on me, her breasts resting on my chest and my prick snugly lodged up her cunt while my arms retained her in position.

"Now are you ready to discuss matters seriously?" I asked with a mischievous smile.

She nodded merrily. "Go ahead, you dear old Jack, my most faithful friend," she added with sudden tenderness as she kissed me with unusual affection.

"Then listen carefully, dear. The gist of my plan is that you must pretend to be what Mrs. Blunt thinks you are, but which is precisely what you are not: an innocent and unsophisticated virgin!"

"Oh, you beast!" hissed Alice in pretended indignation but with laughing eyes. "And who's responsible for that, Sir?"

"I'm delighted to say that I am, dear!" I replied with a tender smile to which Alice responded by kissing me affectionately. "Anyhow, you've got to pretend to be what you're not! You must get Mrs. Blunt to chaperone you here to lunch. When we all are here afterwards, we'll manage to make her sit down in the Chair of Treachery"—(Alice's eyes lit up)—

"which of course will at once pin her. Immediately I'll collar you and fasten you to one pair of pulleys—I'll have two pairs working that day—and I'll fasten Mrs Blunt to the other pair, so that you will face each other." (Alice's face was now a study in rapt attention) "You both will then be stripped naked in full sight of each other"—(Alice blushed prettily)—"and you both will also be tortured in front of each other! You must agree to be tortured dear, to keep up the swindle!"—("I shan't mind, Jack!" Alice whispered, kissing me)—"But there will be this great difference to your former experience, both when you were done by yourself and when we did Fanny together, the girl that is being tortured is to be first blindfolded." (Alice's eyes opened widely with surprise.)

"I shall keep Mrs. Blunt fastened in the usual way, but for you, I shall use a new and most ingenious set of straps which can be put on and taken off in a jiffy by anyone knowing the trick. So when I have fastened Mrs. Blunt for, say, cunt tickling, I'll blindfold her, then I'll silently let you loose and let you tickle her!"—("Oh Jack! how lovely!" ejaculated Alice delightedly, again kissing me)—"and tie you up quickly when you're finished, then I'll take off the bandage. She is sure to think it was me." (Alice laughed merrily.) "I must blindfold you, dear, when it's your turn, for your eyes may give you away, while your mouth will be quite safe!" (Alice nodded her head approvingly.)

"I don't, however, propose to give you girls much torture. After you both have had a turn, I'll tie Mrs. Blunt to this couch just as we did Fanny. Then I'll threaten you with a whip, and you must pretend to be terrorized and consent to do everything I tell you. I'll first set you free and blindfold Mrs. Blunt, then order you to feel her, then to suck her and then to fuck her!" ("Jack, you're a genius!" ejaculated Alice admiringly.)

"After you've fucked Mrs. Blunt, I'll have her while you look on!" (Alice blushed.) "Then it will be your turn. I'll terrorize Mrs. Blunt in reality and then make her operate on you, and then I'll have you in front of her!" Alice here kissed me with sparkling eyes, then, in her delight, began to agitate herself on my prick. "Steady, dear!" I exclaimed, slipping my hands down to her heaving bottom to keep her still, "I can't think and talk and fuck at the same time! Let me do the first two now and the third afterwards if you don't mind!"

"I'm very sorry, Jack!" Alice replied demurely but with eyes full of merriment: "I'll try and lie still on you, but your magnificent plan is exciting me most awfully! The very idea of having Connie, oh, Jack!" and again she kissed me excitedly.

"Where were we?—oh, yes," I continued. "I'll compel Mrs. Blunt to perform on you and then I'll have you in her presence. Then, under the threat of the whip, I'll make you both swear that you'll never let out what has been happening, and send you home! You must choose some day when you are staying with her, dear, for then you'll go back together and pass the evening together; and if you don't establish a sexual relation with her, I'm afraid I can't help you! Now, what do you honestly and frankly think of my plan, dear?"

"Just splendid, and lovely, Jack!" she replied enthusiastically, then in a different tone of voice she whispered hastily: "Jack, I really must, now…" and began to work herself up and down on me. I saw she was too erotically excited to think seriously and so let her have her way. She fucked me most deliciously, quivering voluptuously when she spent and when she felt my warm discharge shoot into her. After the necessary ablutions, we dressed, as Alice had to leave early to keep a dinner engagement.

"Think it over carefully, dear," I said as I put her in a taxi, "let me have your opinion from the point of view of a girl." And so we parted.

Next day, as I was about to commence my solitary lunch, who should appear but Alice and Fanny. I greeted them warmly, especially Fanny, whom I had not seen since the never-to-be-forgotten afternoon when Alice and I converted her. She blushed prettily, as we shook hands.

"Have you had lunch?" was my natural enquiry.

"No," replied Alice, "but we didn't come for that; I wanted to discuss with you certain points about Connie."

"Lunch first and Connie afterwards!" I said laughing. "Sit down, Alice, sit down, Fanny, and make yourselves at home."

We had a merry lunch. I noticed with great approval that Fanny did not in any way presume, but was natural and respectful, also that she worshipped Alice!

In due course we adjourned to the Snuggery where we settled ourselves down comfortably.

"Now, Alice, let's get down to business. Have you found some holes in my plan, or have you brought some new ideas?"

"Well, neither," she said smiling, "but there are one or two things I thought I ought to tell you. I hope, Jack, dear, you won't mind my having told Fanny—she is as gone on Connie as I am and so is keen on helping me in any way she can!"

Fanny blushed.

"Two heads are always supposed to be better than one, dear," I said with a smile, "and in a matter like this I am sure that two cunts should be better than one!" (Alice playfully shook her fist at me.)

"Well, Jack, Fanny says that she talked to Connie's maid and that her mistress is a virgin! Will this matter?"

I looked enquiringly at Fanny. "She was with Mrs. Blunt before her marriage and has never left her, Sir," said Fanny respectfully, "and she told me she was certain that marriage had never been...I forget the word, Miss!" she added, looking at her mistress.

"Consummated, Jack!" said Alice. "Do you know that I believe it must be so; it explains certain things!"

"What things, dear?" I asked innocently.

"Things that you're not to know, Sir!" she retorted, coloring slightly, while Fanny laughed amusedly. It was delightful to me to note the excellent terms on which the two girls were and to think of my share in bringing about this "entente cordiale!"

"I don't see how it can matter!" I said reflectively. "It will certainly make the show more piquant, a virgin widow is a rarity, and if I am able to carry out my programme as planned, it will fall to you, dear, to show her how her cunt works!"

Both girls laughed delightedly. "It will be very interesting!" I added.

"This brings me to the second point nicely, Jack," said Alice. "Fanny would like awfully to be present. Can it be worked, Jack?"

"It shall be worked if it is possible," I said as I smiled at Fanny's eager expression. "I consider I am in debt to her for the delicious time she gave me when last here!" Fanny colored vividly while her mistress laughed merrily. "Let me think!"

It was a bit of a poser, but my fertile imagination was equal to the occasion.

"By Jove!" I exclaimed as a sudden idea struck me, "I think it can be done! Listen you two." The girls leaned forward in pretty eagerness.

"You and Mrs. Blunt must come here together, Alice! That's inevitable. You'll be here by one o'clock, for we must have an early lunch and a long afternoon." Alice nodded significantly.

"Let Fanny follow you in half an hour's time, lunching at home, as I don't see how I can give her lunch here. She must not be seen by Mrs. Blunt, or the latter will be suspicious! When you arrive, Fanny, come straight into this room and hide yourself in my alcove! There's a peephole there, from which you will be able to see all that passes. If Mrs. Blunt's curiosity should lead her to wish to see my alcove, I will choke her off by saying it is my photographic dark room and there is something there which would spoil if light is admitted now. So you'll be certain to see the fun, Fanny." (She smiled gratefully, as did also Alice.) "When you see that I have worked my plan successfully and your mistress and Mrs. Blunt are fastened to the pulleys, take off your clothes noiselessly, even your shoes, and when I have blindfolded Mrs. Blunt, you can slip out and share with your mistress in the pleasure of torturing her! You mustn't speak and you must move noiselessly, for her senses will be very acute. What do you say to this, Alice?"

"Jack! it will be just lovely!" exclaimed Alice, while Fanny, too respectful to speak, looked her satisfaction and gratitude. "What a time Connie will have between the three of us!" she added, laughing more wickedly.

"Now, what's the next point?" I asked. Alice looked towards Fanny, then replied: "There is nothing more, is there, Fanny?"

"No, Miss!" she answered.

"Then we'll be off! Thanks awfully, Jack, I'm really very grateful to you for arranging about Fanny. Come, Fanny!" and they rose.

"Where to now?" I asked. "You are a pair of gadabouts!"

Alice laughed. "My dentist's, worse luck!"

"Poor fun!" I said. "For you or Fanny?"

"Me, unfortunately. Fanny will have to sit in the waiting room."

I glanced at her maid, and a sudden desire to have her again seized me. "Look here, Alice," I said, "I'm going to ask you a favour! Will you allow me to have the company of your maid this afternoon?"

Fanny blushed rosy red over cheeks and brow. Alice laughed merrily, as she regarded her blushing maid and caught her shy glances.

"Certainly, Jack, as far as I am concerned!" she replied: "What do you say, Fanny? Will you stay and take care of Mr. Jack?"

Fanny glanced shyly at us both. "Yes, Miss, if you don't mind!" And vivid blushes covered her face, as she caught Alice's amused and half-quizzing look.

"Then I'll be off!" Alice exclaimed. "Don't trouble to come down, Jack. Bye-bye, Fanny, for the present!"

But of course I wasn't going to let Alice leave unescorted, so I accompanied her downstairs and saw her into a taxi, under a shower of good-natured chaff from her. Then, two steps at a time, I hurried back to the Snuggery, where I found Fanny standing where we had left her, evidently very nervous at being alone with me.

I took her gently in my arms and kissed her blushing upturned face tenderly, then sat down and drew her onto my knees.

"It is sweet of you to be so kind, dear," I said looking lovingly at her. She blushed, then raising her eyes to mine she said softly: "I couldn't refuse, Sir, after you had been so very kind to me about Mrs. Blunt."

I laughed. "Not for my own sake then?"

"Oh, I didn't mean that, Sir!" she exclaimed hastily in pretty confusion.

"Then it is for my own sake, dear?" I asked with a smile.

"Yes, Sir!" she whispered bashfully as she looked into my eyes timidly but lovingly. I drew her to me and kissed her lips passionately. Then I gently began to unbutton her blouse.

"Do you wish me to...undress, Sir?" she murmured nervously.

"Yes, please, dear!" I whispered back. "Use your mistress's room; does your mistress...have you naked, Fanny?" I asked softly.

"Yes, Sir," she nodded blushing.

"Then I'll do the same!" I replied with a smile as I freed her and led her to Alice's alcove, then undressed myself in mine.

Presently Fanny emerged, stark naked, a delicious object, her face covered with blushes, one hand shielding her breasts and the other over her cunt! I sprang to meet her and led her to the couch and made her sit on my knee, thrilling at the touch of her warm, firm, soft flesh.

"What shall we do, Fanny?" I asked mischievously as I slipped my hand down to her cunt and lovingly played with it. My caress seemed to set her on fire; she lost her restraint, suddenly threw her arms around my neck and kissing me passionately murmured: "Do anything you like to me, Sir!"

"Then may I suggest a little sucking first, and then some sweet fucking?" I said softly. Her eyes beamed assent.

I laid her flat on her back, opened her legs widely, and after feasting my eyes on her lovely cunt, I applied my lips to it and tongued her till she quivered and wriggled with delight. Alice had evidently taught her this delicious pleasure. Then I got on her and thrust my prick well up her; she clasped me delightedly in her arms, and letting herself go, passed from one spending to another, wriggling voluptuously, till she had extracted from me all I could give her, and which I shot into her excited interior with rapturous ecstasy—and between fucking and sucking we passed a delicious afternoon!

In the enforced intervals for rest and recovery I learnt from her all about her sexual relationship with her mistress. She described the sensation of being provoked into spending by the sweet friction of Alice's cunt against hers as something heavenly, so much so that the girls seldom did anything else but satisfy their lustful cravings and desires in this way. One evening, Alice apparently was very randy and insisted on frigging Fanny, first tieing her down to the four bedposts, then made Fanny tie her down similarly and tickle her cunt with a feather till she spent three times. It was clear that the girls were devoted to each other. I asked Fanny what she thought would be the arrangement if we succeeded in converting Mrs. Blunt to their ways; she blushed and said she didn't think it would affect her and Alice's relations and she hoped Connie would sometimes spend the night at Alice's and give her a chance!

6.

A few days later I received a note from Mrs. Blunt saying that Alice was staying with her and she would be delighted if I would dine there with them quite quietly. I naturally accepted the invitation.

I was somewhat of a stranger to Mrs. Blunt. I had met her more than once and admired her radiant beauty, but no more. Now that there was more than a possibility that she might have to submit herself to me, I studied her closely. She was more voluptuously made than I had fancied and was a simply glorious specimen of a woman; but she was something of a doll, rather shallow and weak-willed; and I saw with satisfaction that I would not have much trouble in terrorizing her and forcing her to comply with my desires.

During the evening Alice brought up the subject of my rooms and their oddity and made Mrs. Blunt so interested that I was able naturally to suggest a visit and a lunch there—which was accepted for the following day, an arrangement that made Alice glance at me with secret exultation and delighted anticipation.

In due course my guests arrived, and after a dainty lunch which drew from Mrs. Blunt many compliments, we found ourselves in the Snuggery. The girls at once commenced to examine everything, Alice taking on herself the role of showman while I, in my capacity of host, did the honors. I could see that Fanny was at her post of observation—and now awaited, with some impatience, the critical moment.

In due course Mrs. Blunt and Alice finished their tour of inspection, and made as if they would rest for a while.

"What comfortable chairs you men always manage to get about you," remarked Mrs. Blunt as she somewhat critically glanced at my furniture. "You bachelors *do* study your creature comforts—and so remain bachelors!" she added somewhat significantly, as she was among our deluded friends who planned a match between Alice and me.

"Quite true!" I replied with a polite smile—"so long as I can by hook or by crook get in these rooms what I want, they will be good enough for me—especially when I am permitted to enjoy the visits of such angels!"

"That's a very pretty compliment, isn't it Alice?" exclaimed Mrs. Blunt as she moved towards the Chair of Treachery which stood invitingly close; then gracefully sank into it.

Click!—the arms folded on her. "Oh!" she ejaculated as she endeavored to press them back.

"What's the matter, Connie?" asked Alice, quickly hurrying to her friend—but in a flash I was onto her and had tightly gripped her. "Oh!" she screamed in admirably feinted fright, struggling naturally; but I picked her up and carrying her to the pulleys, made them fast to her wrists and fixed her upright with hands drawn well over her head, to Mrs. Blunt's horror! As I approached her she shrieked, "Help...help!" pressing desperately against the locked arms and striving to get loose.

"It's no use, Mrs. Blunt!" I said quietly, as I commenced to wheel the chair towards the second pair of pulleys. "You're in my power! You'd better yield quietly!"

Seizing her wrists one at a time, I quickly made the ropes fast to them, set the machinery going—and just as she was being lifted off her seat, I released the arms and drew the chair away, forcing her to stand up. In a very few seconds she was drawn up to her full height, facing Alice, both girls panting and gasping after their struggle!

"There, ladies," I exclaimed, as if well pleased with my performance, "now you'll appreciate the utility of this room!"

"Oh! Mr. Jack!" cried Mrs. Blunt in evident relief, "how you did frighten me. I was sure that something dreadful was going to happen!"

Then with a poor attempt to be sprightly, "I quite made up my mind that Alice and I were going to be..." she broke off with a silky, self-conscious giggle.

"I gladly accept the suggestion you have so kindly made, dear lady," I said with a smile of gratitude, "and I will do you and Alice presently!" She started, horrified—stared aghast at me as if she could not believe her ears; she seemed to be dumb with shocked surprise, and went deadly pale. I was afraid to glance at Alice lest I should catch her eye and betray her.

With an effort, Mrs. Blunt stammered brokenly: "Do you mean to say...that Alice and I...are going to be...to be...?" she stopped abruptly, unable to express in words her awful apprehension.

"Fucked is the word you want, I think, dear Mrs. Blunt!" I said with a smile. "Yes, dear ladies—as you are so very kind I shall have much pleasure in fucking you both presently!"

She quivered as if she had been struck, then she screamed hysterically: "No, no! I-I won't! Help! Help!...help!"

I turned quietly to Alice (who I could see was keenly enjoying the trap into which Mrs. Blunt had fallen) and said to her: "Are you going to be foolish and resist, Alice?"

She paused for a long moment, then said in a voice that admirably counterfeited intense emotion: "I feel that resistance will be of no avail—but I'm not going to submit to you tamely. You will have to...force me!"

"Me also!" cried Mrs. Blunt, hysterically.

"As you please!" I said equably. "I've long wanted a good opportunity of testing the working of this machinery; I don't fancy I'll get a better one than you are now offering me, a nice long afternoon—two lovely rebellious girls! Now, Mrs. Blunt, as you are chaperoning Alice, I am bound to begin with you." And I commenced to unbutton her blouse.

"No, no, Mr. Jack!" she screamed in dismay as she felt my fingers unfastening her upper garments and unhooking her skirt—but I steadily went on with my task of undressing her, and soon had her standing in her stays with bare arms and legs—a lovely tall slender half-undressed figure, her bosom heaving and palpitating, the low-cut bodice allowing the upper half of her breasts to become visible. Her flushed face indicated intense shame at this indecent exposure of herself, and her eyes strained appealing towards Alice as if to assure herself of her sympathy.

"Now I will give you a few minutes to collect yourself while I attend to Alice!" I said as I went across to the latter, whose eyes were stealthily devouring Mrs. Blunt's provoking dishabille. "Now, for you, dear!" I said, as I quickly set to work to undress her.

She (very wisely) was adopting the policy of dogged defiance and maintained a sullen silence as one by one her clothes were taken off her, till she also stood bare-armed and bare-legged in her stays. But instead of pausing, I went on, removed her corset, unfastened the shoulder straps of her chemise and vest and pushed them down to her feet, leaving her standing with only her drawers on, a sweet, blushing, dainty, nearly-naked girl, on whose shrinking trembling figure Mrs. Blunt's eyes seemed to be riveted with what certainly looked like involuntary admiration!

"But I myself was getting excited and inflamed by the sight of so much unclothed and lovely girl-flesh, so eagerly returning to Mrs. Blunt, I set to work to remove the little clothing that was left on her. "No, no, Mr. Jack!" she cried piteously as I took off her stays. "Oh!" she screamed in her distress when she felt her chemise and vest slip down to her feet, exposing her in her drawers only, which solitary garment, she evidently concluded, from the sight of Alice, would be left on her. But when, after a few admiring glances, I went behind her and began to undo the waist-band and she realized she was to be exposed naked, Mrs. Blunt went into a paroxysm of impassioned cries and pitiful pleadings; in her desperation she threw the whole of her weight on her slender wrists and wildly twisted her legs together in the hope of preventing me from pulling her drawers off. But they only required a few sharp tugs—down to her ankles they came! A bitter cry broke from her, her head with its wealth of now disordered golden hair fell forward on her bosom in her agony of shame—Connie Blunt was stark naked.

I stepped back a couple of paces, then exultingly gazed on the vision that met my eyes. Close in front of me was revealed the back of Mrs. Blunt's tall, slender, naked figure, uninterrupted from her heels to her up-drawn hands, her enforced attitude displaying to perfection the voluptuous curves of her hips, her luscious haunches, her gloriously rounded bottom, her shapely legs. Facing her stood Alice, naked save for her drawers—her face suffused with blushes at the sight of Connie's nakedness, her bosom heaving excitement not unmixed with delight at witnessing the nudity of her friend and trepidation at the approaching similar exposure of herself. I saw from the stealthy gloating glances she shot at Connie that she was longing to have a good look at her but dared not do so, lest her eyes should betray her delight—so I decided to give her the opportunity. I went over to her, slipped behind her, passed my arms around her and drew her against me—and holding her thus in my embrace, I gazed at the marvellous sight Connie Blunt was affording to us as she stood naked!

She was simply exquisite! Her pearly dazzling skin, her lovely shape, her delicious little breasts standing saucily out with their coral nipples as they quivered on her heaving bosom, her voluptuous hips and round smooth belly, her pretty legs; her drooping head exhibited her glorious golden hair, while, as if to balance it, a close clustering mass of silky, curly, golden-brown hairs grew thickly over the region of her cunt hiding it completely from my eager eyes!

In silent admiration I gloated over the wonderful sight of Connie Blunt naked—till a movement of Alice recalled me to her interests. She was keeping her face steadily averted from Connie, her eyes on the floor, as if unwilling to distress her friend by looking at her in her terrible nudity.

"Well, how do you like Connie now?" I asked loud enough for Mrs. Blunt to hear. She shivered; Alice remained silent.

"Aren't you going to look at her?" Alice still remained silent.

"Come, Alice, you must have a good look at her. I want to discuss her with you, to have your opinions as a girl on certain points. Come, look!" And I gently stroked her naked belly.

"Oh! Don't, Jack!" she cried, affecting a distress she was not feeling. Connie glanced hastily at us to see what I was doing to Alice, and blushed deeply as she noted my wandering hands, which now were creeping up to Alice's breasts.

I seized them and began to squeeze them. "Don't, Jack!" again she cried.

"Then obey me and look at Connie!" I said sternly.

Slowly Alice raised her head, as if most reluctantly, and looked at Connie, who coloured hotly as her eyes met Alice's. "Forgive me, darling!" cried Alice tearfully, "I can't help doing it!" But her throbbing breasts and excitedly agitated bottom told me how the little hypocrite was enjoying the sight of Connie's nakedness!

"Now, no nonsense, Alice!" I said sternly—and I gave her breasts a twist that made her squeal in earnest and immediately rivet her eyes on her friend lest she should get another twist. And so, for a few minutes, we silently contemplated Mrs. Blunt's shrinking form, our eager eyes greedily devouring the lovely naked charms that she was so unwillingly exhibiting to us!

Presently I said to Alice, (whose breasts were still captives in my hands) "Now, the plain truth, please—speaking as a girl, what bit of Mrs. Blunt do you consider her finest point?"

Alice blushed uncomfortably, pretended to hesitate, then said shame-facedly: "Her...her...private parts!"

Connie flushed furiously and pressed her thighs closely together as if to shield her cunt from the eager eyes which she knew were intently looking at it! I laughed amusedly at Alice's demure phraseology and said: "I think so too! But that's not what you girls call it when you talk together. Tell me the name you use, your pet name for it!"

Alice was silent. I think she was really unwilling to say the word before Mrs. Blunt, but I mischievously proceeded to get it out of her. So I gave her tender breasts a squeeze that made her cry, "Oh!" and said, "Come, Alice, out with it!"

Still she remained silent. I let go of one of her breasts and began to pinch her fat bottom, making her wriggle and squeal in grim reality—but she would not speak!

Seeing that Mrs. Blunt was watching closely, I moved my hand away from Alice's bottom and made as if I was going to pass it through the slit in her drawers.

"Won't you tell me?" I said, moving my hand ominously.

"Cunny!" whispered Mrs. Blunt in hot confusion.

"You obstinate little thing!" I said to Alice with a laugh that showed her that I was only playing with her. "Cunny!" I repeated significantly. "Well, Alice, let Mrs. Blunt and I see your cunny!"—and as I spoke I slipped the knot off her drawers, and down they tumbled to her ankles before she could check them with her knees, exposing by their disappearance the lovely cunt I knew so well and loved so dearly, framed so to speak by her plump rounded thighs and her sweet belly.

I sank on my knees by Alice's side, then eagerly and delightedly inspected her delicious cleft, the pouting lips of which, half-hidden in their mossy covering, betrayed her erotic excitement! She enduring with simulated confusion and crimson cheeks my close examination of her 'private parts,' to use her own demure phrase! At last I exclaimed rapturously: "Oh! Alice, it *is* sweet!" then as if overjoyed, I gripped her by her bottom and thighs and pressing my lips on her cunt, I kissed passionately! "Don't, Jack!" she cried, her voice half-choked by the lascivious sensations that were thrilling through her; and seeing that Alice was perilously near to spending in her intense erotic excitement, I quitted her and went across to Mrs. Blunt, by whose side I knelt in order to study her cunt.

"Oh, Mr. Jack! Don't look, *please* don't look there!" she cried in agony of shame at the idea of her cunt being thus leisurely inspected by male eyes—and she attempted to thwart me by standing on one leg and throwing her other thigh across her groin.

"Put that leg down, Connie!" I said sternly.

"No, no," she shrieked, "I won't let you look at it!"

"Won't you?" said I, and drew out from the bases of the pillars between which she was standing two stout straps, which I fastened to her slim ankles in spite of her vigorous kicking. I set the mechanism working. A piercing scream broke from her as she felt her legs being pulled remorselessly apart—and soon, notwithstanding her desperate resistance and frantic struggles, she stood like an inverted Y with her cunt in full view!

"Won't you?" I repeated with a cruelly triumphant smile as I proceeded to blindfold her, she all the while pitifully protesting. Then I noiselessly set Alice loose and signalled to Fanny to join us, which she quickly did, stark naked as directed; and the three of us knelt in front of Connie (I between the girls with an arm around each) and with heads close together delightedly examined her private parts, Alice and Fanny's eyes sparkling with undisguised enjoyment as we noted the delicate and close-fitting, shell-pink lips of her cunt, its luscious fleshiness, and its wonderful covering of brown-gold silky hairs! she all the time quivering in her shame at being thus forced to exhibit the most secret part of herself to my male eyes.

I motioned to the girls to remain as they were, detached myself from them, leant forward and gently deposited a kiss on Connie's cunt. Taken absolutely by surprise, Mrs. Blunt shrieked: "O-h-h!" and began to wriggle divinely, to the delight of the girls, who motioned to me to kiss Connie's cunt again—which I gladly did. Again she screamed, squirming deliciously in her fright. I gave her cunt a third kiss, which nearly sent her into convulsions, Alice and Fanny's eyes now sparkling with lust. Not daring to do it again I rose, slipped behind her noiselessly and took her in my arms, my hands on her belly!

"No, no, Mr. Jack!" she cried, struggling fiercely, "don't touch me!...Oh-h-h!" she screamed as my hands caught hold of her breasts and began to feel them! They were smaller than Alice's but firmer, soft, elastic and strangely provoking, most delicious morsels of girl-flesh; and I toyed and played with them squeezing them lasciviously to the huge delight of the girls, till I felt it was time to feel her cunt. So, releasing her sweet breasts, I slipped my hands over Mrs. Blunt's stomach and her cunt!

"Oh! My God!" she shrieked, her head tossing wildly in her shame and agony as she felt my fingers wander over her private parts so conveniently arranged for the purpose. Over her shoulder I could see Alice and Fanny's faces as they watched every movement of my fingers, their eyes humid, their cheeks flushed, their breasts dancing with sexual excitement! From the fingers' point of view, Alice's cunt was the more delicious of the two because of its superior plumpness and fleshiness—but there was a certain delicacy about Connie's cunt that made me revel in the sweet occupation of feeling it.

Presently I inserted my forefinger gently between the close-fitting lips. The girls' eyes glistened with eagerness and they bent forward to see if Fanny's information was true—and I smiled at the disappointment expressed in their faces when they saw my finger bury itself in Connie's cunt up to the knuckle! She was not a virgin! But she was terribly tight, much more so than Fanny was when I first felt her—and Mrs. Blunt's screams and agonized cries clearly indicated that, for want of use, her cunt had regained its virgin tightness.

Keeping my fingers inside her, I gently tickled her clitoris, in order to test her sexual susceptibility. She gave a fearful shriek accompanied by an indescribable wriggle, then another—then bedewed my hand with her sweet love-juice, her head falling on her bosom as she spent, utterly unable to control herself. I kept my finger inside her till her ecstatic crisis was over and her spasmodic thrills had quieted down—then gently withdrew it as I lovingly kissed the back of her soft neck and then left her to herself.

As I did so, Alice and Fanny rose, their eyes betraying their intense enjoyment of the scene. With an unmistakable gesture they indicated each other's cunts, as if seeking mutual relief—but I shook my head, for Alice had now to be tortured. Quickly I fastened her up again while Fanny noiselessly disappeared into my alcove; then I removed the bandage from Connie's eyes. As she wearily raised her head, having scarcely recovered from the violence of her spending, I clasped her to me and passionately showered kisses on her flushed cheeks and trembling lips. I saw her eyes seek Alice's as if to learn her thoughts as to what she had witnessed—then both girls blushed vividly as if in symphony. I pushed a padded chair behind Connie, released her legs and then lowered her till she could sit down in comfort and left her to recover herself—while I went across to Alice, who was now to be the prey of my lustful hands.

But I was now in an almost uncontrollable state of lust! My erotic senses had been so irritated and inflamed by the sight of Mrs. Blunt's delicious person naked, her terrible struggles, her shame and distress during her ordeal, that my lascivious cravings and desires imperiously called for immediate satisfaction. And the circumstances that all this had taken place in the presence of Alice and Fanny, both stark naked both in a state of intense sexual excitement and unconcealed delight at witnessing the torturing of Mrs. Blunt, only added further fuel to the flame of my lust. But to enjoy either Connie or Alice at the moment did not suit my programme—and my thoughts flew to Fanny now sitting naked in my alcove and undoubtedly very excited sexually by Mrs. Blunt's struggles and cries!

So slipping behind Alice, I took her in my arms, seized her breasts, and said not unkindly while watching Mrs. Blunt keenly, "Now, Alice, it's your turn! You've seen all that has happened to Mrs. Blunt and how in spite of her desperate resistance she has been forced to do whatever I wanted—even to spend! Now I'm going to undress." (Mrs. Blunt looked up in evident alarm.) "While I am away, let me suggest that you consult your chaperone as to whether you had not better yield yourself quietly to me!" And I disappeared into my alcove, where Fanny, still naked, received me with conscious expectancy, having heard every word!

I tore off my clothing, seized her naked person and whispered excitedly as I pointed to my rampant prick, "Quick, Fanny!" She instantly understood. I threw myself into an easy chair—in a moment she was kneeling between my legs with my prick in her mouth; and she sucked me deliciously till I spent rapturously down her throat! Having thus delightfully relieved my feelings, I drew her onto my knees, then whispered as I gratefully kissed her, "Now, dear, I'll repay you by frigging you, while we listen to what Alice and Connie are saying." Then slipping my hand down to her pouting and still excited cunt, I gently commenced the sweet junction, she clasping silently but passionately as my active finger soothed her excited senses. From our chair we could clearly see Connie and Alice and hear every word they said.

Their embarrassed silence had just been broken by Alice, who whispered in admirably simulated distress: "Oh, Connie! What *shall* I do?"

Connie coloured painfully, then with downcast eyes (as if fearing to meet her friend's agitated glances) replied in an undertone: "Better yield, dear! Don't you think so?"

"Oh! no! I can't!" cried Alice despairingly, playing her part with a perfection that brought smiles from Fanny and me; then with a change of voice she asked timidly: "Was it *very* dreadful Connie?"

Connie covered her face with her hands and replied in broken agitation: "I thought I should have died!...The awful feeling of shame! the terrible helplessness!...the dreadful position into which I was fastened!... the agony of having a man's hand on my... cunny!...Oh-h-hh!"

Just then, Fanny began to wriggle deliciously on my knees as she felt her pleasure approaching! Her eyes closed slowly, she strained me against her breasts—then suddenly she agitated herself rapidly on my finger, plunging wildly with quick strokes of her buttocks. Then she caught her breath, murmured brokenly: "Oh-h-h!" and inundated my finger as she spent ecstatically! My mouth sought hers as, little by little, I slowed down the play of my finger in her cunt, till she came to, deliciously satisfied!

"Now I'd better go to them," I whispered, and after a few more tender kisses I went out. My appearance, naked save for my shoes and socks, caused Mrs. Blunt to hurriedly cover her face with her hands as she hysterically cried: "Oh!...Oh!...Oh!"

I ignored her, and took Alice into my arms as before, then said to her encouragingly: "Well, dear, what is it to be?" whispering inaudibly in her ear, "You're to be tickled!"

Alice stood silent with downcast eyes. In her anxiety to hear Alice's decision, Mrs. Blunt uncovered her face and looked eagerly at us!

At last it came! "No," spoken so low that we could just hear her.

"Oh, Alice! You are a silly girl!" exclaimed Mrs. Blunt, now afraid about herself. Alice cast a reproachful glance at Connie, then said almost in tears (the little humbug!): "I can't! Oh, I can't!"

Without a word I fastened straps to Alice's pretty ankles and dragged her legs apart—till she stood precisely as Mrs. Blunt had done. Then I carefully blindfolded her and seated myself just below her on the floor, within easy reach of her—and began to amuse myself with her defenseless cunt, knowing that Mrs. Blunt could see over my shoulder all that passed.

With both hands I felt all of Alice's private parts, touching, pressing, stroking, parting her lips, even pulling her hairs, every now and then, and peering into her interior—an act invariably followed by an ardent kiss as if in apology, she squirming deliciously. She submitted herself to the sweet torture in silence, till I pretended to be trying to push my finger into her cunt, when she screamed in horror: "Don't, Jack, don't!" as if unable to endure it!

"Hurts, does it, Alice!" I said smiling meanly. "Then I won't do it again!"

I'll try something softer than my finger!" And, after fetching a feather, I resumed my position on the carpet.

Alice's colour now went and came and her bosom began to heave uneasily, for she guessed what was now going to be done to her; and although she rather liked having her cunt tickled, the existing conditions were not what she was accustomed to—she awaited her ordeal with a good deal of trepidation.

Quietly I applied the tip of the feather to her cunt's now slightly pouting lips, with a delicate yet subtle touch "O-h-h!" she ejaculated, quivering painfully. I gave her three or four more similar touches, after which she began to wriggle vigorously, crying: "Oh!...Oh!... Don't, Jack!"—and I was just beginning to tickle her cunt in real earnest when Connie, horrified at the sight, shrieked: "Stop!... stop!...oh, you awful brute!...you coward!...to torture a girl in that way!...oh! my God!" she moaned, quite overcome at the sight of Alice being tortured!

How thankful I was that I had blindfolded Alice! I am sure that she otherwise would have given the game away—she must have laughed! In fact some of her convulsions were undoubtedly caused by suppressed laughter and not by her torture!

"There's no better way of curing a girl of obstinacy than by tickling her cunt, Connie," I said unconcernedly, and I again commenced to tickle Alice.

"No, no, stop!" Connie shrieked frantically. "Oh! You cruel brute!...you'll kill her!"

I laughed. "Oh, no! Connie, she's all right—only a little erotic excitement!" I explained equably as I resumed the tickling, this time making Alice wriggle and scream in real earnest. She had not been allowed to satisfy her lustful cravings, induced by the sight of Connie's agonies, and by now she was in a terrible condition of fierce concupiscence and unsatisfied desires, dying to spend, but so far unable to do so for want of the spark necessary to provoke the discharge! More and more hysterical became Connie's prayers and pleadings, shriller her cries of genuine horror at the sight of Alice's cunt being so cruelly tickled— wilder and wilder became Alice's struggles and screams, till suddenly she shrieked: "For God's sake, make me spend!" Immediately I thrust the feather well up her cunt and rapidly twiddled it, then tickled her clitoris! A tremendous spasm shook Alice, her head fell back, then dropped on her bosom as she ejaculated: "A-h-h...ah-h-h!" in a tone of blessed relief, quivering deliciously as the rapturous spasm of the ecstasy thrilled through as she spent madly!

As soon as she came to herself again, I said to her: "Well, will you now yield yourself to me, or do you want some more?"

"Oh, no! No!—my God, no!" she cried, feigning to be completely subdued.

"You'll then be a good girl?"

"Yes!" she gasped.

"You'll do whatever I tell you to do?"

"Yes! Yes!" she cried.

"You'll let me...fuck you?"

"Oh, my God!..." she moaned, remaining silent. I touched her cunt with the feather. "Yes! Yes!" she screamed. "Yes!"

"That's right, dear!" I said encouragingly, then quickly I released her and put her into a large and comfortable easy chair in which she promptly coiled herself up, as if utterly exhausted and ashamed of her absolute surrender—but really to escape the sympathetic and pitying glances from Connie. It was as clever a piece of acting as I had ever seen!

I then went across to Mrs. Blunt and without a word, I touched the springs and set the machinery at work. "Oh! Oh!" she cried as she felt herself drawn up again and her legs being remorselessly dragged asunder till she had resumed her late position. When I had her properly fixed, I said to her: "Now, Connie, I am going to punish you for abusing me—you'll have something to scream about!" And I applied the feather to her lovely, but defenseless, cunt!

"Don't, don't!...Oh, my God!" she screamed. I saw we were about to have a glorious spectacle—so I stopped, blindfolded her, and beckoned to Fanny, who promptly came up, Alice also. Handing a feather to each, I pointed to Connie's quivering cunt.

Delightedly both girls applied their feathers to Connie's tender slit, Alice directing hers against Connie's clitoris, while Fanny ran hers all along the lips and as far inside as she could, their eyes sparkling with cruel glee as they watched Connie wriggle and listened to her terrible shrieks and hysterical ejaculations. It was a truly voluptuous sight! Connie naked, struggling frantically while Alice and Fanny, also naked, were goading her into hysterics with their feathers! But soon I had to intervene—Connie by now was exhausted, she couldn't stand any more; so reluctantly, I stopped the girls, signalled to Fanny to disappear and Alice to return to her chair while I released Connie's bandage.

She looked at me seemingly half-dazed, panting and gasping after her exertions.

"Now will *you* submit yourself to me, Connie?" I asked.

"Yes! Yes!" she gasped.

"Fucking and all!"

"Oh, my God!...Yes!"

Then I set her free. As she sank into her chair, Alice rushed to her as if impelled by irresistible sympathy; the two girls fell into each other's arms, kissing each other passionately, murmuring: "Oh, Connie!..."

"Oh, Alice!" The first part of the play was over!

7.

I produced a large bottle of champagne, and pretending that the opener was in my alcove I went there—but my real objective was to satisfy in Fanny the raging concupiscence which my torturing of Alice and then Connie had so fiercely aroused in me.

I found her shivering with unsatisfied hot lust. I threw myself into a chair, placed my bottom on the edge and pointed to my prick in glorious erection. Instantly Fanny straddled across me, brought her excited cunt to bear on my tool and impaled herself on it with deliciously voluptuous movements, sinking down on it till she rested on my thighs, her arms 'round my neck, mine 'round her warm body, our lips against each other's; then working herself divinely up and down on my prick, she soon brought on the blessed relief we both were thirsting for—and in exquisite rapture we spent madly.

"Oh! Sir! Wasn't it lovely!" she whispered as soon as she could speak.

"Which, Fanny," I asked mischievously. "This!—or that!" pointing to the room.

She blushed prettily, then whispered saucily: "Both, Sir!" as she passionately kissed me.

I begged her to sponge me while I opened the champagne, which she did sweetly, kissing my flaccid prick lovingly, as soon as she had removed from it all traces of our bout of fucking. I poured out four large glasses and made her drink one (which she did with great enjoyment)—then took the other three out with me to the girls.

I found them still in each other's arms and coiled together in the large armchair, Alice half-sitting on Connie's thighs and half resting on Connie's breasts, a lovely sight. I touched her, she started up, while Connie slowly opened her eyes.

"Drink this, it will pull you together!" I said, handing each a tumbler. They did so, and the generous wine seemed to have an immediate good effect and to put new life into them. I eyed them with satisfaction, then raising my glass said: "To your good healths, dears-and a delicious consummation of Connie's charming and most sporting suggestion!" then gravely emptied my tumbler. Both girls turned scarlet, Connie almost angrily—they glanced tentatively at each other but neither spoke.

To terminate their embarrassment, I pointed to a settee close by, and soon we arranged ourselves in it, I in the centre, Alice on my right, and Connie on my left, their heads resting on my shoulders, their faces turned towards each other and within easy kissing distance, my arms clasping them to me, my hands being just able to command the outer breast of each! Both girls seemed ill at ease; I think Connie was really so, as she evidently dreaded having to be fucked by me, but with Alice it was only a pretense.

"A penny for your thoughts dear!" I said to her chafingly, curious to know what she would say.

"I was thinking how lovely Connie is, naked!" she murmured softly, blushing prettily. I felt a quiver run through Connie.

"Before today, how much of each other have you seen?" I asked interestedly. Silently, both girls pointed to just above their breasts.

"Then stand up, Connie dear, and let us have a good look at you," I said, "and Alice shall afterwards return the compliment by showing you herself! Stand naturally, with your hands behind you."

With evident unwillingness she complied, and with pretty bashfulness she faced us, a naked blue-eyed daughter of the gods, tall, slender, golden-haired, exquisite—blushing as she noted in our eyes the pleasure the contemplation of her naked charms was giving us!

"Now in profile, dear!"

Obediently she turned. We delightedly noted her exquisite outline from chin to thigh, her proud little breasts, her gently curving belly, its wealth of golden-brown hair, standing out like a bush at its junction with her thighs, the sweep of her haunches and bottom, and her shapely legs!

"Thanks, darling," I said appreciatively. "Now Alice!" And drawing Connie onto my knees, I kissed her lovingly.

Blushingly Alice complied, and with hands clasped; behind her back she faced us, a piquant, provoking, demure, brown-eyed, dark-haired little English lassie, plump, juicy, appetizing. She smiled mischievously at me as she watched Connie's eyes wander approvingly over her delicious little figure!

"Now in profile, please!"

She turned, and now we realized the subtle voluptuousness of Alice's naked figure, how her exquisitely full and luscious breasts were matched, in turn being balanced by her glorious fleshy bottom and her fat thighs, the comparative shortness of her legs only adding piquancy to the whole; while her unusually conspicuous Mount Venus, with its dark, clustering, silky hairs, proudly proclaiming itself as the delightful centre of her attractions!

"Thanks, darling!" we both exclaimed admiringly as we drew her to us and lovingly kissed her, to her evident delight and gratification.

"Now, Connie darling!" I said. "I want you to lie down on that couch!" And I removed my arm from her waist to allow her to rise.

"No, Jack!" she begged piteously and imploringly, her lovely eyes not far from tears, "Please, Jack!…Don't insist!"

"You must do it, darling!" I said kindly but firmly as I raised her to her feet. "Come, dear!" and I led her to the couch and made her lie down.

"I must put the straps on you, Connie, dear," I said, "not that I doubt your promise, but because I am sure you won't be able to lie still Don't be frightened, dear!" I added, as I saw a look of terror come over her face, "you are not going to be tortured, or tickled or hurt, but you will be treated most sweetly!"

Reluctantly Connie yielded. Quickly Alice attached the straps to her wrists, while I secured the other pair to her ankles; we set the machinery to work and soon she was lying flat on her back, her hands and feet secured to the four corners—the dark-brown upholstery throwing into high relief her lovely figure and dazzling fair hair and skin! I then blindfolded her very carefully in such a way that she could not get rid of the bandage by rubbing her head against the couch; and now that Connie was at our mercy, I signalled to Fanny, who gleefully rushed to us noiselessly and hugged her mistress with silent delight.

"Now, Alice, dear!" I said, "make love to Connie!"

"Oh-h!" cried Connie in shocked surprise, blushing so hotly that even her bosom was suffused with colour. But Alice was already on her knees by Connie's side and was passionately kissing her protesting mouth in the exuberance of her delight at the arrival at last of the much-desired opportunity to satisfy her lusts on Connie's lovely person, cunt against cunt.

I slipped into a chair and took Fanny on my knees, and in sweet companionship, we settled ourselves comfortably to watch Alice make love to Connie! My left arm was 'round Fanny's waist, the hand toying with the breasts which it could just command—while my right hand played lovingly with her cunt.

After Alice had relieved her excited feelings by showering her kisses on Connie's lips with whispered fond endearments, she raised her head and contemplated, with an expression of intense delight, the naked figure of her friend which I had placed at her disposal! Then she proceeded to pass her hands lightly over Connie's flesh. Shakespeare sings (substituting the feminine pronoun for the masculine one he uses):

> To win her heart she touched her here and there,
> —Touches so soft that conquer chastity!

This is what Alice was doing! With lightly poised hands, she touched Connie on the most susceptible parts of herself: her armpits, navel, belly, and especially the soft tender insides of her thighs—evidently reserving her breasts and cunt for special attention. Soon the effect on Connie became apparent—her bosom began to palpitate in sweet agitation, while significant tremors ran through her limbs. "Is it so nice then, darling?" cooed Alice, her eyes dancing with delight as she watched the effect of her operations on Connie's now quivering person; then she rested her lips on Connie's and gently took hold of her breasts!

"Oh, Alice!" cried Connie—but Alice closed her lips with her own, half choking her friend with her passionate kisses. Then raising her head again, she eagerly and delightedly inspected the delicious morsels of Connie's flesh that were imprisoned in her hands. "Oh, you darlings!" she exclaimed as she squeezed them. "You sweet things!" as she kissed them rapturously. "Oh, what dear little nipples!" she cried, taking them in turn into her mouth, her hands all the while squeezing and caressing Connie's lovely breasts till that worthy woman faintly murmured: "Oh, stop, darling!"

"Oh, my love! Was I hurting you, darling?" cried Alice with gleaming eyes, as with a smile full of mischief towards us, she reluctantly released Connie's breasts. For a moment she hesitated, as if uncertain what to do next—then her eyes rested on Connie's cunt, so sweetly defenseless; an idea seemed to seize her—with a look of delicious anticipation, she slipped her left arm under Connie's shoulders so as to embrace her, placed her lips on Connie's mouth, extended her right arm—and without giving Connie the least hint as to her intentions, she placed her hand on Connie's cunt, her slender forefinger resting on the orifice itself!

"Oh-h, Alice!" cried Connie, taken completely by surprise and wriggling voluptuously. "Oh-h-h, Connie!" rapturously murmured Alice, between the hot kisses she was now raining on Connie's mouth—her forefinger beginning to agitate itself inquisitively but lovingly! "Oh darling! Your cunny is sweet!" she murmured as her hand wandered all over Connie's private parts, now stroking and pressing her delicate Mount Venus, now twisting and pulling her hairs, now gently compressing the soft, springy flesh between her thumb and forefinger, now passing along the delicate shell-pink lips, and finally gently inserting her finger between them into the pouting orifice! "I must!…I must look at it!" Quickly she with drew her arm from under Connie's shoulders, gave her a long, clinging kiss, then shifted her position by Connie's side, till her head commanded Connie's private parts; then she squared her arms, rested herself on Connie's belly, and with both hands proceeded to examine and study Connie's cunt, her eyes sparkling with delight.

Again she submitted Connie's delicious organ of sex to a most searching and merciless examination, one hand on each side of the now slightly gaping slit, stroking, squeezing, pressing, touching! Then with fingers poised gently but firmly on each side of the slit, Alice gently drew the lips apart and peered curiously into the shell-pink cavity of Connie's cunt—and after a prolonged inspection, she shifted her finger rather higher, again parted the lips and with rapt attention she gazed at Connie's clitoris which was now beginning to show signs of sexual excitement, Connie all this time quivering and wriggling under the touches of Alice's fingers.

Her curiosity apparently satisfied for the time, Alice raised her head and looked strangely and interrogatively at me. Comprehending her mute enquiry, I smiled and nodded. She smiled back, then dropping her head, she looked intently at Connie's cunt, and imprinted a long clinging kiss in its very centre.

Connie squirmed violently. "Oh-h-h!" she ejaculated in a half-strangled voice. With a smile of intense delight, Alice repeated her kiss, then again and again, Connie at each repetition squirming and wriggling in the most delicious way, her vehement plunging telling Alice what flames her hot kisses had aroused in Connie.

Again she opened Connie's cunt, and keeping its tender lips wide apart she deposited between them and right inside the orifice itself a long lingering kiss which seemed to set Connie's blood on fire, for she began to plunge wildly with furious upward jerks and jogs of her hips and bottom, nearly dislodging Alice. She glanced merrily at us, her eyes brimming with; mischief and delight, then straddled across Connie and arranged herself on her, so that her mouth commanded Connie's cunt, while her stomach rested on Connie's breasts and her cunt lay poised over Connie's mouth, but not touching it. Her legs now lay parallel to Connie's arms and outside them.

Utterly taken aback by Alice's tactics, and in her innocence not recognizing the significance of the position Alice assumed on her, she cried, "Oh, Alice! What are you doing?" Alice grinned delightedly at us, then lowered her head, ran her tongue lightly half a dozen times along the lips of Connie's cunt and then set to work to gamahuch her!

"Oh-h-h!" shrieked Connie, her voice almost strangled by the violence of the wave of lust that swept over her at the first touch of Alice's tongue. "Oh-h-h!...Oh-h-h..." she ejaculated in her utter bewilderment and confusion as she abandoned herself to strangely intoxicating and thrilling sensations hitherto unknown to her, jerking herself upwards as if to meet Alice's tongue, her face in her agitated movements coming against Alice's cunt, before it dawned on her confused senses what the warm, moist, quivering hairy object could be! In wild excitement Alice thoroughly searched Connie's cunt with her active fingers, darting deeply into it, playing delicately on the quivering lips, sucking and tickling her clitoris—and sending Connie into such a state of lust that I thought it wise to intervene.

"Stop, dear!" I called out to Alice, who at once desisted, looking interrogatively at me. "You are trying her too much! Get off her now, and let her recover herself a little—or you'll finish her, which we don't want yet!" Quickly comprehending the danger, Alice rolled off Connie, turned 'round, contemplated for a moment Connie's naked wriggling figure, then got onto her again, only this time lips to lips, bubbies against bubbies, and cunt against cunt; she clasped Connie closely to her as she arranged herself, murmuring passionately: "Oh, Connie!...At last!...At last!..." then commenced to rub her cunt sweetly on Connie's.

"Oh-h-h, Alice!" breathed Connie rapturously as she responded to Alice's efforts by heaving and jogging herself upwards: "Oh-h-h...darling!" she panted brokenly, evidently feeling her ecstasy approaching by the voluptuous wriggles and agitated movements, as Alice now rubbed herself vigorously against her cunt with riotous down-strokes of her luscious bottom. Quicker and quicker, faster and faster, wilder and wilder became the movements of both girls, Connie now plunging madly upwards, while Alice rammed herself down on her with fiercer and fiercer thrusts of her raging hips and buttocks—till the delicious crisis arrived! "Connie!...Connie!" gasped Alice, as the indescribable spasm of spending thrilled voluptuously through her. "Ah-h-h...ah-h-h!... AH-H-H!..." ejaculated Connie rapturously, as she spent madly in exquisite convulsions! dead to everything but the delirious rapture that was thrilling through her as she lay tightly clasped in Alice's clinging arms!

The sight was too much for Fanny! With the most intense interest, she had watched the whole of this exciting scene, parting her legs the better to accommodate my hand, which now was actually grasping her cunt, my forefinger buried in her up to the knuckle, while my thumb rested on her clitoris—and she had already spent once deliciously. But the spectacle of the lascivious transports of her mistress on Connie set her blood on fire again: she recollected her similar experience in Alice's arms, the sensations that Alice's cunt had communicated to hers, the delicious ecstasy of her discharge, and, as the two girls neared their bliss, she began to agitate herself voluptuously on my knees, on my now active finger, keeping pace with them—till with an inarticulate murmur of, "Oh!...Oh-h, Sir-r," she inundated my hand with her love-juice, spending simultaneously with her mistress and her mistress's friend.

As soon as she emerged from her ecstatic trance, I whispered to her inaudibly: "Bring the sponge and towel, dear!"

Noiselessly she darted off, sponged herself, then returned with a bowl of water, a sponge, and a towel just as Alice slowly raised herself off Connie, with eyes still humid with lust and her cunt bedewed with love-juice. I took her fondly in my arms and kissed her tenderly, while Fanny quickly removed all traces of her discharge from her hairs, then proceeded to pay the same delicate attention to Connie, whose cunt she now touched for the first time.

Presently we heard Connie murmur: "May I get up now, Jack!"

"Not yet, darling!" I replied lovingly as I stooped and kissed her. "You have to make me happy now!"

"No, Jack! Please," she whispered, but Alice intervened. "Yes, darling, you must let Jack have you! You must taste again the real article," she cooed. "Let me work you into condition again!" And she signalled to Fanny, who instantly knelt by Connie and began playing with her dainty little breasts and feeling her cunt, her eyes sparkling with delight at thus being permitted to handle Connie who not noting the difference of touch (as Fanny's ministrations to her cunt had accustomed Connie to her fingers) lay still in happy ignorance of the change of operator!

Soon Fanny's fingers began to bring about the desired recovery; Connie's breasts began to stiffen and grow tense, and her body began to tremble in gentle agitation. She was ready—and so was I!

Without a word I slipped onto her. "Oh, Jack!" she murmured as I took her into my arms, holding up her lips to be kissed—no reluctance now! My rampant prick found her sweet hole and gently made an entrance; she was terribly tight, but her discharge had well-lubricated the sweet passage into her interior, and inch by inch, I forced myself into her till my prick was buried in her cunt, she trembling and quivering in my clasp, her involuntary flinchings and sighs confessing the pain attending her penetration! But once she had admitted me all the way into her and I began the sweet up-and-down movement, she went into transports of delight, accommodating herself deliciously to me as, with lips closely against each other, we exchanged hot kisses! Then I set to work to fuck Connie in earnest. Straining her to me, till her breasts were flattened against my chest and I could feel every flutter of her sweet body, I let myself go, ramming into her faster and faster, more and more wildly—till, unable any longer to restrain myself, I surrendered to love's delicious ecstasy and spent madly into Connie just as she flooded my prick in rapturous bliss, quivering under me in the most voluptuous way!

We lay closely clasped together, till our mutual ecstatic trance slowly died away, then, with a sign, I bade Fanny disappear. As soon as she had vanished, Alice removed the blindfold from Connie's eyes. As they met mine, bashfully and shamefacedly, blushing deeply at thus finding herself naked in my arms, Connie timidly held up her mouth to me—instantly my lips were on hers and we exchanged long lingering kisses till we panted for breath. Gently I released her from my clasp and rose off her, and, with Alice's help, unfastened her. Alice gently led her to her alcove where she sedulously attended to her, while Fanny silently but delightedly did the same for me.

It was now only four o'clock—we had a good hour before us. There was now no possible doubt that Connie had surrendered herself to the pleasures of Tribadism and Lesbian love as far as Alice was concerned. So when the girls rejoined me—Connie with a tender look on her face—and we had refreshed ourselves and recovered our sexual appetites and powers, I said to Connie: "Now, dear, you are entitled to take your revenge on Alice—will you…?"

She cast a look of love at Alice, who blushed sweetly, then turning to me she murmured, "Please, Jack!" at the same time giving me a delicious kiss.

"Come along, Alice!" I said as we all rose, and I led her to the couch—the veritable Altar of Venus. "How will you have her, Connie?" I asked, as Alice stood nervously awaiting the disposal of her sweet person.

Connie blushed, then with a glance at Alice, she replied; "Tie her down, Jack, just as you did me!"

Blushingly Alice lay down, and soon Connie and I had her fastened down in the desired position.

"Will you have her blindfolded, dear?" I enquired.

Connie hesitated, looking oddly at Alice—then replied, "No, Jack! I want to see her eyes!" so significantly that Alice involuntarily quivered as she coloured hotly again.

"May I do just whatever I like to Alice, Jack?" asked Connie almost hesitatingly with a fresh access of colour.

"Anything within reason, dear!" I replied with a smile. "You mustn't bite her bubbies off, or stitch up her cunt, for instance." Alice quivered while Connie laughed. "And you must leave her alive, for I am to follow you!" ("Oh, Jack!" exclaimed Alice at this intimation, blushing prettily.)

Connie turned eagerly to me. "Are you going to fuck her?" she asked with sparkling eyes. I nodded, smiling at her eagerness.

"And may I watch you?" she demanded.

"Why, certainly, dear—and perhaps help me! Now what are you going to do to Alice? See how impatiently she is waiting!"

Both girls laughed, Alice a trifle uneasily. Connie looked intently at her for a moment, then seating herself by Alice's side, she began playing with Alice's breasts, keeping her eyes steadily fixed on Alice's.

"Your bubbies are too big for my hands, darling!" she said presently, as she stooped to kiss her. "But they are lovely!" And she squeezed them tenderly for a while—then she deserted them, shifting her position and began to feel Alice's cunt, which she lovingly stroked and caressed.

"Your cunny *is* fat, darling!" she exclaimed presently with heightened colour as she held Alice's cunt compressed between her finger and thumb and gently squeezed the soft springy flesh, while Alice squirmed involuntarily.

Suddenly Connie leant forward, took Alice's face in her hands and whispered: "Darling, I'm going to fuck you twice, eh?" and lovingly kissed her while Alice's eyes sought mine shamefully.

Quickly Connie got onto Alice, took her into her arms, then keeping her head raised so as to look right into Alice's eyes, she began to rub her cunt against Alice's, gently and slowly at first with a circular grinding sort of movement. Presently her action quickened then became more and more irregular. Soon Connie was rubbing herself up and down Alice's cunt, with quick agitated strokes of her bottom, all the while intently watching Alice's eyes as if to gauge her friend's sensations. Soon both girls began plunging and heaving riotously, Alice especially, as they both felt the crisis approaching—then came a veritable storm of confused heaving, thrusting and plunging. "Kiss…me…darling!" ejaculated Alice, now on the verge of spending. But Connie only shook her head with a loving smile, rammed her cunt against Alice's fiercely, intent on Alice's now-humid eyes, and apparently restraining her own discharge! A frantic heave from Alice—"Ah-h-h, dar-r-ling" she gasped as her eyes half closed in ecstasy—then she spent with delicious quivering. Immediately Connie glued her lips to Alice's, agitated herself rapidly against Alice's cunt. "Alice!" she breathed in her delirious frenzy, as a spasm thrilled through her, and Alice's cunt received her love-juice as she spent ecstatically.

For some moments the girls lay silent, only half-conscious, motionless save for the involuntary thrills that shot through them. Then Connie raised her head and with the smile of the victor surveyed Alice, whose eyes now began to open languidly. She blushed deliciously as she met Connie's glances and raised her mouth as if inviting a kiss. Instantly Connie complied with passionate delight. "Wasn't it nice, darling?" I heard her whisper. "Oh, Connie, just heavenly!" murmured Alice tenderly and with loving kisses. "Are you ready again, darling?" whispered Connie eagerly. "Yes! Yes!" replied Alice softly, beginning to agitate herself under Connie.

"Our mouths together this time, darling, eh!" whispered Connie with excitement. "Don't stop kissing me, darling!" she added tenderly as she responded to Alice's movements under her and set to work to rub her cunt against Alice's. Soon both girls were hard at work with their cunts squeezed against each other, slit to slit, clitoris against clitoris—Connie's bottom and hips swaying and oscillating voluptuously while Alice jerked herself up madly. With mouths glued to each other they plunged, curvetted, wriggled, squirmed, till the blissful ecstasy overtook them both simultaneously, when madly they bedewed each other with their love-juice to the accompaniment of the most exquisite quivering, utterly absorbed in rapture!

With a deep-drawn sigh of intense satisfaction, Connie presently rose slowly off Alice, and tenderly contemplated her as she lay—still fastened by her widely extended limbs—to the four corners of the couch, her closed eyes and her involuntary tremors indicating that she was still tasting bliss. Then Connie turned to me and whispered rapturously: "Oh, Jack, she *is* sweet!" I kissed her lovingly and resting her on my knees, I sponged and dried her, then begged her to perform the same office to Alice, whose cunt was positively glistening with her own and Connie's spendings. As soon as Alice felt the sponge at work, she dreamily opened her eyes, and, on recognizing me, she made as if to rise; but when she found herself checked by her fastenings and realized that she was now to be fucked by me, she smiled somewhat uneasily as our eyes met—for as often as she had tasted love's ecstasy in my arms, she had invariably, after that first time, been free; now she was tied down in such a way as to be absolutely helpless, and in this equivocal position, she had to accommodate herself to me and to satisfy my lustful passions and desires. But I smiled encouragingly back to her, seated myself by her side, and tenderly embracing her defenseless body, I whispered: "Darling, may I have you like this?"

Her eyes beamed gratefully on me, full of love; she was now perfectly happy because I had left it to her to say whether or not she would be fucked while tied down in the most shamelessly abandoned attitude in which any girl could be placed in. So with love's own light in her shining eyes and with pretty blushes on her cheeks, Alice whispered back tenderly, "Yes, darling, yes!"

Promptly I got on her, took her in my arms, and gently drove my prick home up her cunt. "Do you like it like this, darling?" I murmured softly. "Shall I go on?" She nodded sweetly, our lips met, and I began to fuck her.

Tied down as she was, she was simply delicious! I had had first

Fanny and then Connie in precisely the same attitude, but voluptuous as was the act of fucking them so, the pleasure fell short of what I was now tasting! To a certain extent, both Fanny and Connie were unwilling recipients of my erotic favours—Fanny was really ravished and Connie practically so, and their movements under me were the outcome of fright, shame, and even pain; but Alice was yielding herself sweetly to my caprices and was doing her best to accommodate her captive body to my movements. Perhaps her little plump rounded figure suited the attitude better than the taller and more slender forms of Fanny and Connie—but whatever may have been the reason, the result was undeniable, and Alice, fucked as a helpless captive, was simply delicious. Her double spend under Connie made her usual quick response to love's demands arrive more slowly than was customary with her; and as this was my fourth course that afternoon, our fucking was protracted to a delicious extent, and I adopted every method and variation known to me to intensify our exquisite pleasure.

Commencing slowly, I fucked Alice with long strokes, drawing my prick nearly out of her cunt and then shoving it well home again, a procedure which always delighted her and which she welcomed with appreciative and warm kisses. Then I agitated myself more rapidly on her, shoving, pressing, thrusting, ramming, now fast, now slow, holding her so tightly clasped that her breasts were flattened against my chest—while she, panting and gasping, plunged, wriggled, and heaved herself wildly under me, in her loyal endeavors to cooperate with me to bring about love's ecstasy. Presently she thrilled exquisitely under me! Fired by her delicious transports, I re-doubled my efforts, as did she also—I began to feel my seminal resources respond to my demand on them; soon we both were overtaken by the tempestuous prelude to the blissful crisis—and then came the exquisite consummation of our wildly sexual desires! With a half-strangled, "Ah-h...Jack" Alice spent in rapturous convulsions just as I madly shot into her my boiling tribute!

Oblivious to absolutely everything except the delicious satisfaction of our overwrought feelings, we lay as if in a trance! We were roused by Connie's gentle warning voice, "Alice!...Alice!...Alice, dear!" as she set to work to undo Alice's fastenings. Taking the hint, I rose after giving Alice a long lingering parting kiss, then we helped her to get up and Connie tenderly took her off at once to the girl's alcove, while I retired to mine—where Fanny deliciously attended to me, her eyes sparkling with gratified pleasure at the recollection of the voluptuous spectacle she had been permitted to witness through the peep-hole.

As it was getting late, we all dressed ourselves, and after a tender parting, I put Connie and Alice into a taxi and started them off home. On returning to my room, I found Fanny ready to depart. She was full of delighted gratitude to me for having managed that she should see all that went on and also have a share in the afternoon's proceedings; and when I slipped a couple of sovereigns into her hand, I had the greatest difficulty making her accept them. Finally she did so, saying shyly and with pretty blushes: "You've only got to call me, Sir, and I will come." I kissed her tenderly, put her into a hansom and sent her home; then wended my way to my Club, where I drank to the three sweet cunts I, that afternoon, had enjoyed, and their delicious owners; Alice, Connie, and Fanny!

8.

I did not see anything of Alice for some little time after the conversion of Connie, but I did not distress myself; for I knew she would be in the first flush of her newly developed Tribadic ardour and newly born passion for her own sex and would be hard put to satisfy Connie and Fanny—and I felt sure that she would, of her own volition, come to me before long. Meanwhile, another matter began to occupy my serious attention.

A few months ago, I had made the acquaintance of Lady Betty Bashe at the house of a mutual friend; she was a consolable widow of something under forty and was busy introducing her daughter into Society, and for some perverse reason, she took it into her head that I would make an excellent son-in-law and proceeded to hunt me persistently, her daughter aiding, and abetting her vigorously—till they became a real nuisance.

I had taken a dislike to both mother and daughter from our first meeting, although they both were decidedly attractive. Lady Betty was a tall, robust, buxom woman of under forty, after the type of Ruben's fleshy females, but somewhat over-developed, and owed a good deal to her corseter—I guessed that without her stays she would be almost exuberant, but nevertheless a fine armful. Molly, her daughter, was a small and dainty edition of her mother, and with the added freshness and juiciness of her eighteen years. She was really a tidbit. But both mother and daughter were silly, affected, insincere, and unscrupulous, and Lady Betty's juvenile airs and youthful affectations only tended to confirm my distaste for her.

I had told Lady Betty plainly one day that I was not in the matrimonial market; but she nevertheless continued to pursue me pertinaciously till it became intolerable—and I determined I would stop her at any cost.

Matters culminated at a dinner given by the same hostess whose kindly suggestion brought about the reconciliation of Alice and myself, as already related in the first chapter. She, of course, again gave me Alice as my dinner partner, an arrangement that did not commend itself to Lady Betty. I think she must have taken a little too much of our hostess' champagne, but in the middle of dinner she called out in a tone that attracted everyone's attention and checked the conversation, "Jack, we're coming to lunch day after tomorrow; mind you're in!"

I was intensely annoyed, first by the use of my Christian name and then by the intolerable air of proprietorship she assumed; but the look of distress on my dear little hostess's face impelled me to face the music. So I promptly responded with a smile: "That will be very nice of you, Lady Betty; you shall have some of my famous souffle, and you will be the first to see my new curios!" The conversation then turned on my curios and soon became general, much to my hostess's relief, and the rest of the dinner passed off pleasantly.

As I was driving Alice home, she said sympathetically: "Poor Jack, what a bad time you'll have day after tomorrow."

"Not at all, dear," I replied cheerily, "somebody else will have the bad time—for unless I am greatly mistaken, there will be a lot of squealing in the Snuggery on that afternoon, her Ladyship will be made to remember the pleasures of married life, and there will be one virgin less in the world!"

Alice started in surprise. "You don't mean to say, Jack, that you mean to...to..."

"I do!" I said stoutly. "I'm sick of this annoyance and mean to stop it. Will you come and see the fun, dear?"

"I will, gladly," Alice replied energetically. "But, Jack, do ask Connie also, for we both have a certain bone to pick with her Ladyship."

"Why not include Fanny as well, dear?" I asked mischievously.

"Jack! That would be just lovely!" Alice exclaimed with sparkling eyes. "Yes, Jack! Please let Fanny come! We'll then be three couples, very convenient, Sir—and we'll be three couples in the undressing and the...the...sponging! Yes, Jack! Let's have Fanny also—then we can have a regular orgy with Lady Betty and Molly as the main attraction!" she added, eagerly hugging me in her excitement while one hand wandered down to the fly of my trousers.

I was hugely taken by her idea—a luscious woman and a voluptuous maiden on whom to exercise our lustful ingenuity! "A most excellent idea, darling," I replied, "you bring Connie with you, let Fanny follow and hide in my alcove till she's wanted, as before—and we'll give Lady Betty and Molly an afternoon entertainment they won't easily forget, and also have a heavenly time ourselves!"

Alice smiled delightedly; then cuddling up to me she whispered: "Now, Jack, I'm going to ask a favour: I'm longing to be fucked in my own little room in the middle of my own familiar things, on my own bed! Come in tonight, darling, and do me!"

"Yes!...yes...yes!" I whispered passionately, punctuating my reply with kisses and noting with delight how she thrilled with sweet anticipation. Soon we arrived at her flat; soon Fanny, with pretty lashes, ushered me into Alice's dainty bedroom; and on her little bed in the quaint surroundings of her most intimate self, Alice, stark naked, received me in her arms and expired deliciously five times, while I twice madly spent into her. So excited was I by my voluptuous experience of fucking an unmarried girl in her bedroom, and on her own bed, that I began a third course but Alice murmured: "No, Jack, darling! Not again!...I've got to console Fanny presently, and she'll be very excited!" Whereupon I reluctantly rose off her, dressed, and after a hundred kisses (not confined to her mouth by any means) I went home, imagining on my way Fanny in her mistress's arms, the cunts of both in sweet conjunction.

The eventful afternoon came around. Lady Betty was disgusted at finding that she and Molly were not going to have me at their mercy by myself all the afternoon, and vented her spite on Alice and Connie more than once in her ill-bred way. But they knew their vengeance was at hand and they took her insulting impertinence with well-bred indifference. In due course we were all collected in the Snuggery, Fanny concealed in my alcove.

"Jack, why don't you have those nasty pulleys taken down, they are not pretty, they're useless, and they're horridly in the way!" exclaimed Lady Betty, after she narrowly escaped coming up against one.

"Why, they form my gymnasium, your Ladyship!" I replied. "I couldn't do without them!"

Molly now joined in eagerly. "How do you work them, Jack?" she asked. "What's the idea of the loops? I'm a dab at gymnastics but never saw this arrangement before."

"The loops are wristlets, Miss Molly," I replied. "You must fasten them 'round your wrists and then grasp the rope with your hand—thus you divide your weight between wrist and hand instead of it all coming on the fingers, as in a trapeze."

Of course all this was arrant nonsense and rubbish—yet this "dab in gymnastics" believed it all solemnly; it was a fair sample of her ways.

"Oh, how clever!" Molly exclaimed in her affected fulsome way. "Let me try, Jack! Alice, please fasten me!" Alice complied demurely, with a sly glance at me.

"I used to be the best girl at gymnastics in school," said Lady Betty complacently. "Molly takes after me." By this time, Alice had fastened the ropes to Molly's wrists and the latter began to swing herself slowly and gently, backwards and forwards.

"Oh, Mother, it is jolly!" cried Molly. "Do try it!"

Ever anxious to show herself to be a juvenile, Lady Betty rose briskly. "Will you fasten me, Jack?" she said as she raised her arms for the purpose. "I'm afraid I'm too old and heavy for this sort of thing now! Will the ropes bear me, Jack?"

"They carry me, Lady Betty," I replied as I fastened the wristlets to her arms. "Why malign yourself so cruelly?"

Lady Betty glanced at me approvingly for my pretty speech, little dreaming that she and Molly were now our prisoners by their own actions. Alice and I exchanged exulting looks—we had our victims safe!

Following Molly's lead, Lady Betty swung herself gently to and fro a few times, then stopped, remarking: "I can't say I like it, dear, but I'm not as young you are! Let me loose, Jack!"

Instead of doing so, I passed my arms 'round her buxom waist, and drew her to me as I replied: "Not yet, dear Lady Betty—we're going to have some fun with you and Miss Molly first!"

Something significant in my voice or in my eyes told her of what was in store for her and her daughter! She flushed nervously, then paled, while Molly, startled, stopped swinging herself, as Alice and Connie quietly took up positions, one on each side of her.

For a moment there was dead silence, then Lady Betty said somewhat unsteadily: "I don't follow you at all Jack. Loose us both at once please; I don't mind a joke in the least, but you're going too far, Sir!"

"Will this help you to understand our ideas, dear Lady Betty?" I rejoined with a mischievous smile, as I slipped my hand under her clothes and pulled them up till they rested on her fat thighs.

"Oh!" she screamed, utterly taken aback by the quickness of my action and its most unexpected nature. "How dare you, Sir!" she shrieked as she felt my hand forcing its way upwards and between her legs. "Stop!...Stop!" she yelled, now furious with rage at such an outrage, while Molly screamed sympathetically, horror-stricken!

I withdrew my hand. "You're awfully nice and plump dear Lady!" I remarked cruelly, as I watched her flustered face and heaving bosom. "If the rest of you is like what I have just had the pleasure of feeling, you'll give us even a more delicious time than we expected! We really must undress you to see; you won't mind, will you?"

"WHAT!!" cried Lady Betty, staring wildly at me as if unable to believe her ears, while Molly shrieked hysterically: "No, no!"

"Make Molly comfortable in that easy chair, dears, till we want her," I said quietly to Alice and Connie, who instantly pushed the Chair of Treachery up to Molly and gently forced her into it till the arms firmly held her prisoner; then they took the ropes off her wrists, as she was sufficiently under control now, Molly, all the time struggling frantically, shrieking: "Oh, Mother!...Help! Help!" But Lady Betty had her own troubles to attend to, for to her bewilderment, Fanny suddenly appeared before her in response to my signal—and the sight of this trim smart lady's maid ready to commence to undress her, was evidently an awful proof that we intended to carry out our intentions as to her and her daughter.

"Undress Lady Betty, Fanny," I commanded quietly, and Fanny instantly began to do so!

"I won't have it! I won't have it! Stop her Jack," screamed Lady Betty, now purple with wrathful indignation and the sense of her powerlessness, for her frantic tugs at the ropes availed her nothing. "Mother! Oh mother dear!" yelled Molly in an agony of dismay as she saw Fanny deftly remove Lady Betty's hat, and then proceed to unfasten her dress. Intent on going to her mother's aid, she made desperate efforts to drag the heavy armchair after her, but Connie easily frustrated her attempts at rescue; and seeing that Molly was safe in Connie's hands, I signalled to Alice to assist Fanny—which she was delighted to do. Between the three of us, Lady Betty's clothes slipped off her in a way that must have been marvellous to her; by the time we had reduced her to her stays, bare-legged and bare armed, she evidently saw she was doomed, and in place of threats she began to plead for some mercy. But we were deaf to her prayers and entreaties; off came her stays, then her chemise and vest, leaving her standing with only her drawers on!

"For God's sake, Jack, don't strip me naked!" she shrieked in terrible distress, her face crimson with shame. I simply nodded to Alice; a twitch at the tape, and down came the drawers—leaving Lady Betty standing naked from head to foot!

"Oh!" she wailed, as her agonized eyes instinctively sought Molly's and read in her daughter's face her horrible anguish at the sight of her naked mother.

"Cover me up! For God's sake, cover me up, Jack!" she piteously pleaded as she involuntarily squeezed her legs together in a despairing attempt to shield her private parts from view. Just then, I touched the spring and made the ropes draw her off the ground, so that Alice and Fanny could remove the tumbled mass of her garments. "Oh-h-h!" she shrieked, as she found herself dangling by her wrists, her struggles to touch the ground exposing her person deliciously. Quickly Fanny cleared away Lady Betty's clothes; then I let her down till she could stand erect comfortably, and joined Alice and Connie at Molly's side, my intention now being to compel Molly to inspect her naked mother and to harrow her already tortured feelings by criticizing Lady Betty's naked charms!

She must have been a simply magnificent woman in her prime; even now, in spite of an exuberance of flesh, Lady Betty was enough to provoke any man, into concupiscence with her massive, though shapely, arms and legs, her grand hips and round fat thighs, her full ample belly, and her enormous breasts, which though naturally pendulous, still maintained their upstanding sauciness to a marvellous degree. But what attracted all our eyes (even her daughter's) was the hair which grew over her cunt. I do not think I ever saw such an enormous tract—a dinner plate would not have covered it! It seemed to spring from somewhere between Lady Betty's legs, it clustered so thickly over the cunt itself that her crack was quite invisible, it extended all over her groin and abdomen and reached her navel—closely curling and silky and fully two inches deep all over her Mount Venus! A simply wonderful sight!

In spite of the attraction of Lady Betty's naked figure, I closely watched Molly. She had been terribly distressed during the undressing of her mother, especially when the naked flesh began to be exposed, and she hysterically joined in her mother's futile prayers and piteous pleadings as she watched her quickly growing nudity with a fascination she could not resist; but when the terrible climax arrived and Lady Betty stood naked, the poor girl uttered a heart-broken shriek as she buried her face in her hands. But I could see that every now and then she glanced stealthily through her fingers at her mother's naked body as if unable to resist the fascinating temptation.

I turned to the three girls, who with gleaming eyes were devouring Lady Betty's naked charms, their arms around each other. Our eyes met. "Isn't she splendid, Jack!" cried Alice enthusiastically. "What a lovely time she'll give us all!" And they laughed delightedly as Lady Betty shivered.

"And you, my pet!" cooed Connie to Molly, "are you anything like Mummy?" And she began to pass her hands over Molly's corsage as if to sample her body. The girls' individual predilections were clear even at this early stage—Alice was captivated by lady Betty's fleshy amplitude, while Connie coveted Molly's still-budding charms.

"Oh, don't, Mrs. Blunt, please, don't!" cried Molly, flushing deeply as she endeavored to protect herself with her hands, thereby uncovering her face. This was what I desired—I intended that Lady Betty should now be felt in front of her daughter, and that Molly should be forced to look at her mother—and witness her shame and anguish and involuntary struggles—while my hands wandered lasciviously over Lady Betty's naked body and invaded her most private parts.

"Sling Molly up again, girls," I said quietly. "No, no," screamed Molly in an agony of apprehension, but in a trice she was standing upright, with her hands secured over her head, her eyes full of silent terror!

"Do you think you could slip Molly's drawers off her without disturbing the rest of her garments?" I asked.

"Yes, of course!" replied Connie—and the three girls dropped on their knees 'round Molly; their hands disappeared under her skirts, her wriggles and cries and agitated movements proclaiming how she was upset by their attacking hands. Then came a shriek of despair from her—and Connie rose with an air of triumph, waving Molly's drawers.

"Good!" I exclaimed, a smile of congratulation on my lips, "Now, Connie, take Molly in your arms and hold her steady; Alice and Fanny, slip your hands under Molly's clothes and behind her, till you can each command a cheek of her bottom!" Merrily the girls carried out my commands, Molly crying, "Don't, don't!" as she felt the hands of Alice and Fanny on her bottom.

"Now, Molly, I'm going to amuse myself with your mother! You must watch her intently! If I see you avert your eyes from her, whatever may be the cause, I'll signal to Alice and Fanny—and they will give you such a pinching that you won't repeat the offence. Now be careful!" and I turned towards Lady Betty who (having heard every word) was now trembling with nervous apprehension as she brokenly ejaculated, "Don't touch me!" But ignoring her pleading, I passed behind her, slipped my arms 'round her and caught hold of her large, full breasts!

"Oh-h-h!" shrieked Lady Betty.

"Oh, Mother!" screamed Molly, colouring painfully as she watched her mother writhing in my embrace with her breasts in my hands.

"Don't Jack," again shrieked Lady Betty, as I proceeded to squeeze and mould and toy with her voluptuous semi-globes, revelling in their exquisite fleshiness, now pulling now stroking, now pressing them against each other—causing her intense distress, but affording myself the most delicious pleasure!

I glanced at the group of four girls facing Lady Betty. Alice, Connie, and Fanny were simply beaming with smiles and gloating at the sight of Lady Betty's sufferings, while poor Molly, with staring eyes and flushing face, gazed horror-sticken at her tortured and naked mother, not daring to avert her eyes!

After a few more minutes of toying with Lady Betty's huge breasts, I suddenly slipped my hands downwards over her hairy, fat belly and attacked her cunt! "Mother! Oh, Mother!" shrieked Molly hysterically, as she saw my eager fingers disappear in the luxuriant growth that so effectually covered her mother's cunt—and utterly unable any longer to endure the sight of her mother's shame and agony, she let her head drop on her heaving bosom.

"Oh, my God! Don't, Jack!" yelled Lady Betty, her face crimson with shame, her eyes half-closed, as she frantically attempted to defeat my hands by squeezing her plump thighs together. But it was useless! With both hands, I set to work to thoroughly explore the fattest and longest cunt I had ever touched—at the same time nodding meaningfully to Alice. Instantly came a series of ear-piercing shrieks from Molly, whose wiggles were almost more than Connie could subdue; she continued to keep her face averted for a few seconds, then the agony of the pinches became more than she could endure—and slowly and reluctantly she nerved to again contemplate her mother, who now was writhing and wriggling frenziedly while filling the room with her inarticulate cries as my fingers tortured her cunt with their subtle titillation, one indeed being lodged up to the knuckle! For a minute or so I continued to explore and feel Lady Betty's delicious private parts till it was evident I was testing both her and her daughter beyond their powers of endurance—for Lady Betty was now nearly in convulsions while her daughter was on the verge of hysterics—and unwillingly, I removed my hands from her cunt and left the tortured lady to recover herself, first gently placing her in the Chair of Treachery and releasing her arms.

"What does she feel like, Jack?" cried Alice and Connie excitedly, as I joined them by Molly.

"Gloriously ripe flesh, dears," I replied, "and the biggest cunt I ever came across!" They looked joyously at each other, their eyes sparkling with pleasurable anticipation.

"And Molly?" I asked in my turn.

"Just delicious, Jack!" replied Alice delightedly. "Do let us undress her now!"

"Certainly!" I replied. Whereupon Molly screamed in terror: "No, no, no, oh, Mother, they're going to undress me!"

"Oh, no, Jack! For pity's sake, don't!" cried Lady Betty, now fully roused by the danger threatening her daughter. "Do anything you like to me, but spare my Molly, she's only a girl still."

But Connie, Alice, and Fanny were already hard at work on Molly's clothes, the stays of which were now visible in spite of her frantic exertions to thwart their active hands. As the girls did not require any help from me, I returned and stood beside Lady Betty, who with the intense anguish in her face, was distractedly watching the clothes being taken off her daughter. "For God's sake, Jack, stop them," she cried agonizingly, stretching her clasped hands towards me appealingly, as if unable to endure the sight.

"No, Lady Betty!" I replied with a cruel smile. "Molly must contribute her share to the afternoon's entertainment! We must have her naked!"

"Oh, my God!" she wailed, letting her head drop on her agitated bosom in her despair. Just then Molly screamed loudly; we looked up and saw her in her chemise struggling in Connie's grasp, while Alice and Fanny dragged off her shoes and stockings. Promptly, they then proceeded to undo the shoulder fastenings of her two remaining garments and stepped quickly clear—down these slid, and with a bitter cry of, "Oh-h-h, oh, Mother!" poor Molly stood naked.

"Oh, my God," Lady Betty shrieked again, frantically endeavoring, chair and all, to go to her daughter's rescue—but I quietly checked her efforts. "My darling! I can't help you," she wailed, hiding her face in her hands in her anguish at the sight of her daughter's helpless nakedness. My eyes met the girls'—they were gleaming with delight; they joined me behind Lady Betty and together we stood and critically inspected poor shrinking Molly's naked person!

Alice had chosen the correct word—Molly naked was just delicious, so exquisitely shaped, so perfectly made, so lithe and yet so charmingly rounded and plump, so juicy and fresh, so virgin! She took after her mother in her large, firm, upstanding breasts with saucy little nipples, and few girls could have shown at eighteen the quantity of dark moss-like hair that clustered so prettily over her cunt—which like her mother's, was peculiarly fat and prominent; and I noticed with secret pleasure how Connie's eyes glistened as they dwelt rapturously on Molly's tender organ of sex.

For a minute or so we gazed admiringly at Molly's charming nudity—then Alice whispered, "Jack, let us put them side by side and then examine them."

"An excellent idea!" I replied, rewarding her with a kiss. We moved Molly's pulleys closer to the pillar on her left, then wheeled Lady Betty across to Molly's right and quickly slung her up in spite of her stubborn resistance—then mother and daughter stood naked side by side!

They formed a most provoking, fascinating spectacle. It was delicious to trace how Molly's exquisite curves were echoed by her mother's exuberant fleshiness—how both the bodies were framed on similar lines—how the matron and the virgin were unmistakably related! Conscious that our eyes were devouring them greedily and travelling over their naked persons, both mother and daughter kept their faces down and stubbornly averted their eyes from us.

"Turn them so that they face each other," I said presently. Quickly Connie and Alice executed my order, Connie taking Molly. "Oh, how can you be so cruel!" moaned Lady Betty, as Alice forced her 'round till she faced Molly. There was just space to stand behind each of them while mother and daughter were about four feet apart. I saw their eyes meet for a moment, horrible dread visible in both.

Their profiles naked were an interesting study—Molly: lithe, graceful, with exquisite curves—Lady Betty: paunchy and protuberant, but most voluptuous. One striking feature both possessed: the hair on their cunts stood out conspicuously like bushes.

After we had to some extent satisfied our eyes, I said to the girls: "I've no doubt Lady Betty and Molly would like to be alone for a few minutes, so let us go off and undress." And we disappeared into the alcoves, Fanny coming into mine so as not to crowd her mistress and Connie.

We undressed quickly in silence, being desirous of hearing all that passed between our naked victims, and presently we heard Molly whisper agitatedly, "Oh, Mother, what are they going to do with us?"

"Darling, I can only guess!" replied Lady Betty faintly. "Their going off to undress makes me fear that you and I will have to satisfy their...lust! Darling, I'm very afraid that Jack will violate you and outrage me, and then hand us over to the girls—and girls can be very cruel to their own sex."

"Oh, Mother!" stammered Molly, horror-stricken. "What shall I do if Jack wants me?" And her voice shook with terror.

Before Lady Betty could reply, Connie appeared, naked save for shoes and stockings. She went straight up to Molly, threw her arms 'round the shrinking girl and passionately kissed her flushed face, gently rubbing her breasts against Molly's and murmuring: "Oh, you darling! Oh, you sweet thing!" Then she slipped behind Molly and gently seized her lovely breasts.

"Don't, Mrs. Blunt!" shrieked Molly, now turning and twisting herself agitatedly. Just then Alice emerged, and seeing how Connie was amusing herself, she quickly slipped behind Lady Betty and caught hold of her huge breasts and began to squeeze and handle them in a way that drew cries from Lady Betty. It was delicious to watch the mother and the daughter writhing and wriggling—but I did not want their cunts touched yet by the girls and so appeared on the scene with Fanny, whom I had refrained (with difficulty) from fucking when she exposed herself naked in my alcove.

"Stop, darlings!" I commanded, and reluctantly Connie and Alice obeyed. Under my instructions they pushed the padded music-bench under the skylight—then we released Lady Betty's wrists from the pulleys and forced her onto her back on the bench, where I held her down while Alice and Connie and Fanny fastened first her arms and then her legs to the longitudinal bars of the bench, in fact, trussed her like a fowl, her arms and legs being on each side of the bench, her knees being separated by the full width, thus exposing her cunt to our attack!

Having thus fixed the mother, we turned our attention to her trembling daughter. We placed a chair in a position to command a view of Lady Betty; I seated myself on it, and the girls then dragged Molly to me and forced her onto my knees with her back to me. While I held her firmly, they drew her arms backwards and made them fast to the sides of the chair, then, seizing her delicate ankles, they forced her legs apart and tied them to the chair legs. In short, they tied Molly onto the chair as she sat in my lap, thereby placing her breasts and cunt at my disposal and in easy reach of my hands.

It is needless to say that this was not effected without the most desperate resistance from both Lady Betty and Molly. The former struggled like a tigress, till we got her down on the bench, while Molly had really to be carried and placed on my knees. But now both were satisfactorily fixed, and nervously awaited their fate, their bosoms panting and heaving with their desperate exertions.

"Now, my darlings, Lady Betty is at your disposal!" I said with a cruel smile. "I'll take charge of Molly! My pet," I added, as the girls hastily arranged among themselves how to deal with Lady Betty, "I'll try and make you comprehend what your mother is feeling, from time to time!"

"Let me have charge of Lady Betty's breasts," cried Connie.

"Excellent!" said Alice. "Fanny and I want her cunt between us! Now, your Ladyship," she added as Fanny knelt between Lady Betty's legs and Connie stationed herself by her shoulders, greedily seizing Lady Betty's breasts in her little hands, "you're not to spend till we give you leave!" And kneeling down between Connie and Fanny and opposite the object of her admiration, she placed her hands on the forest of hair and while Fanny's fingers attacked Lady Betty's crack, Alice proceeded to play with Lady Betty's cunt.

"Oh, my God! Stop!" yelled the unhappy lady as her breasts and private parts thus became the prey of the excited girls. "Mother! Oh, Mother!" shrieked Molly at the sight of her naked mother being thus tortured. Just then I seized Molly's breasts. "Don't, Jack!" she screamed, agitating herself on my lap, her plump bottom roving deliciously on my thighs and stimulating my prick to wild erection. Molly's breasts were simply luscious, and I handled them delightedly as I watched her mother's agonies and listened to her cries.

Steadily and remorselessly, Connie's hands worked Lady Betty's breasts, squeezing, kneading, stroking, pulling, and even pinching them; she simply revelled in the touch of Lady Betty's ripe flesh, and while she faithfully attended to the duties committed to her, she delightedly watched Alice and Fanny as they played with Lady Betty's cunt. Every now and then they would change positions, Alice then devoting herself to the gaping orifice itself, while Fanny played with the hairs. It was while they were thus dividing the duty that Alice suddenly rose and fetched the box of feathers.

Connie's eyes glittered delightedly as Fanny lent herself to Alice's caprice by carefully parting the dense mass that clustered on Lady Betty's cunt and thus cleared the way for the feather. With a finger on each side of the pouting slit, she kept the curling black hairs back—then Alice, poising her hand daintily, brought the tip of the feather along the tender lips.

A fearful shriek burst from Lady Betty, followed by another and another, as Alice continued to tickle Lady Betty's cunt, now passing the feather along the slit itself, now inside, now gently touching the clitoris! Every muscle in Lady Betty's body seemed to be exerting itself to break her fastenings and escape from the terribly subtle torture that was being so skillfully administered. She wriggled her hips and bottom in the most extraordinary way, seeing how tightly we had fastened her—then she would arch herself upwards, contorting herself frantically and disturbing Connie's grasp of her breasts—all the time shrieking almost inarticulate prayers for mercy. It was a wonderful sight—a fine voluptuous woman, naked, being tortured by three pretty girls, also naked—and my lust surged wildly in me.

So far, I had confined my attentions to Molly's delicious breasts so that she should not have her attention distracted too much from her mother, by her own sensations; she was wild with grief and terror at the sight of the cruel indignities and tortures being inflicted on her naked and helpless mother, and with flushed face and horrified eye, she followed every movement. But when she saw the feather applied to her mother's cunt and heard her fearful shrieks and witnessed her desperate struggles, she completely lost her head. "Mother, dear, dear! Oh! My darling!..." Stop them, Jack! Stop, Alice, you're killing her!... Oh, my God, stop!..." she yelled as she desperately endeavored to get loose and go to her mother's aid. I really had to hold her tightly, lest she hurt herself in her frantic efforts. But it was now time for me to intervene, for Lady Betty was fast being driven into madness by the terrible tickling of so sensitive a part of herself; so I called out to Alice, who reluctantly stopped, Connie and Fanny at the same time ceasing their attention.

"Oh-h-h!" moaned Lady Betty with evident heartfelt relief as she turned her head unconsciously towards us, her eyes half-closed, her lips slightly parted. The three girls gloatingly watched her in silence while

I soothed poor Molly; and, before long, both Lady Betty and her daughter regained comparative command of themselves.

I intercepted an interrogating glance from Lady Betty to her daughter as if seeking to learn what had happened to the latter. I thought it as well to answer. "Molly is all right, Lady Betty. She was so interested in watching you that I haven't done more than play with her breasts; but now that you are going to have a rest and can watch her, we'll proceed!" And I slid my hand down to Molly's virgin cunt!

"Oh!" the girl shrieked, utterly upset by the sensation of a male hand on her tender organ.

"No, Jack, don't!" cried Lady Betty, again horrified at the sight of Molly's distress. Promptly, the three girls then crowded 'round me to watch Molly, taking care not to interfere with Lady Betty's view of her daughter.

"Oh, don't Jack!" Molly again shrieked, as she felt my fingers begin to wander inquisitively over her cunt, feeling, pressing, stroking, and caressing it tenderly but deliberately and rousing sensations in her that frightened her by their half-pleasant nature.

"Don't be afraid darling!" cooed Connie. "You'll like it presently!" I continued my sweet investigations and explorations, my fingers moving gently all over Molly's private parts, playing with her silky hairs, stroking her cunt's throbbing lips—then as she became calmer and submitted herself more quietly to having her cunt felt, I tenderly tested her for virginity by slowly and gently pushing my finger into her. "Stop, Jack!" she cried agitatedly. "Oh, stop!—You're hurting me!" her face crimson with shame, for it was evident to her what my object was!

I smiled congratulatingly at Lady Betty, whose eyes never left Molly in her maternal anxiety and distress. "I congratulate you, your Ladyship," I said "your daughter is a virgin—and as I haven't had a virgin for some time, I'm all the more obliged to you for allowing me this opportunity and the privilege of taking Molly's sweet maidenhead."

"No, no!...Oh, Mother!" cried Molly in terrible distress, while her mother, now knowing that remonstrances would be to no avail, moaned heartbrokenly, "Oh, Jack! How can you be so cruel?"

Suddenly, Molly seemed to be seized with a fit of desperation. "You shan't have me!...Oh, you brute! You coward!...You shan't have me!..." she shrieked, as she frantically struggled to break loose, "Oh, oh, Molly," I said chidingly. "What a naughty temper, darling."

"Let me loose, you beast!" she cried, making another furious struggle. "You shan't have me! I won't let you, you beast!" she hissed. "Leave me alone! Take your hand away, you cruel lustful brute!... Oh!...Oh!" she shrieked, as again I forced my finger into her cunt and began to agitate it gently. "Help, mother," she yelled, again struggling desperately—then, "Oh! Jack! Do stop! Oh, you're hurting me," as she relapsed into her usual mood.

I nodded to Connie who at once came up. "Get a feather, dear, we must punish Molly—you can tickle her cunt; it will perhaps cure her temper."

Quickly and in huge delight, Alice handed Connie a sharp-pointed feather. "No, no, Mrs. Blunt don't tickle me!" she cried in terror, as the recollection of her mother's agony flashed through her mind. But Connie was now on her knees before us, and with a smile of delight, she applied the feather to Molly's tender cunt!

"Oh, my God!" shrieked Molly.

"Jack, don't!" cried Lady Betty, appreciating, from her recent experience, what her daughter must be feeling.

"Stop, Mrs. Blunt—Mrs. Blunt, do stop! Oh, my God, I can't stand it! Oh, Mrs. Blunt! Dear Mrs. Blunt!...Stop it...Stop! I'll be good. I'll do anything you like, Jack! You can have me, Jack! Oh, Mrs. Blunt! Mrs. Blunt!...," shrieked Molly, mad with the awful tickling she was getting.

"Stop for a moment, Connie," I said, then with a tender forefinger, I soothed and caressed Molly's tortured and irritated cunt till the girl was herself again.

"Now, Molly," I said gravely, "of your own free will, you've declared that you'll be good, that you'll do anything I want, and that you'll let me have you. You were rather excited at the time; what do you say now?"

Molly shivered. "Oh, Jack," she stammered, "I'll be good—but...but...I can't do the rest!"

"Go on, Connie," I said briefly.

"No, no, Jack, not again!" cried Molly, but the feather was now being again applied to her cunt—only this time I pulled its lips apart so that Connie could tickle Molly's delicately sensitive interior, which she gleefully did. Molly's screams and struggles now began to be something fearful; and poor Lady Betty, horror-stricken at the sight of her daughter's agony, cried: "Promise everything darling, you'll have to submit!"

"Yes, Jack! I'll submit!...I'll do it all!...Oh, stop, stop, Mrs. Blunt!...I can't stand it any longer!" shrieked Molly.

Again I stopped Connie and soothed Molly's cunt with a loving finger; and when she had regained her self-control, I said, "Molly, there must be no mistake. You'll have to do whatever I tell you, whether it be to yourself, or to me, or to any of the girls, or even to your mother. Do you promise?"

"Yes, Jack, yes!" she gasped brokenly. Quickly the girls set her free, and she fell half-fainting off my knees into Connie's arms, whose caresses and kisses soon restored her.

By now we all were in a terrible state of sexual excitement. Connie was absorbed with Molly, but Alice and Fanny were casting hungry glances towards Lady Betty as she lay on her back, with widely parted legs, invitingly provocative. I could hardly contain my lust, but to fuck Lady Betty now would be to spoil her for the girls—so I decided to let them have her Ladyship first. So quickly I lengthened the bench on which she was fastened down, by adding the other half; then bending over the agitated woman, I said with a cruel smile: "Now, Lady Betty, we're all going to have you in turn, Alice first!"

"Oh, my God, no! No!" she screamed, but Alice was already on her, and Lady Betty felt herself gripped by Alice's strong young arms as she arranged herself on her, so that her cunt pressed against Lady Betty's fat, hairy organ, and then slowly began the delirious rubbing process which she loved, but which was new to Lady Betty—for, woman of the world though she was, she had never been fucked by one of her own sex.

It was delicious to watch her in Alice's arms, utterly helpless, forced to lend her cunt to satisfy Alice's lust. Her colour went and came, she began to catch her breath, her eyes shot wavering glances at us—especially at her daughter, who, seated on Connie's knees, was watching her mother with undisguised astonishment, blushing furiously as Connie in loving whispers and with busy fingers made her understand all that was happening. Soon she began to feel the approach of love's ecstasy as Alice agitated herself more and more quickly against Lady Betty's cunt—soon Lady Betty surrendered herself to her sexual impulses now fully aroused by the exciting friction communicated to her by Alice's cunt and began to jerk herself upwards wildly as if to meet Alice's downward thrusting—then her eyes closed and her lips slightly parted as the spasm of ecstasy thrilled through her and Alice simultaneously. Alice quivered deliciously as she hugged Lady Betty to herself frantically, caught up in the raptures of spending!

Presently the spasmodic thrills ceased, then slowly Alice rose, her eyes still humid with the pleasure she had tasted on Lady Betty, who lay motionless and only half-conscious, absorbed in her sensations. Mutely I invited Connie to take Alice's place—and before Lady Betty quite knew what was happening, she found herself in Connie's embrace.

"Oh, please don't, Mrs. Blunt!" she ejaculated, flushing hotly as she felt Connie's cunt against hers, and the exciting friction again commencing. Connie was evidently very much worked up, and she confessed afterwards that the consciousness that she was fucking Molly's mother in Molly's presence, sent her into a feverish heat; she plunged furiously on Lady Betty as she frenziedly rubbed her cunt against hers, Lady Betty's hairy tract intensifying the delicious friction, till both were overtaken by the ecstatic crisis, Connie spending with divine tremors and evident rapture.

As she rose, I nodded to Fanny, who by now was just mad with desire. Like a panther, she threw herself on Lady Betty, who had hardly recovered from the spend provoked by Connie—fiercely she clasped Lady Betty to her and began to rub her cunt furiously against Lady Betty's now moist organ. "Don't, Fanny, don't!" cried Lady Betty, utterly helpless in Fanny's powerful grip and half alarmed by Fanny's delirious onslaught—but Fanny was now in the full tide of her sexual pleasure and revelling in the satisfaction of her imperious desire by means of Lady Betty's voluptuous body. With fast increasing impatience to taste the joys of the sweet consummation of her lustful passions, she agitated herself frenziedly on Lady Betty's responsive cunt until the rapturous moment arrived—then spent madly, showering hot kisses on Lady Betty's flushed cheeks as she felt her quiver under her in the involuntary thrills of her third spending!

As Fanny rose, the girls looked significantly at me, evidently expecting to see me seize Lady Betty and fuck her—but I had something else in my mind.

"Sponge and freshen Lady Betty, Fanny," I said quietly, and quickly the traces of her three fuckings were removed, the operation affording Lady Betty a little time in which to recover herself.

"Now, Molly, fuck your mother, dear!" I said.

She looked at me as if she could not believe her ears, then turned to Connie as if seeking confirmation—noting as she did so the look of delightful anticipation on the faces of her companions.

Connie rose to the occasion. "Yes, darling," she said soothingly, as she gently pushed Molly towards Lady Betty, "go and get your first taste of the pleasures of love from your mother's cunt!"

"Oh Mrs. Blunt, I couldn't! It's too horrible!" cried Molly aghast, while Lady Betty, utterly shocked at the idea of being submitted to her own daughter's embraces, frenziedly cried: "No, no!"

"Come along, Molly," I said, as I pointed to her mother, "come along—remember your promise!"

"Oh Jack, no, no, it's too horrible!" she cried, as she buried her face in her hands, shuddering at the idea.

I took her gently but firmly by her shoulders and pushed her towards the bench on which her mother lay in terrible distress: "Now, Molly, please understand that you've got to have your mother," I said sternly. "If you won't live up to your promise, we'll tie you onto her and whip your bottom till your movements on and against her make her spend!"

"Oh, my God!" she moaned, then breaking from me, she threw herself on her knees by her mother and cried agitatedly as she kissed her: "Oh, Mother darling, what shall I do?"

Lady Betty's face became a lovely study of maternal love contending with personal predilections. For a moment she was silent, then she murmured faintly: "Come, darling."

Slowly poor Molly rose—unwillingly she placed herself between Lady Betty's legs, then gently let herself down on her and took her helpless mother in her arms, then lay still as if reluctant to begin her repugnant task.

"Just see that Molly has placed herself properly, Connie!" I said, and delightedly Connie arranged Molly so that her cunt rested on her mother's, Fanny and Alice at the same time arranging Lady Betty's breasts so that her daughter should rest hers on them.

"Now she's fine, Jack," cried Connie excitedly. "Now, my pet, fuck Mummy!"

Unwillingly, Molly complied. Slowly and gently she agitated herself on her mother, cheek to cheek, breast to breast, cunt to cunt. Presently she began to move herself faster, then her sexual passions seemed to begin to dominate her—she clasped her mother closely to her as she strenuously worked her cunt against Lady Betty's, rubbing harder and harder, more and more wildly, till the ecstatic climax arrived—when with an indescribable ejaculation of "Oh-h-h, mother!…Oh-h-h!!" she spent on her mother's cunt in delicious transports, Lady Betty's quivers under Molly showing that she too was spending!

In admiring silence we watched the unusual spectacle of a mother and daughter spending in each other's arms, till their thrillings and involuntary tremors died away. Then Molly seemed suddenly to remember where she was; slowly she raised her face from against her mother's cheek where it had rested while she was absorbed in the bliss of her spending, and wailed: "Oh, Mother, forgive me!...I couldn't help it! They made me do it!" And she passionately kissed her. Lady Betty, who had kept her eyes closed while her daughter was fucking her, now opened them, and, with a look of infinite love, she put her lips up as if inviting a kiss. Passionately Molly pressed hers on them, and for a few moments, mother and daughter showered kisses on each other, a sight which drove my already over-excited self into an absolute fury of lust. Hardly knowing what I was doing, I seized Molly, pulled her off her mother, and pushed her into Connie's arms. Then I threw myself on Lady Betty, and with one excited stroke, I drove my prick right up her cunt as I madly gripped her luscious, voluptuous body in my arms and clasped her tightly to me.

"Oh-h-h!" she shrieked, as she struggled wildly under me, her cunt smarting with the sudden distention caused by the violent entrance of my rampantly stiff organ into it: "No, no, Jack! Don't have me!" she cried, as she felt herself being genuinely fucked. I heeded nothing but my imperious desires and rammed madly into her, revelling in the contact with her magnificent flesh and the delicious warmth of her excited cunt, inflamed as it was by the four girl-fuckings she had just received, which however, had not exhausted her love-juice—for I felt her spend as my prick raged wildly up and down her already well-lubricated cunt. Clenching my teeth in my desperate attempts to restrain the outpouring of my lust, and to prolong the heavenly pleasure I was tasting, I continued to fuck Lady Betty madly, her quivers and tremors and inarticulate ejaculations along with her voluptuous movements under me, telling me that her animal passions now had control over her and that she had abandoned herself absolutely to the gratification of her aroused lust—but soon I could no longer control myself. Just then I felt Lady Betty spend again with delicious thrills, inundating my excited prick with her hot love-juice. This broke down all my resistance; wildly I rammed into her till our hairs intertwined, then clutching her against me in a frenzy of rapture, I spent madly into her, flooding her interior with my boiling essence, she ejaculating brokenly: "Ah!...Ah!...Ah!" as she felt the jets of my discharge shoot into her.

When she came to, she found herself still lying under me and clasped in my arms, my prick still lodged in her cunt, for I was loathe to leave so a delicious armfuls. The storm of lust that had overwhelmed her had died away with the last quivers of her ecstasy, and she was only conscious of the appalling fact that she had been forcibly outraged. In an agony of grief and shame she wailed: "Oh, Jack, what have you done?" her eyes full of anguish.

"I've only fucked you, dear Lady Betty!" I replied, with a cruel smile. "And I found you so delicious, that after I've taken your daughter's maidenhead, I'll have you again!" And I laughed delightedly at the look of horror that came into her eyes, then continued: "Molly must now amuse us while you rest and recover yourself sufficiently to allow you to endure the further tortures and outrages we've arranged for your amusement—and ours!" And with this appalling intimation, I rose off Lady Betty, unfastened her, and made her over to Alice and Fanny to be sponged and refreshed, while I went off to my alcove for a similar purpose.

When I returned after a few minutes, I found Lady Betty in the fateful armchair with Molly's arms around her, the girls having allowed mother and daughter a little time to themselves. Connie eagerly advanced to meet me, asking excitedly: "What now, Jack?"

"Would you like to fuck Molly now, dear?" I asked with a smile.

"Oh, yes! Please let me, Jack! I'm dying to have her," she exclaimed, blushing slightly at her own vehemence.

"Very, well," I replied, "but don't take too much out of her just now; I'll violate her as soon as I'm myself again—and then we'll just work them both for all we can. Do you approve, dears?" I asked, turning to Alice and Fanny.

They both nodded delightedly. "Jack, please turn Lady Betty over to Fanny and me—Connie wants Molly left to her; and you can fuck them both whenever you wish. We want to do the torturing!" said Alice softly, looking coaxingly at me.

"Just as you please, dears," I said with a smile, distinctly pleased with the arrangements and delighted to find the girls so keen on exercising their refined cruelty on their own sex! Then, together we approached Lady Betty and Molly, who had not heard a word, being absorbed in the terrible fate indicated by me as awaiting them, regarding which they no doubt were whispering to each other softly.

"Molly, Mrs. Blunt wants to fuck you—come along!" I said quietly, as Connie advanced to take her.

"Mother! Oh, Mother!" cried Molly, clinging apprehensively to Lady Betty. "Come, darling!" cooed Connie, as she gently passed her arms 'round Molly's shrinking trembling body and drew her away from her distressed mother who moaned in her anguish as she watched her daughter forced to lie down and separate her legs. Connie then arranged herself on her, breasts to breasts, cunt to cunt. Shocked beyond endurance, Lady Betty covered her face with her hands, but Alice and Fanny (who had now assumed charge of her) promptly pulled them away and shackled her wrists together behind her back, thus compelling her to witness Molly's martyrdom under Connie, who now was showering hot and lustful kisses on Molly's trembling lips, as she lasciviously agitated herself on her unwilling victim.

To the rest of us, it was a lovely spectacle. The two girls fitted each other perfectly—while the contrast between Connie's look of delighted satisfaction as she gratified her lust after Molly, and the forlorn, woebegone, distressed expression of the latter, as she passively let her cunt minister to Connie's concupiscence, was enough to rekindle my ardour and determined me to ravish Molly as soon as Connie had finished with her.

She did not keep me waiting unnecessarily. After testifying by her hot salacious kisses her satisfaction at holding Molly in her arms, cunt to cunt, she began to girl-fuck her ardently and with fast increasing erotic rage, rubbing herself raspingly against her victim's cunt, till she felt Molly beginning to quiver under her—then redoubling her efforts, she went into a veritable paroxysm of thrusts and shoves and wild friction, which quickly brought on the delicious spasm of pleasure to both herself and Molly, whose unresisting lips she again seized with her own as she quivered and thrilled in the delicious consummation of her lust.

"There, Lady Betty, Molly has spent!" cried Alice gleefully, as she gloated over the spectacle with eyes full of desire, which she then turned hungrily on Lady Betty and then on me, as if begging leave to inflict some torture on her. But I shook my head: Lady Betty had now to witness her daughter's violation.

Presently Connie rose, after giving Molly a long clinging kiss expressive of the most intense satisfaction. Molly then began to raise herself, but I quickly pushed her down again on her back and, lying down myself beside her, I slipped my arms 'round her so that we rested together, her back against my chest, her bottom against my prick, while my hands commanded her breasts and cunt.

"Let me go, Jack!" she cried in alarm, hardly understanding, however, the significance of my action; but it was quite patent to Lady Betty who screamed, "No, Jack, no!" while Alice and Fanny exchanged smiles of delight.

"Lie still, Molly dear!" I said soothingly, gently seizing one of her delicious breasts, while with my remaining hand, I played with her cunt.

"Oh, Jack, don't!" she cried, quivering exquisitely as she submitted reluctantly to my wishes and let my hands enjoy themselves, still not comprehending what was to follow!

Presently I whispered loud enough for the others to hear: "Molly, you're quite ready now, let me have you, darling!"

She lay still for a moment—then, as her fate dawned on her, she made one desperate furious spring, slipped out of my hands, and rushed to Lady Betty; she fell at her mother's knees and, clasping her convulsively, cried: "Don't let Jack have me, Mother! Oh, save me!...Save me!" Alice and Fanny again exchanged delighted smiles with Connie, all three girls intently watching for the order to bring Molly back to me.

I rose from the couch and nodded to them. Like young tigresses, they threw themselves on Molly and dragged her away from her mother's knees, in spite of her frantic resistance as she shrieked: "Mother, save me," while Lady Betty, frantic at her helplessness and distracted by her daughter's cries as she was being thus dragged to her violation cried hysterically: "Jack! For God's sake, spare her!"

The girls had by now forced Molly on the couch again. I saw she would not yield herself quietly to me, so while they held her, I fastened the corner cords to her ankles and wrists and set the machinery to work. As soon as the girls saw the cords tightening, they let go of Molly, who immediately sprang up, only to be arrested and jerked onto her back on the couch—then, inch by inch, she was extended flat with widely parted arms and legs as she shrieked with terror, while Lady Betty went into hysterics, which Alice and Fanny soon cured by twitching a few hairs off her cunt.

I seated myself by Molly, bent over her, and said gravely, "Now you've again broken your promise, Molly—I shall consequently amuse myself with you before I violate you!"

"No, no, Jack!" she shrieked as she again struggled to break loose. "Let me go!...Don't...shame me!...Oh! Don't...have me!"

I ignored her pleading and began to play with her breasts, which I caressed and squeezed to my heart's content, finally putting her little virgin nipples into my mouth and sucking them lovingly—at which the three girls laughed gleefully as they now knew that another part of Molly would also be sucked while virgin. Then I tickled her navel, a proceeding which made her squirm exquisitely. After that, I devoted myself to her cunt!

First I stroked and caressed it, she all the while frantically crying out and jerking herself about in vain endeavors to escape my hands. The girls now wheeled Lady Betty alongside the couch; her hands were still tied behind her back so that she could not use them to shut out the dreadful sight of Molly spread-eagled naked, and was forced to look on and witness the violation of her daughter right in front of her eyes!

When Lady Betty had been properly placed so as to see all that went on, I leant over Molly, seized one of her breasts with my left hand, and while squeezing it lovingly, I gently ran my right forefinger along the tender lips of her cunt, intently watching her telltale face as I did so.

A great wave of colour surged furiously over her cheeks, even suffusing her heaving bosom, as she screamed: "Don't, Jack, don't!" her eyes full of shame—while her involuntary movements of hips and bottom betrayed her sexual agitation. It was simply delicious to have her thus at my absolute disposal, to know that the feeling of utter helplessness and the knowledge that her private parts were utterly defenseless was intensifying the mental and physical agony that my proceedings were making Molly suffer—and despite her prayers and her mother's imploring, I continued delightedly to tickle Molly's cunt with my finger till I considered she was sufficiently worked up to be sucked—when I quietly rose, placed myself between her thighs and began to kiss her cunt, keeping my eyes on Lady Betty, so as to note the effect on her of this fresh torture to her daughter.

Lady Betty's eyes opened wide in shocked surprise—then as a half-strangled shriek broke from Molly, she screamed, "Oh, my God! Don't Jack! You'll drive Molly mad!" Just then my tongue commenced to play on Molly's cunt, working along her lips, darting between them when they began to pout and every now and then caressing her clitoris, the subtle titillation sending Molly into shrieking convulsions as she felt she was being slowly driven against her wishes to spending point! Again Lady Betty screamed: "Stop, Jack, for God's sake, stop!" as she saw her daughter squirming and quivering and heard her now half-inarticulate cries. I made a sign to the girls and promptly Alice and Fanny seized Lady Betty's breasts, while Connie forced her hand between Lady Betty's thighs and tickled her cunt! "Oh, my God! Leave me alone!" she shrieked, struggling frantically but unavailingly—her eyes remaining fixed on her daughter's now violently agitated body, for I had forced her to the verge of spending. Then a great convulsion shook Molly—

"Oh-h-h," she ejaculated, then spent with exquisite tremors and thrills, while an unmistakable shriek from Lady Betty proclaimed that Connie's fingers had brought about an unwilling but neverless delicious discharge.

Impatiently I waited till the thrills of pleasure had ceased, then I sprang on her, seized her in my arms, brought my prick to bear on her cunt, and with a vigorous shove, I succeeded in forcing its head inside her maiden orifice in spite of her cries and frantic struggles. There her virgin barrier blocked the way. Gripping her tightly to me, I rammed fiercely into her, evidently hurting Molly dreadfully, for her shrieks rang through the room as I strove to get into her, Lady Betty, also terribly upset by the sight of her daughter's agonies and cries, frenziedly crying: "Stop, stop!" Molly was very tight, and, in spite of her being tied down, she wriggled her strong young body so desperately that it was some little time before I could get a real good thrust; but presently I managed to pin her for a moment, then shoving furiously in her, I burst through her virgin defenses. A fearful shriek announced her violation, Lady Betty (whose breasts and cunt were still being handled and fingered by the girls) crying hysterically: "Oh, my darling!...My darling!..." as with eyes dilated with horror, she watched her daughter being ravished right in front of her and, indeed, recognized the very moment when Molly lost her maidenhead!

Now firmly lodged inside Molly, I drove my prick up to its roots in her now-smarting cunt, then lay motionless on her for a moment, till her cries ceased. Then I set to work to fuck her in real earnest, first with long slow strokes, then with quicker and more excited ones—Molly submitting passively, as if recognizing that resistance now was useless; the deed had been done, her virginity had been snatched from her! Presently however, she began to agitate herself under me involuntarily, as she succumbed to the imperious demands of her now fully aroused sexual emotions and erotic impulses; as my movements on her became more and more riotous and unrestrained, she responded half-unconsciously, half-mechanically, by jogging and heaving her bottom and hips upward as if to meet my vigorous down-strokes. Soon our movements became a tempest of confused heaves, shoves, thrusts, and wiggles, then the heavenly climax overtook us! I felt a warm discharge from her as she quivered voluptuously in my arms, then I spent madly, pouring my boiling essence into her virgin interior in rapturous ecstasy as I deliciously consummated Molly's violation, revelling in her exquisite thrills and tremors as she felt my hot discharge shoot into her—her movements being astonishingly like those of her mother when I spent into Lady Betty. But such was the violence of the sexual orgasm that shook Molly for the first time in her life that she went off into a semi-trance!

9.

As soon as I had recovered from the delirious ecstasy of my spending, I kissed Molly's still-unconscious lips, rose gently off her and cruelly displayed my blood-stained prick to Lady Betty and the excited girls. After exulting over Lady Betty's distress and the sight of this evidence of her daughter's violation, I said, "I fancy you would like to attend to Molly yourself, your Ladyship. If I let you both loose for that purpose, will you promise to allow yourselves to be fastened again in such a way as I may indicate?"

"Yes! Yes!" she cried feverishly, in her maternal anxiety to attend to Molly.

Immediately we set them free. Hastily, Lady Betty caught up Molly in her arms, and, after passionately kissing her, she led her away to the girls' alcove, while they delightedly bathed and sponged away the marks of my victory from my rejoicing prick, kissing and caressing it as if in sweet congratulation.

"Now we'll wind up with a great orgy of cruelty, dears," I said. "You heard Lady Betty's promise?" They nodded excitedly. "It would hardly have been possible for us to have forced them into the soixante-neuf position, at any event it would have been very difficult—we'll now make them place themselves so, on the half-bench, then tie them down, Lady Betty on Molly. We then can command their cunts for feeling and fingering and tickling and frigging; by slightly moving Lady Betty backwards we could suck them and I could fuck them, standing upright—but you won't be able to do so. Do you want to do it?"

They glanced at each other for a moment, then shook their heads: "We shall be quite content to satisfy our desires when they get too imperious by fucking each other, Jack!" said Alice merrily. "Connie and Fanny haven't tried each other yet and will be delighted to do so presently." The two girls glanced tenderly at each other and blushed deliciously. "My God, Jack! What a doing the poor things will have had by the time we let them away—do you think they can stand it?"

"Oh, yes, dear!" I replied with a smile. They are very strong. And it is about time we all had a little refreshment."

So I opened some champagne and poured out six tumblers, adding a little brandy to the two glasses meant for Lady Betty and Molly, who just then emerged from the alcove, Molly with both hands shielding her cunt, while Lady Betty covered hers with one hand, while her other arm was passed 'round her daughter. Both looked terribly forlorn and disconsolate as they approached us; and when the girls crowded 'round Molly and congratulated her on having become a woman, poor Lady Betty's eyes sought mine with a look of shocked horror. I handed the champagne 'round and we all partook of it with relish, especially Lady Betty and Molly, who seemed to revive.

"Now let us resume," I cried cheerfully. "Come along, girls, come, Lady Betty, bring Molly with you." And I moved towards the bench with the girls, while our unhappy victims followed slowly and reluctantly.

"Now, Molly, you just lie down on your back on this bench, just as your mother was made to do—open your legs, put one on each side." Reluctantly she obeyed, and soon she was lashed firmly to the bars by her wrists and ankles, a lovely sight.

"Now, Lady Betty, place yourself on your daughter reverse ways, your head between her thighs, her head between your legs. Lie on her, and when we have arranged you properly on her, we'll tie you down!"

Lady Betty flushed painfully, horror-stricken. "Oh, Jack, I can't!... Really, I can't do it!... It's too horrible!" she exclaimed, burying her face in her hands and shuddering at the idea.

"Now remember your promise, Lady Betty," I said somewhat sternly, as if I was annoyed. "Come, no nonsense—lie down on Molly."

"Oh, my God!" she wailed. With an effort, she slowly went up to the bench on which poor Molly was lying, bound down and helpless, and shivering with dread—she stood still for a moment as if struggling with repugnance, then stooping down, she kissed her daughter passionately, whispering: "My darling, I can't help it!" Then reluctantly she passed one leg over Molly's face and laid herself down on her daughter as ordered. Promptly Alice and I adjusted her so that her cunt came within reach of Molly's lips, while her mouth commanded Molly's cunt; then we strapped her arms by the wrists and her legs by the ankles to the cross-bar of the bench, one on each side of Molly, pulling the straps as tightly as we could—thereby further securing Molly, who now lay between her mother's arms and legs and was pinned down by her not-inconsiderable weight.

The pair afforded a remarkable spectacle to us and for some little time we stood in gloating admiration. Neither could move in the slightest degree without the other being instantly conscious of it, and realizing its significance; Lady Betty now had her daughter's freshly violated cunt right under her eyes and only a few inches off; right above Molly's eyes, and also only a few inches off, hung her mother's cunt; neither could avoid seeing what was being done to each other's private parts! Were ever a mother and a daughter so cruelly placed?

After a few moments of gloating, I said quietly, "Molly, dear, I'm going to see how your cunt has been altered by your having been deflowered!" And I knelt down between her widely parted legs, while the girls crowded 'round to watch, Molly crying imploringly: "Don't touch me there, Jack, it's so sore!" at which the girls laughed delightedly.

Critically, I examined Molly's delicious organ of sex. "I think it is swollen a bit, and that the slit is longer—don't you believe, Lady Betty?" I remarked. She only moaned inarticulately, evidently feeling her position acutely. With a gentle forefinger I proceeded to touch and press Molly's soft, springy flesh, each touch producing a cry of pain from her and involuntary writhing which even her mother's weight could not subdue. Then I gently drew apart the tender lips and inspected with curiosity the gash-like opening into which I had, with so much difficulty, effected an entrance, poor Molly crying: "Oh, don't, Jack!" Her cunt was clearly inflamed and she must have suffered a good deal of pain while being ravished, and, as I closed the lips again, I gently deposited a loving kiss on them as if seeing their pardon, Molly ejaculating, "Oh!" and quivering deliciously as my caress tingled through her. Then I slowly and gently introduced my forefinger into her cunt!

"Oh!" shrieked Molly, writhing with pain. "Don't Jack!" cried Lady Betty, her eyes full of agony at the horrible sight she was being forced to witness. But remorselessly I pushed my finger into Molly's cunt till it was buried up to the knuckle, and retained it there gently feeling her interior and revelling in the warm, soft flesh, still moist with my spendings, and noting delightedly how her gentle muscles were involuntarily gripping my finger, as I tenderly touched her clitoris with my free hand and generally excited her. She was still deliciously tight, and the corrugations of her tender flesh clasped my finger in a way that augured exquisite pleasure to my prick when next it was put into her cunt.

After a little while I withdrew my finger, to Molly's great relief; then said to Lady Betty, "Now I'll exhibit your cunt to your daughter, your Ladyship!" She moaned inarticulately, knowing that it was no use asking for mercy.

So 'round I went to Molly's side, the delighted girls following me. When there, I leant over Lady Betty's bottom from one side of her, and as I looked down into Molly's flushed and pitiful face, I said quietly to her, "Now, Molly, remember the pinchings and keep your eyes on your mother's cunt!" Then gently, with both hands, I drew its lips well apart and exhibited the large pink gap through which she had entered the world, saying: "Look, Molly, this is the first thing you came through!"

She was inexpressibly shocked at the sight of her mother's gaping cunt and ejaculated tremulously: "Oh, Jack! How can you be so cruel!" at which the girls laughed amusedly.

Then to her horror I pushed my finger in and began to feel her mother just as I had done to her. "Don't, Jack!" cried poor Lady Betty, agitating herself spasmodically on Molly, as my curious finger explored her sensitive interior, revelling in her luscious flesh which throbbed in the most excited fashion. But after Molly's exquisite interior, her mother's seemed almost coarse, and very soon I drew my finger out of her, and said softly to Alice: "Get a couple of feathers, dear, and we'll tickle them both at the same time!"

"No, Jack, no!" shrieked Molly in horrible distress, at the approaching dreadful torture.

"What is it, darling?" cried Lady Betty, who had not heard what I said.

"They're going to tickle us together at the same time!" she cried agitatedly.

Immediately a shriek of terror came from Lady Betty. "My God! No, Jack! For pity's sake, don't!" And frantically both mother and daughter tugged at their fastenings in desperate but unavailing endeavors to get free, thereby affording us a delicious sample of the struggles we were about to witness when the feathers were applied to their tender cunts. Just then Alice came back with half-a-dozen long feathers. She picked out one for herself, and Connie selected another and without any prompting from me, Alice placed herself by Lady Betty's cunt while Connie knelt between Molly's legs, then simultaneously applied the feathers to their respective victims' defenseless slits!

Two fearful shrieks filled the room; "Don't, Mrs. Blunt!" cried Molly, wriggling in a perfectly wonderful way, seeing how tightly she had been tied down and that she also had her mother's weight to contend against while Lady Betty writhed and contorted, twisted and squirmed as if she was in a fit—plunging so wildly on Molly as to make the poor girl gasp for breath. She seemed to feel the torture much more keenly than Molly did, possibly because of Alice's skill as torturer and her quickness in realizing the points where the touch of the feather had the cruelest effect—at any event Lady Betty shrieked, yelled, curvetted and wriggled till I thought it wise to stop the torture for a little while, and signalled to both girls to desist—which they unwillingly did, then rose and rushed excitedly to me with eyes glistening with lust and cruelty.

"Oh, Jack! Wasn't it lovely!" cried Alice rapturously. "Fanny, you take a turn now at Lady Betty, I'd like to watch her!" she continued, handing the feather to Fanny, whose eyes gleamed delightedly at the opportunity of torturing Lady Betty. Then she and Connie impatiently took their places by their trembling victims and awaited my signal.

A refinement of cruelty suddenly struck me. "Look here, dear," I said to Alice, "suppose you sit astride on Lady Betty's backside and looking down on Molly—you'll feel Lady Betty's struggles, you'll see the feather play on her cunt, and you'll be able to watch Molly's face at the same time!"

"Jack! You're a genius!" she cried delightedly. "Help me up, darling!" And in a moment she was arranged astride Lady Betty, whose plump, fleshy buttocks she grasped firmly so as not to be dislodged by her Ladyship's struggles and plunges, her weight forcing Lady Betty's cunt almost onto Molly's face, so that Fanny had to poise her hand delicately so as not to bring the feather into play.

"Go ahead, dears!" Fanny cried, and immediately both feathers were applied to their respective cunts. Again Lady Betty and Molly shrieked frantically as their cunts were slowly and cruelly tickled and irritated and goaded almost into spending, but not allowed to taste the blessed relief! Lady Betty was going nearly mad, and, in spite of Alice's weight, plunging so wildly that Alice had some difficulty in sticking on, while poor Molly, whose chest had now to bear the weight of her mother as well as Alice, had scarcely enough breath to keep her going and so had to endure the terrible torture absolutely passively. Soon both of our victims had again been pushed to the extreme point of endurance, Molly being nearly in hysterics, while Lady Betty was fast going into convulsions—whereupon I stopped Connie and lifted Alice off.

"Hadn't we better soothe the poor things by stroking their cunts?" asked Alice, as she watched our panting, quivering, trembling victims.

"I'm going to force them to suck each other now, dear," I whispered with a smile.

"Jack, how lovely!" she ejaculated in rapture, eagerly eyeing Lady Betty and Molly—who by now were getting more normal, though the involuntary heaves and tremors that ran through them showed significantly the nature of the relief they were craving for.

I leant over Lady Betty and whispered: "You can tell by your own feelings and by the sight of Molly's cunt what she wants! Suck her!"

"Oh," she ejaculated, shocked beyond expression.

"Suck her, Lady Betty!" I repeated. "Then she'll understand and she'll suck you!"

"Oh, I couldn't!" she cried. "Suck my own daughter?"

"Yes, suck your own daughter, Lady Betty, and she'll then suck her own mother! You've got to do it! So you'd better do it quietly at once without further nonsense. Now suck Molly!"

"No, no!" she cried. "I can't!...I can't!"

I turned to Alice. "Get me that cutting riding whip dear," I said quietly. Quickly she brought it. I swished it through the air close to Lady Betty, who trembled with fright.

"Now, Lady Betty, please understand me clearly. You've got to do whatever I tell you—if you refuse you'll be whipped into submission! Now suck your daughter's cunt!"

"Oh! Jack! I can't!" she wailed.

Down came the whip across her splendid bottom. She shrieked wildly as she writhed with the pain. I dealt her another cut—more shrieks; then a third—yet no compliance, but I could see that her obstinacy was giving way. I did not want to hurt her unnecessarily so I aimed the fourth cut crossways, making the lash curl around her buttock and flick her cunt. A fearful yell of pain broke from Lady Betty: "Stop, Jack!" she screeched, then hurriedly she commenced to lick Molly's cunt!

"That's right!" I said encouragingly. "Keep on till I tell you to stop, Lady Betty!" Then delightedly we all watched the piquant spectacle of a daughter being licked by her mother! Their faces were a study—Lady Betty's showing her disgust and repugnance at thus having to apply her tongue to her daughter's cunt, while Molly's was full of shame at being thus forced to spend by her mother. Heroically, she tried to retain herself—to refrain from spending—but in vain; soon her control of herself broke down, and in sheer despair, she ejaculated brokenly: "Oh!...I can't...help it!...Ah!...Ah!..." as she spent frantically!

The sight was more than the girls could stand. Alice and Connie flew into each other's arms—too excited to rush to the couch, they fell on the soft thick carpet and madly cunt-fucked each other till their feelings were relieved. Fanny, hardly knowing what she was doing, threw her arms 'round me and clinging closely to me whispered excitedly: "Oh, Mr. Jack, please frig me!" which I delightedly did. I would have gladly fucked her, but I had determined to have Lady Betty as she lay on Molly, making Molly lick my balls during the process, so I could spare nothing at the moment for Fanny.

Presently Alice and Connie rose, looking somewhat sheep-faced, but their countenances cleared when they saw that Fanny had been also obliged to relieve her excited feelings by means of my finger; and they exchanged sympathetic and congratulatory smiles as we again clustered 'round Lady Betty and Molly, whom we had left tied down and who began to tremble with dread as they saw that they were to be submitted to further indignities and tortures.

"Now, Molly, It's your turn, dear—suck your mother's cunt!" I said to her, as I flicked her tender cunt sharply with the lash of my riding whip so as to stop the useless protest and pleadings I knew she was sure to make at receiving such a demand.

"Don't, Jack!" she screamed with pain. Then, with loathing horror in her face, she placed her mouth on her mother's cunt and commenced to tongue its lips.

"Oh! Molly, don't!" cried Lady Betty, involuntarily wriggling her bottom and hips voluptuously as her daughter's tongue began to arouse her sexual appetites in spite of herself; but Molly was too terrified by my whip to disobey me and so continued to tease and torture her mother's cunt with her tongue for some little time till I stopped her— then straddling over her head with my balls just touching her face, I shoved my rampant prick into Lady Betty's now gaping cunt till I had buried it inside her, up to its root. As I did so my balls travelled over

Molly's face, till they rested on her mouth, my thighs then holding her head so firmly gripped between them that she could not avoid the shocking contact with my genital organs.

"Now, Molly, you're to lick my balls while I fuck your mother!" I said with a smile at the delighted girls, who in turn peeped between my thighs to view the extraordinary conjunction of Lady Betty's cunt, my prick and balls, and Molly's mouth. Lady Betty all the while inarticulately moaned in her distress at being thus fucked by me so unexpectedly and in such a position!

I heard stifled cries come from Molly; I could feel her warm breath on my balls but not the velvet of her tongue—so I again sharply flicked her cunt. A smothered shriek of agony—then something exquisitely warm, soft, and moist began to caress my scrotum. It was Molly's tongue—the poor girl was licking my balls!

Oh! My delicious sensations at that moment as my prick luxuriated in the cunt of the mother while the mouth of the daughter reluctantly, but deliciously, was exciting me into spending! For some moments, I remained motionless save for thrills of exquisite pleasure, until I could no longer control my imperious desires—then with piston-like strokes I began to work myself backwards and forwards in Lady Betty's cunt, moving faster and faster and getting more and more furious, till I spent rapturously into her, just as her quivering, wriggling backside proclaimed that she too was discharging, her head unconsciously resting on her daughter's cunt as the spasm of her pleasure vibrated through her!

When I had become myself again, I drew out my prick, and after gloating cruelly over the sight of poor Molly's flushed, shame-stricken, quivering, face and tearful, but tearless eyes, I pointed to her mother's cunt now visibly wet and bedewed from my discharge and said, "Now go on, again, Molly!"

She closed her horrified eyes with an expression of sickening, loathing and repugnance and moaned, "Oh, my God!...Jack, I can't!...I simply can't!..."

"You can, and you shall, Molly!" I replied sternly, as I sent the lash of my whip sharply across her tender cunt, drawing from her a terrible shriek which brought Lady Betty out of her semi-stupor.

"Go on, Molly!" I said, pointing to her mother's cunt as her eyes sought mine as if imploring mercy. Again she dumbly refused—again I caught her a sharp cut full on her cunt.

She yelled in agony, then slowly and with horrible repugnance, she nerved herself to touch her mother's greasy and sticky cunt with her lips, nearly choking as her tongue slowly transferred the remains of my spend from her mother's gaping slit into her own mouth and down her throat! As soon as I saw she was fairly started, I put her in charge of Connie with instructions to keep her at it, whatever happened—then placing myself between Molly's legs, my prick all wet and semen-soiled close to Lady Betty's face. I touched the latter with my whip and said: "Now suck me clean, Lady Betty!"

"Oh!" she cried in horror, shuddering violently as she let her head again fall on her daughter's cunt. Raising the whip, I slashed her fiercely right down her left buttock, then along the other, my lash cutting well into her soft, plump flesh and evidently giving her intense pain from the lovely way in which she writhed and screamed. "Suck me clean, Lady Betty!" I sternly repeated, as I sent cut after cut on her wriggling plunging backside till she could no longer endure the pain, and half-hysterically raised her head and opened her mouth. Instantly, I ceased the flagellation and popped my humid prick between her unwilling lips, which then closed softly but reluctantly on it, as a look of intense repulsion passed over her agonized face!

For some time, Lady Betty simply held my prick in her mouth passively and in shamefaced confusion, for she had never before sucked a man and really did not know what to do! But I didn't mind! Her mouth was deliciously warm and moist, while the touch of her lips was voluptuousness itself—and as I watched her, gloating over her misery and shame, I could see her throat convulsively working, as from time to time she forced herself to swallow the accumulated saliva, now highly impregnated with our mingled spendings.

With the stimulus afforded by Lady Betty's mouth, my virility began quickly to revive. "Pass your tongue over and 'round my prick, Lady Betty," I recommended. "Lick and suck simultaneously!" Painfully, she complied. The action of her tongue was something exquisite, so much so that in a very short time my prick began to swell and stiffen (to her silent horror) till her mouth could just hold it! I was ready for action again. Should I spend in Lady Betty's mouth or fuck Molly again? Hurriedly, I decided in favour of Molly!

Quickly, I pulled my prick out of Lady Betty's mouth. "Untie her," I cried to the girls, as I pushed up the second half-bench and fastened it to the piece on which Molly was lying, still tied. Soon the girls freed Lady Betty and lifted her off her daughter, then guessing what was coming, they held her between them in such a way that she was compelled to see what happened to her. As soon as Molly caught sight of me, with my prick in rampant erection, she instinctively divined that she was again to be ravished, and screamed for mercy. But I threw myself on her, took her in my arms, brought my prick to bear on the orifice of her cunt, and fiercely rammed it into her, forcing my way ruthlessly into her, while she shrieked with a pain hardly less keen than had accompanied her violation. Mad with lust and the exquisite pleasure of holding the voluptuous girl again in my close embrace, and stimulated by the spectacle of the lovely naked bodies of Alice, Connie, and Fanny. The three girls controlled Lady Betty's frantic struggles to go to her daughter's assistance, while they made free with her breasts and her cunt. Watching the spectacle, I let myself go, and, ramming myself furiously into the still shrieking Molly. I fucked her exquisitely, self rapturously, till love's ecstasy overtook me, when I spent deliriously into her, flooding her smarting interior with the soothing balm of my boiling love-juice, which she received into her with the most voluptuous thrills and quivers, the sudden transition from the pains of penetration to the raptures of spending sending her into a semi-swoon as she lay locked in my arms!

Reluctantly I quitted her, unfastened her, and made her over to her mother, who quickly took her off to the girls' alcove, while said girls crowded 'round me with delicious kisses as they congratulated me on my prowess in having fucked mother and daughter twice, each in each other's presence, and to the accompaniment of such exquisite licentiousness. Then, solicitously and tenderly, they bathed and sponged my prick and generally refreshed me.

"Now, what next?" I asked.

"I'm afraid we must be going, Jack," said Connie, "as we have to dine out!"

"And I think you've had enough, Sir," said Alice archly.

"Miss Molly looked quite played out, Mr. Jack," said Fanny, who had gone to offer her services but evidently had been brusquely refused.

"Well, perhaps we had better let the poor things off now!" I said musingly, "I don't think they will offend any of us again!" They laughed. "Well, dears, thank you all very much for your help today; we've had a lovely orgy, punished our enemies, and had a fine time ourselves. Now run away and dress; perhaps you won't mind Fanny attending to Betty and Molly as they resume their clothing, Alice?"

Just then Lady Betty and Molly came out. They were evidently utterly exhausted. I hastily poured out some champagne for them, which greatly revived them, then as they tremblingly awaited the resumption of their tortures, I said gently: "Now you can go, Lady Betty, with your daughter. Fanny will help you to dress yourselves. Now, if ever you breathe a single word as to what has happened here this afternoon, or if in word, or deed, or suggestion, you say or do anything to harm or wound these girls or myself, I'll get you both brought here again and what you've undergone today will be mild compared to what you'll then taste. Now each of you kneel in turn before Alice first, then Connie, then Fanny, and then me—kiss each cunt three times, also my prick three times, in token of apology and in promise of good behavior—then dress yourselves."

We arranged ourselves in the order indicated, standing in a line with our arms 'round each other. Shamefacedly, Lady Betty and Molly performed their penance, my prick quivering as their lips touched it. Then we all resumed our clothing; I put Lady Betty and Molly into a taxi, only breaking the contained silence with the remark: "Now don't forget!" then returned to the girls whom I found chatting eagerly and delightedly, all now daintily dressed.

"I'd like to fuck you all just as you are, dears!" I said as I eyed them lasciviously in their provoking daintiness.

"Think what our clothes would look like!" laughed Connie.

"Jack, we owe you a lot!" said Alice, more seriously. "Now Connie and Fanny, let's say good-bye in a new way. One by one, Jack, we'll let you suck us just as we are, through our drawers; then we'll make you lie down take your prick out through your trousers, and suck you good-bye! I claim last turn so as to receive all that you've left in you!"

Delightedly, Connie and Fanny complied. One by one, they seated themselves in an easy-chair, while the other two pulled up the clothes and I, kneeling between their legs, sucked a tender farewell to each cunt through the opening of their dainty frilly drawers; then I lay down on my back on the couch. With a trembling hand, Connie excitedly opened my fly and gently pulled out my prick, then kissed and sucked it lovingly; Fanny followed suit, her tongue provoking it into life again. Then Alice took charge and sucked and tongued me till she forced my seminal reserves to yield all they held, receiving in her sweet mouth my love-juice as I spent in quivering rapture. Then we all four entered the waiting taxi and the girls drove me to my Club, where they left me with tender and insistent injunctions to "Do yourself well, darling!"

Fanny Hill's Daughter

*W*hen last I was engaged in setting down my history for your perusal, I was still in full possession of my virginity, at least in body if not in mind. But it was not to be thus for long. I had passed the legal age at which it is now permitted that a young female may without hindrance of the law enter the profession of whoredom, and there was no longer need of hesitance.

It was simply a matter of Madame Berkley finding the best offer for my preciously guarded maidenhead and then striking a bargain. In my youthful dreams I had hoped that when this long-awaited event took place, the instrument of my deflowering would be one of the young and handsome gentlemen who frequented the establishment. More often than not I had feasted my young eyes on the stalwart body of this one or that one when I chanced in one of the occupied rooms with a ewer of warm water or fresh hand linen. With such a one, I often mused, any momentary hurt would be well worth the joy that must most certainly follow.

Madame Berkley quickly disabused me, dashing these innocent hopes to the ground.

"Would that it were so, child," she told me when I broached the subject. "Unfortunately, life is not so arranged. Those gentlemen—at least, such of those as most often frequent establishments the like of this—who are favored by Nature with comely looks and healthy bodies are not overly burdened with coin of the realm. Many, truth to tell, are hard press'd to meet the price of a night of pleasure, as I have far too many chits to show. It is the old and ofttimes ugly who had the gold with which to indulge their flagging passions, and a good thing it is for the likes of us."

Without knowing it, and certainly quite without intention, for such would not have been seemly, I must have made a sour face.

"Don't let your thoughts dwell on it," Madame Berkley advised. "I assure you that there are far worse things in life than servicing the old and ugly, most particularly when they can pay well for that service. You are most fortunate, child, never to have known dire poverty. An empty belly would willingly lay with the ugliest ogre on earth for a crust of bread to fill it."

It was but a few days after this conversation that Madame Berkley sought me out, coming herself to my little top floor room, followed by her personal blackamoor serving boy. The latter carried an armful of clothes which he placed most carefully over a chair and then stood back, waiting his mistress's further orders.

"I have good news for you, Nellie," Madame Berkley informed me. "At last someone has offered what I consider a suitable price to be the first to savor your innocent charms."

"So soon?" I could but stammer.

"So soon, indeed!" Madame Berkley said brusquely. "It is high time that you were settled down to business. I had nigh given up hopes of ever getting the price which I consider you worthy of. It is twenty-five guineas, and that is not to be sneezed at."

She ordered me then to rid myself of my clothes so that I could be properly attired for the event that was shortly to take place. I got out of my everyday dress of brown homespun and then, after a hesitant moment, rid myself of my shift. I stood there, naked as the day I was born, while Madame Berkley studied me with an appraising eye. "A very choice morsel," she murmured. "Well worth the price it is fetching."

I felt my cheeks become aflame, but it was not solely because of Madame's words of praise. For I was also well aware of the blackamoor's eyes studying me covertly. He was a young and stalwart youth. His skin rippled like black silk over his muscular body. He was wearing only short white breeches, and it was clear to see that the sight of my naked charms had had a positive effect on his manhood. I could only hope that Madame Berkley did not notice his enlargement, for it was quite well known in the establishment that the young man served Madame Berkley in more ways than one.

And, in truth, if I were about to lose my maidenhead, I would much have preferred that he be the instrument of my deflowerment. I suspicioned that the same thought was lurking somewhere inside his kinky dark head.

"Get on with it," Madame Berkley ordered. "Don't stand there like a ninny with nothing in your head." Then she laughed. "You will have something within yourself elsewhere than your head soon enough to keep you busy."

So I got into the linen petticoats and the dress of flowered cambric and the small lace cap she had brought me. When I had finished, Madame Berkley herself draped a lace kerchief about my shoulders and then crossed it over my budding bosom. Then she made me turn about several times, eyeing the result, and finally nodded her head in approval.

You can imagine with what nervousness and inner trepidation I followed Madame Berkley down the stairs to a private parlor on the first floor, a room reserved for the most important of the clients that sought out our establishment. I followed her into the room and then stopped short a few steps behind her while she addressed herself to the individual who sat—or, better said, overflowed—a chair placed to one side of the crackling fire in the grate. He was, indeed, a most monstrous creature, of a formidable weight I would hesitate to guess. Not a single hair sprouted on his gleaming scalp, which was the color of yellow tallow. But from his little pig eyes nearly lost behind puffy eyelids on down, his body seemed a succession of overlapping ridges of sagging flesh. His cheek jowls hung down like overweight dewlaps; he had more hanging chins, each one larger than the other, than I could count. His enormous belly hung over his lap, and his thighs and buttocks in turn hung over the edges of the chair on which he reclined. And I thought to myself in sudden affright and consternation, whatever will happen to me with such a weight pressed down on my frail and delicate body? It was that horrendous thought, and not the idea of any tool he might possess penetrating my tender maidenhead, that most disturbed and frightened me.

I became aware that Madame Berkley was addressing this mountain of flesh in a most respectful manner that she reserved for gentlemen not only of title, of which there were many who came to our place, but those of wealth as well.

"Here is the little darling of whom I spoke, my lord," she was saying. "As fresh and unsullied as a rosebud first unfolding its delicate petals in the morning dew."

A deep throaty sound that I decided was a laugh rumbled out from the mountainous pile of flesh. "I am not paying for fancy words, you old harridan. If I wished for poetry, I would remain home in the comfort of my library."

"You will see for yourself," Madame Berkley told him, not at all affronted by his manner of addressing her.

"I intend to do more than see," he countered.

"I shall leave you to your pleasure, then," Madame Berkley said and left the room, leaving me there to whatever Fate held in store for me. And, in truth, I was none too happy at the prospect before me.

Suddenly I was alone with the monster, so petrified that I knew not what to do or say. My fears were in no way eased when, all at once, the object of my concern heaved himself with many a grunt and groan from the chair and crossed over and lowered himself onto the couch at one side of the fireplace. When he spoke, his voice came as a wheeze as the result of his exertions. "Don't stare at me so wide-eyed, little one," he instructed. "I am not about to gobble you up." He patted a place beside him on the couch. "Come here and sit beside me. And tell me again; what is the name they call you by?"

"Nellie, sir," I found my voice sufficiently to say.

Again he indicated the space on the couch beside him. With lagging footsteps, I approached. No sooner was I within arm's reach than he thrust out a hand and grabbed me. I have heard much of the impetuousness of youth, but it cannot even approach the haste of old age reaching for a sweetmeat that by all rights Nature should deny it.

I tried to elude him, but without sufficient swiftness. His fat fingers, that were like uncooked sausages except for the jeweled rings that adorned them, fastened about my wrist. I was so put on imbalance that I stumbled and fell against him. "A little kiss, now," he wheezed. "I'd like my dollies to show proper affection."

"Sir," I begged, seeking desperately for a moment of respite. "You give me no time. I am but scarce acquainted with you, my lord."

"That is a circumstance that can be altered in a moment. I intend that you should become *most* well acquainted with me."

With sudden force, he pulled me closer to him with his other hand holding my head imprisoned, so that he was free to press his fat lips down on mine. His breath was so ripe with the fumes of strong spirits and heaven knows what rich foods that I nearly swooned then and there. Truth, it would have been a relief had I done so, for I then would have been blissfully unaware of all that was happening and about to happen. Although I knew that I should not do so, as it was contrary to all the teachings of my future profession that Madame Berkley had so painstakingly imbued in me, I nevertheless struggled to free myself. My weak struggles seemed only to further excite the monstrous creature that held me in his grasp.

"Faith, but I have myself a spirited little vixen," he grunted heavily. With a movement surprisingly quick for one of his ponderous size, he tumbled me back on the couch so that my legs were spread apart in a most undignified posture. He had flipped up my petticoats so that not only were my thighs bare, but also that tender nest between them that was the goal of his desires. His fingers tweaked at the silken tendrils that outlined my little port of entry, and I feared me that he might plunge one of his thick digits therein; but for the moment he seemed content to no more than toy with my exposed treasure, much like one of our giant tomcats playing with a helpless mouse.

"Oh, sir," I beseeched. "Be not so hasty, I beg of you. Give me but a little time to compose myself."

He grunted something unintelligible in reply. But if I could not understand his words, the intent of his actions was clear enough. While one hand continued to fondle my most private parts, with his other hand he was fumbling with his own clothes, undoing the buttons of his waistcoat and breeches, until his own shaft of lust was firmly exposed. It wasn't such a fearsome thing to behold, although in truth it was not a puny digit, either. It was betwixt and between, it was not duly long, but of a distressing thickness. I shivered inwardly at the thought of having that stubby shaft land within me by sheer force and twisted my buttocks desperately to free myself.

My lord and master was having none of such maidenly protests. With a grunt and wheezy groan, he half-arose and then smothered me with his ponderous weight. I could no longer remain there, helpless and motionless as a squashed insect while he snorted and groaned over my defenseless body. I could feel the shaft of his manhood pumping and probing between my thighs, seeking entrance to that which Nature had provided to guard my maidenhead. I tightened my muscles as best I could, striving to postpone that fatal moment.

It was, in truth, my very inexperience that saved me. For I was still lamentably ignorant of the vast differences between men when they are having their pleasure with a female. I had yet to learn that while desire may be strong, the flesh may be woefully weak. And most particularly is it so with gentlemen who are no longer young. What they most desire in their mind they cannot always execute with their bodies. That was how it was with this monstrous creature, Lord R., the first to purchase permission to assail the portals of my so carefully and preciously guarded virginity. For while I was still fearing the penetration of his stubby shaft that would tear me apart, he suddenly gave a most thunderous groan. A shudder shook his body so that every pound of his flesh quivered over me. I feared for a frightened moment that he had suffered a fatal attack as the result of his strenuous exertions that ill-befitted a man of his size and years, thinking that he might have passed beyond this life into another. But it was not so. Even as he began to ease his bulk up from me, I became aware of the sticky effusions which his lust had left on my tender thighs. I glanced towards his still-unbuttoned breeches and saw that what I had feared in its rigid state was now no more than a pendulous bit of drooping flesh. Some bit of unsuspected cunning which I am sure, Madame, I must have inherited from you, made me quickly lower my petticoats so that he would not be aware of where he had spent the product of his lust.

"That old harridan was telling me no lie when she insisted that you were untouched," he muttered, tucking his wilted member within his breeches. "Did I enter you well, lass?"

"Too well," I lied without a single blush on my cheeks. "It hurt most frightfully."

"That is as it should be. But at another time there will be less pain."

"Oh, kind sir!" I cried out. "You are not about to assault me again? I could not stand it!"

"Nor could I." He gave a hoarse, wheezy chuckle that had the sound of wooden wheels rumbling over the cobblestones. "Though there was a time when I could have kept you well occupied through the night until you begged for mercy."

"I beg for mercy now, sir," I said. "I fear that you are much too big a gentleman for such a tiny mite as I."

He grunted and wheezed some more, but it was clear to see that he was pleased. That is one of the strange quirks of gentlemen that I have since come to know so well; a doxy can praise a gentleman's carriage or mind or manners and her words are taken with a grain of salt, but let her speak in vain words of the artful way in which a gentleman handles his lance of love, or of his size no matter how diminutive Nature may have fashioned it, and he swells up like a pouter pigeon with pride. It is most strange that even the gentlemen most highly renowned elsewhere for wit and wisdom have this curious weakness. Well it is for those of us in this profession, for where else could false praise garner such handsome returns?

Pacified for the moment, my lord and master finished with the buttons on his breeches and waistcoat that threatened to burst asunder again at any moment from the exertion of his heavy breathing. I took advantage of the occasion to sit up and arrange my own disordered clothes. I was uncomfortably aware of the stickiness between my thighs, but for the moment could do nothing to rid myself to it without arousing the suspicion of the gross creature responsible. I said hesitantly, "Should I not advise Madame Berkley of what has taken place? Perchance you would care for some refreshment after your so strenuous efforts."

He murmured something that I took for assent. 'Twas most clear that his exertions, brief though they had been on the battlefield of lust, had been far too much for one who had so clearly spent too many years in self-indulgence. His massive head began to droop over his sagging chins; the sound of his breathing became heavier until it was cluttered with little rasping snorts. I stood watching him for a careful moment and then slipped out of the room and sought out Madame Berkley.

With some hesitance I appraised her of what had taken place, somewhat fearful that she might consider me remiss in my duties inasmuch as the gentleman who had purchased my virginity had not, in truth, taken that which he had bought. But she seemed not to be surprised. All that concerned her was whether or not Lord R. was aware of what had actually occurred. "Was he of the opinion that he had made entry?" she queried.

"He was, indeed," I assured her. "He was even concerned, in a small way, of the degree to which he might have caused me pain."

Madame Berkley nodded in a pleased way. "You did well, my dear. You will learn as time goes on that with gentlemen who have passed a certain age in life, it is not what actually takes place but what they think has happened that is most important."

I then learned that the gentleman had paid a full twenty-five pounds to be the first to assail my virginity; or, as I heard the estimable Dr. Johnson once say, to render asunder the veil protecting my innocence. With a gesture of generosity that was not always common to her, Madame Berkley informed me that half of that sum would be mine. It would be used, she told me, to purchase such clothes and finery as were most suitable to one in the profession in which I was now full embarked.

"But how can you maintain that I am a whore when yet I still possess my maidenhead?" I asked with some puzzlement.

"Because you have already sold yourself," Madame Berkley informed me. "The fact that your purchaser was unable to make full use of that which he bought is beside the point."

So no, indeed, though still unsullied, I was full embarked upon the profession for which the Fates had destined me. Or, to be more exact, I was on the brink of that profession, still awaiting to be fully immersed. And waiting with more than a little impatience, if the truth be told, for it is a most vexing experience to go through the motions of whoredom without actually enjoying such pleasures as are a part of it.

Yet that was to be my fate for some time to come. As Jenny had previously forewarned me, Madame Berkley was most astute in striking up a good bargain for the merchandise she had to offer. Indeed, she was able to sell the same special merchandise over several times, without any of the purchasers being privy to the fact.

So it was with my darling maidenhead. Three times in the fortnight that followed, Madame Berkley put it on the auction block, so to speak, and three times the doddering gentlemen who had paid dearly for the pleasure trip spent their efforts long before reaching the journey's end. My buttocks were sore pressed from these encounters, but my precious treasure chest remained unopened.

As befitted my new position in life, I had now been moved from the small attic room I had previously shared with Jenny to a room of my own on a lower floor. I was not as yet considered worthy of having a young blackamoor servant of my own, but Madame Berkley assured me that I would be so rewarded when I reached the proper height in my profession, which meant when I was sufficiently in demand to further swell the already bulging coffers in which Madame Berkley by all accounts was piling up a considerable fortune for her old age.

Secretly, I was most anxious for that moment to come. I well knew what I would do when I had a little black servant of my own.

Several times, since the occasion some years before when Madame
Berkley had first caught me at it and severely chastised me for so
doing, I had managed some stolen moments of innocent play with
one of the little black boys. The dark silken sheen of their skin
delighted my touch, and I obtained an exciting pleasure from teas-
ing them, opening their tight white breeches and letting my fingers
explore their private parts until suddenly an ebony lance sprang
out and stood at rigid attention. I had many a private and pleasurable thought over what I should do with such a delightful and
pleasure-promising toy once I had obtained my full status as a
whore.

I know not, respected Madame, how it was with you when first
you surrendered your maidenly treasure to the lance of some
gentleman. Whether you were taken by force or surrendered willingly is but naturally unknown to me, although I trust you will not
take it amiss and think it forward of me if I suspect it was the latter.
Likewise I know not at what age your virginity was assailed and
successfully conquered, and whether or not you were impatient for
that moment to come. I have my own ideas on the subject, but it
is not my place to express them.

I know only of myself, and that my patience was becoming
frayed in waiting for the event so often promised and that Nature—
or rather, the nature of those gentlemen who paid Madame Berkley
well for the privilege—seemed to deny to take place.

I was, indeed, most eager to experience to the full that of which
I had so far only heard and seen. For more than once I had ventured
into a room when love's sport was in full play. I had stood unob-
served and watched while some young gallant more fully endowed
and capable than the timeworn gentlemen it had so far been my
sad lot to service, forced an erect machine with practiced skill
between the parted thighs of Molly or Polly or one of the other
doxies of the establishment. I had watched naked bodies heave and
strain, and listened to the groans and cries of delight which such
exertions always seemed to evince.

I well realized that Madame Berkley was going to postpone as
long as possible the moment when I became one of the regular
doxies in the house. My as-yet-intact maidenhead made me a

special—and far-higher-priced—attraction. And, as she continued to point out, it was the gentlemen of advanced years who had the wealth to pay most dearly for the privilege of opening that little treasure chest.

I mention all this only to explain my own most unprofessional conduct in what shortly took place. Even so, and I am certain you will agree with me, Madame, from what I have heard concerning your own escapades, being a whore whose duties are to others has yet the right, at times, to indulge in her own pleasures.

It chanced that one of the more practiced doxies in the establishment, by name Louisa, had the room next to the one to which I had been so recently assigned. It chanced, too, that a small peephole had been made in the wall separating the two rooms, for what purpose I then knew not. But once I discovered it, you may be sure I made good use of it.

Late one afternoon I was in my room, occupying myself with the mending of a lace bodice that had been torn the night before by an impetuous but inadequate assault on my virginity, when I heard sounds of an unmistakable nature from the adjoining room. I put down my mending, got to my feet, and peered through the peep-hole.

There, stretched out on a couch that was well within my field of stolen vision, was Louisa, stark naked as the day she first appeared in this world of ours. Even my natural envy forces me to admit that she was one of the most attractive girls in the house. She had yet to pass her twentieth birthday, and her blonde beauty was not as yet marred by the ravages of worldly experience. Her features were clear cut and regular; her body most delightfully proportioned. Her breasts were full and ripe and firm, crowned with rosy-hued nipples. The gentle curve of her belly led the eyes downward to the meeting of white thighs, well-marked by the golden triangle of fur with which Nature guards our most precious treasure.

But it was not the sight of Louisa's naked charms, which I had seen often enough before, that held my eyes but rather the enchanting spectacle of her companion. Standing by the couch gazing down at the body of Louisa was truly the most handsome young gallant I had ever feasted my eyes upon. He was tall and well-limbed, with square shoulders and a broad chest. His features were finely chiseled, like those of a Greek god, and his skin had the golden bronze that is truly the gift of Apollo.

He was standing in naught but his shirt when first my eyes feasted on him, but almost in that very instant he rid himself of it. I could scarcely stifle a gasp of astonishment at what I saw then; as though at a signal the machine of his love sprang forward, seeming to rise out of a thicket of curly hair that spread from the root of that delectable machine up round his muscular thighs and belly, right up to the navel. It was of a size most impressive and awesome to behold, and I could not but wonder how Louisa would ever manage to receive it entire within her without most grievous hurt. But that fearsome thought seemed not to concern her; to the contrary, she seemed almost impatient to feel its compelling force.

Her legs spread wide, so wide, indeed, that I could see the red-centered cleft of flesh, whose lips were vermillioned inwards, that was the mark of her sex.

And now the young gentleman postured himself between Louisa's wide-spread thighs, and holding that fierce erect machine of his in one hand, guided it towards its goal. With her own hands Louisa herself assisted by drawing apart the lips of her treasure slit. Then came the first thrust, that went but partway, and I gasped again and shivered deliciously at the thought of what the force and feeling must be. But Louisa seemed not to mind. Rather, with upward motions of her hips she seemed to assist, so that on his next thrust, the enormous lance was full ensheathed, most completely buried within her, and I could not but wonder where it had gone.

And then began such exercising as never did I witness before; with each powerful thrust downward and inward, Louisa heaved upward, at first slowly and gently and then in a more regular cadence to match that of the gentleman above her. The two seemed to be keeping time to some unheard melody, a melody that had an increasingly wild and more demanding rhythm. Louisa's legs curled upwards and around the thighs of the stalwart bearing down on her, as though attempting to draw every inch of him within her. She began to cry out aloud, with words and phrases that she scarce could finish. "Oh, oh…give me more, my darling, give me more…I cannot stand it, I cannot stand it…in one more moment I am going to—I am going to—" These, and suchlike phrases, seemed to be forced form her with every breath.

Then the young god mounted over her gave two or three more powerful thrusts as though in truth he sought to penetrate through her body, and then they both shuddered and shook in an ecstasy of spent passion.

They subsided into languorous rest and I tore myself away from the peep-hole. Though I was dressed in no more than a light cambric shift, I felt as though my body were afire. My skin was hot to the touch, and I could feel the blood coursing through my veins like liquid fire. And I could feel my little treasure chest, nestling inviolate in the silken thicket between my thighs, throbbing with desire, longing to be opened and explored.

I sat myself down on my own couch, my legs tight together, seeking to regain control of my tempestuous feelings. It was a sore temptation to fondle myself, as I had at times done before, and thus gain a certain release; but the very thought of the loneliness of that endeavor depressed me. I found that I could not sit still with comfort, and getting once again to my feet paced nervously about the small confines of my room. I was strong tempted to peer once again through the peep-hole and see what was now taking place in the silence of the room on the other side of the wall, but knew too well that the mere sight of those two naked bodies entwined in an amorous pattern would only further inflame my own passions and add to the burning discomfort which possessed me.

I know not how long I paced my little room, a prey to tumultuous feelings that would not be stilled, before I bethought myself of my dear friend Jenny, with whom for so long I had shared a bed. Jenny was well versed in the cunning ways of bringing ecstasy to a peak of fulfillment, although such fulfillment always left something to be desired. Even so, it was better than a solitary session with oneself. I could only hope that Jenny was not occupied with some gentleman in the common rooms below and could be found in the attic retreat we had once shared.

With this in mind, I crossed my room and opened the door onto the hallway. At that very moment, the door of Louisa's room opened, and the young gallant I had so admired, and whose performance had so stirred the very core of my being, stepped out into the hallway. He turned and saw me standing there in my doorway, clad only in my sheer shift, through which I am most certain every line and curve of my body was clearly visible. His eyes widened at the sight. Then with a quick backward glance over his shoulder to make sure that the door to Louisa's room was well closed, he advanced toward me.

"And what a fetching sight you are, my lass," he said lightly. "Where did you so suddenly appear from?"

"Nowhere, sir," I half-stammered. "That is, I have been here all my life."

"Impossible!" he insisted. "How is it that I have never encountered you with the other doxies below?"

"Because Madame Berkley has kept me in reserve for—" I started to say that she had kept me in reserve in order to sell my maidenhead to the highest bidder, but some devil's prompting stilled my words in time. Instead I finished, "In reserve for special occasions."

"I'll wager that she has," he murmured, his eyes still feasting on my nearly exposed charms. "The occasion being a well-filled purse, if I know my Madame Berkley."

As I continued to slowly, but not too slowly, retreat within my room, the young man followed me. I well knew that I should send him speedily on his way; that Madame Berkley would be most angry if she knew what was happening. Or, to be more exact, what was about to happen. For, to be quite honest, I must say that even without putting it into exact words in my mind, I was well aware that he was going to do more with me than merely politely pass the time of day.

But I did say, "You had best close the door behind you. It would be most unfortunate for us both if it were known you were here."

"Do you think it unfortunate?" he queried, approaching ever closer to me. For answer, I only shook my head, not wanting to be thought forward by expressing aloud my innermost thoughts. I had retreated backward across the small confines of the room. Now, suddenly, the back of my legs struck hard against the edge of the couch, and I tumbled backward. So unexpected was it that when I landed on my back, my legs flew upward, as did my thin cambric shift, so that I was full exposed to his appreciative and searching glance.

"Oh!" I gasped, and with a hurried hand tried to repair the damage to my modesty. "Whatever will you think of me?"

He just stood there, laughing down at me, his dark, thickly lashed eyes bright and merry. "Whatever you wish me to think, my dear," he promised. "Just give me a moment's time to join you in your natural state."

Even as he spoke, his hands were busy undoing the buttons of his breeches. In less time than it takes to write of it, he had stripped them off. He hesitated for a moment, still clad in his shirt, and then divested himself of that garment. I had feared that because of the lusty session with Louisa that he had just consummated, and to which I had been secret witness, he might quite naturally be somewhat depleted in his virility. But happily it was a fear without foundation. His machine of love, standing out at erect attention, was even grander and more awesome than I remembered from seeing it but moments before through the peep-hole. Hesitantly, almost without my own volition, I stretched out my hand to touch it, and then drew my fingers quickly away.

My action seemed to please and amuse him. He bent over me, and with a quick movement, caught hold of my shift and drew it quickly up and over my head so that I rested there on the couch bare naked before his eyes. "Ah," he murmured. "And what a choice morsel you are. Sufficiently so to tempt a monk out of the monastery or even a corpse out of the grave."

His fingers began to artfully caress my nipples and, when they sprang full erect, he bent his head down and teased them with his lips and tongue. Little shivers that were at the same time both icy cold and burning hot rippled through my body, and I twined my fingers tightly in his hair, holding his head close. "Oh, God!" I sobbed. "Oh, dear God…you know not what you do to me…."

For answer he shifted his body about, positioning himself

between my parted thighs. He held his lance in one hand, directing it with practiced skill at the fur-fringed little cleft that was his goal. It found the right spot—and probed—and probed and thrust again—and stopped.

"Oh, sir!" I cried out partly in minor pain and partly in expectation. "I fear me I neglected to tell you that I am yet a virgin!"

"God's truth, you are!" he exclaimed. "And God knows I shouldn't be here!"

But he made no move to leave me. The knowledge of my virginity only seemed to increase his desire. Again he probed at my virgin flower that was still unplucked, again he thrust more forcefully with his lance. There was more pain this time, almost enough to make me sob out in protest, but still no penetration. He swore under his breath, round and rich curses of frustration and at the same time my own inner being churned in an agony of desire. Then an idea, doubtless gained from some previous experience, came to him. He reached for the pillow at the head of the couch, raised me up, and placed it under my hips. It was instinct now, and not experience, that prompted my movements to aid him in his onslaught. I spread my thighs as wide as possible and placed my hands down so that they could part the lips of my waiting cleft. Once again I felt the burning head of his shaft of love pounding for admission. A trifle, and then another trifle, and then his carefully prodding patience was drowned in hot desire. With a final all-powerful thrust, he broke through.

I could scarce stifle the cry that threatened to burst from me. Only the fear that such a scream would be overheard and bring others running to my room stilled my voice, forcing me to bite my lower lip until it, too, bled.

The Autobiography Of A Flea

*B*orn I was—but how, when, or where I cannot say; so I must leave the reader to accept the assertion "per se," and believe it if he will. One thing is equally certain: the fact of my birth is not one atom less veracious than the reality of these memoirs, and if the intelligent student of these pages wonders how it came to pass that one in my walk—or perhaps I should have said jump—in life became possessed of the learning, observation, and power of committing to memory the whole of the wonderful facts and disclosures I am about to relate, I can only remind him that there are intelligences, little suspected by the vulgar, and laws in nature, the very existence of which have not yet been detected by the advanced among the scientific world.

I have heard it somewhere remarked that my province was to get my living by bloodsucking. I am not the lowest by any means of that universal fraternity, and if I sustain a precarious existence upon the bodies of those with whom I come in contact, my own experience proves that I do so in a marked and peculiar manner, with a warning of my employment which is seldom given by those in other grades of my profession. But I submit that I have other and nobler aims than the mere sustaining of my being by the contributions of the unwary. I have been conscious of this original defect and, with a soul far above the vulgar instincts of my race, I jumped by degrees to heights of mental perception and erudition which placed me forever upon a pinnacle of insect-grandeur.

It is this attainment to learning which I shall evoke in describing the scenes of which I have been a witness—nay, even a partaker. I shall not stop to explain by what means I am possessed of human powers of thinking and observing; but, in my lucubrations, leave you simply to perceive that I possess them and wonder accordingly.

You will thus perceive that I am no common flea; indeed, when it is borne in mind the company in which I have been accustomed to mingle, the familiarity with which I have been suffered to treat persons the most exalted, and the opportunities I have possessed to make the most of my acquaintances, the reader will no doubt agree with me that I am in very truth a most wonderful and exalted insect.

My earliest recollections lead me back to a period when I found myself within a church. There was a rolling of rich music and a slow monotonous chanting which then filled me with surprise and admiration, but I have long since learned the true import of such influences, and the attitudes of the worshippers are now taken by me for the outward semblance of inward emotions which are very generally nonexistent. Be this as it may, I was engaged upon professional business connected with the plump white leg of a young lady of some fourteen years of age, the taste of whose delicious blood I well remember, and the flavor of whose—

But I am digressing.

Soon after commencing in a quiet and friendly way my little attentions, the young girl, in common with the rest of the congregation rose to depart; and I, as a matter of course, determined to accompany her.

I am very sharp of sight as well as of hearing, and that is how I saw a young gentleman slip a small folded piece of white paper into the young lady's pretty gloved hand, as she passed through the crowded porch. I had noticed the name "Bella" neatly worked upon the soft silk stocking which had at first attracted me, and I now saw that the same word appeared alone upon the outside of the billet-doux. She was with her aunt, a tall, stately dame, with whom I did not care to get upon terms of intimacy.

Bella was a beauty—just fourteen—a perfect figure, and although so young, her soft bosom was already budding into those proportions which delight the other sex. Her face was charming in its frankness; her breath sweet as the perfumes of Arabia, and, as I have already said, her skin as soft as velvet. Bella was evidently well aware of her good looks and carried her head as proudly and as coquettishly as a queen. That she inspired admiration was not difficult to see by the wistful and longing glances which the young men, and sometimes also those of more mature years, cast upon her. There was a general hush of conversation outside the building, and a turning of glances generally toward the pretty Bella, which told more plainly than words that she was the admired one of all eyes and the desired one of all hearts—at any rate among the male sex.

Paying, however, very little attention to what was evidently a matter of everyday occurrence, the young lady walked sharply homeward with her aunt and, after arrival at the neat and genteel residence, went quickly to her room. I will not say I followed, but I "went with her" and beheld the gentle girl raise one dainty leg across the other and remove the tiniest of tight and elegant kid boots.

I jumped upon the carpet and proceeded with my examinations. The left boot followed, and then Bella sat looking at the folded piece of paper which I had seen the young fellow deposit secretly in her hand.

Closely watching everything, I noted the swelling thighs, which spread upward above her tightly fitting garters, until they were lost in the darkness, as they closed together at a point where her beautiful belly met them in her stooping position; and almost obliterated a thin and peachlike slit, which just showed its rounded lips between them in the shade.

Presently Bella dropped her note and, being open, I took the liberty to read it.

"I will be in the old spot at eight o'clock tonight" were the only words which the paper contained, but they appeared to have a special interest for Bella, who remained cogitating for some time in the same thoughtful mood.

My curiosity had been aroused, and my desire to know more of the interesting young being with whom chance had so promiscuously brought me in pleasing contact, prompted me to remain quietly ensconced in a snug though somewhat moist hiding place. It was not until near upon the hour named that I once more emerged in order to watch the progress of events.

Bella had dressed herself with scrupulous care and now prepared to betake herself to the garden which surrounded the country house in which she dwelt.

I went with her.

Arriving at the end of a long and shady avenue, the young girl seated herself upon a rustic bench and there awaited the coming of the person she was to meet.

It was not many minutes before the young man whom I had seen in communication with my fair little friend in the morning presented himself.

A conversation ensued which, if I might judge by the abstraction of the pair from aught besides themselves, had unusual interest for both.

It was evening, and the twilight had already commenced: the air was warm and genial, and the young pair sat closely entwined upon the bench, lost to all but their own united happiness.

"You don't know how I love you, Bella," whispered the youth, tenderly sealing his protestation with a kiss upon the pouting lips of his companion.

"Yes I do," replied the girl, naïvely. "Are you not always telling me? I shall get tired of hearing it soon."

Bella fidgeted her pretty little foot and looked thoughtful.

"When are you going to explain and show me all those funny

things you told me about?" she asked, giving a quick glance up, and then as rapidly bending her eyes upon the gravel walk.

"Now," answered the youth. "Now, dear Bella, while we have the chance to be alone and free from interruption. You know, Bella, we are no longer children?"

Bella nodded her head.

"Well, there are things which are not known to children and which are necessary for lovers not only to know, but also to practice."

"Dear me," said the girl seriously.

"Yes," continued her companion, "there are secrets which render lovers happy and which make the enjoyment of loving and of being loved."

"Lord!" exclaimed Bella. "How sentimental you have grown, Charlie; I remember the time when you declared sentiment was 'all humbug.'"

"So I thought it was, till I loved you," replied the youth.

"Nonsense," continued Bella. "But go on, Charlie, and tell me what you promised."

"I can't tell you without showing you as well," replied Charlie. "The knowledge can be learned only by experience."

"Oh, go on, then, and show me," cried the girl, in whose bright eyes and glowing cheeks I thought I could detect a very conscious knowledge of the kind of instruction about to be imparted.

There was something catching in her impatience. The youth yielded to it and, covering her beautiful young form with his own, glued his mouth to hers and kissed it rapturously.

Bella made no resistance; she even aided and returned her lover's caresses.

Meanwhile the evening advanced: the trees lay in the gathering darkness, spreading their lofty tops to screen the waning light from the young lovers.

Presently Charlie slid onto one side; he made a slight movement, and then, without any opposition, he passed his hand under and up the petticoats of the pretty Bella. Not satisfied with the charms which he found within the compass of her glistening silk stockings, he essayed to press on still further, and his wandering fingers now touched the soft and quivering flesh of her young thighs.

Bella's breath came hard and fast, as she felt the indelicate attack which was being made upon her charms. So far, however, from resisting, she evidently enjoyed the exciting dalliance.

"Touch it," whispered Bella. "You may."

Charlie needed no further invitation: indeed, he was already preparing to advance without one and, instantly comprehending the permission, drove his fingers forward.

The fair girl opened her thighs as he did so, and the next instant his hand covered the delicate pink lips of her pretty slit.

For the next ten minutes the pair remained almost motionless, their lips joined and their breathing alone marking the sensations which were overpowering them with the intoxication of wantonness. Charlie felt a delicate object, which stiffened beneath his nimble fingers, and assumed a prominence of which he had no experience.

Presently Bella closed her eyes and, throwing back her head, shuddered slightly, while her frame became supple and languid. She suffered her head to rest upon the arm of her lover.

"Oh, Charlie," she murmured, "what is it you do? What delightful sensations you give me!"

Meanwhile the youth was not idle. Having fairly explored all he could in the constrained position in which he found himself, he rose; and, sensible of the need of assuaging the raging passion which his actions had fanned, he besought his fair companion to let him guide her hand to a dear object, which he assured her was capable of giving her far greater pleasure than his fingers had done.

Nothing loath, Bella's grasp was the next moment upon a new and delicious substance; and, either giving way to the curiosity she simulated, or really carried away by her newly roused desires, nothing would do but she must bring out and into the light the standing affair of her friend.

Those of my readers who have been placed in a similar position will readily understand the warmth of the grasp and the surprise of the look which greeted the first appearance in public of the new acquisition.

Bella beheld a man's member for the first time in her life, in the full plenitude of its power; and although it was not, I could plainly see, by any means a formidable one, yet its white shaft and red-capped head, from which the soft skin retreated as she pressed it, gained her quick inclination to learn more.

Charlie was equally moved; his eyes shone, and his hand continued to rove all over the sweet young treasure of which he had taken possession.

Meanwhile the toyings of the little white hand upon the youthful member with which it was in contact had produced effects common under such circumstances to all of so healthy and vigorous a constitution as that of the owner of this particular affair.

Enraptured with the soft pressures, the gentle and delicious squeezings, and artless way in which the young lady pulled back the folds from the rampant nut and disclosed the ruby crest, purple with desire, and the tip, ended by the tiny orifice, now awaiting its opportunity to send forth its slippery offering, the youth grew wild with lust; and Bella, participating in sensations new and strange, but which carried her away in a whirlwind of passionate excitement, panted, for she knew not what kind of rapturous relief.

With her beautiful eyes half-closed, her dewy lips parted, and her skin warm and glowing with the unwonted impulse stealing over her, she lay the delicious victim of whomsoever had the instant chance to reap her favors and pluck her delicate young rose.

Charlie, youth though he was, was not so blind as to lose so fair an opportunity; besides, his now-rampant passions carried him forward despite the dictates of prudence which he otherwise might have heard.

He felt the throbbing and well-moistened center quivering beneath his fingers. He beheld the beautiful girl lying invitingly to the amorous sport. He watched the tender breathings which caused the young breast to rise and fall and the strong sensual emotions which animated the glowing form of his youthful companion.

The full, soft and swelling legs of the girl were now exposed to his sensual gaze.

Gently raising the intervening drapery, Charlie further disclosed the charms of his lovely companion until, with eyes of flame, he saw the plump limbs terminated in the full hips and palpitating white belly.

Then also his ardent gaze fell upon the center spot of attraction—on the small pink slit which lay half-hidden at the foot of the swelling Mount of Venus, hardly yet shaded by the softest down.

The titillation which he had administered, and the caresses which he had bestowed upon the coveted object had induced a flow of the native moisture which such excitement tends to provoke, and Bella lay with her peachlike slit well bedewed with Nature's best and sweetest lubricant.

Charlie saw his chance. Gently disengaging her hand from its grasp upon his member, he threw himself frantically upon the recumbent figure of the girl.

His left arm wound itself round her slender waist; his hot breath was on her cheek; his lips pressed hers in one long, passionate, and hurried kiss. His left hand, now free, sought to bring together those parts of both which are the active instruments of sensual pleasure, and with eager efforts he sought to complete conjunction.

Bella now felt for the first time in her life the magic touch of a man's machine between the lips of her rosy orifice.

No sooner had she perceived the warm contact which was occasioned by the stiffened head of Charlie's member then she shuddered perceptibly and, already anticipating the delights of venery, gave down an abundance of proof of her susceptible nature.

Charlie was enraptured at his happiness and strove eagerly to perfect his enjoyment.

But Nature, which had operated so powerfully in the development of Bella's sensual passions, left yet something to be accomplished ere the opening of so early a rosebud could be easily effected.

She was very young, immature, certainly so in the sense of those monthly visitations which are supposed to mark the commencement of puberty; and Bella's parts, replete as they were with perfection and freshness, were as yet hardly prepared for the accommodation of even so moderate a champion as that which, with round intruded head, now sought to enter in and effect a lodgment.

In vain Charlie pushed and exerted himself to press his excited member into the delicate parts of the lovely girl.

The pink folds and the tiny orifice withstood all his attempts to penetrate the mystic grotto. In vain the pretty Bella, now roused into a fury of excitement and half-mad with the titillation she had already undergone, seconded by all the means in her power the audacious attempts of her young lover.

The membrane was strong and resisted bravely until, with a desperate purpose to win the goal or burst everything, the youth drew back for a moment; and then, desperately plunging forward, succeeded in piercing the obstruction and thrusting the head and shoulders of his stiffened affair into the belly of the yielding girl.

Bella gave a little scream, as she felt the forcible inroad upon her secret charms, but the delicious contact gave her courage to bear the smart in hopes of the relief which appeared to be coming.

Meanwhile Charlie pushed again and again; and, proud of the victory which he had already won, not only stood his ground, but at each thrust advanced some small way farther upon his road.

It has been said, *"Ce n'est que le premier coup qui coute,"* but it may be fairly argued that it is at the same time perfectly possible that *"quelquefois il coute trop,"* as the reader may be inclined to infer with me in the present case.

Neither of our lovers, however, had, strange to say, a thought on the subject; but, fully occupied with the delicious sensations which had overpowered them, united to give effect to those ardent movements which both could feel would end in ecstasy.

As for Bella, with her whole body quivering with delicious impatience, and her full red lips giving vent to the short excursive exclamations which announced her extreme gratification, she gave herself up body and soul to the delights of the coition. Her muscular compressions upon the weapon which had now effectually gained her, the firm embrace in which she held the writhing lad, the delicate thighs of the moistened, glovelike sheath, all tended to excite Charlie to madness. He felt himself in her body to the roots of his machine, until the two globes which tightened beneath the foaming champion of his manhood pressed upon the firm cheeks of her white bottom. He could go no further and his sole employment was to enjoy—to reap to the full the delicious harvest of his exertions.

But Bella, insatiable in her passion, no sooner found the wished-for junction completed, then relishing the keen pleasure which the stuff and warm member was giving her, became too excited to know or care further aught that was happening; and her frenzied excitement, quickly overtaken again by the maddening spasms of completed lust, pressed downward upon the object of her pleasure, threw up her arms in passionate rapture, and then, sinking back in the arms of her lover, with low groans of ecstatic agony and little cries of surprise and delight, gave down a copious emission, which finding a reluctant escape below, inundated Charlie's balls.

No sooner did the youth witness the delivering enjoyment he was the means of bestowing upon the beautiful Bella, and became sensible of the flood which she had poured down in such profusion upon his person, then he was also seized with lustful fury. A raging torrent of desire seemed to rush through his veins; his instrument was now plunged to the hilt in her delicious belly; then, drawing back, he extracted the smoking member almost to the head. He pressed and bore all before him. He felt a tickling, maddening feeling creeping upon him; he tightened his grasp upon his young mistress and, at the same instant that another rapturous enjoyment issued from her heaving breast, he found himself gasping upon her bosom, and pouring into her grateful womb a rich tickling jet of youthful vigor.

A low moan of salacious gratification escaped the parted lips of Bella, as she felt the jerking gushes of seminal fluid which came from the excited member within her; at the same moment the lustful frenzy of emission forced from Charlie a sharp and thrilling cry as he lay with upturned eyes in the last act of the sensual drama.

That cry was the signal for an interruption which was as sudden as it was unexpected. From out the bordering shrubs stole the somber figure of a man who stood before the youthful lovers.

Horror froze the blood of both.

Slipping from his warm and luscious retreat, and essaying to stand upright, Charlie recoiled from the apparition as from some dreadful serpent.

As for the gentle Bella, no sooner did she catch sight of the intruder then, covering her face with her hands, she shrank back upon the seat which had been the silent witness of her pleasures and, too frightened to utter a sound, waited with what presence of mind she could assume to face the brewing storm.

Nor was she kept long in suspense.

Quickly advancing toward the guilty couple, the newcomer seized the lad by the arm, while, with a stern gesture of authority, he ordered him to repair the disorder of dress.

"Impudent boy," he hissed between his teeth, "what is it that you have done? To what lengths have your mad and savage passions hurried you? How will you face the rage of your justly offended father? How appease his angry resentment when, in the exercise of my bounden duty, I apprise him of the mischief wrought by the hand of his only son?"

As the speaker ceased, still holding Charlie by the wrist, he came forth into the moonlight, which disclosed the figure of a man of some forty-five years of age, short, stout, and somewhat corpulent. His face, decidedly handsome, was rendered still more attractive by a pair of brilliant eyes which, black as jet, threw around fierce glances of passionate resentment. He was habited in clerical dress, the somber shades and quiet unobtrusive neatness of which drew out only more prominently his remarkably muscular proportions and striking physiognomy.

Charlie appeared, as well indeed he might, covered with confusion when, to his infinite and selfish relief, the stern intruder turned to the young partner of his libidinous enjoyment.

"For you, miserable girl, I can only express my utmost horror and my most righteous indignation. Forgetful alike of the precepts of Holy Mother Church, careless of your honor, you have allowed this wicked and presumptuous boy to pluck the forbidden fruit. What now remains for you? Scorned by your friends and driven from your uncle's house, you will herd with the beasts of the field and, like Nebuchadnezzar of old, shunned as contamination by your species, gladly gather a miserable sustenance in the highways. Oh, daughter of sin, child given up to lust and unto Satan, I say unto thee—"

The stranger had proceeded thus far in his abjuration of the unfortunate girl when Bella, rising from her crouching attitude, threw herself at his feet and joined her tears and prayers for forgiveness to those of her young lover.

"Say no more," the priest continued. "Say no more. Confessions are of no avail, and humiliations do but add to your offense. My mind misgives me as to my duty in this sad affair; but if I obeyed the dictates of my present inclinations, I should go straight to your natural guardians and acquaint them immediately with the infamous nature of my chance discovery."

"Oh, in pity, have mercy upon me!" pleaded Bella, whose tears now coursed down her pretty cheeks, so lately aglow with wanton pleasure.

"Spare us, father, spare us both. We will do anything in our power to make atonement. Six masses and several patermusters shall be performed on our account and at our cost. The pilgrimage to the shrine of St. Engulphus, of which you spoke to me the other day, shall now surely be undertaken. I am willing to do anything, sacrifice anything, if you will spare my dear Bella."

The priest waved his hand for silence. Then he spoke, while accents of pity mingled with his naturally stern and resolute manner.

"Enough," said he. "I must have time. I must invoke assistance from the Blessed Virgin, who knew no sin, but who, without the carnal delights of mortal copulation, brought forth the Babe of Babes in the manger of Bethlehem. Come to me tomorrow in the sacristy, Bella. There, in the precincts, I will unfold to you the Divine will concerning your transgression. I will expect you at two o'clock. As for you, rash youth, I shall reserve my judgment and all action until the following day, when at the same hour I shall likewise expect you."

A thousand thanks were being poured out by the united throats of the penitents, when the priest warned them both to part.

The evening had long ago closed in, and the dews of night were stealing upward.

"Meanwhile, good night and peace; your secret is safe with me, until we meet again," the priest spoke and disappeared.

Subrban Souls

July 2, 1898

On my way to the rue de Leipzig, where I was to meet Lily, I bought a light bamboo switch or riding stick, preferring this to walking through the streets with a whip.

When she arrived, as she did punctually, and coquettishly dressed, showing that she had taken great trouble with her toilette, her first words were:

"Where is your whip?"

I showed her my switch.

"This is for you, Lily, and my dogs afterward."

She had in her hand *The Yellow Room*, which she had understood I wanted back at once. I told her she could keep it as long as she liked and not hurry through it. She had been reading it in the train. She said she liked it. It had made her "naughty," and she had been obliged to finish herself with her finger. I replied that I thought she had told me she never did that.

"I do not as a rule, but now and again I can't help myself."

I warned her to beware and not give way to the habit. When I went on to inform her that habitual masturbation deprives the sexual organs of women of their tone and elasticity, causing the secret slit to gape and the inner lips to become elongated, she thanked me for the advice and told me she would resist the temptation, so as not to wither that pretty part of her body.

"I like my pussy," she said, "I like to look at the hair on it. I love to play with my hairs."

I informed her that she had a very pretty one and it would be a pity to spoil it. The two large outer lips should close themselves naturally, but if Lily gives way to onanism they will do so no longer.

I asked her to show me the paragraph which had brought about this crisis. She did so:

"He inserted his enormous affair in her burning c—, etc."

It was not exactly that sentence alone which so unduly excited her, but what led up to this termination. She did not understand certain words, but guessed them from the context. She thought that the extreme and bloodthirsty long-drawn-out cruelty, described in the volume, was impossible, but thoroughly appreciated the idea of man's domination over a woman, and to bend her to his lewd will, a little brutality appealed to her imagination. She wanted more books later on, but not tales of lesbianism. Anything, simple lust or cruelty, as long as it took place between men and women. She thought that everything and anything was possible and agreeable, if a male and a female were fond of each other. This was far from bad philosophy, springing naturally from a virgin of twenty-two. How changed she was now with me!

During our conversation, I had made her sit by my side on the sofa, with her clothes well up, as I wanted to see and feel her legs, calves, and knees. I made her open and close her thighs and cross and recross her legs, as I chose to command.

I kissed her passionately. My lips wandered all over her face. I kissed her eyes and licked and gently nibbled her ears. This last caress pleased her very much.

I made her stand up in front of me, and by threats of ill-usage and pinching the fat part of her arms, I got her, after a little resistance, to let me put my hands up her clothes, lift her chemise out of her drawers, and put my hand between her thighs, entirely grasping her center of love. In this manner, my hand still gripping her plump, hairy lips, I walked her round the room, in spite of her blushes and protestations. It was an agreeable sensation for both of us. I had great enjoyment in feeling the movement of her soft thighs as she walked, my hand clasping her furry retreat. I halted in front of the looking glass of the wardrobe, and forced her to look at the strange group we thus formed. She hid her face on my shoulder and I could feel she was now quite wet, heated and ready for anything.

I asked her if she could take off her drawers without undressing. She replied in the affirmative.

"An English girl could not, but my drawers are fastened to my stays."

I reclined on the sofa and told her to take them off slowly, without sitting down. She did so with docility, and I enjoyed the sight of seeing her get her legs out of her beribboned undergarments. I called her to me and stood her up again in front of me and close to me, as I sat on the chaise lounge, while my hands, up her clothes, now for the first time roved without hindrance over her belly, bottom, thighs, and Nature's orifice. It was a delicious moment for me. I put my left index finger as far as possible up her crisp fundament, gradually forcing it up with a corkscrew motion, as I felt her pleasure in front increasing, for I was masturbating her scientifically the while, with the middle finger of my left hand. I had great difficulty in piercing her anus; but to my astonishment, she did not complain of pain. She afterward told me that she liked the feeling of my finger in the posterior aperture. The crisis came quickly for her, and she could no longer stand upright, but soon sank gradually to her knees, all in a heap, sighing with satisfied lust, her head pillowed on my breast. I kissed her sweet neck and finished her as quickly as my wrist would let me, until she tore herself from my grasp.

Now I tell her to disrobe before me, until she is entirely naked. She refuses indignantly. The moment has now arrived for me to take hold of my cane and, as she still refuses, I give her two or three stinging cuts over biceps and shoulders. Smarting with pain, she consents to undress until she is in her shift. I kiss and lick again all the charms of the upper part of her frame, which is now quite bare, and I teach her how to suck my lips and tickle my cheeks and forehead with the point of her tongue, not forgetting my neck and ears.

Sufficiently excited, I order the chemise to be taken off.

"Never!" she exclaims.

I get my stick again, and show her how silly she is to refuse, as it is already nearly down to her navel. But she still will not consent, and I cut her, not too severely, over her back, shoulders, and arms. I love to see the dark stripes raised by the whistling bamboo. She hardly winces at each blow. I am certain she likes the chastisement of the male. Suddenly I twist her round and tell her to remain quiet and take three cuts on her naked bottom. I pull up her shift, fully exposing her plump posteriors and she is quiet on her knees, leaning over the sofa. I do not hurry, but count slowly: "One, two, three!"

And the poor little bottom receives three severe cuts, stretching across both posteriors and equaling, although I do not tell her so, six stinging blows. I have tamed her, for she rises with a wry face, and drops the offending chemise to her feet. She is naked at last before me, in the full light of a sunny summer day. I kiss her and caress her again, admiring her flat belly and her splendid bush, as black as night.

She seems uneasy, but I soon bring a smile to her face again, by telling her that I will never do anything to her by surprise.

"I will always let you know beforehand, what I want, and if what I propose to do displeases you, tell me and I will then see if your master should give way or not."

And now I make her plainly understand what I intend to do to her:

"I shall lick you all over and then suck you, and you shall suck me until I discharge boldly and without reserve in your mouth. But I want to tell you something which is very important. The first time I had you, you expectorated my elixir. That is an insult to the man who is loved by a woman. You must swallow all to the very last drop and remain with your mouth on the instrument until told to go. If you cannot perform the operation as I describe, it shows you do not love me, as nothing coming from me—however seemingly dirty—can cause disgust in you."

"But I can't. I shan't be able. Perhaps I shall be sick?"

"You must try, and if you really love me, you will succeed."

I now stripped quite naked and took her in my arms, as if she were a baby. She was as light as a feather. I lifted her up until her body was on a level with my chin, and threw her from me onto the bed with all the strength I could muster. It was a pretty sight to see her naked body tumble down all in a heap.

We were soon entwined together, outside the bedclothes, and I cannot describe our mutual kisses, caresses, and pressures. I licked her face all over and sucked her neck, her nipples, and waggled my tongue under her arms, while her belly, navel, and thighs came in for their share of the kisses of my eager mouth. She uttered little shrieks of pleasures, and anon cooed like a turtledove or purred like the rutting kitten she was. I turned her round onto her belly, and the nape of her neck, her shoulders, spine, loins, and bottom were soon wetted by my saliva. I wished to get my tongue between her round posteriors, but she would not consent. I was now too feverish and unnerved to press the point. It was a very hot day. So I lay over her, and started pretending to copulate, and the end of my dagger went in a little.

"Oh! you hurt down there. On the top it is nice."

"Take hold of it yourself and put it where you like."

She placed the head just on her sensitive button, and I moved gently, the swollen tip rubbing against her clitoris. This she approved of. I told her that a woman could be enjoyed in the hole of her bottom. Would she let me? She answered me affirmatively without hesitation. I warned her that it hurt the first time.

"What a pity it is that everything hurts the first time!"

She turned her posteriors to me, freely offering them with a loving look.

"I must lick you there to make it wet."

"No! No!"

So I wetted my arrow with my saliva, and began to push between her rotund cheeks.

"You are not right!" she exclaimed.

"Guide it yourself, Lily."

She did so, and I thrust home.

"Oh!" she shrieked, piteously. "It hurts! You do hurt me so, Papa!"

At these words, a wave of pity broke over me. It would be a cowardly trick, I thought, to sodomize my confiding sweetheart. So I desisted, and my organ grew limp.

"Try again," she said. And she seized my weapon. "Oh! you are not excited enough now!"

I did not tell her what had crossed my mind. And I never did. I often thought since of warning her against ever yielding up her anus to a man, but the idea to speak of this escaped my memory. I am afraid it will be too late when she reads this book.

I was hot, tired, and perspiring, but still full of desire. I rested and gave her a little lesson in the art of manualization, teaching her how to hold the manly staff, the way to move the wrist, slowly or quickly, and so on. She was an apt pupil.

Then she got up to arrange her hair and, taking out the combs and pins, let her long black tresses escape in freedom. They fell below her tiny waist.

She seized my bamboo switch and began to tease me as I lay on the bed, giving me slight blows with it. I jumped up to catch it, but the task was an impossible one. I chased her round the room and I must have looked a ridiculous sight with my semierection, and my testicles dangling as I ran. When I was about to seize her, she would spring on the bed and, landing on the other side, always get the couch between us. So, I, panting, lie down again and say coolly:

"It is disgusting to see a young lady jumping about a room stark naked. Lily, are you not ashamed?"

She took my words literally and rushed to pull on her chemise.

"Of course I'm naked! I forgot that!"

And she sat on the sofa trying to hide her pussy. I soon laughed her out of her chemise again, and she was in my arms once more.

Then I gamahuched her seriously, reversed over her sideways, while she felt my spear and stroked the appendages, masturbating me as I had just taught her. I did not ask her to touch me thus while I sucked her. She did it of her own accord. I opened the big lips of her little shaded slit and looked well at it and inside it. It was small and pink, rather tight and thin inside, but seemingly little. The vagina was clearly closed up. She was a perfect virgin. She spent, and we rested awhile.

"Now you!" she said.

"How?"

"As you like!"

I opened my legs, and placed her on her knees between my outstretched thighs. She bent her head and engulfed her playfellow. After a few hints, she sucked me like a professional. Her large mouth and sensual thick lips proved that she was born to be a sucker of men's tools all her life. I took her cheeks in my two hands and held her head still, as I moved slowly in and out of her mouth, telling her that I was having connection with her in a vile, unnatural manner. I then took it out of her mouth and made her suck the balls alone, and tickle the erect member up and down the shaft with the pointed end of her tongue. While she was busily engaged on the little olives in their purse, I rubbed my organ, all wet as it was, on her flushed cheeks, and informed her I should emit one day on her face, and in her hair, and in fact all over her, until every part of her body had been sullied by me. She got very excited by listening to this filthy talk as she performed her task and worked fast and furiously. I put my thigh between her legs and rubbed it against her furrows. At last I felt I could bear the touch of her tongue no longer. I held her head and pushed up and down myself, talking to her in a most disgusting manner, as the storm burst, and she tickled my member with her tongue until I was forced to push her away.

She looked up and talked to me very gravely and seriously.

"You see, it is all gone!"

I praised her, and she asked me timidly to be allowed to drink a little water. That I graciously permitted, and the voluptuous vestal begged me to let her suck again! She liked doing it!

It was five o'clock. We had been in the room since a quarter to three. I was dead beat, and I had not yet packed up my things for my departure the next day. We kissed and said good-bye effusively.

The Pearl

*T*he following day in the afternoon, Manette came into my room and asked me to follow her to her chamber, whither she led, saying, "I have something to show you that will please and satisfy you much more than your mistress could do."

I followed to her chamber which, after entering, she locked. I stood looking out of a window while Manette went behind the bed, the curtains of which were drawn. Hearing a light step advancing toward me, I turned round, and Manette stood before me entirely naked; she sprang into my arms, clasping me round the neck, and led me to the bed, on which she seated herself.

I now saw what it was she had to show me, and being in no way loath to enter into the combat with her, to which she had invited me, I threw off my coat and vest, while she let down my pantaloons and drew out my blunt but ever-ready weapon; then, falling back on the bed, she drew me on top of her. My cock soon ran its full length into the soft and luscious sheath which Nature intended for it. Twice before I got off her did I open the floodgates of love's reservoir, and pour into her a stream of fiery sperm, as each time she met me, letting down the very cream and essence of her body so copiously that our thighs were bedewed with it.

From this time till my cousin left the castle did I enjoy Manette in the same manner each day.

At the end of the second week after his coming, my uncle announced his departure for Paris on the following day and told me to make all preparations to go with him. When this was announced to my cousins and myself, we determined to make the best possible use of the day by spending it in the woods on the banks of a small creek, with our respective mistresses.

On Sunday morning, Raoul, myself, and Julien (for although I have not mentioned him in connection with our love affairs, it must not be supposed that he was idle in such things all the time, far from it; while Raoul and myself amused ourselves with Manette and Rose he consoled himself in the arms of Marie, one of the dairymaids, a large, lusty brunette, and very good-looking, to whose bedchamber he stole every night) set out, meeting the three girls at the place appointed, they having gone on some time before us carrying provisions and wine.

Having saluted our beauties, we proceeded to arrange matters for a lunch, and sat down—or rather reclined—on the greensward, and discussed the merits of some of the good things they had provided for us, and after satisfying our appetites felt inclined to taste of the other good things they had left, but which were not visible.

Accordingly, as a preparatory note, we would slip our hands in their bosoms and, dallying awhile, would roll them over on their backs; but in spite of our endeavors we could not raise a petticoat, more than to just get a glimpse of a thigh, resisting all our endeavors to get further into matters, saying they would not consent to such naughty things in sight of each other, and if we did not behave better, they would run off and leave us.

I then proposed we should undress and have a swim. "We will strip ourselves to our shirts and then strip you, and at the word of command, each shall throw off their nether garments."

To this there was some demurring on the part of our young

ladies, as they felt some shame at being seen by each other thus, especially Marie, whom neither Raoul nor myself had seen till the present time; but we overruled their objections and stripped to our shirts, then each going up to his mistress, commenced unhooking and unlacing, and taking off frock and petticoats, till nothing but their shorts were left on them. I gave the word of command. "Off shirts." We threw our shirts off, but on looking at our girls found them still standing in their shifts.

Finding they would not take their shifts off, I proposed that one after the other throw off and stand naked, and each as they did so to be examined in all parts by the men, and their relative beauties compared, and offered to the one that would first do so a handsome diamond ring.

Manette agreed, saying that having come there to meet and enjoy ourselves with our lovers, and they having thrown off all covering, she would not spoil the sport, as she was not ashamed to let them see all what she had, for she was sure she had as pretty a leg and as sweet a little cunt as any girl in Brittany.

I was so much taken with the lusty Marie, Julien's mistress, her immense titties, her extraordinary large hips and thighs, above all, her beautiful cunt, which was covered up and hidden in a most luxuriant growth of jet-black hair, which hung down fully eight inches long, and from out of which peeped two large red pouting lips, which looked most temptingly luscious, that I proposed we should each, after our first swim, change mistresses, so that each one should have enjoyed the mistresses of the other two.

To this my cousins consented—with it, the girls were much pleased, as Manette was very anxious to have me once more bury myself within the juicy folds and recesses of her cunt; and Marie was also very willing, as she had whispered to me while examining her, telling me that although she was large she had a little cunt, but that Julien's prick was too small to give her much pleasure when he was in her; that mine was nearly twice as large as his, and she was sure that if I would consent to try her, I would like her much better than Rose.

I now led the way into the brook, leading Rose by the hand, the others following us. Once in, we played and sportively wantoned in the water, playing all manner of tricks, plunging them in over head and ears, and provoking them in every possible way, and under pretense of washing our fair partners, we gave our hands every liberty, going over every part, the breasts, squeezing and molding their titties, their soft bellies, rubbing their thighs, their cunts, and all other parts; the girls at the same time going over us in pretty much the same manner.

As we thus stood in the water, which was only about waist deep, our engines erect and in good working condition, with my arm around Rose's waist, I tried to insert the nozzle of my engine into the mouth of her watertight furnace, for the purpose of putting out the fire which was raging within it, but could not succeed, as we were unable to support one another.

My attention was drawn to a considerable splashing I heard, and on looking round, I perceived that Raoul and Julien had laid their nymphs down on the edge of the water, their heads resting on the bank, and had got into them in that manner, the motions of their backsides and bellies coming together making the water fly all over them.

This was an example set before us which Rose and I could not resist; so leading her out of the water, we sat down on the grass, under the shade of a tree, there setting her across my thighs, her legs lapping around my backside, her soft, beautiful white belly rubbing against mine. I dallied with her ruby-nippled titties, firm and springing to the touch, with one hand, while with the other I was trying to make out the entrance to the harbor of love, in order to make room for my masterpiece of Nature, that stood reared up between her thighs and pressed hard against her belly, as if demanding admittance and shelter within the soft and luscious sheath, which Nature had so bountifully supplied to a woman, and of which Rose possessed a most lovely specimen. She, in a fit of humor, affected to elude my efforts to gain entrance into her, trying to protract the desire she was wishing for, but managing her maneuvers so that they made the fire which was burning in us rage fiercer and redoubled my excitement.

I covered her with burning kisses, and her eyes shot forth humid fires, and, languishing, seemed to melt beneath her long dark silken lashes which half-concealed them. We rolled and twined about on the greensward, locked in each other's arms, till at last got her under, with my knees between her thighs, and I was soon fairly into her; while she, feeling the dart of love entering into the very depths of the retreat, gave up, and lay at my mercy. But as the fight grew fiercer and fiercer, she soon brought me to a crisis, at the same time paying down her own tribute to man.

Closing her eyes and breathing a sigh, she stretched out her limbs with a faint shudder, the muscles instantly relaxing gave me to know that she had experienced the greatest pleasure that woman is capable of receiving or man of giving.

We had not recovered out of our trance when the others came up, and slapping us on our bare backsides soon brought us to.

Immediately on coming out of the water, we changed partners: Raoul taking Rose, Julien Manette, and I Marie, and on receiving her, I lay down between her beautiful legs, my cheek pillowed on the mossy hair that surmounted the gaping lips of the delicious entrance below.

Reclining thus for some time, sipping wine, eating bonbons and sweetmeats, we dallied away an hour or two, till our passions began to rise in such a manner as to be not long kept in subjection. My cousins, I suppose, thinking that being in the water added to the pleasure they received from the girls while fucking them, or from the novelty of the thing, proposed our going into the water again, and there enjoying our mistresses. They did so, but I remained under the tree with Marie. When the others got under the bank, I rose up, and spreading down all the dresses and petticoats, and making a pillow of a coat, I made a comfortable bed for Marie to lie on. I invited her to the combat. She got up and lay on the bed I had prepared for her, placing herself in an excellent position to favor my entrance. I lay myself down on her gently, she taking hold and guiding the head of the instrument into the opening, which was to pierce her to the very vitals. After she had lodged the head between the lips of her cunt, I titillated her with it for a moment and then slowly drove it into her, so slowly that it was a full minute before it was all in, so tight was her cunt and so large was my prick that they were stretched and gorged to the fullest extent.

Marie's cunt was small—very small indeed—most lusciously tight, and slowly drawing my rod out to the head—the tightness of it causing so great a suction that it sent a thrill of most exquisite pleasure through my whole body—then darting it into her, and again drawing it out, and darting it in till I could no longer master myself, my motions became so rapid and vigorous that we soon let down and mixed the essence of our souls together.

Although I loved my little Rose, with her dear little cunt and all her charms, although I found great pleasure when in the arms and enjoying the riper beauties of her sister Manette, yet the sensations of delight and pleasure I had just received from Marie were, in my mind, superior to them both.

I was the second time tasting and sipping of the sweets to be had in the arms of Marie when the rest of the party broke in upon us, but we did not mind them and kept on till we had finished our work. After resting from our labors for some time, and our appetites being sharpened, we got our nude sirens to rearrange the luncheon; then, after satisfying our appetites, and taking another swim, we dressed and set out for home. On the way, I called for a consultation as to whether our exchange of mistresses should stand good for the night or not.

Raoul answered that as we had spent the day together so we ought to do the night; for all of us to lie together in one room, and if either of the girls wished to be fucked by either of us, that she should say so, and be accommodated, and vice versa, to which we all consented.

That night we met in my chamber at eleven o'clock, the girls fetching in beds from another room and making them up on the floor. I stretched myself naked on a pallet, and Manette ran up and lay down by me. Raoul took Marie for trial, and Julien Rose.

After I had given the plump Manette a double proof of the powers within me, another change was made, and I got the lusty Marie. Toward daylight we were each lying with our own particular mistress and, after making all arrangements for the future, we fell asleep, I in my favorite position, laying between the legs of Rose, having them thrown over me, my head pillowed on her soft white belly, my cheek resting on the silken mossy hair that surrounded her cunt.

We breakfasted at ten o'clock, after which I slipped up to Manette's room, where I found her, Rose, and Marie. To each I made handsome presents and told them if they would be true to me, that on my return from Paris, I would take and keep the whole three of them. Each one of them was anxious to have me tumble her once more on the bed, but as I could do only one, they drew lots for my last fuck, which fell to Marie. She lay down across the bed, and while I let down my pants, the other two girls threw up her clothes, and each raised a leg, and after I had made good my entrance they rested her thighs on my hips, so that I soon put her in ecstasy by the delicious maneuvers of love's pistonrod.

Half an hour after, I was on the road to Paris, where I will introduce myself to you in new scenes in a new chapter.

The Romance Of Lust,
Or Early Experiences

A happy thought seized me. I put my finger to my lips to give the hint to Florence, slipped out into the passage, and peeped through the keyhole, which commanded the whole of the narrow room. I beheld a handsome man fucking a superbly stout woman, kneeling with her head down low, but toward the door. Her arse uncovered and held aloft was a remarkably fine one, wriggling indeed to perfection.

I slipped back, described it to my dear wife, and suggested our speaking to them through the partition as soon as they were done, to avow that we had heard all their goings-on, as they had ours, and to propose that we should form a *partie carrée*.

Florence jumped at the idea, just as their sighs and shaking of their couch against the partition announced the grand final crisis.

We allowed them some minutes for the after-satisfaction; we then heard the lady beg him to do it again, as she felt his cock was stiffening within her cunt.

"No wonder," said he, "when your delicious tight cunt is giving
me such exquisite pressures."

We thought this a happy moment, as they were both in a state
of lasciviousness; so, tapping at the partition, and raising my voice
just sufficient to be clearly heard, I said, "You have been following our example and seem as lustful as we are. Suppose we join
parties and exchange partners? I am sure you must be two desirable persons, and you will find us worth knowing. It will be a
novelty exciting to all, and will lead or not, as it may be, to a
further acquaintance or just a momentary caprice. What say you?"

A pause and a whisper was followed by *"Eh, bien, nous accep-
tons."*

"Come to us, for I am half-undressed," cried the gentleman.

We rose and went in unto them, even in a biblical sense. My
slight peep had given me an idea of two handsome persons, but a
full view proved them to be eminently so. He was still up to the hilt
from behind. She lifted her head to look at us on entering, but left
her splendid arse exposed and did not for the moment alter her
position. We handled and pressed it. The gentleman, feeling my
wife's arse, cried out to his dearie, "Here's an arse equal to yours."

Meanwhile, as I stood by her side feeling hers, she slipped her
hand into my flap, and in answer to his exclamation, said, "There's
a prick bigger than yours. Oh, I see we shall all be delighted."

She rose and pulled out my standing prick to show it to her
husband for, like us, they turned out to be a most salacious couple
of married people.

My wife laid hold of the husband's prick, and declared it to be
a very fine one, and a delicious variety, which was always charming.

As the room and couch could accommodate only one couple, I
proposed that I should take his wife into our room and leave mine
with him; and, as the two couches were close to the partition
between, we could excite each other by our mutual sighs and
bawdy exclamations. This was at once agreed to.

We all of us stripped to the buff; my new companion was
magnificently made—very much of my aunt's figure, with a splendid arse, although not so enormously developed as dear aunt's. Her

cunt was delicious, a grand mons veneris, sweetly haired with silky curls; her pouting cunt had the true odor and was very tight, and her pressures and action left nothing to desire.

I gamahuched her first—her clitoris was well defined and stiff. Her bubbies were superb and stood firmly apart, face charming with lovely and lovable blue eyes, full of the sparkle of lust; lips red and moist, inviting a tongue.

We indulged in delicious preliminaries; she had a good look at my prick, declared she had thought her husband's could not be beaten, but admitted mine was longer and larger. She sucked its head. Then, lying back on the couch, she begged me to mount on her belly, as she liked to commence in that pose. I mounted upon her, got my prick gradually up to the crushing of the two hairs, and then alternately tonguing her sweet mouth or sucking a nipple of her lovely bosom, ran a most delicious course, making her spend thrice to my once.

Our other equally occupied couple had evidently got a course ahead of us and were changing into the position in which we had first fucked our wives.

We, too, followed in the same attitude, and really, the fine arse of my *fouteuse*, her naturally small waist, seen to perfection in this position, and her noble shoulders beyond could hardly be excelled, and were most inviting and inciting. I plunged with one fierce thrust up her reeking cunt and, by the very violence of my attack, made her spend on finding it up to the cods, giving me at the same time a cunt pressure almost equal to my beloved wife's.

She was so delightful a fucker that I fucked her thrice more before drawing out of that exquisite receptacle.

On comparing notes afterward, I learnt that my wife's fucker had just done as much, and though not so cunt-satisfying a prick as mine, the variety and novelty gave it an extra charm that more than made up for any diminution of size.

We were thus all mutually delighted with our change of partners. An acquaintance begun so delightfully led to a warm friendship and a constant interchange of these most agreeable refinements, including every variety of the gamahuche and *la double jouissance* to all parties.

We all went together to witness some rear operations between two men, for which the old bawd's house, No. 60, rue de Rivoli, was quietly known to be the rendezvous. I made a first visit alone to see whether it would be worth our while, and had an interview with the old bawd, a bold, masculine woman of a certain age, who must have been very desirable in her younger years. For even now, many who frequented her house finished off in her fully developed charms, her habit being, as I was told, to come in to the man after one of the girls had left him to purify herself, and herself to lave his prick from mere love and excitement of handling a prick. And from long practice, she had an art of doing it in a way to raise another perpendicular, which led to its being allayed in the full-blown charms of the bawd herself.

I was shown into her sanctum, and there I told her that I knew she could arrange an exhibition of sodomy. I said that I wanted only to see the operation, as it appeared to me impossible, and I should like the two fellows to be well hung and good-looking, if such she could procure.

"I have the very thing for you under my hand if you can wait a quarter of an hour."

As that exactly suited my purpose, I said I would.

She rose, rang the bell, and when a tap came to the door, went out and gave some orders. When she came back, she said to me, "I have some very fine girls, all entirely without prejudices. Would you like to have one up? I have them of all ages, from twelve to twenty-five; and also one or two handsome boys to have in company with them, to excite the slower powers of elderly men or those who like such additions."

I thanked her but told her my only object at present was to see an actual scene of sodomy. So, to occupy me, she opened a small cupboard, and took out some bawdy books, admirably illustrated. The examination of these was exciting; her experienced eye detected the effect in the distention of my trousers, the extent of which seemed so to astonish her that she laid her hand upon it, gave an exclamation of surprise at its size, and said she must see so noble a prick, unbuttoned my trousers, and pulled it out. She handled it charmingly and looked so lewd that I don't know what might have happened, for I had already slipped a hand up to an enormous big and hard arse, when a tap came to the door, and a voice announced simply that all was ready. This at once recalled me to myself, although the bawd would willingly have made me before adjourning to the other room.

She said, "What a pity not to let me have this magnificent prick into me. I wish the fellows had not come so soon, I am certain I could have got it if we had not been interrupted, and I can tell you you would have found me as good a fuck yet as the finest young woman you could meet with."

I laughed and, to quiet her, said, "We may have that another time, for you are a very fine and desirable woman." With this placebo, she rose and accompanied me to the room where the two men awaited us. They were two tall, good-looking young men, evidently *garçons de cafés*, a class much addicted to this letch, and acting as paid minions to those wanting them.

They naturally concluded that such was my object. They were already stripped, and both their very fair pricks were nearly at full stand. They each turned themselves round and asked which arse I wished to operate on and which prick was to operate upon me.

The old bawd, whose interest it was to induce me to have them, handled their pricks with great gusto and pointed out the firmness and attractiveness of their arses, bid me feel how hard they were, as well as the stiffness of their pricks and the rough crispness of their ballocks.

I felt them and would gladly have had them both, but I knew they had an infamous habit of *chantage* —that is, of denouncing to their gang well-to-do men who were got within their meshes, and go where he would in Europe, he was sure to be waited on and money screwed out of him by threatening to denounce his practices. So shaking my head and refusing to let the old bawd pull out my prick, which might then have become too unruly, I firmly told her she knew I only came there to see what the operation was like and had no idea of having my own person handled by them.

A mutual glance of disappointment was ex-changed between the bawd and them, but they put themselves at my disposal, and asked which was to be the recipient and which the operator. I pointed out the largest prick as the operator. They drew a sofa into the best light, and one knelt on it, presenting a very tempting arsehole to his fellow minion. After moistening it and spitting on it, the old bawd, with apparent relish, guided the prick of the other to the aperture, and it glided with all ease into the well-accustomed receptacle.

I was seated by their side with my eyes on a level and close to the point of junction. A very exciting scene, for he went up to his cods, and fucked right earnestly while the recipient wriggled his arse to perfection and really seemed to enjoy it. They spent with cries of joy in great delight. It excited me very much, and the observant old bawd could see my prick bounding within the confinement of my trousers.

Hoping to overcome my reluctance to take part in the program, she stimulated them to change places; the recipient became the operator, and the other the recipient. I was awfully lewd, but resisted even that; after they had done, I gave them a napoleon apiece in excess of the price paid to the bawd, left them to dress, and retired with the bawd to make other arrangements.

On shutting the door and entering the corridor, I perceived at once some doors opening upon small rooms adjoining the operating room. I guessed their destination; on attempting to open one, the bawd seized my arm in great alarm, and said, "You must not go there."

I smiled and said, "Oh, I understand, come along."

When once more in her sanctum, I said, "I see you have had peepers watching the operations, so it is well I resisted any complicity in the action; but the discovery that you have the peep-holes already simplifies my object. I have come here to report upon the effect of this scene of sodomy. A friend who dares not do as much requires such a stimulant to enable him to fuck a woman he much desires to have, and who is my mistress. Now it so happens I want very much to fuck his mistress, and we have made a compact that if this scene is likely to excite him, we are to come to your peep-holes, and while he is thus enabled to fuck my woman, I shall fuck his. I am thus explicit that you may know our real object. I suppose that now the witnesses to our operations today have left, so let me see the rooms that I may judge how far they will suit and which will favor our object."

The old bawd complied directly, but still longing to have my big prick into her, pulled her petticoats up to her navel, showing an enormous mons veneris, thickly haired and, turning round, a still finer arse, said, would I not like to assuage my excited prick in one or other of her really splendid attractions?

I said, "Not at present, thank you." And, tightening my trousers over it, showed her that it had quite drooped its head and was no longer in the humor.

She undertook to raise it very quickly, but I declined politely, on the play of want of time, to thoroughly enjoy so splendid a woman.

With a sigh of disappointment, for the size of my prick had evidently raised her lewdness to fiery zest, she led the way. Two or three of the peeping rooms were too small for four, but one was arranged for a *partie carrée*. I made an arrangement for the second day from then, and requested, if possible, to have four buggers together, to do it in various positions, and once at least in a chain of three pricks into the arses before them at the same time; I paid in advance half of the high price we were to pay and fixed the hour of one o'clock in the afternoon, in order to have plenty of daylight to see and thoroughly enjoy all the excitement.

I left, but allowed the old bawd, just on going away, to take out my prick and give it a suck by the way of allaying a little the great desire she had for it. She doubtless expected to raise such a heat as would compel my passions to satisfy her, but I had now sufficient command of it to keep it down.

Dolly Morton

*I*n the summer of the year 1866, shortly after the conclusion of the Civil War between the North and South, in America, I was in New York. To this city I had gone for the purpose of taking my passage in a Cunard steamer to Liverpool, on my way back to my home in one of the Midland counties of England, after a shooting and fishing trip I had been making in the province of Nova Scotia.

My age at that period was thirty years. I stood six feet in my socks, and I was strong and healthy. My disposition was adventurous. I was fond of women and rather reckless in my pursuit of them; so, during my stay in New York, I went about the city very much at night, seeing many queer sights, and also various strange phases of life in the tenement houses. However, I do not intend to relate my experiences in the slums of New York City.

One afternoon, about five o'clock, I had strolled into Central Park, where I seated myself on a bench under the shade of a tree to smoke a cigar. It was a beautiful day in August; and the sun, sloping to the west, was shining brightly in a cloudless sky. A light breeze was blowing, tempering the heat and making the leaves of the trees rustle with a soothing sound, and I leaned back lazily in my seat, looking at the trim and often pretty nursemaids of various nationalities in charge of the smartly dressed American children. Then my eyes turned upon a lady who was sitting on the adjoining bench, reading a book.

She was apparently twenty-five years of age, a very pretty little woman with, as far as I could see, a shapely, well-rounded figure. Her hair was a light golden brown, coiled in a big chignon at the back of her head—it was the day of chignons and crinolines. She was neatly gloved and handsomely but quietly dressed. Everything she wore was in good taste, from the little hat on her head to the neat boots on her small, well-shaped feet, which peeped from under the hem of her wide skirt.

I stared at her harder than was polite, thinking she was quite the type of a pretty American lady of the upper class. After a moment or two, she became conscious of my fixed gaze and, raising her eyes from her book, she looked steadily at me for a short time; then, apparently satisfied with my appearance, a bright smile came to her face, and she shot a saucy glance at me, at the same time making a motion with her hand inviting me to come and sit beside her. I was rather astonished, as I had not thought from her appearance that she was one of the demimonde, but I was quite willing to have a chat with her and also to poke her, if her conversation pleased me as much as her looks.

Rising from my seat, I went over to her, and she at once drew aside her voluminous skirts so as to make room for me on the bench beside her. I seated myself and we began to talk. She spoke grammatically and in an educated manner; and, although she had the American accent, her voice was low and musical. I do not dislike the American accent when I hear it on the lips of a pretty woman, and she certainly was a pretty woman. Her eyes were large, clear, and blue, her complexion was extremely good, her teeth were white and regular, her nose was well shaped, and her mouth was small and red-lipped.

She had plenty to say for herself, chatting away merrily, and using quaint expressions that made me laugh. I took quite a fancy to the lively little woman, so I made up my mind to see her home and spend the night with her. She had at once noticed by my accent that I was an Englishman, and she informed me that she had never before spoken to a man of my nationality. After we had chatted for some time, I asked her to dine with me. She seemed pleased at my invitation, and at once accepted it; so we strolled quietly out of the park to a restaurant, where I ordered a good dinner with champagne.

When the meal was over, and I had smoked a cigar, I took my companion, who told me her name was "Dolly," to a theater. At the end of the performance I engaged a "hack," as the conveyance is called in New York, and drove the woman to her home, which was in the suburbs, about three miles from the theater. As it was a bright moonlit night, I was able to see that the house was a pretty little one-storied building with a creeper-covered veranda, standing in a small garden surrounded by iron railings. The door was opened by a neatly dressed quadroon woman, who ushered us into the drawing room; then, after drawing the curtains and turning up the jets in the chandelier, she went away. The room, which had folding doors at one end, was furnished prettily. There was nothing the least suggestive about it; everything was in good style. The floor was covered with a handsome Oriental carpet, the curtains were velvet, some good engravings were on the walls, and a cabinet contained some choice specimens of old china.

My companion told me to sit down and make myself comfortable; then, begging me to excuse her for a moment or two, she passed through the folding doors into the adjoining apartment, which I saw was a bedroom. In a short time she returned, dressed in a white wrapper trimmed with blue ribbons. She had taken off her boots and put on dainty little French slippers, while her hair was flowing loose over her shoulders, nearly down to her waist. She looked so fetching that I at once took her on my knees and gave her a kiss on the lips, which she returned, at the same time inserting the tip of her tongue in my mouth. Then I put my hand up her clothes, finding that she had nothing on under the wrapper but a fine lace-trimmed chemise and black silk stockings, which were fastened high above the knees with scarlet satin garters, so I was able to feel her whole body with perfect ease.

She was as plump as a partridge; there was not a single angle about her figure. Her skin was as smooth as satin. Her bubbies were rather small, but they were as round as apples, quite firm, and tipped with tiny erect pink nipples. She had a very good bottom with plump, firm cheeks, and the hair on her mons veneris was silky to the touch.

She gave me a brandy and soda, and we chatted while I smoked a cigar. Then we went into the bedroom, where everything was exquisitely clean and sweet. In a short time we were between the sheets, my breast on her bosom, my mouth on her lips, my amatory organ up to the roots in her den of love, my hands grasping the cheeks of her bottom, and I was riding her vigorously, while she was sighing, squeaking, and bucking up under my powerful digs. My member was big; her fissure was small and wonderfully tight. Moreover, she was a good mount, so I enjoyed the "flutter" very much, especially as I had not had a woman for a month. But I had knocked all the breath out of the little woman, and when all was over, she lay panting in my arms. However, when she had recovered her wind, she said with a little laugh, "My gracious! You are very big and very strong. I don't think I've ever had such a vigorous embrace in all my life. You seemed to go right through me. But I liked it."

I laughed, making no remark, but lying quietly resting, still holding her in my arms, and stroking her cool velvety skin until I was ready for action again.

Then, making her kneel on all fours outside the bed, I poked her from behind *en levrette,* again making her wince, squeak, and wriggle her bottom. We then got between the sheets again, and I made her turn on her side with her back toward me, while I lay behind her with my belly and thighs pressed against the cool plump cheeks of her bottom, and with my half-stiff tool resting in the cleft of her thighs. In this position we fell asleep.

Eveline

*P*ercy had been at Eastbourne three days. We had not altogether lost our time. I determined to run up to town. I went by an early train, alone. I entered the station some fifteen minutes before the train started. On the platform was a gentlemanly looking man in a tweed suit. I thought I had seen his face before. We passed each other. He looked pointedly at me. Certainly I knew his features. I never forget, if I take an interest in a man's appearance. I liked the looks of this tall, well-built fellow in tweed. He appeared to be about thirty-five or forty years of age, hale and hearty. I gave him one of my glances as he passed me.

"This way, miss. First-class. No corridors on this train. You'll be all right here. You're alone at present."

"Thank you, guard. Does the train go without stopping?"

"Stops at Lewes, miss. That's all—then right up."

I saw my tall friend pass the carriage. Another glance. He stopped, hesitated, then opened the door and got in. He took a seat opposite me. The newspaper appeared to engross his attention until the whistle sounded.

"Would you mind if I were to lower the window? These carriages are stuffy. The morning is so warm."

I made no objection, but smilingly gave my consent.

"How calm and beautiful the sea looks. It seems a pity to leave it."

"Indeed, I think so—especially for London."

"You are going to London? How odd! So am I."

I could not be mistaken. I had seen him somewhere before.

"I shall miss the sea very much. We have no sea baths in Manchester. I love my morning dip."

It struck me like a flash. I remembered him now.

"You must have enjoyed it very much, coming from an inland city."

"Well, yes, you see, I had a good time. They looked after me well. Always had my machine ready."

"I had no doubt of that."

"Number 33. A new one—capital people—very fine machine."

I suppose I smiled a little. He laughed in reply as he read my thoughts. Then he folded up his paper. I arranged my small reticule. Unfortunately, it dropped from my hand. He picked it up and presented it to me. His foot touched mine. We conversed. He told me he lived near Manchester. He had been to Eastbourne for a rest. His business had been too much for him, but he was all right now. His gaze was constantly on me. I kept thinking about his appearance all naked on the platform of the bathing machine as old David Jones rowed me past. We stopped at Lewes.

My companion put his head out of the window. He prevented the entry of an old lady by abusing the newspaper boy for his want of activity.

"I think Eastbourne is one of the best bathing places on the coast. You know, where the gentlemen's machines are!"

"I think I know where they keep them."

"Well, I was going to say…but…well…what a funny girl you are! Why are you laughing?"

"Because I was thinking of a funny idea. I was thinking of a friend."

His foot pushed a little closer. Very perceptible was the touch.

He never ceased gloating over my person. My gloves evidently had an especial attraction for him. Meanwhile I looked him over well. He was certainly a fine man. He aroused my emotions. I permitted his foot to remain in contact with mine. I even moved it past his so that our ankles touched. His face worked nervously. Poor man, no wonder! He gave me a searching look. Our glances met. He pressed my leg between his own. His fingers were trembling with that undefined longing for contact with the object of desire I so well understood. I smiled.

"You seem very fond of the ladies."

I said it boldly, with a familiar meaning. He could not fail to understand. I glanced at his leather bag in the rack above.

"I cannot deny the soft impeachment. I am. Especially when they are young and beautiful."

"Oh, you men. You are dreadfully wicked. What would Mrs. Turner say to that?"

I laughed. He stared with evident alarm. It was a bold stroke. I risked it. Either way I lost nothing.

"How do you know I'm married?"

My shaft had gone home. He had actually missed the first evident fact. However, he picked it up quickly before I could reply.

"It appears you know me; you know my name."

"Well, yes, you see I'm not blind."

It was his turn to laugh.

"Ah, you had me there. What a terribly observant young woman you are."

He seized my hand before I could regain my attitude. He pressed it with both of his.

"You will not like me any the less, will you?"

"On the contrary. They say married men are the best."

Up to this point, my effrontery had led him on. He must have felt that he was on safe ground. My last remark was hardly even equivocal. He evidently took it as it was intended. I was actually excited. The man and the opportunity tempted me. I wanted him. I was delighted with his embarrassment, with his first and fast-increasing assurance. He crossed over. He occupied the seat beside me. My gloved hand remained in his.

"I am so glad you think so. You do not know how charming I think you. Married men ought to be good judges, you know."

"I suppose so. I rather prefer them."

He looked into my face and I laughed as I uttered the words. He brought his face very close. He pressed his left hand around my waist. I made no resistance. The carriage gave a sympathetic jerk as it rushed along. Our faces touched. His lips were in contact with mine. It was quite accidental, of course; the line is so badly laid. We kissed.

"Oh, you are nice! How pretty you are!"

He pressed his hot lips again to mine. I thought of the sight I had seen on the bathing machine. My blood boiled. I half-closed my eyes. I let him keep his lips on mine. He pressed me to him. He drew my light form to his stout and well-built body as in a vise. I put my right foot up on the opposite seat. He stared at the pretty, tight little kid boot. He was evidently much agitated.

"Ah, what a lovely boot!"

He touched it with his hand. His fingers ran over the soft cream-colored leather. I wore a pair of Papa's prime favorites. He did not stop there. His trembling hand passed on to my stockings, advancing by stealthy degrees. Then he tried to push the tip of his tongue forward.

"How beautiful you are, and how gentle and kind!"

His arm enfolded me still closer; my bosom pressed his shoulder. His hand advanced farther and farther up my stocking. I closed my knees resolutely. I gave a hurried glance around.

"Are we quite safe here, do you think?"

"Quite safe and, as you see, alone."

Our lips met again. This time I kissed him boldly. The tip of his active tongue inserted itself between my moist lips.

"Ah, how lovely you are! How gloriously pretty!"

"Hush! They might hear us in the next carriage. I am frightened."

"You are deliciously sweet. I long for you dreadfully."

Mr. Turner's hand continued its efforts to reach my knees. I relaxed my pressure a little. He reached my garters above them. In doing so he uncovered my ankles. He feasted his eyes on my calves daintily set off in openwork stockings of a delicate shade.

It was a delicious game of seduction. I enjoyed his lecherous touches. He was constantly becoming more confident in his sudden and uncontrollable passion. He strained me to him. His breath came quick and sweet on my face. I lusted for this man's embrace beyond all power of language to convey. His warm hand reached my plump thigh. I made a pretense to prevent his advance.

"Pray, oh, pray, do not do that! Oh!"

There was a sudden jolt as we apparently sped over some joints I relaxed my resistance a little. He took instant advantage of the movement. His finger was on the most sensitive of my private parts. It pressed upon my clitoris. I felt the little thing stiffen, swell, and throb under the touch of a man's hand. His excitement increased. He drew me ever closer. He pressed my warm body to his. His kisses, hot and voluptuous, covered my neck and face.

"How divine you are! The perfume of your breath is so rapturously nice. Do let me—do—do! I love you."

He held me tight with his left arm. He had withdrawn his right. I was conscious that he was undoing his trousers. He had left my skirts in disorder. I saw him pull aside his protruding shirt. I secretly watched his movements out of a corner of my eye while he kept my face close to him. Then appeared all that I had seen in the bathing machine. But standing erect. Red-headed and formidable. A huge limb. He thrust it into full view.

"My darling! My beauty! See this! To what a savage state you have driven me! You will let me, won't you?"

"Oh, for shame, let me go! Pray, do not do that! You must not! Your finger hurts. Don't!"

The jolting of the carriage favored his operations. His hand was again between my legs. His second finger pressed my button. His parts were bedewed with the fluid begotten by desire. He was inspecting the premises before taking possession. I only hoped he would not find the accommodation insufficient.

"Oh, pray, don't! Oh, goodness! What a man you are!"

With a sudden movement, he slipped around upon his knees, passing one of my legs over his left arm and thus thrust me back on the soft spring seat of the carriage. He threw up my clothes. He was between my thighs. My belly and private parts were exposed to his lascivious operations. I looked over my dress as I attempted to right myself. I saw him kneeling before me in the most indelicate position. His trousers were open. He had loosened his clothing so much that his testicles were out. I saw all in that quick feverish glance. His belly was covered with crisp hair. I saw the dull red head of his big limb drawn downward by the little string as it faced my way and the slitlike opening from which men spurt their white sap.

He audaciously took my hand, gloved as it was, and placed it upon his member. It was hard and rigid as wood.

"Feel that—dear girl! Do not be frightened. I will not hurt you. Feel, feel my prick!"

He drew me forward. I felt him, as requested. I had ceased all resistance. My willing little hand clasped the immense instrument he called his "prick."

"Now, put it there yourself, little girl. It is longing to be into you."

"Oh, my good heavens! It will never go in. You will kill me!"

Nevertheless I assisted him to his enjoyment. I put the nut between my nether lips. He pushed while firmly holding me by both hips. My parts relaxed. My vagina adapted itself as I had been told it could without injury to the most formidable of male organs. The huge thing entered me. He thrust in fierce earnest. He got fairly in.

"Oh, my God! I'm into you now! Oh, how delicious! Hold tight. Let me pull you down to me! Oh, how soft!"

I passed my left arm through the strap. My right clutched him round the neck. He pulled down his hand. He parted my strained lips around his intruding weapon. Then he seized me by the buttocks. He strained me toward him as he pushed. My head fell back—my lips parted. I felt his testicles rubbing close up between my legs. He was into me to the quick.

"Oh, dear, you are too rough. My goodness me! How you are tearing me! Oh! Oh! Ah, it is too much! You darling man. Push—Push—Oh!"

It was too much pleasure. I threw my head back again. I grasped the cushions on either side. I could only gasp and moan now. I moved my head from side to side as he lay down on my belly and enjoyed me. His thing—stiff as a staff—worked up and down in my vagina. I could feel the big plumlike gland pushed forcibly against my womb. I spent over and over again. I was in heaven.

He ground his teeth. He hissed. He lolled his head. He kissed me on the lips, breathing hard and fast. His pleasure was delicious to witness.

"Oh, hold tight, love! I am in an agony of pleasure! I...I can't tell you! I never tasted such delicious poking! Oh!"

"Oh, dear! Oh, dear! You are so large...so strong!"

"Don't move! Don't pinch my prick more than you can help, darling girl. Let us go on as long as possible. You are coming again—I can feel you squeezing me. Oh, wait a moment! So! Hold still!"

"Oh, I can feel it at my waist! Oh! Oh! You are so stiff!"

"I cannot hold much longer—I must spend soon!"

Bang! Bang! Bang!

The train was passing over the joints at Reigate. The alarm was sufficient to retard our climax. It acted as a check to his wild excitement; it was too much pleasure. I threw my head back again. I grasped the cushions on either side. I could not speak. I could not gasp again as before.

"Hold quite still, you sweet little beauty! We do not stop; the seed is quickening up again. Now push! Is that nice? Do you like my big prick? Does it stir you up? You are right, my sweet, I can feel your little womb to the tip."

He assisted me to throw my legs over his shoulders. He seemed to enter me farther than ever.

"Oh, you are so large! Oh, good Lord! Go on slowly—don't finish yet. It's so...so...nice! You're making me come again. Oh!"

"No, dear, I won't finish you before I can help it. You are so nice to poke slowly. Do you like being finished? Do you like to feel a man come?"

"Oh, not so hard! There...oh, my! Must I tell you? I...I...love to feel...to feel a man spend...all the sweet sperm."

"You'll feel mine very soon. Very soon, you beautiful little angel. Oh! I shall swim in it. There. My prick is in up to the balls! Oh! How you nip it!"

He gave me some exquisite short stabs with his loins. His thing, as hard as wood, was up in my belly as far as it would go. He sank his head on my shoulder.

"Hold still…I'm spending! Oh, my God!"

I felt a little gush from him. It flowed in quick jets as he groaned in his ecstasy. I opened my legs and raised my loins to receive it. I clutched right and left at anything and everything. I spent furiously. He gave me a quantity. I was swimming in it. At length he desisted and released me.

A few minutes sufficed in which to arrange ourselves decently. Mr. Turner asked me many questions: I fenced some—I answered others. I led him to believe I was professionally employed in a provincial company. I told him I had been ill and had been resting a short time in Eastbourne. He was delicate enough not to press me for particulars. But he asked for an address. I gave him a country post office. In a few minutes more, we stopped on the river bridge to deliver our tickets.

The train rolled into the station. My new friend made his exit. He dexterously slipped two sovereigns into my glove as he squeezed my hand. I was glad. It proved the complete success of my precautions.

I hailed a hansom and drove direct to Swan and Edgars. Outside the station, my cab stopped in a crowd. A poor woman thrust a skinny arm and hand toward me with an offer of a box of matches. I took them and substituted one of the sovereigns. As I alighted in Piccadilly a ragged little urchin made a dash to turn back the door of my cab. He looked half-starved.

"Have you a mother? How many brothers and sisters?"

"Six of us, lady. Muvver's out of work."

"Take that home as quick as you can!"

He took the other sovereign and dashed off. He had never been taught to say "thank you." I discharged the cab. I made sure I was not followed.

The Boudior

*T*was just eighteen and had been in Paris a week. Paris! To me it was a strange and delightful place—with manners and customs free, easy, and uncontrolled, so unlike what I had experienced in Birmingham, where I had passed nearly all my life. I lived in a little avenue branching from the rue Saint-Honoré—a street resembling the Strand in London. Here a friend had taken lodgings for me, and I went in and out just as I liked. The apartments at public hotels are generally kept in order by the garçon, but mine was tended by the maid, the niece of the landlady, whom I shall call Maria. As I had nothing particular to do, I passed my time in sauntering about nearly all day, seeing what was to be seen in the city. When I came in at night, I found the bed made and the room tidied up. The house—although three stories—was comparatively empty. The lower part was occupied by my landlady; I was alone on the first floor, and on the upper portion lived an old Italian artist and a little Frenchwoman, a widow.

One afternoon, while walking along the Champs-Élysées, a woman accosted me in broken English and asked me if I wanted to purchase some "funny pictures." As I felt rather curious to know what she had to dispose of, I asked her to show them to me. I can safely affirm that I had never seen such things before or since. The cool attitude with which she exhibited them I shall never forget. Of course, the reader will understand that they were not precisely the style of engravings you would cover your office screen with, or paste inside your sister's prayer book. I purchased a small book filled with these plates for two francs from the old hag, being glad to get rid of her, and then hurried home. Rushing upstairs, I was about to enter my apartment, intending to examine my purchase. The room, however, was all in a disturbance, and I paused at the door, for I heard someone inside muttering, *"Sacre-diable-peste."* Peeping through the crack of the door, I saw the little French girl, Maria, who, with her back toward me, was busily hunting in her clothes for one of those essentials to a French lodging-house: a flea.

What a hunt—and what a rummage there was. Never shall I forget that little French girl; how she tossed her clothes up, around, and about her. Finally the villainous insect was caught, and a snapping, cracking sound, with the finger and thumb upon the edge of the table, proclaimed that the rude little vagabond had hopped out of this world.

With her back still toward me, I found that Maria's troubles were not over, for her garter had become untied. Unconscious of my presence, she gave herself plenty of room to fasten it comfortably. The view to me was pleasing—for what is more pleasing than a shapely bottom, a rounded thigh, a pretty foot. If the reader thinks I acted wrongly, I am sure he will forgive me when he remembers that I was only eighteen, and the girl about my own age. There she stood, with her tiny foot upon a chair, her small ankle, well-rounded calf and thigh, neat white stocking, and her garter—a ragged one, by the way—plainly shown in the large mirror that faced her. Pulling down the stocking, she commenced scratching her calf, the red mark left by the nasty flea showing plainly upon her white skin. I don't know how long I would have stood looking, but the confounded door (reader, whenever you go upon a love excursion, always oil the door) creaked on its hinges. Maria turned around and, seeing me, blushed, as I believe any and every woman would have done, English, French, German, or American. Before she could say one word, I seized her around the waist and kissed her two or three times on the lips. In the confusion, the little picture book I had purchased fell upon the ground. In stooping to pick it up, Maria broke away from me; not, however, before she had seen a portion of its scandalous contents. Evidently annoyed, she rushed out of the room.

The next day I bought a very beautifully made pair of garters, intending to present them to Maria, but it was nearly a week before I again caught her in my room. Upon my doing so, I told her that I thought she wore very unbecoming garters, and produced those I had purchased. I told her the new garters deserved no less than such a pretty leg as she had, and that she could have them provided I was permitted to put them on her. In reality, I could think of little more than putting her on her back once I'd removed her garments, and plunging my youthful prick— inexperienced as it was—into her warm love-nest.

She looked very mysterious, then laughed, and snatched one of them out of my hands. I was advancing toward her when there was a light tap at the door. Before I could recover from my confusion she seized the other garter and, laughing, rushed out of the room upstairs to her own apartment. Her room being immediately over mine, I could hear her rapping on the floor and laughing at having conquered me. To add to my mortification, I could not discover who had disturbed me by knocking at the door.

Two or three times in the course of the day I saw Maria, and upon each occasion she laughed at me. Once, while talking to her aunt, she, unseen by her, shook her lovely little bottom at me as if to accentuate the fact that she was wearing my garters. At supper-time she inquired, to the surprise of her aunt, if she knew where Monsieur Larpour, the name of the maker of the garters, lived, as a person of that name had been inquiring in the neighborhood about some goods, which had wrongly been delivered. It needed not this last piece of mockery to instill in me a determination to have my revenge, which I executed in the following fashion:

I mentioned that Maria's room was immediately over mine, and that in the afternoon she went upstairs to change her dress. The door of this room I knew remained unlocked during the day. Accordingly, watching my opportunity when the house was quiet, I took off my shoes, coat, and vest and slipped upstairs. I thought I was unseen and concealed myself in a closet in Maria's room. After about half an hour's suspense, I heard her upon the stairs, and almost immediately she entered the room. Unconscious of there being anyone in the apartment, she commenced removing her clothes. She had taken off her gown and drawers—standing in full view resplendently naked—when suddenly she recollected something she had left in the closet.

Her astonishment may be better imagined than described when I jumped from the closet upon her. I bore her onto the bed, running my hands over her pert breasts, squeezing her nipples, and delving into the lightly mossed valley between her thighs. I was going to fuck her, though I scarcely knew what I was about. She struggled violently, and in the confusion the chair fell down.

"For heaven's sake," she exclaimed, "leave the room. My aunt will be here directly, and should she find you here, I am ruined."

The words had scarcely escaped her when I heard footsteps outside the door and someone trying to open it. I rushed to it for the purpose of preventing their entrance, whoever it might be; but before I could do so, it was opened and a female attempted to come into the apartment. It was not Maria's aunt, but the lodger in the apartment above. So, plucking up my courage, I forced her from the door; Maria crouched behind it so as not to be seen. At the same time, I said, "You cannot come in, madame. A gentleman— a friend of mine—is here dressing."

"It's no gentleman you have in the room," she said sharply, "but a woman, and I know who it is."

The conversation had been in French, but I answered instantly in good English, "I'm damned if you do." Before she could prevent me, I seized her around the waist, carried her upstairs, and deposited her upon her own bed, laughing all the while.

I was leaving the room when she called out, "If you go away in that manner, I'll tell Maria's aunt all about the garters…and what you were about to do!"

Here was a pretty dilemma! What was I to do? A few more sentences convinced me that Madame Dufour had been an eavesdropper and knew all about the garters. As I looked at her, the idea struck me that she would not have been very unwilling to receive such a present. She was a pretty little Frenchwoman, apparently about thirty years of age, with a pleasing countenance and lush body I had failed to notice.

"So you'll tell Maria's aunt?" I said, advancing toward her and laughing.

"Yes," she replied, with a roguish leer, "unless you give me something that will keep me quiet."

"A pair of garters, for instance," I continued.

"This for your garters! Give them to your silly girls. A woman like me wants something better than garters," she answered.

I replied, "Perhaps I cannot satisfy you. You must know I am only eighteen, and while I have been here, I have been rather extravagant. I haven't much money."

"I will not put you to much expense," she answered. "I would like something of genuine English manufacture. Something that I can be certain came from that country. As you are an Englishman, you might oblige me."

I told her I felt flattered by her respect for my country.

"I have taken a great interest in you," she continued, "and if you will stay here a short time, I will give you some instructions that will be useful to you as long as you live. If you pursue the path I put you on, you can never miss the road to true happiness."

When she put her hand on the stiffening lump in my trousers, I knew right away what thing of English manufacture she desired. I was only too happy to oblige her, though there was little doubt who was the instructor and who the pupil.

While I stood by, shy and unsure of myself in front of this experienced dark-eyed beauty, she undid my trousers and drew them down to the floor. I stepped out of them. She had me totally naked in a few moments more, and stood back, admiring what I had to offer. She seemed to like the length and thickness of my cock, for she smiled and kneeled in front of me and took it in her mouth.

This I had not anticipated. I trembled and practically lost the strength in my legs as she sucked my rod the way a baby would suckle at its mother's breast. She licked the swollen head and teased the slit in its tip with her tongue, then swept downward and laved the length of my shaft. When she reached my balls, I shuddered again, for she took them in her mouth and rolled them around like marbles.

When she released me, she bade me lie on the bed. I did so, my excited tool sticking in the air like a flagpole. While I watched, she removed her dress, then her undergarments, until she was as naked as I. My cock stiffened still further at the sight of her large, rounded boobs capped with dark protruding nipples. She was shapely and still seemed to enjoy the bloom of youth. Her belly was taut and her thighs smooth. A downy patch of dark hair nestled between her legs and covered her glorious mount.

She grinned, cognizant of my undisguised admiration, and walked slowly over to where I lay. She mounted the bed and straddled my hips, raising herself over my upthrusting spike. She took it in hand and guided the head to the pink gash beneath her ebony fleece. Then she lowered herself upon it, effectively impaling herself. Her eyes rolled back in her head as the full length disappeared inside her. She was now seated on my belly.

I could already feel the stirrings in my loins as she slowly rocked her hips. My God, she was milking me with her delightful pussy! She thrust forward and back, faster and faster, my cock entombed in her cavern. The tingling spread through my entire body; I felt as though I were on fire.

Madame Dufour seemed to take no notice of me, but she certainly took notice of my tool. She used it as she wished, raising and lowering herself on it, squeezing it with the practiced muscles in her quim, milking it by simply shuttling back and forth on top of me. It was exquisite, and far better than I'd anticipated.

Finally, her breath began to come in staccato gasps, and mine matched hers. She writhed and bucked as she drove my cock home, and a wonderful flush spread across her bosom and neck. As for me, I would have erupted just from watching her. Instead, she wrung every drop of sperm from me in a spouting geyser that threatened to overwhelm my every sense and leave me a husk devoid of moisture.

I found the widow as good as her word. I believe, sincerely, that all she preached she practiced, for a better instructress no man could wish for. She never told about the garters. And before I left Paris, I was so pleased with what she'd taught me, I thought it my duty to impart a portion of the information I had learned to my landlady's niece, who, I trust, enjoyed it.

Simplicity Shocked

"Come in," said Coupeau. "No one will eat you."
—*L'Assommoir*

When her widowed aunt, with whom she had been living for several years in York-shire, died, Miss Alice Darvell was sent off to live with her nearest relative and guardian at his house in Suffolk. The change from a small house in a bleak and lonely part of the West Riding to a Baronet's establishment was hailed with rapture by the handsome and healthy girl of eighteen. The only, or at any rate, the principal, advantage gained by her life with her aunt was one she scarcely appreciated. Her life in the country, the bracing air, the long walks, and the rigorous punctuality of the old lady had allowed Miss Darvell to fully develop all the physical charms which so distinguished her. Add to that her fresh complexion, laughing brown eyes, the magnificent contour of her form and her limbs and you may begin to see what a rare beauty Alice possessed. But she also had a distracting air of reckless ingenuousness, picked up, no doubt, in her moorland scampers. Although unconscious of her charms, she sighed for the pomp and vanity of the world, even though they were held up to her by her aunt as perils of the deadliest description—a view regarded by Alice with skeptical curiosity. Her solitude only increased her imaginative faculty, and the fascination it attached to balls, parties, and life generally in the world, was greater than their charm actually warranted, as Alice subsequently found out. The only disquiet she had experienced arose from a vague longing which was satisfied by none of the small events in her puritanical life. She was modest even to prudishness; had long worn dresses of such a length as to make them remarkable; had never in her life had on one of the fashionable low-cut variety. She blushed at the mention of an ankle, and would have fainted at the sight of one. The matter of sex was a perpetual puzzle to her, but she was perfectly unembarrassed in her interaction with men, and quite unconscious of the desire she excited in them. All she knew of her guardian, Sir Edward Bosmere of Bosmere Hall, was that he was her trustee and that he was a widower much older than herself, a cousin some degrees removed from her, but that notwithstanding, she called him "Uncle."

Thither then she went. Sir Edward turned out to be a man of about fifty; very determined in his manner, powerfully built, and of a medium height. But what surprised Alice most was to find herself introduced to a tall, dark girl who looked about two and twenty, who was introduced as his housekeeper. She was dressed in exquisite fashion, but Alice thought most indecently. Even more shocking, she, too, called Sir Edward, "Uncle."

The first few days were taken up in making acquaintance, but Alice was surprised one morning at breakfast to see the housekeeper, Maud, grow very pale when told by Sir Edward, that she was to go to the yellow room after breakfast, and that she was to go straight there. This direction apparently was directly as a consequence of some cutlets which were served at the meal slightly overcooked. When Alice again saw Maud she was flushed and excited, and appeared to have been crying her eyes out. In some consternation, she inquired what the yellow room was. Her curiosity wasn't to be satisfied, though, as the only reply she obtained was that she would find out soon enough. On the same occasion, after Maud had left the breakfast-room, Sir Edward, who had by that time quite accepted Alice into his household, told her he thought she dressed in a very dowdy fashion, and said he had given directions to their maid to provide a more suitable wardrobe for her. Alice was quite flustered. She was covered with blushes and confusion as she listened to her uncle speak of having her dressed like Maud. She was most disconcerted, for Maud showed a great deal of leg—as well as other charms. So Alice tried to pull herself together and replied that she really could do no such thing. Sir Edward looked at her in a very peculiar way, and said he felt sure her present mode of dress hid the loveliest neck and limbs in the world. He went on to ask whether she did not admire Maud's style of dress, and if she had noticed her stockings and drawers.

"I have indeed, uncle; but I could never wear anything like them."

"And why not, pray?"

"I should be so ashamed."

"We will soon cure you of that. We punish prudish young women here by shortening their petticoats. How do you like that idea?"

"I like it not at all; and I will not have anything of the sort done to me."

"I am afraid, miss, you want a whipping."

"I should like," Alice declared defiantly, "to know who would dare such a thing."

Sir Edward again looked at her in a peculiar manner, but said nothing more on the subject. Instead her guardian went on to tell her of his belief that young women should learn how to manage a house before they had one of their own and found themselves not knowing what to do with it. As part of her training as a proper young lady, she and Maud were to take weekly turns in the management of his household. A week from that day she would take the running of the household in hand.

"In the meantime, my dear, you had better learn as much as you can from Maud; especially not to let them burn cutlets like these." Saying which, he left the room.

At this point the narrative can best be continued from the diary of Alice Darvell herself:

Wed., July 3, 1883

As soon as uncle had left the breakfast-table, I felt quite disturbed, but on the whole determined to go on as if nothing had happened. A message from Maud came a little later, delivered by our maid, Janet. The note said that she could not go out riding that morning as we had arranged. What a terrible woman our 'maid' is! Why on earth does uncle have a Scotchwoman with so terrible a disposition for two young girls? She makes me quake if she only looks at me. Well, I made up my mind to go alone; and rode off very soon after.

On my return I met Maud, very red-faced, and looking as though she had been crying dreadfully. I asked her what was in the room to which uncle had sent her. She would not tell me what had happened, although I was struck with an icy chill down my spine when she told me that I should soon learn the secrets of the yellow room for myself.

The rest of the day passed in the usual way. We drove out after lunch, paid some visits, received several, and dressed for dinner. While waiting for the gong to sound Maud came to me, and to my horror took up precisely the same subject Sir Edward had so thoroughly embarrassed me about at breakfast.

"Uncle does not approve of your dresses, you little prude, and Janet has another one for you."

"If Janet," said I, "has a dress for me that shows my neck and breasts and back, as well as my feet, my ankles, my legs—I mean, if she has one for me that is like yours—I declare flatly, I won't wear it."

"Don't be a fool, dear. I am mistress this week; you will be next week, as uncle has explained to you, and if you do not get rid of your ridiculous shame, you will be soundly punished. You may be thankful if you are only obliged to show your legs up to your knees and your bosom down to your breasts."

"I do not care. I have never been punished."

"Very well," said Maud; "have your own way. You will soon know better."

When I arrived for dinner, uncle and Maud were there with three or four young men. Some very handsome women were also present; every one in low dresses. I was the only one in a high dress. Uncle said something to Maud, who in turn whispered to me that I was to go with her. As soon as we got into the hall, she told me I was to be taken to the yellow room and that I was a goose. When I asked her why, she only laughed. Once we arrived there, she said she was very sorry, but that she must obey orders. She then strapped my hands firmly behind my back. My struggles were useless in the end, but kept her so long that she said, "I shall take care that you shall have an extra half-dozen for this." I could not think what she meant but I had plenty of time to ponder the strange comment for I was left alone in that room for a considerable time. It got darker and still no one came. The yellow room was in an out-of-the-way wing, and I could hear not any activity from the party which I knew was still in the dining room. In fact, I heard nothing until the faint sound of the tower clock striking ten reached my ears. My hands tied tight behind me and ached with a dull, throbbing pain. I began to lose my temper. I wondered how long I was to be kept there, and then I wondered who had the right to keep me, trussed up in such a manner. I had nothing to occupy my time so I made a study of my surroundings. I suppose it was called the yellow room because the bed-curtains, the curtains on the windows, and the valances were all yellow damask. I found myself staring at the ottoman and wondering what such an enormous one was doing here, in company with a heavy oak table. That wasn't the only oddity about the room. There was a bar swinging from the ceiling! I puzzled over that for quite awhile and, then, overcome with vexation and impatience, I went to sleep.

I was awakened at about half-past eleven by the sound of carriages driving off. It was pitch dark, and the curtains had been drawn. I know it was about half-past eleven because about half-an-hour later midnight struck. There was a footstep in the corridor, and uncle came in.

Before I could express my anger at being treated in such a manner, my uncle addressed me in a clipped angry voice. "I am extremely surprised at your insubordination, miss, and for that I am about to punish you." What followed I cannot write.

So much for that part of the diary. Later on, by way of penance, as the sequel will show, Miss Alice Darvell was compelled to write out the minutest description of her punishments and her sensations and secret thoughts.

What happened was this; Sir Edward Bosmere at once informed Alice that he would have no more prudish nonsense. He explained that he was going to strip her and flog her soundly. "But you must first promise to take off your own drawers. That is a very important humiliation to which a proud young beauty such as yourself has to be subjected."

She protested in the most vehement manner.

"You have no right to whip me," she said in a cold, tight little voice. She was trying hard to keep control of her speech. She tried not to screech or let her voice tremble, as that would tell him that he had the power to frighten her. "I will not be whipped by any man or anyone else. Undo my hands at once," she said in what she thought was an authoritative voice. "Being kept all the evening in this room without any dinner is quite punishment enough. And what have I done that calls for punishment? Refusing to wear horrid dresses which only serve to make nakedness conspicuous? If I am to be treated in this way, I shall leave tomorrow. As for promising to take off my own drawers before my own uncle, you must be mad, Sir, to think of such a thing. I would rather die first."

She looked lovely in her fury, and an alteration in the surface of Sir Edward's trousers showed his appreciation of her beauty. He longed to see her naked and all her charms revealed.

"I will not dispute with you, you saucy miss, and as your face is too pretty to slap; I will settle accounts with your bottom—yes, your bottom, and a pretty plump white bottom I have no doubt it is. I can promise you, however, it won't be white long. Now lie across that ottoman on your face. What? You won't? Well, across my knee will do as well, and perhaps better."

Putting his arm round her waist, he dragged her with him to the sofa, telling her that her shrieks and struggles in that heavily curtained and thickly carpeted room would bring her no assistance; that even if they were heard no one would pay attention to them. In fact, he told her, the only result, if she persisted, would be to double her punishment. He did not, however, at that moment wish to do more than examine the charms that were so jealously concealed, the magnificence of which might be easily guessed from the little that did appear of her figure. He walked her to the sofa and sat down upon it, still holding her by the waist, and then, putting her between his legs, pulled her down across his left one. Her power of resistance was very much lessened because her hands were strapped behind her, but still she managed to slide down upon her knees in front of him instead of being laid across his lap. He then held her tightly between his knees and proceeded to unfasten the neck of her dress. Since the buttons were at the back he was obliged to put his arms round her and draw her so close that he felt her warm pressure upon him. The passion he felt was intensified, and the girl then, for the first time, seemed in a hazy sort of wonder as to whether the treatment she was undergoing was altogether unpleasant. So shocked was she by this unconscious thought, she ceased her useless resistance. At length the buttons were all undone to the waist. The dress was pulled down in front as far as her arms—still strapped behind her back—would allow. It was sufficient, however, to disclose a neck as white as snow and the upper surfaces of two swelling, firm globes. Sir Edward immediately, placed his left arm under his victim's armpit and round her shoulders, and drew her closer to him, spreading his legs wider. Notwithstanding her pretty cries for him to desist, he inserted his right hand in her bosom. At last, succeeding in loosening her corset, he was able to caress the scarlet centre of the lovely, palpitating breast while its owner lay in most bewitching disorder in his lap. Her hair had partly fallen; her bosom was exposed by the dress three parts down and the loose corset—her eyes swam, and her colour was heightened.

"Oh, stop! uncle; oh, do, do, do stop! I never felt like this before. Whatever will become of me? I cannot bear the sensation. You have no business to pull me about so."

"Do you not like the sensation, Alice?" asked he, stooping and putting his face into her bosom; "and being kissed like this, and this, and this? And is this not nice?" Taking her red teat between his lips, he gently played with it, using his tongue and his teeth until she was quite overtaken by strange feelings, the like of which she had never experienced or even imagined.

"Oh! uncle! whatever are you doing to me?" said the girl, flushing crimson all over, her eyes opening wide with amazement while her knees fell wider apart, as she fell slightly back upon his right knee.

"Is it nice? Do you like it? Does it give you sensations anywhere else?" asked he, glancing at her waist—and then, a moment after, putting his hand down outside her dress, asked, "here, for instance?"

She flushed a still deeper crimson shame, but there was a gleam of rapture after the momentary pressure, followed by the exclamation: "How dare you?"

"How dare I, miss? We shall see. Now you will please lie on your face across my knee. You can rest on the sofa."

"Oh, I suppose, you are now going to button up my dress," she said with some disappointment in her tone.

"Am I?"

"Then what are you going to do?"

"Make you obey me, and without any more resistance, or you shall have double punishment. Lie down at once, miss."

"Oh, uncle, don't look at my legs! Oh, do not, do not strip me. Oh, if I am to be whipped, whip my hands or shoulders; just not —not t-there."

"You are a very naughty, obstinate girl, with very much too much prudishness about you. But when you yourself have been forced to expose all you possess in the most unconcealed manner, and have been kept some days in short frocks with no drawers, there will, no doubt, be an improvement. And, as I said before, I shall flog your bare bottom soundly, Miss Alice; and fairly often if you do not mend your ways. Lash your arms and shoulders? Indeed! I shall lash your legs and thighs. Lie down this instant."

The poor girl, although she sensed resistance was useless, made not a move; but the arm put round her back soon cured her inaction. She lay across her uncle's left leg and under his left arm, which he had well round her waist.

"Now," said he, tightening his grasp, "we shall see what we have all along so carefully hidden; eh, miss?" He pulled up her dress behind, despite her struggles and reiterated prayers to him to desist.

"No use struggling, miss," he went on, slipping his hand up her legs and proceeding at once to that organ in front which women delight in having touched.

"Oh, uncle! Oh, leave off. How dare you? How dare you outrage me in this manner? Oh! take your hand away! Oh! oh! oh!"

"So you are a little wet," he said, feeling the hairs moistened by the voluptuous sensations he had caused her by caressing her breasts; "and you hoped that no one would know, no doubt. Now just let me stroke these legs." He ran his free hand up and down her silky thighs, his left arm was still draped over her back, holding her across his lap, although it could be argued that he could have used both hands to explore her form as it was doubtful that she had the strength or inclination to escape. "What a nice fine pair they are," he exclaimed, turning the robe above her waist. "And what a pretty, what a perfectly lovely bottom!" he said, opening her drawers. "What a crime to hide it from me. However, you will make amends for that by taking your drawers off presently."

"Never! Never while I live! You monster! You wretch! If ever I get out of this room alive, I will expose you!"

"My dear, let me try a little gentle persuasion, a novel sensation. If that does not suffice, I can find some better, more striking, argument."

And, again he pressed her down upon him, and slipped his hand up along her thighs. He deviated for a moment to caress her fine plump bottom-cheeks, but he wasn't long distracted from his true purpose. He moved his hand down once more and, while putting his finger in her virgin orifice in front, he positioned his thumb over her rear opening. Upon feeling his finger at the lips of her cunny, she jerked herself upwards, heaving herself off his lap as high as she could manage. Although her movement did manage to dislodge his finger somewhat from her front, she soon realized that she had just facilitated the invasion of her bottom-hole for as she rose up, his thumb, which had been carefully positioned to take advantage of this very reaction, went in. Then, with a little scream, Alice again bounced forward and his finger slid into her cunny as far as her maidenhead would admit. She could do nothing to dislodge either invader, for her hands were all the time still tied. Besides which, she was mortified that she had so unthinkingly assisted in her own undoing.

While she was held motionless by her shock and embarrassment, her uncle kept up a severe use of both his finger and thumb for some moments, moving in and out of the two openings with surprising ease. Soon, she was unable to contain herself, and was ultimately obliged to abandon herself to the sensations he provoked. Her legs were stretched out and wide apart; her bottom rose and fell regularly; her lovely neck and shoulders, which were still exposed to his sight, increased his rapture and her dismay; and at last, when the crisis had arrived—pretty nearly at the same moment did it overtake them both—she lay panting and sobbing, almost dead with shame; but for the time subdued.

"Well, dear, how do you like your new experience?"

"Oh, uncle, it is awful, simply awful! I am beside myself."

"When you have rested a moment, will you stand up and take off your drawers before me?"

No answer.

"Answer directly, miss."

"No; I won't! I won't, and I shall not allow you do take them from me."

"I have no intention of removing the pretty garment myself," he said with a wicked twinkle in his eyes. "I believe I can convince you to follow my orders."

Getting up, he went to a chest of drawers, and opening one, took out a riding-whip. Silently, and notwithstanding her violent resistance, he again got the refractory girl over his knee, with his arm round her, her dress up, and her bottom as bare as her drawers would admit. Across the linen and the bare part he gave her a vigorous cut, making the whip whistle through the air. It fell, leaving a livid mark across the delicate white flesh, and causing her to yell in shocked pain. Again he raised it and brought it down—another yell and more desperate contortions.

"Oh, uncle, don't! Oh! No more! No more! Oh! I can't bear it. I will be good. I will obey."

Although he had succeeded in wresting from her the promise he sought, Sir Edward paid no attention. Instead, he raised the whip, made it whistle a third time through the air. A more piercing shriek.

"It is not enough for you to promise to obey; you must be punished and cured of your obstinacy. Here's your reward for calling me a wretch and monster"—swish—swishswish.

"Oh! oh! oh! Don't! Oh, don't! Oh, you are not a wretch! I say you are not anything but what—oh! oh! put down that whip. Oh! please, dear uncle! You are not a wretch! or monster! I was very naughty to call you so, and I liked what you did to me, only I was ashamed to say it. I will take my drawers off before you if you like! I will do anything, only don't whip me any more."

"You shall have your dozen, miss"—swish. "So you liked my tickling your clitty, did you, better than"—swish—"tickling your bottom with this whip, eh?"—swish—swish. "You will expose me if you escape alive, will you?"—swish—swish.

"Oh, stop, stop! You have given me thirteen. For heaven's sake, stop!"

"I have given you a baker's dozen, and"—swish—"there is another because you complained."

Sir Edward was carried away by the passions excited by the punishment he was inflicting upon this lovely girl, and her yells as he brought the whip down again, cutting into her delicate flesh, only stirred his own passion to greater heights. Still holding her, he asked the sobbing girl whether she would be good.

"Yes. Indeed, indeed I will."

"There is a very satisfactory magic in this wand. Now, if I unfasten your hands, will you stand up and take your drawers off so that I may birch your bottom for refusing to wear a proper evening dress?"

"Oh, uncle, you have whipped me already, and punished me severely, too, by what you did to me with your f-fingers. Why should I be put to more shame?"

"Shame! Nonsense. You should be proud of your charms and glad to show them. What I did should give you pleasure. Anyhow, will you take off your drawers?"

"Oh!" she said, flushing and in despair, "however can I? I should have to lift my dress quite up, and I should be all exposed. Besides, it is so humiliating."

"Precisely. You yourself must bare all your hidden fascinations. And the humiliation is to chastise you for your prudishness. You must do it. You had much better be a good, obedient girl, as you promised you would be just now."

"Very well. I will then."

"That is a good girl. You shall have a kiss for reward," and, putting his lips on her beautiful mouth, Sir Edward gave her a long and thrilling kiss, and inserted his tongue between her lips until it came into contact with hers.

"What a delicious kiss," she said, shuddering with delight; and coyly adding "I shall not so much mind taking off my—my—my drawers now," she said in a hushed tone, her eyes averted from him.

"That is right, dear. Now let me undo your hands. There. Now stand before that mirror and let me arrange the light so that it may fall full upon you. You must do this unassisted, I shall sit here."

Miss Alice Darvell walked over to the mirror in a graceful and stately fashion, and started as she saw herself. She turned round and looked shyly at her master, but said nothing. Stooping down, she gathered up her gown and petticoats in her arms and slowly lifted them to her waist. The act revealed a slender and graceful pair of ankles and calves, but the knees were hidden by the garment she was about to remove. After some fumbling with the buttons about her waist—they increased her confusion by not readily unbuttoning, at which she, in a charming little rage, stamped angrily once or twice making the drawers tumble down.

"Keep up your petticoats," cried Sir Edward, "and step out of your drawers. Keep them up," said he, rising, "until I tell you you may let them down. What lovely thighs! what splendid hips! what a lovely, round bottom! Look at it, Alice, in the glass."

"Oh," she said, startled, "I am so glad you think so. I have never looked at myself before."

He laughed at this revelation and stroked the satin skin with his hand, rubbing her limbs in front and behind and all over her bottom until, at last, when he had gradually stroked her all the way up, he put his hand between the cheeks of her backside right through to her cunt. He rubbed that passage also, and kept gently stroking for some minutes until she fell limply against him, uttering inarticulate sounds of delight.

"There," he said at length, "that will do for tonight. You may let your clothes down now. It is so late that the birching shall be postponed until the morning."

"May I take my drawers with me?"

"No, my dear; it will be some time before I shall allow you to wear them again. Not as long as you are still a maiden," he added significantly.

"Oh, that will be years."

"Will it?" he inquired, innocently. "Come," he said, "I will take you to your room. You will, in future, occupy the one I will now take you to, and not your old one."

"Why, uncle? All my things are in the old one."

"That does not matter, my dear. I must keep you under my eye until you are reduced to abject submission."

The room to which he took her was cheery and warm. Although the month was July, a fire had been lighted, and had evidently been recently stirred. And on a small table near the hearth stood a biscuit box and a small bottle of Dry Monopole. Alice would have preferred a sweeter wine, but was told that this was better for her. It was quite plain that either uncle had told someone the precise hour at which he would bring her to the room, or that someone had been watching, for the wine was still frothing in the glass, and therefore must have been poured out the very moment before she entered. What a terrible thought—could anyone have been watching her and have seen her nakedness? Her uncle could not have known at what hour he would take her there. She was for an instant paralyzed at the notion; but the next moment, accidentally catching sight of a bare breast and arm, it caused her a certain voluptuous thrill to think she had been seen by someone besides Sir Edward. As she slowly undressed herself, her uncle having gone off, shutting the door behind him, it struck her that she would herself, for her own satisfaction, have a peep at all she had been compelled to expose to him. Having resolved to so look at herself, she felt delightfully immoral. She stood before one of the large glasses with which her room was furnished, and after letting down her wealth of brown hair, she divested herself of all but her chemise. She stood staring at herself in the glass for a time before she allowed that last garment to slip off her shoulders and arms. She gazed at her naked charms in the glass. But only for an instant. She was then overcome by a flood of shame at her nakedness and, after fully realizing what she had been doing, she hurriedly averted her eyes and looked about for her nightdress. That she could not find; and she then recollected that the room she was in was not the same one she had previously used. She supposed they must have forgotten to bring her things. No; here was her dressing gown. She would put it on, and go to her old room for her nightdress.

She went to the door, and to her utter amazement, found that there was no handle inside! She was a prisoner. She looked about, but there was no other door anywhere to be seen.

"Very well," she said to herself; "I shall have to sleep in my chemise."

She was naked underneath, so taking off her dressing gown made her feel immodest. She didn't feel much better once she had her chemise on as it was cut very low in the neck and left her arms bare. She felt more immodest still when she remembered what she had undergone and was to undergo later in the morning.

Before she got into bed she looked about for the article ladies generally use. There was nothing of the kind in the room, and there was no bell. Then it struck her that the deprivation of her nightdress and of the utensil she now needed to make use of, must have been done deliberately by Sir Edward, and the idea that he had thought of such things so intimately connected with her person gave her a fresh delightful glow of sensuality as she plunged into the cold, silky, linen sheets. The necessary effort to retain her urine, the sense that she was being punished by being made to retain it, and the knowledge that her uncle knew all about it and so was punishing her, excited her to such an extent that she went to bed a very naughty girl indeed.

Circumstances had been such that she found it impossible, even though she closed her eyes, to fall asleep. Her mind was racing with the memories of what had happened to her just a short time ago. As she tossed and turned in her bed in this strange room, unfamiliar sensations again stabbed through her as her sore bottom scraped against the sheets with only the thin chemise to protect her. The feelings that overtook her were new and different, yet strangely similar to what she had experienced when Sir Edward had touched her so intimately. How could she sleep when so many thoughts rushed through her head. It was difficult to believe that she had gone down to dinner just a few short hours ago and, now, only a little while later, she felt as if her whole world had changed. She blushed just thinking about how Sir Edward had touched her. She had been shocked and embarrassed, yet, at the same time, the feelings he had inspired in her had been enjoyable.

In fact, now—as she thought of it—her bottom-hole squeezed, gripping a finger that was no longer there. But, strangely, she could still feel it. Never before had she passed one moment thinking of that embarrassingly personal area. But now, since her uncle's finger had delved inside, she could not help but think of it, imagining again how the tiny hole had expanded to accept his thumb, how it resisted only a little as he pushed in, and then closed again as his digit was removed; closed, but felt surprisingly open still, wanting, waiting to be filled again.

She started awakening, drifting back out of her thought-filled slumber. "I must stop these wicked thoughts," she chastised herself. "I must clear my mind and sleep."

But each time she closed her eyes she imagined her uncle's hands roaming once more over her naked limbs. Her breath caught in her throat as her thoughts drifted to the memory of his lips closing over her breasts. Her nipples swelled as she remembered how her heart leapt in her breast at the sensation. Her thoughts ran wild again and she imagined his tongue encircling her nipple, his teeth nibbling at the bud of flesh. She moaned at the thought and her nipples tautened at the memory. She was amazed that her body, so recently awakened to these sensations, could react so physically to the mere memory of what had taken place. Even as she wondered at this phenomenon, she felt a sudden gush of wetness between her thighs and an intense heat radiated upwards. She blushed at her body's betrayal, even though no one else knew of her shame. She thought of her recently deceased aunt and how she had raged at the sins associated with pleasures of the flesh. She shuddered to think what the prudish old lady would have thought of tonight's activities. Her thoughts didn't rest long, though, on that frigid woman. The reactions of her own body, the throbbing ache and the wetness between her thighs, soon brought her back to the present. Not caring about the propriety of her actions, Alice slid her hand under the sheets and tugged on her chemise until it rested above her belly. She worked her hand between her legs, mimicking the actions her uncle had performed earlier. She slipped one finger into her opening and began to work it in and out. The moisture she had felt earlier facilitated her movements and soon her finger was coated with the slick, warm stuff. Her heart was pounding in her breast and a moan escaped her before she closed her mouth to muffle the sound, wondering if anyone had heard her. Again, as had happened earlier, her legs stiffened and she felt a warmth spread quickly through her. Her back arched as her finger slid furiously over the slick folds of flesh. She tried jamming further into the still-tight opening and was rewarded with an intense shot of pleasure that was quickly followed by a sharp stab of pain. Her finger could go no further within, but exploring deeper did not seem necessary, since the feelings she had unleashed in her explorations were fast coming to an earth-shattering conclusion. She worked her hand even faster between her thighs, switching to a circular motion so that her finger came in contact with the entire circumference of her opening as it made its journey around. Her juices flowed more freely and her hand slipped during yet another joyous trip around. Suddenly, Alice was overcome and her body was wracked with tremors. Her back arched still more, until, exhausted she relaxed back into the soft bed and fell fast asleep.

Initiation

"Don't be afraid; a little bleeding does 'em good."
—*L'ASSOMMOIR*

Awakening next morning about nine o'clock, she caught herself wondering what the whipping would be like, and how it would be administered, and was filled with a delightful sense of shame when she recollected the part of her body that would receive the castigation and she imagined the exposure it would inevitably entail. The thought or anticipation of this did not disturb her much. She even contemplated with pleasure how her legs and thighs would be exposed. She also realized that more would be exposed, specifically that part of her which she could not name to herself. Even though she had been made quite free with that area as she lay in bed the night before, and suffered the examination by her uncle, she could not now, in the bright morning light, bring herself to name it, considering the word immodest; but she did trust that her uncle would not flog her very severely.

As she lay thus occupied with these thoughts there was a tap at the door. Since there was no handle on her side of the door, she sat up in the bed, covering herself as best she could with the sheet, and waited. Within moments, the door swung open and Janet entered carrying a cup of tea and some buttered bread.

"You have just an hour for dressing, miss," she announced, "for breakfast will be served at half-past ten in the blue sitting-room—the one which overlooks the park. Miss Maud will come to show you where it is."

"Thank you, Janet," said Alice, the sheet drawn close about her neck. "There are several things I shall want from my old room—linen and a dress. Will you please bring them?"

"I have the clothes you are to wear all ready, miss, and will bring them to you."

"What do you mean, Janet? I should like to choose my own dress."

Janet did not reply, grimly leaving the girl to find out for herself.

The maid returned presently with an armful of clothing, which she deposited on a sofa.

In the meantime Alice had jumped up and donned the dressing-gown. She then found it necessary to again look about for that piece of furniture which is a feature in most bedrooms. Alas, she could not find it anywhere. She did not know, however, how to broach the subject to Janet, and while she was wondering how to accomplish it, that amiable domestic had left the room. Alice had told her to return in about half an hour to do her hair, and the reply was that her hair was not to be done up that morning—a circumstance which, recalling what was before her, made her blush deeply. Then Janet departed, shutting the door and again leaving her trapped since the door only opened from the outside. Alice, resigning herself to the idea that her bodily needs would have to wait until she was on the way to breakfast, proceeded to wash. In the wall, close to the washstand, was a black marble knob, with the word 'Bath' inscribed upon it in gold letters. It was exactly what she wanted at the moment. Putting her hand upon it, she pressed slightly. To her surprise, a panel slid aside and revealed a marble-floored room surrounded by looking-glasses. There were several large slabs of cork for standing on, and a large bath of green Irish marble in the centre. Proceeding to it, she found that the same knob that had opened the room, filled the bath with water. She soon found the water to be not only perfumed, but deliciously softened. The champagne she had refreshed herself with the previous night and the tea she had just finished made her wish again that she could have got rid of the water she herself contained, but she could not make out how the water ran away or was emptied from the bath—so that little idea was knocked on the head. While bathing, she caught sight of herself continually in the glasses about her, and fell in love with her round, plump limbs and frame. She briefly wondered why she had never looked at herself before. She also noticed with indignation the red marks her uncle had made across her bottom with the cruel whip. She dried herself with the deliciously woolly and warmed towels, as she remembered that she had yet another flogging to undergo. She shuddered as she came to the conclusion that her disobedience deserved punishment; and felt naughty, as she confessed to herself that she really deserved to be whipped.

She had just made this determination when she found her obedience again put to the test. Proceeding to dress, she found that the clothes she had been provided were far worse than the dress she had refused to wear the evening before. They were unfit even for a girl of ten. The chemise was cut abominably low both behind and before, and the petticoats were quite short. So was the dress. And the petticoats were starched in such a way as to stand almost straight out. In other words, instead of hiding her limbs, they would display them. And there were no drawers. What was she to do? Sir Edward was rigid in his expectation of punctuality at meals. If she waited until Maud came she would be too late, and probably receive a worse flogging; besides, in all probability, Maud would only laugh at her again. So, a little indignantly, she dressed herself in the white silk stockings, which reached just halfway up her thighs, fastened them with the rose-coloured garters above her knee, put on the patent leather low-cut shoes, the black and yellow corset, and the white frock with a rose-coloured sash. She tied her hair with a ribbon of the same colour, and then looked at herself. She looked like a great, overgrown schoolgirl, but, she could not help owning to herself, a very lovely one. Her arms were bare, and the frock was so low that she noticed with horror that it would only just concealed her red teats from someone looking at her from straight in front. But if someone were to look straight down from her shoulder they would be quite visible. And the dress stopped at her knees; no amount of tugging or pulling could make it longer. And the petticoats made it stick out so. The only comfort was her hair, which did help to hide her naked back. Dressed at last, but feeling worse than naked, she sat down to wait for Maud. To her horror she noticed, by looking in a glass opposite her, that the dress stuck out to such an extent that not only could her leg be seen to the top of the stocking, but that the rosy flesh beyond was quite visible. After a trial or two she discovered that if she was not very careful how she sat, not only would the whole of both legs be displayed, but the juncture between her thighs would be clearly visible as well. She wondered how she could go about, and whether she would have to; and at last the costume so excited her passions that she was compelled to walk up and down, and became so naughty that she did not know how to contain herself or the water she had been unable to get rid of. While fidgeting about the room in this state of agitation, Maud entered, and immediately applauded.

"How perfectly lovely you are, Alice, with that blush-rose flush!" she exclaimed in the most disingenuous manner. "What a splendid bust! Good gracious! Do let me look at them. What lovely straight beautifully-shaped legs," she giggled, catching hold of the skirt of the frock. "Oh, do let me see!"

"Oh! don't, Maud! Don't!"

"Very well, dear. But you have not done up your hair. That won't do."

"Janet told me I was not to."

"Yes; I know. But that was a mistake. It hides too much."

"That is just why I like it down."

"And just why I do not, dear. You must let me roll it up for you so that your back and neck and shoulders may be fully shown. There; now you look a perfect darling. I thought I should find you quite cured of your anxiety to hide your charms. Do you not now wish you had taken my advice?"

"Yes."

"But," she went on, "it is not of much consequence; for if you had not rebelled, some other excuse would have been made for punishing you."

"Indeed?"

"Yes; and you deserved it, Alice."

As Alice had herself come to this conclusion, she only blushed.

Feeling her bare legs, she said, "Oh, Maud, do you know I have no drawers on; and that when I sit down my legs a-and-and everything else will show? Shall I have to go about in this dress? How long shall I have to wear it?"

"That depends upon how you take your punishment. Until you are given other garments to wear, you will certainly have to go about the house and grounds with it. I suppose you wish you had drawers on?"

"Indeed you may suppose so. Oh, Maud, however can I…"

"We must be going, Alice," Maud interrupted, "or we shall be late."

"Oh, Maud, do tell me, does uncle whip very hard?"

"I should have thought," and Maud's eyes flashed, "you could have answered that question yourself."

"Yes. He hurt me dreadfully with the riding-whip. Have you been birched?"

"Yes. I have."

"Was it very bad?"

"In a few hours you will be able to judge for yourself."

"Where did he birch you?"

"Here," said Maud, slyly putting her hand under Alice's petticoats upon her bare bottom.

"Oh, don't, Maud."

"Silly child, you should be obliged to me for the sensation. Do come along to breakfast."

"Oh, Maud, there is something I want to ask you; but how to do it I do not know. Perhaps," she said with a deep blush, "the best way is to say they have forgotten to put something in my room."

"I know very well what you mean, Alice. You mean you have no pot and you want to pee. All I can say is that I hope you do not want to very badly, because it is not at all likely that you will be allowed to do so until after your flogging. But, of course, you can ask uncle."

"However could I ask him?" replied Alice, aghast and pale at the notion and the prospect of what she would have to endure. "Does he know that this room is so lacking in the necessary furniture?" remembering her thought of the night.

"Yes. Of course he knows; and he does it to punish you and to help to make you feel naughty. Do you feel naughty, dear?" asked Maud, again putting her hand under Alice's petticoats. This time she did not allow Alice to brush her hand away, indeed, she began tickling the shocked girl's clitoris.

"Oh, don't! Maud. Oh, pray don't! Oh, you will make me wet myself if you do. Oh, can't you let me go to your room?"

"My dear girl, if I were to let you pee without permission I would probably be forbidden to do so myself more often than twice a day for a week or a fortnight. And I advise you to say nothing about it to uncle, for if he finds out that you want to very badly, he will probably make you wait another hour. It is a very favourite punishment of his."

"Why?"

"Oh, I don't know; except that it is a severe one. And it is awfully humiliating to a girl to have to ask; but it certainly makes one feel naughty."

"Yes; it does. Do you know, I was nearly doing it in the bath?"

"Lucky for you that you did not. It would certainly have been found out, and you would have caught it. But, Alice, why do you say 'doing it' instead of 'peeing' when you refer to it. When you do ask you will have to use plain language."

"Oh, Maud!"

"Yes; and most likely you will have to do it in front of uncle. One more note of warning: If he finds out you squirm about saying things and calling them by their names, he will make you say the most outrageous things, and write them also. Now hurry, there's the clock chiming half-past ten. Come along."

When they got to the blue room—on the way to which they passed, to Alice's intense consternation, several servants who gazed intently at her—they found Sir Edward there in a velvet coat and kilt. He greeted them cheerily. The view across the park, in the glades of which the fallow deer could be seen grazing, was lovely; the sunshine was flooding the room, and the soft, warm summer air carried the perfume of the flowers in through the wide-open windows from the beds below. Alice was so struck by the view that for a moment she forgot to notice how her uncle was gazing at her. She forgot how she was dressed until she felt the air on her legs, and it provoked a consciousness at which she blushed.

"How do you like your frock, my dear? It becomes you admirably." "Does it, uncle?" Looking coyly at him. "I am glad you like it."

"I am glad to see you are a sensible girl after all. We shall make something of you."

"How long am I to wear it, uncle?"

"For a week."

"For a fortnight," corrected Maud, maliciously. "She is to be mistress next week."

Maud knew very well how difficult it would be to give orders to the staff dressed like that. She revelled in the notion of getting Alice soundly punished.

Sir Edward noticed with a gleam of amusement how fidgety Alice became towards the end of the meal, and Maud smiled gently to herself. Alice thought that after breakfast she would have a chance to relieve herself. She was disappointed. Sir Edward then said, in a severe tone: "I think, Miss Alice, we have a little business to settle together. Your disobedience cannot be overlooked. You must come with me. Your short skirts will punish your prudishness, but the birch is the best corrector of a disobedient girl's bottom." She grew quite pale, and trembled all over, both with fright and at being spoken to so before Maud, who, reposing calmly in her chair, was steadily gazing at her.

She got up. When her uncle had finished speaking, he came up to her and took hold of her left ear with his right hand, and saying, "Come along, miss, to be flogged," he marched her off to the yellow room.

There, to her consternation, she saw straps and pillows on the oak table. In a perfect fright, she said: "Oh, pray do not strap me up, uncle; pray do not. I will submit."

"Undress yourself," he said, having closed the door; "leave on your stockings only."

"Oh, uncle!"

"You had better obey, miss, or you shall have a double dose. Take off your frock this instant."

"Now your petticoat bodice."

"Now your petticoats. Now your corset and chemise. Now, my proud young beauty, how do you feel?"

He had not seen her to such advantage the evening before. She had kept her long dress on the whole time, and while punishing her he had only uncovered a small portion of her legs. It is true she afterwards had been made to take off her drawers; but the skirt and petticoats gathered about her hips had still concealed much. Now she was naked from the crown of her head to her rose-coloured garters. Burning with shame, she put her hands up to her face, and remained standing and silent, while Sir Edward feasted his eyes upon the contemplation of every beautiful curve of the lovely little head poised so beautifully upon a perfect throat; of the dimpled back and beautifully rounded shoulders; of the arms; of the breasts and hips and thighs. She was the most lovely girl he had seen, he said to himself, and then, seating himself, he added aloud, "Come here, miss. Kneel down: there, between my knees; clasp your hands, and say after me: Uncle, I have been"

"Uncle, I have been"

"A naughty, disobedient girl,"

"A n-naughty, disobedient girl,"

"And deserve to be soundly birched."

"And deserve to be s-sound-soundly birched."

"Please, therefore,"

"Please, therefore,"

"Strap me down"

"Oh, no! Oh, no! Oh, please don't strap me down!"

"Say what I tell you at once, miss, or it will be worse for you."

"Strap me down"

"To the table,"

"Oh! oh! oh! To the table,"

"With my legs well apart,"

"Oh, dear! I can't. With—with—I can't. With my—oh, uncle!"

"An extra half-dozen for this."

"Oh, uncle!"

"Say at once: With my legs well apart."

"With my—my oh!—legs" she struggled with the words shuddering deliciously and blushed bewilderingly, "well apart,"

"And give me"

"And give me"

"Please,"

"Please,"

"A dozen and a half"

"Oh, uncle! Please, not so much!" she cried, recollecting the baker's dozen with the riding-whip.

"You will have more if you do not say it at once."

"A dozen and a half"

"On my bare bottom."

"Oh! that!—my—I can never say—"

"You must"

"My bare?"

"You had better say it. Stop; I will improve it. You must say: On my girl's bare bottom."

"Oh, uncle!" she said, looking at him; and seeing his eyes doting upon her and devouring her beauty, and the lust and fire in them, she immediately turned hers away.

"Now, Alice, 'On my girl's bare bottom.'"

"On my girl's b-bare b-bottom."

He moved as he said this, and Alice noticed that he adjusted something under his kilt.

"Well laid on."

"Well laid on."

"Yes; I will, my dear. I will warm your bottom for you as well as any girl ever had her bottom warmed. I will set it on fire for you. You will curse the moment you were disobedient. I will cure you of disobedience and all your silly nonsense. Come along to

the table. There, stand at that end"—Alice began to sob—"put the
cushion before you, so. Now lie over it, right down on the table
No resistance."

As he fixed the strap round her shoulders she made a slight
attempt at remonstrance. The strap went round her and the table
and once it was buckled she could not, of course, get up. He then
buckled on two wristlets, and with two other straps fastened her
wrists to the right and left legs of the table; then another broad
strap was put round the table and the small of her back. This was
pretty tight, as were also those that fastened her at the knees
and ankles. Her legs were wide apart, fixed to the legs of the
table. She was spread-eagled, and her bottom, the tender skin
between its cheeks, her cunt, and her legs were most completely
exposed.

"Now, my dear, you will remain in that position half an hour
and contemplate your offenses, and then you shall have as sound
a flogging as I have ever given a girl."

"Oh, uncle, before you flog me, do let me do something. Maud
told me I should have to tell you, but I do not know how to. I will
come back directly and be strapped down again if you will only
let me. And, oh! please do not leave me in this dreadful position
for half an hour."

"You must say what it is that you want."

"Oh, uncle"—feeling it was all or nothing she whispered, "do
let me go and pee before I am flogged. I want to, oh, so dreadfully.
I have not been able to all the morning, nor all night."

"So you want to very dreadfully, do you, miss?" and going up
to her he put his hand between her legs from behind, and severely
tickled the opening through which the stream was burning to rush.
It was all that Alice could do to retain it.

"Oh, don't! Oh! If you do I shall wet myself. I shall not be able
to help it. Oh, uncle, pray, pray don't! Oh, pray let me go!"

"No, miss, I certainly shall not. It is a part of your punishment. There was an unnatural coldness about these parts of yours
which this will help to warm up. Have you not felt more naughty
since you have had all that hot water inside you?"

"And you are beginning to see how ridiculous prudishness is.

Now, just you think about your conduct and your disobedience until I return to whip you, and remember you owe your present position to those shameful attributes."

Saying this, Sir Edward left the room. Poor Alice, left to herself, all naked save for her stockings; her arms stretched out above her head and tightly strapped; her legs divided and fastened wide apart; the most secret portions of her frame made the most conspicuous in order that they might be punished by a man—did feel her position acutely. She considered it and felt it to be most shameful. Her cheeks burned with a hot, red glow. But all concealment was absolutely impossible; the haughty beauty felt herself prostrate before and at the mercy of her master, and experienced again an exquisite sensual thrill at the thought that she really deserved to have her bottom whipped by her uncle.

Presently Maud came into the room in a low-necked dress, with a large bouquet.

"Well, Alice," she said, "I hope you enjoy your position and the prospect before you."

"Oh, Maud; go away. I can't bear you to see me in this position. I won't be punished before you."

"Silly goose! Young ladies strapped down naked, and stretched out spread-eagle for punishment, are not entitled to say shall or shan't. What a lovely skin and back, Alice. Alas! before long that pretty, plump, white bottom will present a very altered appearance. How many are you to have?"

"I was made to ask for a dozen and a half, well laid on."

"And you may depend upon it, you will have them, my dear, most mercilessly laid on," Maud cooed, stroking her legs and thighs, which caused Alice to catch her breath and shrink away from the pleasure Maud's hand gave her. Maud asked her whether she had tried to induce her uncle to let her go somewhere.

"Yes," replied Alice; "I did. But he would not."

"And I suppose you want to very badly," went on Maud, maliciously placing her fingers on the very spot.

"Yes; I do. Oh, don't, Maud, or you'll make me…"

"Now mind, Alice, whatever you do, hold out till your birching is over. If you do not I warn you that you will catch it."

"I think it is a very, very cruel, horrid punishment," said Alice whimpering.

"It is severe, I know, and it is far better not to be prudish than to incur it. But here comes uncle."

"Now, you bold, disobedient girl, I hope you feel ashamed of yourself," said Sir Edward, entering the room and shutting the door. "Maud will witness your punishment as a warning to her of what she will receive if she is disobedient."

Going up to the wardrobe, he selected three well-pickled birches which had evidently never been used, for there were numbers of buds on them. They were elastic and well spread, and made a most ominous switching sound as, one by one, Sir Edward switched them through the air. Alice shuddered and Maud's eyes gleamed.

"Oh, pray, pray, uncle, do not be very severe. Remember it is almost my first whipping. It is awful!"

"Maud had changed the dress she had worn at breakfast and, as already mentioned, now had on one cut very low in the body; her arms were bare and her skirts short. Between her breasts was placed a bouquet of roses.

"Hold these," said Sir Edward, giving her the rods.

He then put his left arm round Alice, and said: "Now, you saucy, disobedient miss, your bottom will expiate your offenses, and by way of preface"—smack, smack with his right hand, smack, smack, smack. "Ah, it is already becoming a little rosy."

"Oh, uncle! Oh, how you hurt! Oh, how your hand stings! Oh! oh! oh!"

"Yes. A bold girl's bottom must be well stung. It teaches her obedience and submission"—smack! "what a lovely, soft bottom!"— smack, smack, smack.

Maud's eyes gleamed and her face flushed, as Alice, wriggling about as much as the straps allowed, cried softly to herself. When her uncle had warmed her sufficiently, he removed his arm and moved about two feet away from the girl, whose confusion at the invasion of her charms by the rough hand of a man increased her loveliness tenfold. Maud held one birch in her right hand. She, too, looked divine. Her dark eyes flashing, her lovely bosom heaving, she handed it, retaining the other two in her left hand, to her uncle. Alice could not see that as she gave him the birch, as soon as her hand was free she slipped it under her uncle's kilt from the back, and the instant increase of his passion and excitement left no doubt as to the use she was making of it. Sir Edward stood at the left side of his refractory ward. He drew the birch, lecturing her as he did so, three or four times upwards and downwards from back to front and from front to back between the cheeks of the girl's bottom, producing a voluptuous movement of the lovely thighs and little exclamations that he found delightful.

"Oh! oh! oh! don't do that! Oh! oh! how dreadful! Oh, please, uncle!" she shrieked, trying to turn round, which, of course, the straps prevented. He next proceeded to birch her gently all over, the strokes increasing in vigour, but being always confined to the bottom.

"Oh, uncle, you hurt! Oh! how the horrid thing stings! Oh! it is worse than your hand! Oh! stop! Have I not had enough?"

"We will begin now, miss," said he, having given her a cut severe enough to provoke a slight cry of real pain; "and Maud will count."

Lifting up the rod at right angles to the table on which she was bound down, he brought it down with a tremendous swish through the air across the upper parts of her hips.

"One," said the mellow voice of Maud—her right hand and a portion of her arm hidden under her uncle's kilt, the movements of its muscles under the delicate skin and the wriggles of the Baronet showing that Maud had hold of and was kneading a sensitive portion of his frame. The bottom grew crimson where the stroke had fallen, and the culprit emitted a yell and gasped for breath. With the regularity of a steam hammer, he again raised the rod well above his shoulder, and again making it whistle through the air, he gave her another very severe stroke.

"Two," said Maud quietly.

A shriek. "Oh! stop! Oh! stop! Oh! stop!"

Swish. "three," calmly observed Maud.

"Oh! you will kill me. Oh! I can't—I can't—"

Swish. "Four, uncle."

"Oh, ah! Oh, I can't bear it! Oh, I will be good! Oh, Maud, ask him to stop."

Swish. "Five."

Maud had given her uncle an extra pull when Alice had appealed to her, and this stroke was harder in consequence. Spots of blood began to appear where the ends of the birch and its buds fell, especially on the outside of the thigh. The yell which followed number five was more piercing, and choking sobs ensued; but Sir Edward, merely observing that she would run a very good chance of extra punishment if she made so much noise, without heeding her tears or contortions or choking, mercilessly and relentlessly gave her six, seven, eight, and nine, each being counted by Maud's clear gentle voice.

"Now, miss, you've had half of your punishment..."

"Half! Oh! oh! oh! I can't bear more! Oh, I can't bear more! Oh, let me off! You will kill me! Oh, let me off! I will—I will I will indeed be good."

"I suppose you begin to regret your disobedience."

"Oh, don't punish me any more," cried the girl, wriggling and struggling to get free—of course ineffectually, but looking perfectly lovely in her pain.

"Yes! You must receive the whole number. It is not enough to promise to obey now; you should have thought of this before. You are now having your bottom punished, not only to make you better in the future, but for your past offenses."

And Sir Edward walked round to the right side of his niece, and there, in the same place, but from right to left, gave her three sharp cuts. Alice yelled and screamed and roared and rolled about as much as she possibly could, perfectly reckless as to what she showed.

The next three were given lengthwise between her legs. Her bottom being well up, and the legs well apart, the strokes fell upon the tender skin between them, and the long, lithe ends of the rod curled round her cunt, causing her a great deal of pain.

"There is nothing like a good birching for a girl." Swish.

"One," said Maud, moving voluptuously. "Oh! oh! yah! Oh! my bottom! Oh! my legs! Oh! how it hurts! Oh! oh! oh!"

"They are all the better for the pain!" Swish.

"Two," said Maud.

"Oh! oh! oh! Oh, don't strike me there!" as the birch curled round her cunt.

"And the exposure. I do not think you will disobey." Swish.

"Three," said Maud, apparently beside herself, her eyes swimming.

"Oh! oh! oh! yah! Oh! I shall die! I shall faint! Oh! dear uncle! I will—please forgive me I will never disobey. I will do anything—anything—ANYTHING!"

"I daresay you will, miss; but I shall not let you off"—swish—"there's another for your cunt."

"Four," said Maud.

"Oh! Oh! not there! Oh! I am beside myself! I shall go mad! I shall die or go mad!"

"You will not do anything of the sort, and you must bear your punishment." Swish.

"Five," counted Maud.

The cries gradually lessened, and the culprit seemed to become entranced, whereupon the uncle, at whom Maud looked significantly, directed the single remaining stroke to the insides of her thighs, leaving the palpitating red rose between them free from further blows, for the present.

Alice's moans were then succeeded by piercing shrieks, but her uncle, perfectly deaf to them, continued the flogging. When the eighteenth stroke, given lengthwise, had been completed, Sir Edward put down the birch he had used and took a second from Maud.

Seeing this, Alice earnestly implored him to let her go, since the promised dozen and a half strokes had already been administered.

For reply, he again took up his station at her left side, saying: "No, miss; I shall certainly not unstrap you; you have been far too naughty. I will punish you, and your lovely legs and bottom, to the fullest extent. I'll teach you to be good, you bold hussy! I'll give you a lesson you won't forget in a hurry." He gave her nine more blows; but this time, instead of being administered on the upper part of her bottom, perpendicularly, they were given almost horizontally on its lower part, where it joins the thigh. Alice's renewed shrieks were to no avail. In her agony she lifted up her head, her shoulders being fastened down with the strap, and prayed her uncle, in the name of heaven, to spare her. But the relentless rod still continued to cut into her tender flesh, as she was told she would receive no mercy.

The girl's head dropped again. "No mercy," she whispered; "no, nor justice either, nor even fair play. Indeed, why pretend at all?"

Maud's even voice continued to number the strokes, and Maud herself seemed aflame, and the sight of the agony her uncle was inflicting seemed to excite her sensuality in an extraordinary degree. Her lips were moist; her eyes swam; the eyelids drooped; and all the indications of a very lovesick girl appeared in her. The bleeding bottom, the tightly strapped limbs, the piercing cries, and the relentlessly inflicted punishment excited her strongest passions, She could have torn Alice limb from limb; and she encouraged her uncle, by rolling his balls and pulling and squeezing his prick, to continue the punishment in the severest manner.

She gloated over the numbers as she called them out.

Sir Edward, too, seemed beside himself. His eyes were as two flames as he watched every motion of Alice's body; gloated upon all she displayed. He could have made his teeth meet in her delicate flesh, which he lacerated with the rod yet more severely as his organ, already excited to an enormous size, was still further enlarged by Maud's hand.

At length he judged that, Alice's lower bottom having been striped from right to left as well as from left to right, there remained but nine last lengthwise strokes to be given.

For these, Sir Edward took the third birch from Maud, who by this time was standing with her legs wide apart, uttering little sounds and breathing little sighs of almost uncontrollable desire.

The unhappy culprit's yells had somewhat lessened, for shock had relieved pain; it had been so severe that her sensitiveness to it had much diminished. But now, feeling the rod curling round her cunt, which, being pulled open, was more exposed than ever, she yelled in a perfectly delirious manner.

After some few of these strokes had been given, her uncle

asking her whether he was a wretch and a monster, as she had called him last night, she replied with vehement denials:

"No! oh, no! oh! oh! oh! oh, no! Not a monster! Not a wretch! My own dear uncle, whom I love! Oh! oh! oh! My bottom burns! Oh! oh! It is on fire!"

"Will you be a good, obedient girl miss?"

"Yes! Yes! Yes! Oh! indeed—"

"And thank me for whipping you?"

"Yes; indeed I do."

"Whip well in, uncle," said Maud quietly, in her rich voice.

And he did so. Alice, thus betrayed, shrieked; flooded the floor with urine, and fainted!

Maud, beside herself, threw herself backwards on the long and broad divan, her breasts jiggling, her legs— unhampered by drawers—thrown wide open. Sir Edward, throwing down the birch, fell upon her with a fury. He inserted his enormous appurtenance into her burning cunt, sighing as the lengthy tool was eagerly accepted and drawn deep within the panting girl. Once he had made his entrance, he began fucking her so violently that she almost fainted from delight. As Sir Edward worked himself against her body, Maud looked kindly upon the still unconscious Alice, knowing that the punishment she had undergone was responsible for the pleasure Maud herself was now receiving. Maud sighed delightedly and wrapped her long legs around Sir Edward's back, allowing him to penetrate still deeper within her heaving body. After the long pleasurable minutes spent whipping his beautiful niece, Sir Edward could not long contain himself. His body was wracked with shudders as he grabbed Maud's hips and slammed into her even more furiously. They both exploded and collapsed in a heap on the couch.

When Alice came round, Sir Edward rose from Maud's breast, and then Maud said, in slightly breathless tones:

"Uncle, I told Alice yesterday evening, when she kept me so long before I could succeed in tying her hands, that I would take care it secured her an extra half-dozen."

"Oh, uncle! I beg Maud's pardon. Oh! after all I have gone through, let me off that half-dozen. Oh, dear Maud! do ask uncle to let me off. Oh, do! If I am birched any more I shall go mad! I shall—I shall indeed!"

Maud, still lying backwards on the couch, supported by a big, square pillow, said nothing. Her hands were clasped behind her head. But Sir Edward said, "No miss; you can never be let off! You must have the half-dozen. It will be a lesson to you." And taking up the birch, he gave her six severe strokes, distributed evenly all over her bottom.

As they were being administered, Maud's left hand stole down to her waist and found its way between her legs.

While Alice was smothering her sobs and cries after her last half-dozen, Sir Edward again threw himself upon Maud and enjoyed her.

About ten minutes or a quarter of an hour later he proceeded to unstrap Alice.

She could not stand without Maud's help. The cushion and carpet were soaked with her urine.

"You will tomorrow have a dozen on the trapeze, miss, for disgracing yourself in this beastly manner; you will write out fifty times, 'I peed like a mare before my uncle.' And for the next fortnight you will only pee twice every twenty-four hours. And now come and kiss the rod and say: 'Thank you, my dear uncle, for the flogging you have given me.'"

Quite docilely she knelt down before him, kissed the rod he held to her lips, and repeated the words.

"Will you be a good, obedient girl in future?"

"Yes, dear uncle; indeed I will!"

"That's a good thing. There is, you see, nothing like a good, sound flogging for a girl. Were the rod more in use how very much better women we should have. Now go with Maud and get some refreshment. I have various engagements, and shall not be in 'till dinner. After lunch you had better have a sleep." And so saying, he packed the two girls off to Alice's room, shut the door to the yellow room, and ringing for a footman, gave orders that the estate steward and horses should be in attendance at the front door in half an hour.

Maud and Alice went to the latter's new room. By Maud's advice,

Alice, who was so sore that she could scarcely move, got into bed and had some strong broth and Burgundy, and presently fell asleep. Maud spent her afternoon at an open window reclining in a lounge chair, pretending to read a novel, but in reality revelling in the reminiscences of the morning and meditating upon its delights—and wondering when she would get whipped next herself. The afternoon passed in this manner until she was disturbed by some afternoon visitors.

School Days In Paris

My dearest Ethel,

I told you in my last letter that I would describe the second meeting of our Lesbian Club, but now I come to think of it, it was very little more than a repetition of the first, with the exception of the fact that being no longer the innocent that I was on the first occasion, I was better qualified to play my part as a giver, as well as a receiver, of pleasure. The third meeting, however, was of a very different kind, and well merits a description, which I will now endeavor to give you.

The Sunday started well, for being a very fine day, we had taken exceptional care with our church costumes, which, as you may well believe, caused somewhat of a sensation during the service, to Madame's great delight.

When we went to our rooms to dress for dinner, we found that Madame's feeling of satisfaction had shown itself in placing a lovely bouquet of flowers in each of our rooms; and when we reached the dining room, duly arrayed in our strongly scented bouquets, we found that a still further surprise was waiting for us, for Madame had ordered up a plentiful supply of champagne—a luxury hitherto almost unheard-of in the establishment!

Thanks to the fact that Madame plied us, as well as herself, liberally with this fascinating beverage, we were all very lively by the time dinner was ended; and I was therefore a good deal surprised when, immediately after dinner, Madame proposed that we should all, herself included, go at once to bed. On Sunday nights, I must tell you, we are let off everything in the way of "night toilette," which was the reason why the Lesbian Club chose that night for meetings.

When I got to my room I quickly undressed, but to my surprise the other girls did not arrive for nearly half an hour. Throwing off their hastily put on dressing gowns, they explained that the reason for their delay was that they were waiting to give Madame time to get to bed, so that she might not come and disturb us. They were all crowding round in a naked group, admiring my figure, etc., when to my horror, in walked Madame, wearing a lovely pink and white opera cloak instead of a dressing gown, and bearing in her hand a birch rod.

To my surprise the other girls, on seeing her, did not seem in the least astonished or dismayed, but took her arrival quite as a matter of course.

"What is the meaning of this, girls?" she asked in a severe voice. "Not only do I find you in Blanche's room, but you are all huddled together naked, which is most indecent."

Immediately the girls ran to the bed and bent over it, with their backs to Madame, motioning to me to do the same.

She then applied the birch to the plump cheeks and thighs of each of us in turn, but it was done so gently that, without hurting in the least, it made the blood run toward our Pussies, making us feel awfully hot and naughty. When we were all writhing, not with pain but with randiness and lust, she put down the birch, saying "There, that will do for the present."

Saying this, she threw off her opera cloak and disclosed a costume which amazed me more than anything in the world. It consisted of openworked silk tights of a deep violet hue, the openwork being so wickedly arranged as to leave her Pussy, with its fringe of flame-colored hair, completely exposed to view. Above the tights she wore a tiny evening-corset of white satin, above which her large, rounded breasts stood out firm and high like twin hills of snow. A pair of high-heeled white satin shoes and white satin garters just above the knee completed the costume, except for her hands and arms, which I now for the first time perceived were delicately gloved in white kid, sewn with broad violet stitching at the back to match the tights.

Nothing could have displayed her magnificent figure to better advantage, and I found it hard indeed to realize that this glorious-looking Angel of Vice, with the gleam of lust fired by champagne in her eye, was really our staid schoolmistress, whom I had looked upon as a model of propriety and virtue!

From a pocket inside the opera cloak, one of the girls produced a large morocco case, which, with smiling permission from Madame, she proceeded to open. The contents consisted of three rods of ivory of various sizes, rounded at one end, while to the other end were attached two India-rubber balls, like small tennis balls.

I was at a loss to imagine what these could possibly be, when my friend Daniela exclaimed, "Oh, Madame, you have brought the dildos! How charming of you!"

At this you may be sure I pricked up my ears, for Daniela had several times explained to me the nature of a dildo, which is nothing more nor less than an artificial model of a man's Prick.

The smallest was only about three inches long, not much thicker than my forefinger, and had a much sharper point than the others. This I gathered was nicknamed The Wee One, for it was evidently not the first time the girls had seen and handled these treasures.

The next one, known as The Schoolboy, was about half as large again, being covered all along its length with obscene carvings in low relief, the object of which was to cause a greater amount of tickling than a smooth surface would have done.

The third was The Captain, which was quite twice as long and more than twice as thick as The Wee One, being covered like the last with carvings, while the Balls were of a considerably larger size.

After a short consultation with Madame, Daniela darted off to the latter's bedroom, whence she re-turned bearing a lighted Etna, which evidently contained some steaming liquid.

Under her arm she carried another leather case, this time looking like a large pistol case, at the sight of which Madame pretended to be much displeased; but she nevertheless opened it and displayed its contents to all of us, the evident astonishment of the girls clearly showing that this, at any rate, was something they had never seen before.

It was a dildo made exactly like The Captain, but of such gigantic proportions that it positively took our breath away. It was at least ten inches long, and quite as thick as my wrist, the Balls being about the size of cricket balls.

"Surely, Madame," said one of the girls, "no one in the world has a Cunt large enough to admit that!"

It gave me rather a shock of surprise to hear her use such a naughty word as Cunt in speaking to Madame, but I soon found out that the latter could be the smuttiest of us all, when she felt inclined, as it was evident she did on the present occasion; in fact she only smiled at the question and said:

"It comes from South America, where the women are accustomed to being poked by Latin types who, as I daresay you know, have far bigger Pricks than European men."

"But surely no European girl could use it!"

"That all depends on the way in which it is done," Madame answered. "Of course, if a girl were to thrust this into her Cunny in cold blood, she would simply fail to get it in, in the first place, and in the second she would about kill herself if she succeeded. But if the Cunt had previously been excited, first of all by Lesbian kisses, and then by an ordinary dildo, you would find, I think, that, with the help of some love-oil and a good deal of pressure, The Giant, as I have named it, would not only go in, but would cause the most exquisite pleasure to the Pussy, in which it would undoubtedly be a most amazingly tight fit!"

While she was saying this, Daniela had taken out The Schoolboy, and had filled the balls with the hot liquid, which, I gathered, was a mixture of milk and white liquor.

I had forgotten to tell you that each of the dildos had straps attached to them for the purpose of fastening them round a female's body, so as to make her resemble a man. The Wee One was fastened to one girl, while Daniela made herself into a pretty boy by means of The Schoolboy.

"Now, Blanche," said Madame, approaching me, "as we do not allow virgins in this society, we are going to take your maiden-head."

I was laid on the bed, my Titties were kissed as before by two of the girls, while Madame herself, putting her head between my legs, began, with a far more expert tongue than Daniela's, to tickle my Pussy. Her tongue several times touched my membrane of virginity, which was to be pierced by The Wee One.

She parted my hot, swollen love-lips and dipped her tongue into the Valley of Virginity, licking my hymen and the rim of my Cunthole, as if to fully lubricate me for the kill.

Her tongue found my clit, as well, and she lingered there for quite some time to generate a generous amount of sex heat.

When I was wet and once my hips were wiggling and gyrating against her face, Madame gently rose, held her palms on either side of my inner thigh, and motioned for the senior who wielded The Wee One to bring it to the entrance of my Cunt.

I felt the cool, tiny dildo head at my opening, yet my pleasure focus moved to my inner thigh, where Madame played my flesh like a piano.

The heat of sexual excitement swelled in my groin until I was quite beyond myself with pleasure; that's when Madame nodded to the girl holding the dildo by my Cunt. She pushed it in, hold-ing it with her hand and twisted it about in such a way that it felt like a man fucking me. This was all causing me an exquisite sense of pleasure, which made me clasp her toward me with all my force, and in a moment I felt a thrill, half of pleasure and half of pain, and I knew that my virginity had gone.

As soon as Madame perceived this she signaled to The Wee One girl to come out of me so as to make room for Daniela, who, with the larger dildo strapped onto her as if she were a man, penetrated into regions which were now entered for the first time; she gave me the liveliest pleasure, and caused me to come with a feeling of exquisite enjoyment, different from the enjoyment I had felt when the girls had kissed me there. I now experienced for the first time something that rocked my insides like a volcano—I was coming. When she saw that the supreme moment had arrived, Daniela gripped the Balls between her legs, and squeezing them again and again, squirted the hot liquid up through the tube in the center of the dildo, so as to produce exactly the same effect inside my Cunt as if a man's sperm were being poured into me.

Madame was delighted to see how much I enjoyed the experience, and assured me that, for her part, she much preferred a dildo to a man, because one can make the dildo spend when one chooses, whereas the man has to come when he can.

The girls were now all begging Madame to let them try if they could get The Giant into her in the way she had explained, and, though she at first resisted, she soon took my place on the bed, where she lay with her legs apart, still in her fancy costume, panting with the anticipation of the voluptuous experience she was about to undergo.

Two of the girls started at once to suck her Titties, while I began with tongue and finger to tickle her delicious Cunt, and very soon had the satisfaction of seeing that we were causing her to thrill with delighted sensuality.

Daniela and another girl were meanwhile filling the immense Balls of The Giant with liquid, and getting The Captain ready to be used first.

When I had started Madame successfully upon her voyage of pleasure, I motioned to The Captain girl, who at once got on top of her, and, inserting the dildo, proceeded to work it up and down as knowingly and as quickly as if she had been a man.

Meanwhile, I was aiding Daniela to gird on The Giant, with the result that, when it was adjusted, she looked like a delicate boy endowed by nature with the most monstrous Prick that ever was seen. I smothered the point in love-oil, and we then stood and waited by the bed. Very soon it was evident from Madame's lascivious movements that The Captain was rapidly conducting her to the supreme pleasure of coming, and a few moments later, we saw that The Captain, as he slid in and out of her Pussy, was covered with a thick frothy moisture, showing that the flow of sperm had begun. This was evidently the moment for The Giant, and as The Captain slipped out, I instantly inserted my fingers, so that the sensation of pleasure might not slacken for a moment.

With wonderful speed and adroitness, Daniela took the place vacated by the other girl, and while I held the lips of the Cunt as wide apart as ever I could with my two hands, Daniela pushed and shoved with all her force, until to our great satisfaction, it began to move inward slowly. Then followed the most extraordinary scene that can possibly be conceived. Madame, having already reached the highest pitch of enjoyment to which she had ever attained, could scarcely believe that there was still greater delight yet to come; but as Daniela pushed The Giant steadily onward, at the same time working it gently in and out in the proper manner, the distention and irritation of the Cunt was so extreme and the delightful feeling of tickling so immensely in excess of anything she had ever felt before, that her body rocked and swayed about in a perfect agony of enjoyment, and her voluptuous movements caused us onlookers to feel as randy as possible. As The Giant went steadily farther in, Daniela quickened the movement, and finally, pushing it right home, she squeezed the balls repeatedly, sending into her very soul a flow both far hotter and far more plentiful than any man's Prick could possibly have produced. As Daniela withdrew the dildo from Madame's palpitating Pussy, our schoolmistress swooned away in a dead faint, utterly exhausted by the immensely prolonged and artificially exaggerated scene of enjoyment, of which she had been the delighted heroine.

On seeing this, one of the girls ran downstairs and soon returned with some champagne, which speedily revived her, and she immediately began to give us an account of the exquisite sensations she had been experiencing. She assured us that from the moment The Giant began to make its way in, the pleasure was absolutely heavenly, causing her to come twice before the final injection of the fluid, but that at times the feeling became so strong as to be scarcely bearable.

This recital, in addition to the voluptuous scene we had witnessed, aroused our sensuality to a high pitch of expectation; and Madame herself, having recharged The Captain with liquid and having fastened it on, was very soon on top of Daniela, vigorously poking her, while I did the same to one of the other girls with The Schoolboy; and, as the other three girls were doing the Trio of the Graces with mutually tickling fingers, the goddess of sensuality was soon reigning supreme over our naked bodies.

When I was at last left alone in bed, I could not get to sleep for a long time, owing to the heated and excited state of my brain and blood, and as I lay awake, I could not help feeling amazed at the part our dignified schoolmistress had taken in the proceedings. Later on, however, I found that she had long been an ardent devotee of Lesbianism.

There, my dear Ethel, you have a full and true account of our third meeting, and if it does not make your hair stand on end, fringe and all, I shall be surprised! I wonder, by the way, if my earlier letters have made you sufficiently curious to induce you to try the experiment of tickling your own Pussy? If so, I have no doubt you have discovered the little button, the inciting and tickling of which causes such exquisite pleasure. At the same time I can tell you from experience that it is not half so nice to do it to oneself as to get someone else to do it, and I am told that to have it done by a nice man is the most voluptuous thing of all.

Good-bye, dearest, for the present, and I hope you will not be shocked by this awfully naughty letter from

Your ever-loving
Blanche

My dearest Ethel,

I am afraid this is going to be rather a long letter, but I hope you will nevertheless find it both instructive and amusing!

The morning after the scene related in my last letter, I was not very much surprised to receive a message from Madame when the maid came to call me, saying that, as she was rather tired, we need none of us get up till our twelve o'clock brunch.

When therefore I had finished my chocolate and tea sandwiches, I nestled down once more into the warm bedclothes to enjoy myself for at least two hours.

Just as I had done so the door opened, and in came a girl named Edith—the one who is a family friend of the Countess de B——, whom I have already mentioned in connection with the book Le Demi-monde des Jeunes Filles. As a general rule, she is very quiet and demure, but I had heard from the other girls that, when you get her alone, she is very smutty and wicked, so that I was delighted when she said she had come to have a chat. She began by taking off her chemise de nuit, making me do the same, and we then lay together in the warm bed, her naked body cuddled close against mine, while the strong pressure of our Pussies against one another, with a little aid from her slender fingers, soon put us in a good condition for naughty conversation!

She began asking me if I knew why it was that girls are taught to pay so much attention to their dress and appearance?

I told her I had never thought about the subject; and she then told me that it is all done simply to arouse the sensuality of the male sex. A pretty face, and even a voluptuous figure, so she assured me, do not appeal successfully to a man's instinct of vice unless they are accompanied by the accessories of fashionable luxury, such as smart dresses, hats, boots, gloves, etc.

Above all, she said, our evening dress, with its display of naked breasts, arms and shoulders, the hair elaborately dressed, the hands delicately gloved, and our bodies breathing out the scent of lascivious perfumes, has such a powerful effect upon the other sex that often, especially in dancing, when their hands are clasping the tightly corseted waist, and their eyes and nostrils are almost touching our nude and panting busts, a girl can feel her partner's Prick forcing out his trousers to such an extent as to make its pressure distinctly felt against her leg!

When I asked her how she found this out, she told me that the Countess, an old family friend, has two sons, who are now twenty-three and twenty-four—a few years older than herself—and as the Countess since the untimely death of her own parents has lived nearby, these two males, have come to speak to her of their vices without any restraint. And there have been times when the three have explored together sexually.

She went on to tell me that, whereas in England young men are supposed by their parents to be pious, and have therefore to do their poking with tarts on the sly, in France the parents recognize the necessity of a young man having a mistress of his own, to keep him from running after the cocottes who throng the streets and music-halls, and from whom he might catch some disease. In fact, men were encouraged to bed servants of the house.

When these young men—the Countess's sons— were about eighteen and nineteen, she declared that one morning, when they were together in the bathroom drying themselves after their morning tub, the Countess's maid, who was then only twenty-six and looked about ten years younger, should become mistress to the two young men. The Countess declared this after the maid one day calmly walked in upon them, wearing nothing but a transparent chemise de nuit, which, moreover, was unfastened all down the front in such a way as to leave her opulent breasts, big hips and smiling Pussy fully exposed to view.

The young men, somewhat amazed, especially to see a servant so lasciviously dressed, with natural modesty held their towels in such a way as to hide as much of their nakedness as possible, but the maid, when she had given her charms time to work up on them, told them with a bawdy smile to put their towels down, and noticed with delight their Pricks standing up big and erect with desire, aroused by the sight of her attractive nudity.

This pleased her. Looking approvingly at their quivering Pricks, she said, "Ah! I thought my boys must be becoming men by this time, though I scarcely expected to find you so well developed already, and it is for this purpose that I have come to talk to you. The maid, Nilda, blatantly made her case, saying: "Your mother has asked me to chat with you about things of a sexual nature and about your sexual futures. You see, she does not want to have you two running around after stray young women, and fucking everything you can get your big Pricks into and thus, she has asked me, her faithful servant, to avail myself to your sexual instruction and your sexual needs. She hopes you find this a satisfactory arrangement. And I might add that I look forward to it being quite pleasurable!"

With that she ran a polished fingernail around her ripe red nipple and lightly toyed with the tiny bud so the young men could get a taste of what they had coming to them and both young men hungrily watched her roving hand with their eager eyes; she could see a slight reaction in their Pricks, which seemed to grow with lust with her every word.

"Your mother has taken two very nice apartments, one for each of you, with connecting doors, and in each she has installed a personal maid to assist you in all you need for the game of sexual evolution—they will purchase toiletries, sexy stockings and outfits that will excite you and in general arouse your senses with their great beauty. But you are to focus on sexual education through my tutelage; I will work with you individually and together; and I will call in the two personal maids for assistance when needed.

"At the end of a few weeks, you will be free to fuck any of the great ladies of Society you desire— but you will know by then how to choose a woman, woo her, treat her well, and satisfy her pleasure with as much enthusiasm as you satisfy your own!

"Your mother stresses she is not trying to control your sexuality, merely provide you with proper sex education, as a parent should for her children. But she will not discuss this with you, nor will she acknowledge your activities. You are to bring all your questions to me."

Still toying with her nipples as she spoke to her new sexual charges, Nilda was getting excited with the thoughts of teaching two randy young men how to properly pay homage to a woman's flesh.

While she had been saying all this, her Pussy was throbbing beneath the lustful gaze of the two boys; very soon, almost automatically, she found herself clasping the two stiff Pricks, one in each of her hands, the tickling of which inflamed still further the boys' passionate desires.

She was getting extremely aroused.

The boys, who had long been friends of Edith's because their families were close, told Edith of this scene when she was old enough to appreciate it!

"It would be ever so tempting to have you both at once, but I believe you each deserve my full attention; I will begin with you," she said, pointing to the oldest young man. Eyeing his younger brother she said: "I will come to your apartment next."

The moment the eighteen-year-old departed, the nineteen-year-old was on top of the maid in a flash, his big Cock hard and ready to penetrate her. He had pushed her down on the bed, mounted her, and put his long tool at her entrance when suddenly she pushed him off her and said sternly:

"Never force a woman back onto a bed, or fuck her before she's ready. First, you pleasure her with long, leisurely strokes of your tongue on her Pussy. Have you tasted Pussy before?"

"No," he said.

"Then come here between my legs and look what I have here—a juicy, wet Cunt that needs attention. Bend your head...that's right...and stick out your tongue...no, not so hard...relax it yes yes-tongue up and down...ah...yes, that's very nice...very nice."

It didn't take him long to catch the rhythm of loving a woman's inner lips, and he did a good job of licking Nilda into a state of ecstasy.

"Now, press your lips around the Clitoris and suck me," she instructed, "and press one finger into the wetness of my opening...yes, ah...that's nice." He licked, flicked and sucked her Clitoris deliciously while finger-fucking her opening, and soon, the maid told him she was about to come; and when a woman was coming, she explained, he should lick and suck harder and poke faster.

"Now, ah...it's coming in your mouth, dear one...suck it...lick it...ah, take it all."

Furiously, his mouth worked to fully pleasure his instructress, and he lost track of his own huge erection, which was bursting to plow inside her juicy folds.

Sensing his urgency, Nilda instructed him that now he could mount her, enter her, and fuck her. He did, climbing atop her sweating form and slipping his hardness into her wet opening. She writhed in pleasure as her hips moved up to meet him; he plunged into her with a rapid pace until she slowed his hips and whispered:

"A woman likes it slow. Pace yourself and fuck slowly; plunge and poke when you're both ready to come!"

He heeded her words and gave her a slow, sensual fuck until he could feel his sperm about to burst.

"May I come?" he asked, panting as Nature began to carry him toward his climax.

"You may...and pull it out as you are about to shoot and shower my belly with your sperm."

He humped and pumped until finally the juicy jism funneled through his Prick and out it came—slippery, wet and covered with her juices. She grabbed hold and helped him jerk the final drops out onto her flesh. Then she affectionately laid the tired tool on her leg and caressed it.

"Very good for a first time," she said, in a sexy yet somewhat tutorial tone. "And now, it's off for your brother's lesson!"

With that, she was gone to the younger man's apartments, where, it was said, she did the same!

And just as relaying it to me got me excited, that was Edith's reaction the day the boys, by then men, shared their tales of being sexually tutored by the sexy maid, Nilda! And told her, too, of further escapades with their personal maids!

Edith was about eighteen when she first heard the tales of lust and, in the telling, the brothers would again relive the excitement and the lust. Ultimately, she ended up becoming the occasional lover to them both, at different intervals, because they had shared such naughty secrets.

But she also became quite close with the personal maids of both the boys, and perhaps that is where a large part of her sexual education came to be—learning and practicing with the two young women who were close to her age. This is also what made her a prime candidate for the Lesbian Society at school. She shared with them the tale of her first time experience with Lesbian love:

She was at first treated with great respect as a young Society lady. However, as soon as the maids discovered her smutty tastes, they arrayed themselves in the most fascinating of their indecent costumes, and then they went through a series of all the most lascivious forms of vice that they could think of for her amusement.

Besides this, they showed her all sorts of books of extraordinary smutty pictures and photos, and lent her some stories to read of the kind described as "Erotic and Ultra-gallant." In fact, they did everything to corrupt her completely, and encouraged her to have sex with one or another of the Countess's sons, right before their eyes so as to render her altogether shameless, in which they had quite succeeded, for she said she was longing to be poked by lots of different men and that it was her intention to let the men know it too!

These maids had a little rhymed Prayer to the Virgin to be used before enjoying a poke:

> Holy Mother, we believe
> Without sin Thou didst conceive,
> Grant that we, in Thee believing,
> Now may sin without conceiving.

After these initial visits to mistresses of her own dear friends and occasional lovers, Edith was very anxious to be taken to see one of the more fashionable of the immoral houses, which are to be found of a more luxurious character in Paris than anywhere else in the world. The young men, however, refused to run the risk of taking her there, and so she had to be content with a description of the most luxurious and voluptuous of them all. She then described it to me as follows:

The inside of the house is decorated with exquisite pictures and carvings, while the large marble staircase and all the rooms are carpeted so thickly that no sound of footsteps is ever heard.

Visitors are received by a gorgeously dressed lady, who, when she has ascertained their wants, hands them over to the care of pages, of whom there are a great number in the establishment, all exquisitely dressed in fancy tights costumes. They are of both sexes, but, as they all have their hair elaborately dressed with flowers in it, and all alike wear corsets, long kid gloves, and dainty feminine shoes, it is hard to tell the sex of the pages, except that the close-fitting tights, if looked at carefully, will generally reveal a Prick in the case of male pages. These conduct the visitors to a large room surrounded with mirrors, in which a large number of lovely women, absolutely naked, except for transparent chemises and stockings, are placed in lascivious groups, whose suggestive poses are reflected by the mirrors on the walls.

From these groups, one or more partners are chosen by the visitors, who are then conducted to the sumptuous bedrooms, where, if desired, the pages still remain to aid them in undressing, and to excite them during their acts of sensuality by tickling, etc.

There are also rooms specially set apart for the vice of Lesbianism, where only women are admitted, though men are allowed to peep through hidden windows to watch the obscene movements and poses of the ladies within!

On one occasion the Countess's two sons came into the establishment, where people were clearly watching—through the secret spy-hole—their mother—the Countess—reveling with the keenest enjoyment in an orgy of this fascinating but unnatural vice.

Edith says, however, that despite her fondness for vice of all sorts, the Countess was most particular about going to church on Sundays, where she could not only display her own smart clothes, but study those of her neighbors; and she also showed her religion by aiding various charities. The way in which she preferred to do this was by acting in plays or tableaux got up in aid of the charity, in which case she always began by protesting that she would act any part they liked, provided it was not a maillot (tights) part; and yet she always allowed herself to be persuaded that with her lovely figure, etc., she would thereby induce more people to come to the entertainment and so benefit the poor, and ended by not only wearing the tights, but by wearing very little else besides. In fact, in one comic opera, she played the part of a boy, but wore a costume consisting of a sleeveless bodice of the thinnest possible pink kid, with knickers—or, rather, drawers—of the same material; and as the points of the breasts, as well as the shape of her thighs and hips, stood out as plainly as if she had been stark naked, it is evident that few people can have mistaken her for the boy she was supposed to represent, especially as she finished her costume with sixteen-button pink kid gloves.

On another occasion, she posed in a tableau as Venus, after much protesting and resistance; and, though it was known to the audience that she wore a tight-fitting suit of the thinnest possible pink silk all over her body, anyone seeing her in the brilliant light of the stage would have sworn that she was as naked as Eve, for it revealed not only every curve, but every hair on her body.

Edith spoke to me also of the French watering places, and I am now longing to go to Trouville, which, as I daresay you know, is the Brighton of France. She says that there the men and women all bathe together and have the most splendid fun. There are, it seems, two distinct classes of women at Trouville: those who wear bathing costumes to bathe in, and those who like to show off their figures without the bother of going into the water. The latter wear a costume consisting of a sleeveless bodice, silk tights, high-heeled shoes, and very often long kid gloves. A big picture hat with a parasol to match the costume completes a toilette which would be ruined by going into the water; and so they sit on the beach, smoking cigarettes and flirting, or listening to the men's very risqué stories.

On the other hand, the bathing girls who really swim generally wear a sort of silk jersey combination, something like the men's, only much lower in the neck, sleeveless, and much thinner. The "knowing" girls have these made so tight that when they get wet and shrink, the stitches begin to stretch and gape, thereby allowing the pink skin and other charms to show through as distinctly as if they were perfectly nude. In this way, they get a distinct score over the other girls, who do not go into the water.

Edith tells me she wears dark blue suits of this sort through which her pink skin looks awfully fetching, but they sometimes shrink so much that, on coming out, her maid cannot get them off without cutting them! She says the best fun is to spot a man with a big Prick—it is apparently easy enough to see them under the tights—and ask him to teach you to swim. While 'he is holding you up, you slide your hand down and tickle his Dolly, which has probably come up already, if your body, and especially your Titties are of a voluptuous character. As soon as he feels your fingers at work, he returns the compliment by tickling your Pussy with one hand, while with the other he strokes the points of your breasts.

This sounds awfully good fun, and I mean to try it when I go to Trouville.

I came to the conclusion that Daniela had only done her justice when she said, "You will find that sly little monkey, Edith, who seems so pious, the most delightfully smutty talker in the world, when you get her by herself."

So entranced was I by her conversation that we did not notice how quickly the time slipped by, and, to our dismay, one of the seniors arrived with a message from Madame asking why we were not down, just at the very moment when we had allowed the mutual tickling of our fingers, which had been gently going on nearly all the time, to quicken into a regular frig.

As I am not anymore the little shamefaced thing I was when I first came here, and as Edith is, as you may have gathered from all she has told me, quite shameless, we continued our little game without taking any notice of the presence of the other young woman, finding, in fact, in the sense of our shamelessness, an increase of sensual gratification.

So our fellow student, a very pretty girl of eighteen, saw from our movements what was going on, and, pulling down the bedclothes, she watched with eager eyes the lascivious heavings of our naked bodies, which were rapidly approaching the spasm of supreme pleasure. Seeing this, she began to tickle us down our spines, laughing all the time with delight at our voluptuous movements.

When we had finished, she said to me, "Dearest Blanche, do let me come and do that with you some day; my friends and I often do it at home, and they say my fingers are simply made for a 'frigging.'"

She is so pretty and daring that I could not refuse, and so she is to creep up some night, when everyone is asleep, and stay the whole night with me. When I told her this, she began in her excitement to kiss me all over my naked body in a way which showed she was no novice in the arts of sensual pleasure.

We told Madame we had fallen asleep again, an explanation

which she accepted, though I think she guessed the truth.

And now, dearest Ethel, good-bye for the present. I am afraid this is a very disjointed letter, the contents of which will probably shock you very much, but some of it I daresay will instruct you as well as amuse you. After perusing it, I think that you will say like me, that it is no wonder Edith is filled with insights and lusty tales!

Ever your most loving
Blanche

My dearest Ethel,

Since my last letter we have had our half-term vacation, which is a short holiday lasting from Saturday morning to Tuesday evening. To my great delight Edith very kindly got the Countess to write to Madame, asking if I might be allowed to spend the holidays with her, as Edith would be staying with a close family friend during this time. The invitation was most readily accepted, as Madame assured me that the Countess was a leader of the very best Parisian Society. After what Edith had told me, I rather smiled at this, but I nevertheless departed joyfully on the Saturday morning with Edith, having first of all carefully packed up the smartest of my new dresses and hats to wear on Sunday, as well as two very low-necked evening dresses to wear at dinner.

The Countess, who is marvelously young-looking for her age, received us most kindly, though with very much the air of a "grande dame." Edith declares that her youthful appearance is entirely due to make-up, but if so, her maids must be most marvelously skillful, for she would easily pass for ten years younger than her true age, while her exquisitely corseted figure looks quite girlish. Talking of figures, by the way, it is very curious to notice how very differently shaped French women's figures are from the English. The two chief points of difference are that the breasts, which English girls wear almost in their natural position, are always forced upward by the French corsets, so as to stand out quite straight from the body without hanging down in the least. This has a very suggestive appearance, especially in evening dresses, which thus expose to view far more of the Titties, even if they are cut no lower than an English gown.

It is most amusing to see the way the men will keep their eyes fixed on a well-filled bustier, watching for the moment when some forward movement of the wearer shall expose the naughty little breast-points to their eager gaze. I have now learnt how to expose them or to hide them just as I please, with such slight and imperceptible motions as to give a man the idea that I am all the time perfectly unconscious of what he is so anxiously looking out for.

The other point of difference in the French and English women's figures is that in England women always try to keep the stomach in as much as possible, and have their corsets made so as to force it in, out of sight, if they can.

In Paris, however, a prominent ventre is as much admired as a big behind, and just as we used to wear bustles to make the latter look unnaturally large, so some French women actually wear a small cushion in front, if their ventre is too flat by nature.

I am even amused to notice how much the shape of my own figure has changed, for the extra pressure at the waist caused by my thirteen-and-a-half-inch stays has of course caused the flesh to expand below the waist, and this, encouraged by the shape of the corsets, now stands out—so round and plump and firm that, when you next see me, you will think I have got a football under the lower part of my stays. It is in fact so prominent that in England I am afraid people will think I am enceinte but here it is considered a great beauty, especially by men. Moreover, Edith declares that there is no part of a girl's body which it gives a man so much pleasure to kiss as a ventre, provided it is firm and round.

They treated me with the greatest politeness, and I was so fortunate in pleasing the Countess that she gave permission for her sons to escort Edith and me to the theater in the evening.

Instead, however, of going to this classical theatre, the idea of which did not please any of us, we spent half the evening watching the lascivious dances at the Moulin Rouge, and the other half at the Folies Bergères, where the open attempts of the cocottes to arouse the sensuality of the different men they met amused me immensely.

By this time, Edith's male friends had thrown off all restraint, and told us all sorts of stories of the different cocottes we saw.

One they pointed out to us had, it seemed, a passion for younger men, and, finding a difficulty in gratifying this lust, she adopted the expedient of sending numbers of telegrams to herself every day. In Paris, I must tell you, telegrams are always delivered by the telegraph boys in person. They are usually young men of nineteen or twenty. When one of these knocked at her door and was told to come in, he found her lying in a chaise longue, with nothing on but a thin silk dressing gown which, being carefully left unfastened all down the front, would fly open at the slightest movement, allowing the young man to feast his eyes upon her naked Cunt and Titties. After looking at these for a few moments, it generally did not require much persuasion to induce him to take off his regulation trousers and place his strong Prick at her disposal.

If he was a novice in the art of vice, her enjoyment was of course all the greater, for there is no greater pleasure for a depraved woman of forty than to teach a young man all the different ways of satisfying sensual passion and to make him adept at the vice.

The following morning, I breakfasted in my bedroom and then proceeded to dress for church, naturally choosing some of my prettiest things.

When I came downstairs, I found the party waiting for me. The Countess stood so astonished at what she termed this "vision of loveliness" that at first she seemed speechless; then, however, lifting up her own veil and my own, she gave me a long passionate kiss, which told me how the elegance of my figure had excited her Lesbianism. All the way to church and all through the service, she was feasting her eyes on me, and when we got home afterward, she instantly carried me off to her bedroom, where she gave orders that luncheon was to be served for herself and me.

Edith and her two male companions smiled at what they knew was going to happen, but did not complain at having their own lunch together by themselves.

The Countess, with the aid of her maid, rapidly undressed, till she had nothing on but her stockings and chemise. The maid then came to undress me, and I was beginning to unbutton my long gloves when the Countess stopped me and said to the maid, "Leave the hat, gloves, boots, stockings, corset and chemise, but remove everything else." And when this was done, I must confess that the image of myself reflected in the glass looked extraordinarily wanton and lascivious. In this costume we lunched, being waited on by the maid, who was evidently an adept in the art of vice, and who constantly refilled our glasses with champagne.

After lunch the Countess and her maid together laid me on the bed, and lifting up my chemise, they exhausted the French language in their compliments of my ventre, thighs, Pussy, etc. "Never," so the Countess assured me, "has the mere sight of a girl made me feel so hot!" And I was soon able to return the compliment by telling her that never before had I been so skillfully kissed, tickled and frigged, while it was evident the maid enjoyed the scene almost as much as we did.

To the horror of the Countess, Edith came in, in the middle of this ultra-Lesbian scene, but she soon showed that, so far from being shocked, she quite appreciated the voluptuous nature of the performance, for she undressed at once and very soon joined in the fun so heartily as to prove that she too was no novice in the arts of vice.

It was quite a sight. My body was stretched out upon the bed, and the Countess was between my legs, deliciously eating my Cunt, and our dear friend Edith was now undressed, straddling my face with her Cunt. I licked her with delight as the Countess lapped away at me and soon I could feel the swell of my sexflesh, letting me know an orgasm was near. I came in the Countess's mouth and she licked up every bit. Next, Edith let loose a small torrent of love-juice in my mouth. The maid, who was watching all the while from a corner, was coming as well from masturbating. The only Pussy needing dire attention was the Countess's, and Edith and I were more than glad to please her.

I took the sweet lips of her Cunt as my challenge—spreading them apart so I could see and taste the salty dew of her love-juice; Edith worked on her nipples, kneading and rubbing and nibbling on her Titties. And soon she began to frantically shove her Cunt against my mouth, pressing herself and pushing herself until the come began to dribble from within.

She whispered something to her French maid and the maid returned with a pot of cleansing water and three sponges. She cleaned us all up and allowed us to rest, until the latter-day activities were to begin.

Edith then led me to another apartment, where I found the Countess's youngest son, his Cock harder than a rock and ready for fucking. I was shocked, for I'd never seen a male's exposed flesh, let alone one so big and hard. I looked at him with great interest, and felt my Cunt getting wet. My virginity having been removed with the swift thrust of a dildo, I was aching to fuck the real thing. Edith left me with the youngest brother and bid adieu as she entered the apartment of the older one. Within moments I could hear groans and moans and the slapping of Balls against female assflesh; they were fucking wildly, inspiring me to do the same.

In spite of the voluptuous scenes in which I had already taken part, the sight of his hard tool caused a fresh thrill of sensuality to run through my body and made me long for those boys to throw me down on the bed or on the chaise longue and I felt that all sense of shame had left me and that the fire of my animal passions had been kindled to such a pitch that henceforth I would have to satisfy those passions at all costs.

So, like a young harlot, I quite offered myself to the young man before me, who was very soon on top of me as his mighty Prick slid softly up and down in my throbbing Cunt, exerting more and more pressure as he twined his muscular legs around my stockinged limbs, I learnt for the first time the superiority of the real article over the artificial poking of the dildo! The delicious enjoyment of this, my first real poke, was still further increased with tickling fingers and burning kisses; he did all in his power to augment our lascivious sensations of sensual pleasure.

When everyone at the house was all thoroughly exhausted by our very "religious" Sunday afternoon, we put on the most transparent of costumes, and then went down to a sumptuous dinner, the rich meats and wines of which were specially well suited to invigorate bodies that were fatigued by sensual pleasures.

Just before dinner, the Countess dispatched her maid with a whispered message, which turned out afterward to have been sent to the immoral house described in my last letter, asking the head of the establishment to send back with the maid two of the most experienced pages in the establishment.

Accordingly, after dinner we found a young man and woman of nineteen awaiting us in the drawing room, both deliciously dressed in the most indecent manner, while their bodies exuded the most exquisite perfumes.

Their beautiful faces were all aglow with the anticipation of the scene they were going to enact, their eyes flashing with the excitement caused by the champagne with which the maid who fetched them had taken care to prime them.

We had all partaken liberally of the same wine at dinner, and in fact, an observer might probably have decided that we were all half-drunk.

Added to this we were all of us so lightly clad that every movement of our bodies disclosed some attractive nudity or another.

The moment the young man caught sight of me, he came toward me. His long hair was dressed with flowers exactly like a woman's, and his chief garment was a pale blue satin corset, which made him look so feminine that his Prick below seemed quite out of place. His openwork silk stockings, long kid gloves and high-heeled shoes all exactly matched the color of his tightly laced corset. Pulling open my dressing gown, he plunged his face into my snowy ventre, kissing it again and again in a most passionate manner. Flushed as I was with wine, I could not help being flattered to see the pleasure which this gave him, revealed beyond all doubt by the instant stiffening of his dear Prick, which was rather small, but quite beautiful! After toying with it, I took the point of the little Cock between my lips, and endeavored to gamahuche this lover in the way Edith had described. And while this was taking place the young woman was doing the same for the two men, exciting the two Pricks alternately with lips and fingers; meanwhile the Countess and Edith, closely embraced and mouth to mouth, were masturbating one another, while looking at us.

After this preliminary, we had some more champagne, and then the two pages, who had been carefully trained in vice in the most immoral house of luxurious sensuality in the world, gave us a lascivious performance of sensual wickedness. There was not a single item omitted in the whole category of vice. A couch was brought forward to the middle of the room for them, which, like a fairy bride and bridegroom, they approached, the man doing the poking of his pretty partner with astonishing vigor and lascivious movements. He poked her in front and behind, frigged her dainty little Cunt with tongue and fingers, sucking her Titties till she swooned with pleasure. Then she laid him upon the bed and took his place, kissing his Prick while she inserted her finger into the opening of his behind, and finally ended with a triumphant "St. George," which is like an ordinary poke, only that the male lies underneath, while the female sits down on him in such a way that his Dolly, as she does so, slides into her Pussy.

When they had finished their exhibition, all of us being thoroughly exhausted by the excesses we had indulged in, and moreover being all too drunk for anything, we retired to bed, I sleeping with the Countess's younger son, while Edith went to bed with the Countess and the male page. Her older son stole off with the female page.

The next day we were told we need not get up till lunchtime, but after breakfast Edith came to share my bed with the Countess's young son and I. The Countess wished to rest herself, so Edith brought me a lovely book which the Countess had lent her especially for my benefit.

It had wonderfully nasty photos of men and women in all sorts of erotic poses; looking through it kept us busy for many delicious moments until the stimulation roused us to fuck in a three-way fashion—introducing me to yet one more decadent act during my stay at the Countess's home!

This has been a very long letter, my dear Ethel, and I hope I have not shocked you too much in describing to you so many lascivious scenes.

By the way, when you try tickling yourself, be sure and take up a position in front of a big looking-glass, so that you can watch the action of the fingers in the Cunt, as well as the motions of the body. You will find this adds greatly to the spiciness of a solitary frig, and if you can read a naughty book at the same time so much the better, as it will make you feel nice and randy and will ensure your coming properly.

Ever your loving
Blanche

My dearest Ethel,

I am afraid it is a long time since I have written you one of my long letters, which is all the more disgraceful of me, as I know there are several jolly letters of yours unanswered. In a very little while now, however, I shall be back for the holidays, and then we can have a really good time together.

I was very much interested in your account of your first attempts to "tickle" yourself, and I am not at all surprised that you describe your sensations as "perfectly lovely," as you say that you had no difficulty in finding the little button in your Pussy, the fondling of which causes such exquisite pleasure, and that it stood up firm and stiff under the touch of your fingers, almost like the point of one of your Titties. That is good news, dearest, for it means that you have a disposition specially inclined to all the pleasures of sensuality, and I am certain that, when I am there to teach you all about it, you will get the same heavenly enjoyment that I have been experiencing ever since my first initiation.

Do you remember my telling you of the little eighteen-year-old girl, who was so delighted at my promise to let her sleep with me one night? Her name is Suzette, and she is the dearest young woman imaginable. When she is in bed with me, her soft kisses and slim tickling fingers go all over my body in the most delicious way, and when her dear right hand at last finds my center of delight, the effect is perfectly indescribable, for she has such a slim hand that all four fingers go in at once, and she knows how to cause a separate and special pleasure with each one of them. Her own little nest is so small that I have to return the compliment with my little finger, and even that is rather a tight fit. I am hoping that I can bring her to England to spend part of the holiday with me.

It is a funny thing how different girls are! Suzette is as naughty as ever she can be in act, and yet in word, she is the most perfectly modest and innocent young woman imaginable! Edith—the Countess's dear family friend—on the other hand, is just the opposite, and at the last Lesbian meeting, she kept us all in fits of laughter with some of her droll stories, which are not exactly smutty, but are generally awfully suggestive, which for my part I think much nicer. I can only remember one or two of them, but you can be sure each tale is ripe with sexual tension and sexual innuendo.

And now I want to tell you about rather a curious thing that has happened, only you are so delightfully innocent that I scarcely know how to explain it to you. You know that it is quite a common thing for a man to keep a girl as a mistress or cocotte on whom he lavishes money and presents, while she in return ministers in every possible way to his sensual desires! Even in pious London this goes on, and in St. John's Wood and at Richmond many a dainty little house with an exquisitely dressed mistress bears witness to the genuine piety of the London County Councilors! In Paris, on the other hand, every man without exception who can afford it, keeps one or more cocottes, and these are to be seen driving every day in the most splendid carriages, or displaying their beautiful busts and shoulders in the most gorgeous costumes at the Theatre or Opera.

Their photos are in every shop window, their doings are freely discussed in the papers, some of which make a specialty of giving full accounts of their midnight supper parties, which start with all the guests most correctly and beautifully dressed, and end with them all being still more beautifully undressed. Ladies of fashion discuss them quite freely, pointing out to one another the frail beauties kept by their respective husbands, and imitating them not only in dress and manner, but, as far as they know how, in their lascivious behavior in the privacy of their bedroom. And now, I suppose, you will exclaim, "What is the girl driving at?"

Why just at this, my dear Ethel, which I could not very well explain without leading up to it rather gently. In Paris it is getting almost as common for a beautiful girl to be kept by some leading Society woman, as by a man! Does that take your breath away, dearest? Because if so, prepare for another gasp. The fact is that the Countess has fallen completely in love with me; and though she cannot have me altogether to live with her, as she would like, Madame allows me to spend a day and a night with her every week, during which she lavishes on me the "economies of love" that she has been saving up all the week. She has had a lovely bedroom fitted up in her house especially for me, the walls and ceiling of which are covered with mirrors, interspersed with the most suggestive and voluptuous pictures. The floor is carpeted so thickly that one might sleep on it without discomfort, and is strewn everywhere with the softest and most luxurious satin cushions. The bed itself is a triumph of voluptuous elegance, and the room is filled continually with the most delicious and intoxicating perfumes. The large hanging-cupboards and chests of drawers are filled with the most lovely improper costumes—transparent chemises, openwork tights, lace drawers, satin corsets, etc.—in which we array ourselves when we retire there for an evening's pleasure. When I tell you that she has taken into her service the naughty young man and woman whose performance I described in my last letter, and that their special duty is to wait on me when I am there, you can imagine that we have a most delightfully naughty time when we are together.

I generally go to her on Friday evening, and stay with her till Saturday night. When I arrive, I find the two waiting for me dressed as pages in tights and low satin bodices, with their long hair hanging almost to their waists.

They conduct me to my bedroom and undress me—a task which pleases them both immensely, but especially the young man, whose tights instantly betray the movements of his delicious little Flute.

When I am quite undressed, they conduct me to the splendid

bathroom that opens out of the bedroom, and there the Countess's own maid helps me to enjoy the delicious sensations of a hot and heavily perfumed bath. After this I am dried and massaged by a masseuse, and my hair is carefully done up in the latest fashionable style. I then select the costume that I am going to wear, and to give you some idea of the way we dress at these select little dinners, I will describe to you what I wore the last time I went there.

The colors I decided on were pink and black, and accordingly a chemise of the thinnest black chiffon was brought to me, with big bows of pink ribbon to act as shoulder-straps, and with a trimming of the same 'round the neck. Black openwork silk stockings with pink and black satin garters were finished off with very pointed shoes of pink kid with high Louis XV heels. A pair of pink kid gloves sewn with black and reaching to the elbow completed a costume which sounds perhaps rather gloomy, because there seems to be a good deal more black than pink in it; but if you ever try wearing a thin black chiffon chemise, you will find that your body supplies the pink, which the faint black of the chiffon only serves to heighten.

When I was thus arrayed, the pages ran off to fetch their mistress, who was impatiently waiting in her own room. She arrived in similar costume, only the colors she wore were light blue and a very pale shade of café au lait.

In a moment, we are clasped in one another's arms, the contact of our nearly naked bodies—for chiffon is as good as nothing—causing the most delightful shivers of pleasure to run all over us as we imprint long and lascivious kisses on one another's lips.

We do not, however, take any further liberties with each other yet, as the dinner is served almost immediately, at which we are waited on by the two pages, though the male finds the sight of our beauties so entrancing that he can scarcely walk, owing to the pressure of his Dolly against the tights.

Meanwhile we excite ourselves with the highly seasoned viands, washed down with liberal draughts of champagne in which the pages share, until we are all in such a state of fire that we rush into each other's arms in an absolute fury of sexual desire. Then follow a series of the most voluptuous scenes that can possibly be imagined. The Countess is continually discovering some new means of heightening the pleasure.

On the Saturday morning the Countess generally drives me out in her carriage, and we make a tour of the shops, in the course of which she is only too delighted to buy me anything and everything that I may take a fancy to. The result is that I have now a large collection of the loveliest hats, stockings, handkerchiefs, gloves, etc., that you can possibly imagine, and I am sure you will be perfectly enraptured when you see them. The other girls in the Lesbian Club were at first quite mad with envy of me on account of my good fortune, but as I often pass on some of the Countess's presents to them, they are beginning to get reconciled to my intimacy with her.

Thanks to her various introductions, I have been going into Society a good deal, and I am gradually learning what an immense amount of sensuality there is underlying almost every Society function. At a ball, for instance, everything that can possibly excite the passions is carefully provided. The soft but brilliant lights, the heavy perfume of the flowers and the slow, languorous strains of the waltz music, all tend to arouse the sexual portion of the brain. The costly dresses of each woman, leaving the bust and shoulders naked so that the maddening perfume of her very body rises to the nostrils of her partner, tend to excite the men to the utmost pitch; while the soft touch of the delicate kid gloves and the thrill of the warm body inside the tightly laced corset as his arm encircles her waist, still further heightens the lascivious effect.

One lovely evening gown which the Countess gave me is really shockingly low-cut, and so thin that when I waltz the movement of the air holds it against my body in such a way that the outline of the legs and ventre show as plainly as if they were in tights. The Countess's favorite amusement is to watch me dancing in this dress with some hard, young male of my own age whose trousers soon begin to assume a more and more distorted appearance, until, by a slight turn of my body, I let him see the rosy points of my Titties, erect and firm at the thought of the effect I am producing. This generally fetches out his Dolly so far that I can feel its head against my leg, and at that stage I generally think it safer to let him conduct me into a quiet corner, where his conversation, as a rule, soon betrays the hot and passionate lust that is consuming him.

All this is great fun, both in exciting the men oneself and also in watching the intrigues and flirtations of other naughty couples. One thing, by the way, that I have learnt from the Countess, is that when you sit out with a man on the stairs, you should always sit a step or two below him, for then a dexterous bend or two will open your corsage in such a way that he can see not only your Titties, but far down below them—a sight which is certain to cause him keen enjoyment. On the other hand, if you are entertaining a man in your boudoir, you should lie on a sofa or on a long chair and let him sit in a low chair at your feet, when by a little thoughtless lifting of the knees, etc., you will give him a view of quite a different, but no less enchanting, portion of your person.

Another thing the Countess has taught me is in dressing for a ball to wear plenty of soft frothy petticoats but no drawers; for when a man's hands begin to wander gently up your leg toward the garters and higher—as often happens to me when I am at a ball and am sitting out a dance with some nice fellow in a quiet corner— he loves to come in contact with the delicate texture of luxurious petticoats, but is sadly disappointed if his fingers cannot at last find the cave of delight for which they are seeking. If he does this when you are lying on a sofa or chaise longue, I need not warn you that you must protest most vigorously, and entreat him to desist, while at the same time a few cunning movements will serve to lift your petticoats higher and higher, so as to give him a better view of the treasures concealed within, thereby inflaming him to a more vigorous attack upon your "virtuous" scruples.

In fact, as you may imagine, I am now doing everything to induce men to take improper liberties with me and try to be poked by as many different Pricks as possible, and I must now describe to you a delightful scene which took place one day when I reached the Countess's house a good deal earlier in the afternoon than I was expected.

The pages conducted me to my bedroom, and there I lay down upon a most luxurious couch to read the Don Juan, a very wicked paper, until the Countess came in from her drive. Presently the door was opened by the pages to admit a very pretty boy between nineteen and twenty years old, who I learned was a new servant of the Countess's. The pages shut the door and left him all alone with me, blushing very charmingly with embarrassment at his unexpected situation.

I had only thrown off my hat, which lay on a chair, and was otherwise dressed just as I had come in from the street. My tiny arched shoes with their sharp points and tall slender heels were thrust negligently out of a froufrou of white petticoats, which were pulled up high enough to disclose the skin of a dainty pink ankle, peeping through the windows of a black openwork stocking.

I saw his gaze wander gradually up from there to my very tightly corseted waist, above which my bust stood out most voluptuously, being lifted up by one of the cushions on which I lay in such a manner that the big round globes and erect nipples showed plainly and attractively beneath the thin, well-fitting corsage. My hands were gloved to the elbow in spotless lavender kid that fit without a wrinkle, and the slight disorder of my hair did not, I fancy, serve to make it look any less attractive.

From his increasing blushes, I saw that he was somewhat troubled in the seat of his emotions, and so I asked him to sit down, and chatted with him on various topics, leading them gradually 'round to the paper I held in my hand, the illustrations of which, being mainly of pretty women all in attractive forms of undress or no dress at all, were calculated to increase rather than diminish the vague desires with which he was beginning to burn. When I could see from the flash in his lovely eyes that he was beginning to feel really naughty, a fact which my sly glances at his trousers fully confirmed, I suggested that he should help me to take off my gloves, as it was rather hot.

The voluptuous feeling of the soft kid, warm with the glow of the feminine hand it had so tightly clasped, caused him such exquisite thrills of pleasure and desire that he lingered a long time over this evidently delightful task.

I laughingly complimented him on being so excellent a lady's maid, and suggested that perhaps he would like to take off my shoes as well. His sensuality was now so thoroughly aroused that he took the tiny slipper in his hand, and, having gently and caressingly drawn it off, he imprinted a long lascivious kiss upon my rosy instep, which stood arched up beneath its flimsy covering.

In doing this to the second foot, he lifted it so high to his lips that he caught a glimpse of the pink and black satin garters clasping my leg above the knee. "May I not take off those as well?" he asked, with a still more violent blush; to which I of course replied, "Certainly not, you dreadfully naughty man." But as I smiled at him while I said it, and at the same time gently pulled up my skirts so as to give him a full view of these dainty circlets, being a young man of good sense, in spite of his shyness, he took this as being the permission it was meant to be, and in a few minutes my garters were off, and, having kissed them, he placed one upon his head as a sort of crown, while he continued from time to time to caress the legs from which he had taken them.

Now, it is a whim of my protectress that I should always wear very long opera stockings, reaching right up to my—ahem (as I have become a shameless Society whore, I was going to say my Arse, but remembering you are so delightfully innocent yet, I have been afraid to shock you, dear!). So, when I had tantalized my pretty boy a little longer, I said, "Well, aren't you going to finish the job and take off my stockings, too?"

He looked about quite bewildered as to how to begin, so at last I said, "Well, don't you know how to take off a pair of stockings yet?"

"I—I know how to take off my own," he stammered.

"How do you do it?" I inquired.

"Peel them downward from the top," he answered in a very low voice.

"Quite right," I said. "Why don't you do it?"

His look of puzzled modesty at this was most amusing, and I don't think that I ever in my life felt anything so delicious as my sensations during those next few minutes. Very slowly and cautiously, his hands stole up my thighs, expecting every moment to find the stockings come to an end, and going slower and slower the nearer they got to my love-nest, which was by this time getting so hot that the scent of Rhine violets, with which I always perfume it in accordance with the Countess's wishes—and by no means against my own—was wafted so strongly in his face as to almost overpower him with the voluptuous and lustful feelings which it excited in his mind. For my part, his modesty and blushing awkwardness made the pleasure caused by the soft tickling of his fingers as they gradually approached my burning grotto a thousand times greater than if he had been the most knowing expert of vice in existence.

At last, just at the warm spot where the body meets the thighs, his fingers touched the top of the stocking, while at the same moment his hand came in contact with the curves of my over-hanging ventre, and brushed against the soft tufts of down that fringe the entrance to my Pussy. The start which he gave at this quite unexpected discovery showed clearly enough that this was his first introduction to the mysteries of the mechanism of the feminine person, while the shivers of pleasure that ran all over his body showed how strongly they affected him.

As he pulled gently at the rim of my stocking, I pressed my thighs close together to prevent his being able to draw the stocking downward, and in so doing I imprisoned his little finger, thereby obliging his hand to remain in its soft warm resting place, his faint struggles to get free causing me the most exquisite tickling that can possibly be imagined.

Glancing coquettishly at him, I said, "Why don't you pull my stockings down?"

"Because I can't," he answered, blushing more than ever.

"Perhaps something has caught them, and you had better look and see what it is," I said, and gently lifting up the skirt and petticoats and releasing at the same time his naughty hand, I opened my legs wide apart and gave him a full view of the beauty spot where it had been imprisoned.

I remained like that with my clothes up for a few minutes, fully exposing myself, and noticed with delight the sudden bound given by his Ramrod inside the trousers, which now stood out in so frank and undisguised a fashion that I could not refrain from putting out my hand and feeling its sturdy head, the throbbing of which was plainly felt through his trousers. Then, with a hasty movement of assumed modesty, I pulled down my skirt, and said, "I am afraid you are dreadfully naughty—I hope you did not look right up under my petticoats!"

For a moment, he did not know what to do, but at last, seeing my smiling face and outstretched arms, he embraced me, returning with all the ardor of which he was capable the burning kiss that I imprinted, with all the lascivious sensuality that the scene had aroused in my breast, on his panting lips.

"And now you must go," I said to him, "for I am really going to undress in earnest." And saying this, I rose from the couch and began unbuttoning my corsage.

"Mayn't I help you?" he asked wistfully, as he perceived that a few moments would serve to set free the two great globes, which were already straining to get free from the restraint of the corset.

"Certainly not," I answered, throwing open the bodice, so that the beginning of my bust showed plainly under the lace of the chemise. On this he greedily fixed his eyes. Another moment or two served to unfasten my skirt, so that I stood before him in corset and petticoats—both being of the most exquisite and voluptuous kind that Paris can produce.

"What? Still there?" I said, as I noticed that he showed no signs of departing. "Very well; then you must sit down and turn your head the other way, because it would never do for a young man like you to know what a woman of my charms looks like when she is undressed." Saying this, I turned him 'round and, after giving him a voluptuous kiss on his rosy lips, sat him down in a chair straight opposite a mirror in which I had been all the time contemplating myself, next unfastening the petticoats, I held them up with my hands for a few moments, telling him that he must not look in the glass, as I could not allow him to see me in my drawers. As I intended, this had the effect of making him glue his eyes to my reflection in the glass and, as I let the dainty underwear sink to the ground, "Oh dear!" I exclaimed, "I quite forgot that I had no drawers on!" But he had, I fancy, discovered that fact in his previous explorations.

I was now clad in a pink satin corset, clasping my tiny waist over a perfectly transparent chemise of black gauze, through which my long stockings were perfectly visible, while the tinted marble of my ventre showed up in voluptuous contrast to the curly home of Venus between my thighs.

Feasting his eyes on the reflection of this in the mirror, he remained absolutely entranced by the sight of this spectacle of female nudity.

My efforts to unlace my very tight corset were of course quite fruitless, and so I had to ask my companion whether he was good at untying knots. At this he turned round, and positively staggered when he came near enough to perceive the intoxicating perfume, half-natural, half-artificial, that poured forth from my warm body.

Presenting my back to him, I could see in the glass his eyes fall lovingly upon my two plump cheeks, while his hands fumbled, not so clumsily as I expected, at the stay lace. Presently it was really undone, and as the pressure on my body slowly relaxed, I unfastened the front hooks, and was left in the most naked of all states of nudity: a transparent chemise.

Luckily for me, I knew I had nothing to fear from the loss of the corset, for my breasts stand up as high and firm, and my waist is almost as slender without them as with them. And as I looked in the mirror, I could not help thinking that this lucky houseboy was decidedly to be envied in making his discoveries of sexual mysteries under such unusually voluptuous circumstances in the home in which he was newly employed. At every movement my plump nudities stood out in such a way as almost to brush against him, while the feelings which his modesty excited in me brought it about that I looked far prettier at the moment than I had ever looked before.

In an ecstasy of excited passion, he flung himself at my feet, and began once more to kiss them through my stockings with hot, burning kisses. Lifting him up and seeing the pitiable state of his staff of manhood, I—yes, dear, with my own hands—gently began to unfasten his trousers, which soon fell off, and were quickly followed by everything else except a skimpy little jersey scarcely reaching to his hips, below which his pretty instrument stood up, apparently bent upon doing its duty manfully whenever it should be called upon.

Standing hand in hand before the mirror, I bade him notice the difference between us, though I observed that his eyes were so busy looking at my private domain that he had no eyes for his own sturdy Trunk with its wild, dark undergrowth.

In a short time both our eyes were so flashing with amorous desire that it seemed a shame to make him wait any longer.

"Get into bed, lover," I said, "and I will join you in a minute."

He did not require much pressing, and in another moment he was nestling in the luxurious down cushions of the most voluptuous bed that money could buy.

Without delay I crept in beside him, and lifting up the chemise to the height of my loins, I clasped him in my arms, so that the point of his Dolly was gently kissing my thighs close to my Pussy.

In this position, we kissed and cuddled for some time, until I plainly perceived that he was slightly inexperienced in how to fulfill his share of the task. Thereupon I slid my hand down, and, gently clasping his Dolly, I tickled and caressed it until it was nearly double its former size. Then, guiding it to the lips of my glowing nest, I clasped my arms round him, very gently drawing him toward me, thereby causing his bowsprit to slide very slowly onward into its haven. Never shall I forget the look of pleasure which now began to overspread his face, when he at last found his manly spade digging in its proper soil. To prolong his pleasure as much as possible, I made him work very slowly at first, softly tickling his spine, and kissing his lips in the most lascivious manner possible. Soon, however, the frenzy of love began to overtake him, and his movements quickened as my eager Pussy sucked him further and further in, our bodies twisting and writhing in our exquisite and unsuspected, contest of delight.

You cannot imagine how delicious it was to feel his firm white boy-like limbs pressing against mine, while the plumpness of my breasts, thighs and ventre evidently caused him the most voluptuous sensations.

Just as we were reaching the supreme moment, the door opened and in walked the Countess, much to my horror, for I knew that she was very jealous of my allowing anyone to have the enjoyment of my charms except herself.

Our look of ecstasy at the delightful sensations we were experiencing, however, caused her sensuality to get the better of her jealousy, and tearing the bedclothes off us, she was just in time to see us in the full transports of coming together—an experience so novel for the young man that he could at first hardly realize its full rapture.

She was so delighted with this spectacle, and her sensuality was so much aroused that she quite forgave us; and, after kissing us both and ordering the pages to bring in several bottles of champagne, she got her maid to undress her and soon joined us in bed, my new lover being placed between her and myself, so that we might both cuddle him.

Meanwhile the pages had brought the champagne, so, kissing and caressing the pretty young man, we began to prime him with it, while the Countess and I took good care to have our full share of the wine, and soon we became most lively and in the proper mood to enjoy anything most licentious.

We now began to initiate him to all the mysteries and most refined practices of love. But soon the wine made us mad with lust and I will not relate to you, dear, all that took place, for it would shock you too much! Suffice it to say that we took a sensual delight in sharing this young man—and that we both showed ourselves as expert in all the forms of vice as if we had been professional prostitutes instead of being only Society whores. As for "our" lover, he was called upon to perform prodigies of lustful valor, of which, considering he was essentially a beginner, he acquitted himself most nobly; but at last he was quite done up and, as the Countess was gamahuching him for the third time, while I was frigging his bottom-hole with two of my fingers, which I had inserted as far as they would go, he fainted right off.

And now, dear, I must really bring this letter to an end, as I shall be seeing you soon and shall be able to give you some practical illustrations, which are far better than any amount of description. And as among other lovely presents which the Countess has given me is a morocco case containing a set of four beautiful dildos—the most perfect that Paris can produce, and varying in size—with the smallest one I am intending, if you are willing, to initiate you into the mysteries of poking, while the largest, which I have not yet dared to use, I am saving up in the hope that you will help me to summon up the courage to allow you or someone to put it into me. Besides this she has given me a whole box of beautifully bound books on the most erotic and voluptuous subjects, which you will certainly read with interest, and the reading of which is sure to increase your sensuality; and as to naughty clothes, I have got simply dozens of openwork tights, stockings and transparent chemises, and some of these, I hope, you will condescend to wear.

In fact, I intend to make you as lascivious as I am myself, and hope that we shall soon find some nice boys to poke us both. And don't be afraid, dear, that by showing yourself rather loose and by allowing men to take the fullest liberties with your person, you might compromise your future, and will not be able later to find a husband, for, on the contrary, a girl who is very fast attracts men as honey draws flies, and by becoming a little Society whore like me, you are sure to have all the more men to propose to you. For my part, since I got into Society here in Paris, I have had lots of proposals, and some of them came from men who had "had" me and who knew that other men had poked me as well; some men went even so far as to tell me that if I married them they would leave me the fullest liberty to enjoy myself and poke with whoever I should take a fancy to. This, I know, will seem quite incredible to you, but I assure you it is the perfect truth, and there are many such husbands in Paris who not only wink at their wives' open misconduct, but even do everything to induce them to go in for the greatest excesses and to give way altogether to their sexual passions; and this, which of course seems a very extraordinary way for a husband to act towards his wife, is done in the hope of depraving the wife completely and of making her better "fit" to satisfy her husband's vices! And, by the way, after you have read all the other books given to me by the Countess, I shall lend you one called My Married Life, in which you will read the history of a woman whose husband takes a delight in depravity. The more shameless, the more wicked and the more cruel she becomes, the more attached he gets to her! It is even more abominable than de Sade's works in French. But it is most interesting, first because it is not like any other English erotic book, and principally on account of the strange philosophy pervading the work.

And now, dearest, I hope you do not leave my letters lying about, as I fancy they are scarcely the style of correspondence that young ladies of my age are supposed to indulge in, though I believe lots of other girls are just as bad, only they are afraid of being found out.

Ever your loving
Blanche

The English Governess

*I*t was half an hour before Harriet descended to the library, where Richard had been awaiting her in all the throes of trepidation and uncertainty. On seeing her he became still more disturbed. She, quite at her ease, approached and tapped him lightly under the chin.

"Well," she said, "what have you been doing since I left?"

He blushed and tried to reply, but an excess of shyness strangled his voice. He was silent.

"Come, are you dumb?"

"No, miss…"

"Well?"

"I—I did nothing at all."

"Nothing at all! But that is unheard of. One must do something."

The last words were accompanied by a gaze of such penetration that he shivered, his eyes involuntarily falling to the region of his genitals for assurance that there were no traces of his indulgence. Harriet's shrewd gaze followed his.

"Come now," she said, with a faint note of mockery in her clear, pleasant voice, "tell me what you have been doing. Begin at the beginning."

She sat down, smoothing out her skirt, and taking his hands in hers she drew him close to her.

"I read—a little," he said. "But…"

"But what?'

"I couldn't read—very much…Then I—I looked out of the window."

"A praiseworthy occupation. And after that?"

He was deeply disturbed, The touch of the young woman's soft hands, the contact of her knees distracted him without his knowing why.

"After that," he mumbled, "I—I did nothing at all…'

"Perfect," said Harriet. "You spend your time well. But you know all that is going to be changed from now on, don't you? We shall begin our studies tomorrow, and you will work hard. Where is your room?"

He led her upstairs. His room was only a few steps from her own. She cast a look of disapproval at the slight untidiness she saw there. "What is that jacket doing on the bed?" she asked, pointing. "Hang it up at once." He obeyed. As he opened his closet she saw his short nightgown hanging on the back of the door, and stepping forward she took it from its hook.

"You will not need this any longer," she announced. "From now on you will sleep without nightclothes."

"Yes, miss," he murmured.

"I shall come and see you here this evening, when you are in bed," she said. "You say your prayers at bedtime?"

"No, miss…"

"That is disgraceful. We will say them together in future, in my room."

During the hours until dinner, Harriet and Richard talked together in the library. Thus she learned, almost without his being aware of it, not only of the events of her pupil's own life but the immediate history of his family. From a few naive remarks she also learned of Mr. Lovel's addiction to pleasure and of the existence of his mistress.

The hour for dinner arrived. In her room the table was already set. Harriet seated herself with her back to the lamp, her face in shadow. Opposite her, the pale countenance of Richard was in the full light.

Bridget carried in the dishes and set them on the table with a sullen air; but she altered her manner at once on receiving a single glance from Harriet. The glance was so portentous that the old woman understood in that instant what her position in the household was henceforth to be, and she grasped at the same time the fact that she had everything to gain by making herself Harriet's subordinate. Her air at once became respectful, even obsequious.

The soup was served. Richard hungrily took a spoonful and was carrying it to his lips when Harriet leaned forward and stopped his hand. "What are you doing?"

"M-miss—I'm eating!" he stammered.

"And the Grace before meals? You never say Grace?"

"No, miss..."

"You will do so from now on. I shall say the words now, and you will remember them. Tomorrow you will be made say them by yourself."

His head lowered, he listened carefully while she spoke the benediction. Only when she raised her own spoon did he venture to begin eating.

"You have often been in this room?" she said after a while.

"No, miss."

"You will be from now on. When your work is insufficiently done in the daytime, you will make up the arrears here. And when you are to be punished, it will be in this room."

A curious sensation of fear and fascination went through him as he heard these words and saw her beautiful grey eyes fixed on him; but which of these sentiments was uppermost he could not tell. Already he had felt his whole being profoundly disturbed by the personality of his governess, and now with this disturbance there was mixed a feeling of shuddering attraction towards her, a sense of fear at finding himself so absolutely subject to this young woman, and also something else, something indefinable but sweet, almost too sweet...The meal was finished in silence.

Later, when he gained his room, it was with a feeling of having drunk some heady draught that made his head swim deliciously. A peculiar lassitude invaded his whole body. As he undressed, the touch of his clothes slipping over his skin made him shiver, and as soon as he was between the cool sheets a feeling of profound languor made him relax his naked limbs with an exquisite sense of well-being. Instinctively, he turned his face towards his pillow and curled himself into a ball, as if feeling the need for warmth and physical intimacy. Then he closed his eyes, but wasn't able to fall asleep.

He had been in bed scarcely a quarter of an hour when, very softly, his door was half opened and then closed again. Between these two operations Harriet had slipped into the room without making a sound. She carried a small lamp whose feeble light was further subdued by a heavy shade. On tiptoe she approached the bed and bent over.

The boy was lying on his back now, dozing, his eyes half-closed, lost in a reverie of the one subject that engrossed him—the arrival of Harriet Marwood in the house, and the new life he was entering. But now, thanks to his indulgence of the afternoon, the sensuality of his temperament was no longer aroused by such consideration, and his little penis lay soft and inert between his thighs.

All at once he felt the sheet and coverlet lifted from him; for an instant he felt himself bared to the hips, and then, just a swiftly, the covers were replaced.

He had not time to utter a cry before he recognized his governess. He sat up in bed, shaken by a violent, indefinable fear. But Harriet's hand was laid gently on his head.

"Do not be afraid, Richard," she said softly. "I saw that you were not asleep, and I wished to make sure you were behaving yourself. You were, I see, and all is as it should be. Lie down now, and go to sleep."

He obeyed, stretching himself out, his hand crossed over his chest as if to contain the wild beating of his heart. It was then that he experienced his most intense emotion: Harriet leaned over his bed and kissed him, softly and lingeringly, on the mouth.

"When you have been a good boy during the day," she said, "I will come to you in the evening, like this, to kiss you good-night…"

He had a moment of daring. As the hand that had slipped beneath his chin was withdrawn, he raised his head suddenly and pressed his lips to it. Then, red as a peony, he turned his head to the wall at his bedside.

"Goodnight, Richard," she said.

And she disappeared.

At this moment Mr. Lovel was also in bed, lying beside his mistress in the rosy light of the bedroom in her flat, where he now spent the greater part of his evenings. He had just withdrawn from the warm embrace of her anal sheath, after spending in it with extraordinary satisfaction.

On this occasion Kate was wearing, for the caprice of her protector, the working dress of the high-class Parisian prostitute of the time—a short transparent chemise over a narrow, tightly laced corset with long black silk stockings tightly gartered at mid-thigh and a pair of leather kid boots with immoderately high heels. In this suggestive costume the whiteness and opulence of her superb body had appeared with such striking and voluptuous effect that she had to withstand two separate amorous assaults in succession before her protector's passions were momentarily sated and she was able to revert to the question of Richard's governess.

"Why," said Mr. Lovel, "I suppose you would call her a handsome woman, Kate, but it's a type that makes no impression on me. Miss Marwood is much too straitlaced, I find."

"That's just as well. But did she strike you as likely to break your boy of that habit of his?"

"I don't know. All I can say is that if anyone can do it, she is the one." He laughed. "She looks like a regular martinet, a holy terror. I don't envy the boy."

"Ah well, it's for his own good. He'll thank us all for it some day." And crooking a handsome leg in its tight black stocking, she coquettishly laid the soft kid of her boot in his lap, counting on it making its effect on his sensuality in due time. "Do you think it will take long?"

"I've no idea, Kate. That's a very handsome boot you have on, my dear. Raise it up will you?"

"There you are," she said, raising her bare thigh. "You like my new boots then? I saw them in Dover Street yesterday and bought them with you in mind."

Mr. Lovel bit the toe of her boot softly, then pressed the soft kid of the upper against his cheek. "Ah, you're a dear girl, Kate. Do you know, I find I don't see half as much of you as I'd like. I've gotten into needing you at the oddest times, my dear—in the middle of the night, first thing in the morning, and so on. Yes, that's right, rub your other boot over my genitals..." He kissed the smartly shod foot before him with slowly mounting emotion.

"My poor Arthur," said Kate. "I had no idea you wanted me so often. It seems that whenever you are here you are fucking my bum or my mouth, and I thought that was enough." She reached for his testicles with a warm hand and began kneading them delicately. "Oh, it's a terrible thing for a man to have an erection in his bed all by himself. It's such a waste."

"And with a mistress like you to remember and think of," he said, gripping her leather-shod foot, "one's almost obliged to masturbate as if one were a damned boy oneself. Listen, Kate, I'll tell you what. You must come and sleep at my house. Now that my poor wife has gone, there can be no complications. You'll come, won't you?"

"My darling Arthur," cried Kate, beside herself with joy, "it's what I have always longed for, didn't you know? Oh, many and many's the long night I've tossed and turned in this lonely bed too, with my arse itching to have your prick in it, my hands empty and craving to be holding your sweet balls, and my throat dry with wanting the taste of your seed. Yes, Arthur, let all that be over and done with, and let me share your bed and your pleasure every night as a man's mistress should."

He took her head between his hands and made the rare gesture of kissing her on the lips. "You shall come tomorrow," he said.

"Now who is the happiest woman in the world!" the good creature cried, jumping up. "For that, I must give you the finest frigging ever a man had! Come, sit down on the stool there now, and put your legs apart."

Arthur rose and sat on the low stool with his legs widely spread, while Kate, drawing up a high chair, sat down facing him. Raising her legs and laying her heels on either side of his testicles, she took his half-awakened member between the sides of her boots and began rolling and rubbing it skillfully against the velvety leather of the uppers. Arthur's eyes shone with pleasure as he followed the slow voluptuous movements of her feet.

"That's a grand way to be frigged when you're in the mood for boot, isn't it?" she said archly.

Arthur looked from her flushed face to his member, which was slowly swelling from the soft friction of the leather, and then to her own widespread thighs that, with her chemise now well tucked up displayed the charming slit of her sex opening and shutting with the rotation of her hips as she kept masturbating him in this ingenious manner.

"Dear Kate," he said, "you can frig a man better with your feet than many a whore can do with her two hands, indeed you can."

"Ah, I'm only too glad I can, since you like it so well. But now you've got me so hot I must frig myself, too." She parted the lips of her vulva, and attacked her swollen clitoris with passionate fingers.

The sight completed the process of her lover's erection. As his member throbbed and pulsated between the churning, kneading feet, he kept his eyes fixed, now on it and now on his mistress' masturbation of herself, until he felt the pleasure of the crisis threading his loins imperiously and discharged his sperm freely into the air. Then, sinking back in happy exhaustion, he followed with critical appreciation the course which Kate was following in the achievement of her own orgasm before his eyes.

The next morning at seven o'clock, Harriet, fully dressed, entered her pupil's room again. He was still drowned in slumber, and as on the previous evening she lifted the covers and with a swift glance examined the boy carefully. She at once noted the violent erection of his member, and smiled at this evidence of a temperament so consonant with her plans. Richard had not moved; to waken him she was obliged to shake him by the shoulder. He started up, rubbing his eyes.

"Well, Richard, what do you say?"

"Good—good morning, miss."

"Good morning. It is seven o'clock, the time when you will get up every morning from now on. Come into the bathroom."

He hesitated, all too aware of the distention of his genital.

"Well, I am waiting," she said, her brows knitting in exasperation.

"But—but, miss, I'm not—I mean—I mean, my—my..."

"Your what? Come, up with you now at once." With a swift movement, she pulled the covers from his naked body. His hands went instinctively to cover his member. "Oh, so that is what is troubling you! Really, such false modesty is absurd. Get up at once! We are not going to wait for that morning tension to go down." And she turned away impatiently.

He rose in confusion, seized his dressing gown and followed her into the bathroom.

"I have had Bridget draw your bath," said Harriet. "Get into it now."

He looked at her in embarrassment. "Yes, miss..." But he remained motionless, standing before her uncertainly.

"Well, what are you waiting for?"

"I—miss, I shall have to undress..."

"Of course. You do not make a habit of taking a bath in your dressing gown, I hope. Take it off."

He began untying the cord around his waist, hoping she would leave. Then he understood that she meant to be present when he took his bath. He slipped out of the gown and stood nude before her.

She sat down, examining him with her cool, intent glance. This was the first time she had seen him naked, and for all her air of outward calm she was deeply stirred by the beauty of this adolescent body. Her eyes passed appreciatively from point to point, dwelling with connoisseurship now on the plump shoulders, now on the straight slender legs, now on the almost feminine swell of the hips. She fixed her gaze at last on the firm and nervous rondure of buttocks and thighs, and then centering inevitably on the puerile penis. By now soft and pendent, it had withdrawn coyly between his thighs where it formed, with the small tight testicles, a kind of dainty genital triumvirate in a state of modesty and repose. When he was in the water, she drew her chair beside the bathtub.

"I have been entrusted by your father," she said with a smile, "with the task of supervising your whole upbringing. That comprises more than school work, you know. So I shall be here every morning to see that you take your bath, whether you like it or not. Now hurry. Wash yourself thoroughly all over!"

Richard obeyed. He was reminded more and more of his little schoolmate's governess. How far would the resemblance go? And how downright and domineering this woman was! Suddenly disturbed by the thought that he might even now be keeping her waiting, he finished washing himself and was rising to leave the bath when she stopped him.

"What is this?" she said sharply. "Do you not wash your private parts?"

"No, miss—I mean, yes...I thought that—that—"

"You thought you would omit them this morning, I suppose! I told you to wash yourself all over. Kneel down and do so at once, if you please."

He scrambled to his knees in the bath and began soaping his penis with trembling hands. Harriet watched him closely, noting the accustomed gestures with which he was handling himself as he drew back the prepuce and ran his fingers around the head of the shaft itself.

She spoke suddenly. "You play with yourself a good deal, my boy, don't you?"

He gasped and went red as fire, his hands left their task abruptly. He tried to speak, but could not.

"You need not answer, Richard," she said. She fixed him with the piercing glance of her gray eyes. "I shall have more to say to you on this subject in a few minutes. For the moment, however, you will put your hands behind your head while I finish washing you myself." And rolling up her sleeves she lathered her hands and took hold of his member; in a moment her fingers were firmly palpating its head and neck, while her other hand, passing between his thighs from the rear, grasped his testicles and massaged them briskly.

As her hands plied their double task, the boy's penis, already accustomed to respond instantly to his own manipulations, gradually swelled and stiffened quite independently of his volition. He watched it rising with an indescribable feeling of shame, horror, and pleasure. Harriet, for her part, continued the ablution as if quite unconscious of what was happening. Even when she inserted a smooth finger in the boy's tight anus, the answering throb that elevated his penis to its full height drew no comment from her. Anyone looking at her would have thought she was even ignorant of the very meaning of tumescence. At last she ceased.

"Into the water with you now," she said calmly, "and rinse yourself well...And now get out and dry yourself at once."

The boy obeyed, awkward and embarrassed by the rigid member that was still standing out and swaying before him with an air of arrogance quite out of keeping with his own feelings of shame and confusion. When he finished, Harriet took the towel from him and sat back.

"Come here," she said, drawing him between her knees. "And do not hang your head like that. Yes, look at me. Now, are you listening?"

Her eyes were boring into his. He noted their warm brilliance, so much at variance with the coldness of her tone and the curl of her short upper lip.

"Yes, miss," he whispered.

She settled herself more comfortably in her chair.

"I am going to talk to you very seriously about this habit of yours, Richard. That is because I mean to impress on you the dangers you are running in giving way to it. In the first place, there is the danger to your personality. You are already, I see, quite weak and lacking in character, without this final indulgence of your senses to render you completely spineless. Lacking all will-power, a passive instrument of your own sensuality.

"In the second, there is the danger to your health. Do you know the physical results of constant self-abuse? I do not wish to frighten you, especially when it is not too late for you to turn over a new leaf, but the habit is extremely dangerous. Your present pallor alone is an indication of that.

"And finally there is the moral danger, the danger that this habit may master you to such an extent that you may never be able to find satisfaction in a normal and natural way. Think, Richard: one day you will wish to be married. How will you feel then, facing the woman who you wish to make your wife, if you are already so wedded to a shameful, childish, and weakening habit that you are unable to express your love as God and Nature intended you should?" The governess paused. She had been holding his hands, but now she released them and placed her own hands firmly on his naked hips, drawing him closer to her as she went on. "Those are all reasons for giving up this self-indulgence of yours, and I wish you to think of them constantly from now on. But there is one other reason that is perhaps better than any of those others, Richard, and one that may weigh with you more powerfully than they do." Here she paused again, and suddenly kneading the flesh of his hips with the harsh grip of her strong fingers, she gave him her warm, full-lipped smile. "And that is, Richard, that if I ever catch you playing with yourself I will thrash you to within an inch of your life."

With these words, which fell on him like the blow of a stick, she pushed him away gently and, as if to emphasize her threat, tapped his now subsiding member lightly with her fingers.

"And now, dress yourself, and come to breakfast."

As soon as breakfast was over, Harriet and her pupil repaired to the library, now the schoolroom. She pointed out to him where he was to sit, and sat down herself—not opposite but beside him, and in such a way that she could oversee his work at any moment. Thus the first lesson began.

Richard was nervous, awkward and embarrassed by the smallest difficulty. Not only had he lost the habit of study during his long period of idleness, but the presence of Miss Marwood at his side disturbed him strangely. Truly, the effect this young woman had on his imagination and senses was remarkable!

Sitting beside her, he felt the occasional touch of her knee, her hand, her arm. Her bosom pressed his shoulder when she bent over him. At those moments he became giddy. Her cheek kept brushing his, stray locks of her hair tickled his temples, her breath intoxicated him. So great was his disturbance that sometimes his eyes filled with tears and he wished to break into sobs—and all for no reason. Or what could the reason be? Indeed, she was not threatening him now!

The lesson period lasted three hours, and work was resumed after luncheon without any incident to break the monotony of the day.

For a week matters continued thus. Richard, under the awe he felt for Harriet, was working hard and steadily, doing his best to deserve a word of satisfaction and encouragement—even a caress. Whenever she called him to her chair for him to recite a lesson or explain a problem, if his replies were correct she signified approbation with a few light affectionate taps on his loins, such as one might bestow on an infant.

He still wore the short Eton jacket and white trousers he had worn at school, and the touch of her hand, felt through the tight-fitting serge of the latter, had come to excite and disturb him immoderately. At such moments he had a mad impulse to throw himself into her arms, to crush his face against her breast, to huddle himself against her in absolute abandonment of his whole being to her will. It was then that the fever of his senses rose to a height. He felt the blood beating in his head and a sensation of wild and hopeless craving flooded his loins, while the turgescence of his member and the constriction of his clothing affected him with both the shame and the sheer physical pain of a confined and frustrated erection.

Every night she came to see him in bed. She smoothed his pillow and tucked him in as the tenderest of mothers might have done, then gave him a long kiss on the lips and withdrew, still calm, still apparently cold, leaving him a prey to a thousand confused thoughts and in a kind of ecstasy. And then, alone and naked in his bed, he was left to the torments of his desire and temptation, lying on his back in the dark, his hands pressed tightly to his sides, desperately fighting the impulse to carry out the forbidden self-indulgence that he craved with every nerve in his body and every fibre of his brain. Had it been only the fear of punishment that restrained him, he would have succumbed long before this. But he was bound to this agonizing abstinence by a more imperious taboo, a sense that to give himself this sexual relief would be to commit an act of infidelity to the woman herself. It was often more than an hour before his flesh subsided sufficiently for him to fall asleep, worn out but almost happy in this victory over himself.

By the end of the week he had only one thought, one wish—to be tied always to this woman's apron strings. She was everything to him; he lived only for her. Let us admit it; he was in love with her. And, with the clairvoyance of love, he was aware also of the force and intensity of her own interest in him. Obscurely, he understood that he was a source of frustration for her as well, and this frightened him. He sensed the fact that she was waiting, waiting—but for what? And after a while, obsessed and tormented as he was by the sensuous ordeal he went through twenty times a day, the task of resisting the impulse to give way to his burning desire, he came to believe that it was that very weakness and resumed self-indulgence she was awaiting so she might put her threat of punishment into effect.

This superstition was only half correct. Harriet really desired his abstinence, though for reasons of her own. But it was impossible, after all, for the boy to assess the fact of her mysterious and ardent temperament, to grasp the perverse nature of her love, and the fact that behind her cold and placid demeanor she was inwardly maddened by the desire to begin whipping him.

The New Wave of SM Erotica

Circlet Press specializes in books which expand the erotic imagination. Our anthologies combine science fiction, fantasy, futurism, and magic with sex, bondage, sadomasochism, and more.

Erotic Fantastic: The Best of Circlet Press
$19.95, 388 pages, ISBN 1-885865-44-9
Twenty three stories from the first ten years of Circlet, including Laura Antoniou, Thomas S. Roche, and Cecilia Tan.

The Velderet: A Cybersex S/M Serial
$14.95, ISBN 1-885865-27-9
Cecilia Tan's science fiction adventure where an alien race brings kinky sex to a utopian world.

Sexcrime: An Anthology of Subversive Erotica
$14.95, ISBN 1-885865-26-0
Taking its title from Orwell's 1984, Sexcrime explores the erotic heat and intensity that can come from love under repressive conditions. Underground love and subversive sex flourish in these stories about the intimacy of secrets and the thrill of forbidden pleasures.

To order within the US/Canada, add shipping and handling US$4 for the first book, US$1.50 for each additional, and mail check or credit card information to:
Circlet Press
Order Department MWAM
1770 Mass. Ave. #278
Cambridge, MA 02140

www.circlet.com